D0374826

NIL
UNLOCKED

WITHDRAWN

LYNNE MATSON

NIL
UNLOCKED

HENRY HOLT AND COMPANY | NEW YORK

Henry Holt and Company, LLC
Publishers since 1866
175 Fifth Avenue
New York, New York 10010
macteenbooks.com

Henry Holt® is a registered trademark of Henry Holt and Company, LLC.
Copyright © 2015 by Lynne Matson
All rights reserved.

Library of Congress Cataloging-in-Publication Data
Matson, Lynne.
Nil unlocked / Lynne Matson.
pages   cm.—(Nil series ; 2)
Summary: Trapped on the island of Nil in a parallel universe, Rives is the
undisputed leader of Nil City but raiders, non-human inhabitants, and new arrivals
make it ever harder to maintain order and Rives teams up with Skye, a new arrival
with a mysterious past, in a desperate race to save all the residents of Nil.
ISBN 978-1-62779-293-6 (hardback)
[1. Survival—Fiction.   2. Islands—Fiction.   3. Love—Fiction.
4. Science fiction.]   I. Title.
PZ7.M431506Nm 2015   [Fic]—dc23   2015000566

Henry Holt books may be purchased for business or promotional use. For information on
bulk purchases please contact the Macmillan Corporate and Premium Sales Department at
(800) 221-7945 x5442 or by e-mail at specialmarkets@macmillan.com.

First Edition—2015 / Designed by April Ward
Printed in the United States of America by R. R. Donnelley & Sons Company,
Harrisonburg, Virginia

1 3 5 7 9 10 8 6 4 2

FOR STEPHEN: WITH YOU LIFE IS SO MUCH MORE

INFORMATION IS
NOT KNOWLEDGE.
—ALBERT EINSTEIN

CHAPTER 1

RIVES

DAY 241, JUST AFTER NOON

The ground shook, like Hades had lost his temper.

Or his favorite toy. Or both.

Given the last ten minutes of sheer insanity, I'd pick both.

Three gates, twin exits, and one massive quake, all packed into today's manic noon. Aftershocks tore through the black rock field as the island fought to win, and the battle seemed personal with the devil himself.

Right now I was doing my damnedest not to meet him in person.

Cracks tore through the rock, ripping the ground into a fresh jig-saw puzzle. One lava field away, red blurred like liquid rust. A buffalo lurched awkwardly in the distance, bracing against the very island that held it hostage. Quakes always scared the animals—me included. I scrambled over the trembling rock, aiming to retrieve Charley's gear and not kill myself in the process.

Nil wasn't happy—that was clear.

Another aftershock hit. The ground jerked; black rock splintered on my right. I shifted direction with the wind, already calculating a safer route.

The grizzly roared; I spun to place him. I'd forgotten he was my new sidekick.

I caught the bear in my line of sight and skidded to a sharp halt; my current vector put me on a crash course with the grizzly. He barreled toward me, erratic and unsteady, pointlessly trying to outrun the quake. It was a toss-up as to who was more terrified: me or the jacked-up bear. But it didn't matter. All that mattered was staying alive, a personal mandate that did *not* include me playing chicken with the grizzly.

I backpedaled, unwilling to take my eyes off the bear, and stumbled five steps before I tripped and caught myself one-handed on a large chunk of shifting rock. Three meters out, the ground where I would've been standing cracked into a cruel smile—one with teeth. Jagged black rock, dripping decay, lining a wide hole. The grizzly's eyes were wild, his pace uncontrolled. He hit a patch of gravel and slid—and then he fell. Sideways, into the chasm, a brown blur clawing at empty air. The island jerked, the toothy trap clamped shut. Rock crumbled into the dwindling crack as the island settled, then stilled.

No shake, no quake.

Done.

The only animal left was me.

The stillness was profound. I gingerly let go of the rock and stood. Alone in the field of black, I marveled at the quiet. At the abrupt calm, which was as remarkable as the preceding fifteen minutes of mayhem.

Thad's shocking play.

Charley's escape.

The bear. The quake. Thad leaping toward a gate floating over a deadly black rift, Thad hanging in midair like a crazed long jumper, one heartbeat too long. But he'd made it.

Nothing like cutting it close, bro, I thought.

I exhaled a breath I'd been holding for days.

Days.

I had 124 left.

I took a breath, steady and deep, reveling in the feeling of being alive, then I turned in a slow circle, absorbing the look and feel of the island in the wake of today's noon. The red rock in the distance jutted crisply against the cloudless blue sky, all blurred edges gone. On my right, Mount Nil stretched high like an island sentinel. A near-vertical black rock peak slapped with patches of stubborn green, its tip spearing the only clouds in sight. Wispy steam bleached the sky on the backside, visible if you knew where to look, where hidden vents released deadly pressure. Directly in front of Mount Nil sat the meadow, lush and green and more than a little deadly. I couldn't see the meadow from where I stood, but I knew it was there, just like the rain forest to the northeast and the City due west. So much of Nil was unseen. I understood that now more than ever.

As I stood alone in the wake of today's noon, the island looked exactly the same—and felt completely different. Foreign and new.

I gave a sharp laugh.

Of all the people here, you'd think I'd be the most accustomed to change as the constant, but then again, in my pre-Nil life, the places didn't change; *I* did. *I* moved; *I* traveled; *I* adjusted to new cities and countries as easily as changing my shirt. Here, *I* was the constant, forced to continually reassess the island and everything I knew, which made it impossible to get a handle on where I stood. Every time I thought I had something figured out, it changed.

And with the twin losses of Thad and Charley, things had definitely changed.

Welcome to Nil, Rives, I thought.

Again.

I'd just finished my full rotation when the breeze shifted. Dulled, as if interrupted. Or expectant.

Incoming, I thought.

I soundlessly fell to one knee beside the rock.

A moment later, a gate dropped a few meters away in midair and glittered, a writhing disco ball no one wanted to play anywhere near, especially me.

Perfectly still, I remained crouched by the boulder, once my anchor, now my shield. And I waited.

One second.

Two.

On three, every speck of the disco ball turned matte black. Deep black, the color of a night with no stars, the color of birth on Nil. This gate was an inbound, and now that it churned black, I knew it had a rider.

Friend or foe?

I'd barely finished the thought when the gate coughed out a flash of gold. An animal, with tawny fur the color of the waking sun and a thicker mane of the same, lay motionless on the black rock, his paws facing me.

Foe, I thought.

As the lion lifted his head, another gate popped up a meter farther out and dropped. It too shifted into charcoal black, a dangerous aperture primed to open. One tick later, the second gate dumped another golden animal, only this one lacked a mane.

Lion number two rose to her feet as inbound gate number three appeared and instantly flashed black. Three gates, all inbounds. All with riders.

This time the newcomer wasn't a lion; it was a large, scrawny beast covered with dark splotches and a nasty mop of scraggly fur running down its back. It dropped out of the gate, rolled to a stop, and had barely stilled before raising its wobbly head. It sniffed once, swung its head around toward the lions—*and me*—and bared its teeth.

I didn't move.

With a high-pitched keen, it rose to its feet and took off after the lions at a blistering pace. Hyena, I guessed, although I'd never seen one so large. The trio sprinted away, toward Mount Nil and the meadow, the mangy mutt chasing the lions, an unsettling visual if ever there was one.

On Nil, even the king of the beasts ran in fear.

I stood, alone again.

Assessing again.

Charley, gone. Thad, gone. The grizzly, trapped in rock, lost for good. Three out, three in, the island's balance still intact, only today the Nil scales took a hard tip toward the deadly.

When the trio vanished from sight, I went after Charley's gear. Her clothes, sandals, and satchel lay in a clean pile. Inside the satchel, Charley's maps and fire bow waited, intact and undamaged. Thad's knife glinted like a dull gate, like life and power and something primitively badass. An island offering, just for me.

Thank you, Nil.

I took it all and didn't look back. The City was waiting.

I hoped it was still standing.

CHAPTER
2

SKYE
NOVEMBER 16, 9:00 P.M.

Six weeks ago, my mom gently informed me she'd been chosen to oversee an exciting new dig in Africa, and, oh by the way, I wasn't invited.

Two weeks ago, I moved in with my dad.

Today, he handed me my uncle's journal.

Nothing will ever be the same.

NINE HOURS EARLIER

My dad's official title is Daniel J. Bracken, PhD, Professor of Astrophysics and Solar-Terrestrial Physics at the Institute of Study of Earth, Oceans, and Space, a Department of the University of New Hampshire. His unofficial titles? Island explorer, NASA consultant, stargazer extraordinaire. And the title that fits best? Forty-four-year-old bachelor obsessed with news of the weird.

At least he was consistent.

One step into Dad's home office on the day I moved in confirmed that his last title was still the most accurate. Three walls were completely plastered with overlapping newspaper clippings of unusual happenings and missing-person reports, Internet printouts of similarly odd stories, and Google Earth snapshots. Paragraphs and headlines were circled in various colors; if there was a rhyme or reason for the rainbow-marker madness, it was lost on me. One wall contained a ginormous map of the South Pacific. Chalk lines marked a grid. White tacks dotted the map like stars.

Since my visit last summer, the number of white tacks had grown.

And Dad still insisted I exercise like a fiend. Morning runs, interval workouts, and a ridiculous amount of arm-strength exercises that bordered on fanatic. That's the other thing about my dad: He's a cross between the Nutty Professor and Sarah Connor from *Terminator 2*, only he specializes in Survivorman techniques instead of semiautomatic weapons. Obsessed with fitness, he's pretty ripped for a dad, possibly because he's lived the Paleo lifestyle for as long as I can remember. I've never eaten anything processed at Dad's house. Then again, usually when I visit, we go off somewhere remote where sushi is tame.

I came inside from a run, sweating and tired but feeling pretty good. I'd figured out years ago that my visits with Dad were easier—or at least less painful—if I made a decent effort to stay in shape back home in Gainesville. And by decent I mean sticking to a schedule of regular runs. As a result, I was thin, on the wiry side, but I'd no hope of building big muscles anyway; I had my mom's small-boned build that topped out at a whopping five feet five. I'd also been cursed with the absolute nightmare that was my mom's hair: curly blond ringlets that defied any kind of styling. I relied on massive amounts of ponytail holders and gravity to make it behave, with mixed results. At least I'd inherited my dad's eyes. Neither blue nor green, my eyes were an equal combination of the two, with specks of mica mixed in like salt. My dad said the stars touched my eyes. *It's what makes them shine,* he liked to say. If so, I guess the stars touched my dad's eyes, too. It was the one feature we shared.

"How was it, Skye?" Dad called from his office. "Did you sprint at the end?"

I kicked off my shoes. "Yes, Dad, I sprinted at the end. The last fifty yards, as hard as I could."

"Good girl. How about push-ups? Did you knock those out yet?"

"Not yet."

"Make time for them, Skye. A strong body makes for a strong mind," he continued. "Don't dismiss skills you may need just because you haven't been called on to use them. And hopefully you never will, but better to plan for the worst and hope for the best." His voice lightened. "But if you're not busy with your push-ups, I've got something I want you to see."

"Let me guess," I said, stretching. "Another video on edible plants of the South Pacific? Or a documentary on rudimentary tool making?"

"At least you remember." He laughed.

One thing I'll give my crazy-sweet dad is that he's one of the biggest optimists I've ever met. He wasn't faking his delight in my comments. He wasn't totally balanced, either.

It's why my mom left.

"Seriously, come in here for a sec," he said.

"Coming." I sighed. Nothing in Dad's office ever took just a "sec."

If possible, the walls of Dad's office seemed more covered than usual. A new folding table hugged the wall under the window. Paper coated the table like frosting: piles of white, with handwritten notes scrawled everywhere. Yellow Post-it notes containing hand-drawn arrows pointing to other notes lurked haphazardly among the mess.

As I entered, Dad's eyes lit up like he'd just found leprechauns *and* their pot of gold.

"Skye." He held up a piece of paper and grinned. "I think I'm close."

"To what, exactly?" I tried to muster some enthusiasm and failed.

"To finding the original home of my guide last year. Or rather, his grandmother." He waved the paper animatedly. "According to his stories, his grandmother was relocated from her island birthplace in the late 1940s—a place of secrets and spirits, he said—and that's the island

I need to find." Paper in hand, he walked over to the huge wall map of the South Pacific. "I've narrowed it down to a small cross-section of islands along the equator. I think I'm finally close."

The secret island, I thought, my heart sinking. *Of course.*

Crazy-obsession number one, the one that pushed my mom over the edge and out the door.

"Dad." I spoke slowly, careful to keep my tone level. "I understand you think you're close. But I also love you. And I think"—I paused, making sure he was giving me his full attention—"it's time to stop. You've been fantasizing about this secret island for years. You've fixated on something that doesn't exist—or if it does, it's not part of our life. And you're missing out on this life." He'd gone still as he listened. Maybe that was what encouraged the words I'd been dying to say for the last few years.

"Dad, Mom left because you wouldn't let this island obsession go. She *left*, Dad. Four years ago. And you've been alone ever since. You don't date, barely have friends, and every free minute you're not working at the university or lecturing on solar flares or electromagnetism, you're researching islands or traveling to one. For what, Dad? Where has it gotten you?" I swept my hand around the cluttered office. "Dad, you need to let it go," I said softly. "As your daughter, I'm telling you: Let it go."

"And as your father, Skye, I'm telling you I can't." No judgment, no resignation, just pure astrophysicist matter-of-fact.

He strode over to his desk and picked up a small, worn black journal. With equal purpose, he handed it to me.

"This is your uncle Scott's journal. He wrote it when he was seventeen. Your age. Read it and then we'll talk."

I didn't move. "I want you to think about what I said. I'm serious, Dad. It's time to move on."

His smile was hard. "I know you're serious, Skye. So am I. Read."

"Did Mom ever read this?" I held up the journal.

Dad's voice softened into a pained tone I didn't recognize. "Yes, she did. But she never looked into his eyes. She never saw the truth."

The truth was, I'd never looked into my uncle's eyes, either. I'd never had the chance. My dad's twin brother had died in a freak accident at age eighteen.

I went upstairs, took a quick shower, opened the journal, and began to read.

CHAPTER
3

It was all me, trekking solo.

The last time I'd been this far inland without backup was the day I'd arrived. Just like then, I had zero food, but unlike that hellacious first day, now I had supplies and clothes. Nudity didn't bother me, but that didn't mean I wanted to walk around with my junk on display either.

Because of Charley's escape, I even hauled an extra pair of shorts.

I'd taken for granted that I'd have Charley beside me on the return trip. Taken for granted that she'd be my Second, maybe even the next Leader. Taken for granted that she'd help me decode the rest of Nil, uncovering the secrets that made Nil tick.

Because I knew that Nil was holding back.

Memories flashed, a million fractured mental pixels. *Talla laughing, her blue eyes fierce. Talla whispering, "Be fearless, Rives." Talla silent, lifeless in my arms.*

I needed to stop taking things for granted. Like time, and people.

Got it, Nil, I thought.

I guess I was just a slow learner.

I glanced around, and struck by fierce island déjà vu, I laughed. I was retracing my steps from my Day One. Same solitary hike, right down to the afternoon arrival. I'd woken in this black rock field months ago and made it to the City by nightfall; I'd now spent 241 consecutive days in this deadly arena, more consecutive days than I'd spent in any place ever. Staying in one place so long implied roots, at least to me.

But I damn sure wouldn't call Nil home.

Nil was more like purgatory, a place trapped between Heaven and Hell, with heavy doses of both. Maybe Nil was the devil's playground, maybe it was Heaven's testing ground. Maybe it was both. Or neither. Nobody stuck here had a clue.

But lately I was desperate to find one.

Surviving wasn't enough anymore; I had to know why I was here. Why we *all* were here.

Focus, Rives.

Daydreaming was a dangerous pastime on Nil. Then again, daydreaming was risky anywhere. Daydreaming was what landed me here in the first place, that and blowing off my dad's advice.

Memories ripped through my head, moments I hadn't replayed in months.

Landing in Phuket. My dad laughing, my mom kissing his cheek. The slowing whir of the plane's engines, the lazy wink of the hot flight attendant. The sleek feel of my sick new Canon with a telephoto lens. The annoying weight of the mandatory books on Thai history and culture.

Part extended vacation, part work trip for my dad, it was the three of us, as always. Dad was researching a Thai crime ring, a massive operation with international ramifications and disturbing political ties, or so he'd said. The engine's drone faded, and my dad had seized the vacuum of that moment. *Look around,* he'd counseled as the plane taxied to a stop. *Watch the people. Watch the cues. And watch your back. Never*

12

forget you're a foreigner. Never take your security for granted. Inattentiveness means missed chances and lost opportunities. But, worse, it puts you at risk. Then his eyes had softened. *Got it, son?*

Sure, Dad, I'd said.

I wondered if he'd known then I was all talk.

The next day, I'd gone to Freedom Beach to take pictures. I was checking out some girls chilling on the sand, watching their butts and not my own. A gate caught me from behind; I never saw it coming.

Got it now, Dad, I thought grimly.

On Nil, inattentiveness could get you killed.

I shifted my full focus to my surroundings, to the general post-quake status. *Clear sky, solid ground. No movement.*

A kilometer away, a black rhino marked the intersection of the red and black flows, his head swung toward me. Sweeping wide, I gave him all the space he needed, opting for the "I won't mess with you if you don't mess with me" approach.

The rhino didn't budge.

Win for me, but the closer I got to the City, the more uneasy I grew. No people, no animals. No movement at all. Enough *nothing* to put me on edge.

Stillness on Nil was like the calm before the storm; stillness here felt weighted.

Every muscle tensed, the island's weight pressing on me.

Then I saw it: two skinny boys, dressed in City garb, sprinting barefoot through the Flower Field, running away from the City, carting nets. *Our* nets. The ones Miya just finished last week.

"Hey," I shouted, taking off in their direction. "Stop!"

Of course the boys didn't stop; they didn't even turn. And then they were gone, lost in ribbons of color.

I'd never gotten close.

My concern for the City jacked up to panic level.

I spun back around and stopped. A boy built like a man stood at the edge of the field. His skin matched mine, only his upper left arm and shoulder were laced with lines and swirls of crisp black ink. He wore a ring of flowers around his neck and a brown loincloth low on his waist. A homemade spear in his hand flowed like a deadly extension of him. Facing the field, he studied the raiders' retreat.

Friend or foe?

Like he'd sensed my thoughts, our eyes met, and I'd have sworn his held pity. He turned away first. Away from the City, away from the field, moving toward the southern tip. And then he disappeared into the island like he belonged.

My grip on Nil wavered in the wake of today's noon.

Charley always joked that I was Thad's wingman, but he'd also been mine, and his absence felt like a hole in the fabric of the island itself. Possibly a tear in the fabric of *me.* I'd never realized how heavily I relied on Thad's guidance, or his friendship. Nil was different now. More dangerous, with more variables, and fewer people to lean on to work it all out. Now I had confirmed raiders, a loner, a new Second to appoint, and a City to hold together in the quake's aftermath.

At least I had brought good news back.

The deadleaf plants at the City's edge greeted me first, their bright green leaves broadcasting danger. Green usually meant go, but with these plants it meant death. One plant was trampled, its cracked leaves limp and weeping. I noticed it even as I avoided it, my dad's training instinctual. *Pay attention, Rives. Notice what others ignore.* It's what made him an Emmy-nominated journalist, and it's what made me notice the small things. The odd things, the things out of place—even people. People in the wrong place at the right time, people with tells, tics giving away truths.

Eyes wide open, Thad used to say. I'd smile, even as I'd think, *Always.*

Inside the perimeter, the City was organized chaos. I slowed, relieved to find that no one seemed hurt and all huts were intact. The chicken coop was already reinforced with fresh hemp twine and new logs. By my count only one chicken was lost. The goats roamed loose. One currently nosed around the firepit's edge, scavenging the last of the fish wraps.

Thank God for Dex.

He stood on a black boulder directing salvage teams, his tattoos adding an air of tribal authority to his gestures. Ink was the one accessory that made it to Nil, and Dex's was impressive. Skulls and words paired with flaming crosses and bloody daggers wove together across his torso like a painted shirt, one jacked with color.

Now that I'd seen the kid by the Flower Field, Dex's tats screamed hard-core rocker rather than tribal statesman. To Dex's credit, he held the City's attention like a lead act.

Seeing me, he raised his hand, his expression hopeful.

"He made it." I gave a double thumbs-up. "Thad's gone."

Jason covered his face with his hands, his shoulders shaking. My heart twisted. He'd seen more death than any fourteen-year-old should ever see. Miya gently rested her small hand on his shoulder, as if passing on her quiet strength to him. As I watched her, my heart twisted again, for a different reason.

Because of a different person.

Around Jason, people hooted; Ahmad hugged Jillian; Julio threw his fist in the air as Johan crossed himself, smiling. Macy beamed. Zane, Michael, and a few others clapped, almost politely. They'd barely known Thad. A dark-haired girl with a purple flower tucked behind one ear stood quietly, shoulders back, chin lifted, no clapping. Sy looked relieved.

Dex hopped down and strode over. "Where's Charley?"

"Gone," I said. "Nil sent a triple. Charley caught a ride home, too."

Dex's eyes widened. "A triple? And both Thad and Charley made it? Blimey. Did you go for the third?"

"Never had the chance. Thad missed the first one, so they took the next two." I smiled. "Not my noon, bro." I glanced toward the Flower Field. "Or the City's. I just saw two raiders sprinting east, and they were hauling our nets."

Dex groaned. "Tell me they weren't the new cast nets?"

"Yup."

"Bloody bastards," Dex fumed. "We need those nets." He ran a hand through his half-bleached hair, frustration written all over his face.

"We'll need to set up watch on the Shack again." I sighed. "We can't afford to lose supplies to raiders."

"Maybe." Dex looked thoughtful. "But the nets weren't at the Shack. They were hanging by the firepit to dry." He mumbled a string of expletives, all starting with the word *bloody*.

By the firepit. Near the trampled deadleaf bush.

I dropped my gear and took off at a full sprint, retracing my steps to the Flower Field, but this time I went farther. This time I went *into* the field, starting at the point closest to the City, tracking the trail of crushed flowers.

Sloppy, I thought. *But helpful.*

"What is it?" Jason asked. He'd followed me soundlessly. His innate stealth put the raiders' clumsiness to shame.

I didn't answer until I saw what I was looking for: a large brown net, abandoned in the field, its weight flattening a swath of purple. "Just recovering stolen goods. Sit tight."

I tossed it over my shoulder, and as rocks pressed into my back, I smiled. Small rocks weighted the net's bottom, added kilos that made the difference. The breeze rustled the flowers, whispering without words.

Sensing company, I stilled.

I turned around slowly, fully expecting to see the inked boy's eyes on me. But when I surveyed the field, a lone zebra stared back. Head held high, the zebra stood motionless, ears pricked, its monochromatic stripes a sharp contrast to the brilliant colors of the field. Somehow I knew it was seconds away from being spooked—by us.

We were the foe.

No one else was around.

I turned away. The zebra deserved peace, especially after today's quake.

"How'd you know they dropped it?" Jason pointed to the net when I drew close.

"They didn't drop it; they left it. Too heavy to carry with a numb foot. Or maybe they panicked when they lost feeling in their feet and ditched it to get away faster. Either way, we got one back."

I pointed out the trampled deadleaf plant as we walked back. "Our savior."

Jason laughed. "Nasty plants. I like 'em." He paused. "Thad's idea worked."

I nodded, abruptly choked up.

When Dex saw us, he pointed to the net and grinned. "Pulled out a bit of island magic, did you, Rives?" He clapped me on the shoulder. "Well done, mate."

I returned his grin. "Just a hunch that panned out."

"Right," he said, watching me shrug off the net. "Well, it was a bloody good one." Dex gestured for the net and hefted it over his shoulder, and, with a comical salute, he stepped away. Then he turned back, swallowing hard. "One more thing. I didn't carve for Thad, or Charley. I thought you should be the bloke to do it."

The knot in my throat was back. "I'd be honored." I turned to Jason, fighting to sound chill. "Why don't you carve for Thad, and I'll carve for Charley. Sound good?"

Jason broke into a broad smile, telling me I'd made the right call. "Sounds good."

"Right, then." Dex looked toward the island's interior. "Well, I'm off." But he didn't move.

"Anything else, D?" I asked.

He cocked his head at me. "You didn't spot any leopards out there, did you, Rives? Skulking about the island and such?"

Now I grinned easily. "No leopards, skulking or otherwise. But Nil is now home to a pair of lions and one very ugly hyena. Oh, and a black rhino. Not sure if he's new, though."

"Fantastic," Dex said. "Bloody cats. I may have to change my stance on declawing. My mum was much opposed, but I'm reconsidering in the nature of survival."

I thought of Bart, found with claw marks raked down his back, Nil karma at its best—or worst. "I hear you, bro. But better to just avoid all Nil kitties, especially the big ones." I paused. "Anyway, good news. The grizzly's gone."

"Gone?" Jason asked. "Did the lions get him? Or did he take a gate?"

"Neither. The island ate him for lunch."

"Well, that's not creepy much." Dex paled slightly. "Bears are Nil's lunch? Then what are we?"

"Dinner?" Jason offered.

I laughed. "Entertainment. But at least that gives us a better chance to make it, right?"

"Absolutely," Dex said with feeling. "And better here in the City than out there with the leopards." For an instant, I saw a flash of the shell-shocked boy I'd met on his Day One. But when he leveled his clear eyes on me, he looked every inch my Second. "It's bloody good to have you back, Rives." With a quick nod, Dex strode off, gripping the net with both hands like a weapon.

Jason and I walked toward the Wall in silence.

The Wall was less a wall, more like rows of wooden planks running horizontally, tacked to vertical posts. Both sides were coated with names—first names only. Life on Nil simplified quickly; the Wall was hard proof of that. Beside each name sat a mark. A check, for those lucky enough to win a ticket home. A cross, for the unlucky ones doomed to rest on Nil forever, hopefully in peace. A few other names had marks known only to the owner. Other names begged for a mark, the spaces beside their names conspicuously empty. Some spaces belonged to people still here, like me. Other names had blank spaces long after their owners' days ran out, their fate known only to the island and God himself.

I constantly wondered what became of those people. Maybe because I constantly wondered what would become of *me*.

Without discussion, we stopped in front of Thad's name first. I pulled Thad's blade from my waistband, flipped it around, and handed the knife to Jason, hilt out.

"It's Thad's. The one he used to carve his name."

Jason nodded, and, gripping the knife, he bowed his head before he stepped up to the Wall. A slight move, a show of respect. Even though he was the youngest person on Nil, Jason intuitively understood the island; he always had. It's why he was the best Spotter I'd ever seen, and it's why I'd bet money Jason would catch a gate when it was his time.

Time.

It defined our days and haunted our nights; we were all on the clock. It was one of Nil's rules.

Rules we lived by.

Rules we died by.

Rules we didn't make, rules we were still fighting to figure out. But there were two island rules as unyielding as Nil rock.

First, there's only one way off the island: a gate. Grab one and you're gone—but there's a catch. The moment you open your eyes on Nil, your personal hourglass tips. You've got exactly 365 days to escape, or you're done. Six feet under or lost, but either way, it shook out the same: If you didn't catch an outbound gate by the end of your year, you were toast.

And that was rule number two. Nil gives you one year, with zero chance of overtime. Nobody got an extra grain of Nil sand in their hourglass.

It was a deadline written in blood.

Jason finished carving Thad's check, then pointed the blade at the top of the Wall, where *NIL* was carved in block letters.

"Thank you," he said quietly, blade aimed at the *I*. "For letting him go."

He offered me the knife, the same way I'd offered it to him. Striding to my right, I touched Charley's name, remembering the girl who fought so hard to give us all a better shot at making it home.

"Way to go, girl," I said quietly. "When you find your boy on the other side, you tell him I said he's a dumbass. Shoot, knowing you, C, you'll probably tell him yourself." I smiled, thinking of the piece of her mind Charley would give Thad when he showed up.

Not if.

When.

"And when I get back," I whispered, "I'm going to tell him, too." I kissed my fingers and pressed them against her name in good-bye, knowing Charley and Thad would find each other on the other side. *Believing* it, because I had to. To lose hope was a death sentence, and I refused.

But Thad had scared the crap out of me today with his white knight move, and for one tortured moment, my faith had wavered.

Focus on the good, live in the moment.

Thad's words, a flashback perfectly timed. A stark reminder that if I wanted to live to see tomorrow, I'd better live in the *now*. I'd better get my head straight.

I focused on Charley's check, a mark of victory, fully aware that the last two Wall marks I'd carved had been crosses. One for Li, the first person I'd met in the City. And one for Talla, the last person I'd buried.

The less time I spent at the Wall, the better.

I'd just turned around when Jillian threw her arms around me. She shook like a quake.

"Jills, you okay?" I gently lifted her chin so I could see her face. Half-dried tears stained her cheeks. A twine piece holding her hair had slipped, making one auburn braid unravel. Today Jillian looked younger than sixteen. She also looked conflicted and worried. The rest of her expression I couldn't read, and that worried *me*. "What happened?"

"Nothing. I'm okay." She nodded. "I am." She smiled, as if convincing herself. "It's just—everything, I think. On the way back from the Shack—which is fine, by the way, nothing missing, nothing damaged—I started thinking about Thad and Charley and it's so awesome, but then I thought—what if Rives had caught the third gate? I heard you tell Dex it was a triple. And if you'd caught a gate, it would've been awesome, too, but we'd be totally clueless."

"Clueless about . . . ?" I frowned.

"About *everything*. We wouldn't know whether Thad made it, and we wouldn't know what had happened to Charley or *you*. All three of you would have blank spots on the Wall, and we'd never know if we should be celebrating or mourning or searching for you because you needed help, because there would be no one to tell us." She pressed her cheek against my chest. "Then I felt guilty for being glad you're still here." Her voice dropped to a whisper. "You're my best friend here, Rives. I really want you to make it. But I'm glad it wasn't today."

She looked up at me, her eyes wet again. "Does that make me a bad person?"

"No," I said, pushing her bangs from her eyes. "It makes you human."

We stood unmoving, Jillian's head on my shoulder.

We wouldn't know. Blank spots on the Wall.

Jillian had a point. The unknown was the worst part of Nil. Today, the island had saved the lives of two people and saved the sanity of many more.

Maybe Nil wasn't evil after all.

"I still miss her." Jillian's soft words made me stiffen. "I know you do, too."

I knew Jillian was talking about Talla, Jillian's other best friend on the island. Talla, whose grave lay near the Flower Field. Talla, whose presence I felt near the water. Talla, the first girl who saw through me.

Who saw *me*.

If she had lived, would we be together now?

I didn't know. I'd never know.

I thought of the one night I'd spent with Talla, the one before she'd gone on Search. The night she'd slept in my arms—actually slept, her first full night's sleep since she'd landed. As fierce as Talla was, she'd had her demons, the worst of which was chronic insomnia. On Nil, exhaustion made you vulnerable. And Talla hated feeling vulnerable. It was why she'd pushed herself physically, she'd confided, because she was sure that if she pushed her body to the limits, eventually it would have to cave and rest. Talla was determined to beat even herself.

But the island won. First it broke her body, then her spirit.

I would not let Nil break me.

Maybe the island wasn't evil, but it certainly could be cruel. Then again, cruelty and evil weren't confined to Nil. Neither were love and loss; it was just that Nil's hourglass distilled love, life, and loss into a heightened version of the same.

Today's emotional roller coaster was a ride I hadn't bargained for, but in hindsight, I should've seen it coming, at least with Thad.

Like I said, slow learner.

Jillian pulled away. "I'm so glad they made it. I couldn't have taken another funeral today."

"*Another* funeral?" My blood ran Cove cold.

Jillian's eyes watered as she nodded. "Zeus. You know, the cocker spaniel? He limped into the City yesterday. He'd gotten into a fight. I knew he wouldn't make it; I could just tell. Ahmad and I buried him this morning. And then I found a baby bird on the way back from burying Zeus. It had fallen out of a tree. It was already dead. It was so small, Rives, it fit in my palm. I couldn't just leave it there." Jillian lifted her chin, then sighed again. "So I buried it where I found it underneath the tree. I know they weren't people, but still. If Thad hadn't made it—" She broke off, clearly fighting back tears. "I can't even. Zeus was bad enough. And the bird." She rolled her eyes. "I know you think I'm crazy."

"No," I said softly. "I think you're kind. And I think you did the right thing." On Nil, death rivaled life for attention, and the way we treated the dead said more about us than the deceased. With animals, usually we ate them. But sometimes our humanity was more important than a meal. And we sure as hell didn't eat puppies.

I was also thinking we shouldn't have named the dog Zeus.

"Thanks." Jillian nodded. She bit her lip. "Have you seen Burton lately?"

"Nope. Maybe he hitched a ride home." I smiled.

"Maybe," Jillian said. Only she didn't smile.

Burton was a Nil cat Thad had adopted, much like Jillian had been taken with Zeus. Thad had asked me to keep an eye out for Burton, but I hadn't seen the black cat since Thad left. Not a good sign for Burton.

"So tomorrow night's a Nil Night, right?" Jillian said.

I hesitated.

"Rives, we need this." Her voice was quiet. "Everyone needs this."

I thought of the relief on Jason's face when I announced Thad's fate, and the sleepless bruises under his eyes. I thought of the weight on Dex's shoulders that had nothing to do with the net. And I thought of the girl standing silently near Dex, her face unreadable.

"You're right," I said, unwilling to bring my baggage to the party. Nil Nights *were* a party, a short-lived distraction from Nil's rules. With today's double departure, a Nil Night was definitely in order. "Tomorrow night," I agreed. "We all need a decent night's sleep."

"Rives!" Ahmad's deep voice boomed behind me. "There's something you need to see! You busy?"

"On my way," I called, already moving toward him.

Jillian fell in step beside me. "Does he even need to ask?"

"I hear that," Jason said, jogging to catch up. "With an intro like that, it's got to be good."

"You know it." But it wasn't Ahmad's words that had me stoked; it was his tone: pumped, with absolutely no trace of fear.

Nil had shifted, again.

Time to see how the island wanted to play.

CHAPTER 4

SKYE
NOVEMBER 16, AFTERNOON

The journal handwriting was slanted but neat. Written in black ball-point pen, the printed letters pressed into the paper with an intensity I could touch. No line was skipped.

I began with the first.

> My name is Scott Bracken, and this is my journal.
>
> Dr. Andrews says the first step in my recovery is to write down all my thoughts on paper. That the exercise will help me differentiate between reality and delusion. She tells me that once my thoughts are written down, I'll be able to "separate the wheat from the chaff," as if somehow by turning my thoughts into concrete words, they will magically distill into clear columns of truth and lies, of fiction and nonfiction.
>
> She's wrong.
>
> Because it's all true.
>
> Every word.
>
> My name is Scott Bracken, and this is the truth.

Entry #1

I read once that the most powerful memories are triggered by smell. Not mine. My most powerful memories are triggered by heat.

Blistering, burning, brutal heat—the kind of heat that you think you won't survive and yet you do, and then you spend the next ten months wondering if it would've been easier not to survive after all, even as you spend every waking minute fighting to live. To feel the heat again because it's life. Or maybe it's death, because no one really knows.

But I know now.

It's both.

Yesterday Mom was baking brownies. I was standing next to her when she opened the oven door. Searing, airless heat hit my face—and I choked. I couldn't breathe. Couldn't think. Couldn't stop thinking.

I flinched, waiting for the fiery pain that never came. I didn't want the brownies.

I've been home for 28 days.

Nothing is the same. I am not the same. I feel the fracture inside myself, inside my head, even as I know I'm sane. But if I'm not, it's because the island made me crazy.

My name is Scott Bracken, and this is the truth.

Entry #2

This is how it began.

I was riding my bike to Stephanie's house. I remember how perfect the day was: Stephanie's call inviting me over for lunch, the clear May Connecticut sky. I remember the Van Halen tickets in my pocket. A surprise, setting up the raddest date ever. She was obsessed with David Lee Roth. I like the Police better, but it wasn't about me. It was about her. We'd just started hanging out, and now that I could drive, my world had expanded.

But I wasn't driving that day.

Sometimes I wonder if that would have made a difference. Me driving, instead of biking, me not taking the road less traveled. I read that poem once in school—did a report on it, even. It seemed lame at the time. Now it seems fucking brilliant.

Daniel had the car, which was annoying since we shared the wagon. For all I knew, he'd forgotten I was supposed to have the car that afternoon. After Stephanie's, I was supposed to meet up with Will and Mark to go rent a movie at the new video store down the street. But Daniel was late, and I didn't want to wait. He was always late.

I've never asked him if he forgot. It seems so insignificant now. Sometimes I wonder about the concert tickets. Did anyone find them? Did anyone use them? But like with the car, it doesn't matter.

I never made it to Stephanie's house.

The heat got me first.

Two streets from my house, the road buckled and rocketed straight up into the air ten feet in front of me—then the street dropped away, leaving rippling air in its wake and me with no time to stop. I hit the shimmering air straight on. It burned; it hurt; it was like getting ripped one cell at a time through a

27

white-hot needle. The impact knocked me out, or so I thought. Later I figured out it was the heat.

I woke up on fire.

Literally—my right calf was melting; I lay on warm black rock, sprawled about six feet from a swath of steaming lava, and the skin on my right calf was red and blistering. BECAUSE OF THE FUCKING LAVA. Black and angry, the lava oozed downhill like sludge, its surface cracking into ribbons of fire as it inched forward. Hissing steam billowed to the right; huge mushroom clouds of scalding vapor that I knew would fry my lungs if I got anywhere close.

My bike was gone. My street was gone. MY CLOTHES WERE GONE.

And there wasn't a soul in sight.

But other than my calf, I wasn't burned. I wasn't even scratched.

All those realizations set in within three seconds flat.

Maybe my mind cracked that day after all; maybe it was the part I couldn't see that shattered on landing.

But I know it didn't.

I still have scars on my right calf.

Yeah, I'm still pissed off. Yeah, I'm angry. I have a right to be. Because I was there and NO ONE HERE BELIEVES ME.

My name is Scott Bracken, and this is the truth.

Entry #3

I ran with no idea where I was running to or what I was running from. All I knew was that chilling out with an active volcano was a fast track to death.

I had no clue my fight with death was just beginning.

I ran away from the lava, away from the steam. Over the black rock, which cooled with each step. My calf burned, but I didn't stop to look.

I'm not sure how long I ran. I ran until I slowed. A stitch in my side made me stop. I was sweating, the soles of my feet felt raw—I didn't want to look—and it had just hit me again that I had no clue where I was. I searched for signs, roads, houses—something to tell me where I was, somewhere to get help. On a repeating loop my brain kept screaming, WHERE AM I mixed with the alternative, WAKE THE FUCK UP.

I needed clothes and first aid for my leg, and the farther I walked, the more I needed water.

Soon water was all I could think about.

I followed the coast, heading what I thought was west, because sticking near the sea seemed sensible— not that I was an outdoors expert. My extracurricular activities included golf, a shitty stint as a wrestler, and playing Atari on the weekends. I rocked at Space Invaders.

I wondered if aliens had grabbed me.

The rocky black cliffs went on forever. I broke some large leaves off a low plant, knowing it could collect rain if clouds moved in, but in the meantime, I could collect my urine. I'd seen a documentary on a pilot who crashed in the Sahara and survived ten days alone by drinking his own urine. Granted, he filtered it through his clothes, a luxury I didn't have.

For the record, drinking your own piss sucks. It's warm and foul and yeah—it's URINE. But until I found water, I didn't have many options.

I stopped at the cliff's edge, at the farthest outcropping. Blue-green water crashed against the black rocks below. To my left was the volcano, steaming. To the right, I couldn't see; I'd only know what was there when the cliffs ended. Straight ahead was only water. Endless, glinting water.

And none of it I could drink.

There was a poem about that once, too. Or maybe it was a song. All I know is that it was cruel. And totally right on.

Twilight came, fast and furious and beautiful and frightening. The sea was still too far a drop; the cliffs were vertical black, like slabs of earth chopped straight down. As night fell, I was freezing, shaking with cold and pain. My feet were bloody and my calf burned; one blister had broken open. It was bloody too.

With the stars and moon overhead, I dug a shallow hole with a rock, more like a low hollow, and I lay in it with a few dead palm fronds as coverage. If I slept, I don't remember it.

I got up with the sun. My lips were cracked. Dry, probably sunburned. I sat up, wide-awake in the nightmare that raged in daylight. I tried to pee but lost the few drops I had left; my hands were shaking so badly I dropped the leaf.

I needed water.

Fresh water.

I forced myself up, and when a break in the cliffs

seemed manageable, I climbed down, looking for fresh water as I went. I worked my way around the cliff's base, which was less steep now, more like a black rock bulkhead. It took hours. I moved slowly, wishing there was shade; I'd stopped sweating, which was bad. I kept thinking these low rocks would hold fresh rainwater in the nooks that pitted the edges near the cliff base, but everything was salty. I should've stayed up high, but too late now. I remember thinking that I wasn't thinking clearly, and I remember hoping that when I turned the corner, I'd find docks and houses.

But when I turned the corner, all I saw was a stretch of beach—wide and black, sand not rock, buffered by palm trees, and not a soul in sight. Endless. I managed to make it to the tree line, where I collapsed in the shade of a palm tree and closed my eyes to rest.

Now this is where it gets weird.

Make that weirder.

I woke in that odd wide-awake state that I'd been in since I opened my eyes by the lava. I was still naked. But I wasn't alone. A strange, elongated shadow stretched across the sand.

Fresh fear coursed through me like adrenaline, bringing a rush of jumbled thoughts. I'm-naked-I-don't-want-anyone-to-see-me-but-oh-God-I-need-help-and-I'm-so-thirsty-and-maybe-they-can-tell-me-where-I-am-and-take-me-home-what-if-it's-an-alien-oh-please-God-help-me.

I turned slowly.

A giraffe stepped into the sunlight, working a

leafy green branch in its mouth, regarding me curiously. An honest-to-God GIRAFFE.

I began laughing hysterically, then started coughing. My tongue was swollen and dry. I coughed up blood and no longer laughed.

Maybe I'd inhaled some of the steam yesterday after all. Or maybe the blood was from my tongue.

The giraffe strolled away, bored.

Giraffe Land sucked.

I know what you're thinking. Get a coconut, dude. If there are palm trees, there must be coconuts, too, right? I tried. I shook a dozen trees, but the trees barely budged and the coconuts definitely didn't. None were on the ground, either.

Night fell again, fast. Twilight in Giraffe Land didn't hang around long. The black sand was warm, but the air was cold, and night number two in Giraffe Land was as bad as night number one.

I shook, like I had a fever. Maybe I did, because that night I drifted in and out of a weird sleepy-exhausted-shaky-thirsty state, and woke the same way. The sun came up, and I just lay there. So thirsty. My brain couldn't think, but it could imagine, and here's the one memory that I fully admit might be a delusion: I tilted my head toward the trees and a girl materialized from the brush. She had long dark hair falling around her shoulders, a white skirt and matching white tube top, and a thin halo of white flowers around the top of her head.

I think she was an angel. I'm still not sure she was real.

She was real.

She placed one finger over her lips, came forward, knelt, and placed an oyster shell to my lips. "Slow," she whispered. Brown eyes as warm as chocolate. "Drink."

I drank. Water. The cleanest water I'd ever tasted.

She lifted my hand to take the shell. "Go north," she said. "Find those like you. Find what you seek and Godspeed home."

She went to stand and I grabbed her wrist. "Wait! Who are you? Where am I?"

She shook her head and deftly slid her wrist from my grip. "The answers you seek do not lie with me." She pointed to the sand beside me. "Find what you need. The island helps those who help themselves. And stay away from the meadow."

I looked down, following her finger, and found a piece of dingy white cotton—a loincloth. Beside it rested a gourd. Heavy. Full of water.

When I looked up, she was gone.

I never saw her again.

My name is Scott Bracken, and this is the truth.

Needing a break, I closed the journal, feeling dirty even though Dad had told me to read it. Reading my uncle's journal was like prying into someone's mind—possibly a very fractured, damaged mind.

What Uncle Scott wrote couldn't possibly be real.

Could it?

I ran downstairs, journal in hand.

"Dad!" I shouted.

"In here," he called from his office. He faced the wall map of the South Pacific but turned the moment I entered. "Yes?"

"What is this?" I held up the journal, a private account of *something*. "Was Uncle Scott mentally ill? Is that why he was on that bridge?"

"How far did you get?" he asked. His voice was remarkably calm.

"I stopped after entry number three."

He nodded. "So you know that I was late, and that he might have never made it to that place—" He paused, visibly wrestling personal demons I'd never known he had.

"Giraffe Land," I added helpfully.

Dad tipped his head. "Giraffe Land, if it weren't for me. For my carelessness with time, my utter lack of awareness of it. It's a selfishness of another sort. And that's part of my drive, Skye. Because I'm partially responsible for what happened to him."

I thought about Scott's words. "The road less traveled."

"Indeed."

But Uncle Scott picked the route. I shook my head. "You can't blame yourself. He chose to bike rather than wait. He chose to take that particular street, and for all you know, the same thing would've happened if he'd driven. So to blame yourself for this"—I held up the journal again—"um, no."

"Perhaps I'm not fully to blame, but I shoulder a great deal of responsibility. Call it the butterfly effect, a ripple in time or fate. Our choices define and shape our lives, and our choices impact others. Because I was late—which was my choice, conscious or not—Scott was in the wrong place at the wrong time."

We were discussing the journal as if it were truth.

"So you're saying Uncle Scott wasn't crazy." I paused, trying to wrap my head around Giraffe Land and failing. "You're saying that his journal is fact, not fiction."

"Let me tell you what *isn't* in that journal." Dad sat on the edge of his desk and folded his hands in his lap. "A week after our sixteenth

34

birthday, Scott disappeared. The police never found a single lead except for his bike. Ten months later, Scott was found less than two hours away in Boston on someone's lawn, naked, scratched, and *tan*—mind you, it's March—with old, healed scars on his cheek and calf. He was taken into police custody and refused to talk until our parents arrived. He looked older, in ways I couldn't even begin to describe, and when he told us the story, I'd no doubt he'd survived something both wonderful and terrible. He'd survived Giraffe Land, as he called it."

He pointed at the journal in my hand. "I believe that what he wrote is the truth. Not a delusion, but a reality that he fought to understand after the fact. I looked in his eyes his first day back, Skye. It was all there. Not just the belief, but the depth of sorrow and growth and triumph and strength borne from his experience; it reached all the way to his soul. We were the same age, yet he was so much older. It was in his eyes." His voice softened. "And that's something your mom never had the chance to see."

He looked at me. "I'm the first to tell you I don't understand how he got there, and as a scientist, it's baffling. Maddening. Almost incomprehensible. But I firmly believe Giraffe Land exists. And"—his expression was as fierce and protective as I'd ever seen—"now you know why I've always driven you to be strong. To be resourceful. To be prepared in the event of any sort of catastrophe. So that if you—God forbid—find yourself on that island, you are as equipped to survive as you can be."

A long moment passed.

"The true name of the island is Nil," he said quietly. "And I think I know where to find it."

CHAPTER
5

RIVES
DAY 241, MID-AFTERNOON

Ahmad took point.

He outpaced us quickly, which wasn't surprising given his long stride. Behind Ahmad, Jillian and Jason bantered the whole way to the Cove. I dropped back, intent on filtering the island silence. Trees whispered, their leaves restlessly answering the island breeze. The closer we got to the Cove, the lusher the trees. Bright blue sky flickered through the canopy, a cerulean ceiling free of white.

Past the trees, the Cove broke wide open.

Crisp, clean water fell seven stories into a pristine pool as cold as ice. Black rock, green moss. White water. Blue sky. A photojournalist's wet dream for sure. Not that I had my lens.

"Follow me!" Ahmad waded into the clear pool, elbows high, white froth pooling around his dark waist as he headed straight to the falls. At the final second, he ducked and disappeared under the churning water.

I turned to Jillian and Jason. "You two stay here. Keep watch. Whistle three times if you need us." I wasn't sure we'd hear a whistled warning, but it was worth a shot. I always felt vulnerable behind the falls because I couldn't see what was waiting for me when I came out.

"Ugh." Jillian rolled her eyes. "Fine. We'll stay put. But don't keep us in suspense."

Jason nodded. "We're on it. Just watch your back. And Ahmad's." He crossed his arms, his expression both fierce and anxious.

Grinning, I squeezed his shoulder. "Don't worry, bro. Like you said, it's got to be good, right?"

Jillian snorted. "Don't answer that, Jason. Rives, just be safe."

"Always." With a wink at Jillian, I strode into the pool after Ahmad, gritting my teeth against the icy bite. When the water hit my waist, I switched to freestyle, covered the distance to the falls quickly, and dove. The sound dulled, muffled underwater. The light dimmed, too, but the darkness told me where to go.

I surfaced into cool air. Water roared at my back like a freight train. In front of me, where there used to be a wide ledge at least eight meters wide, now there was a narrow lip butting against a rockslide. Beyond that, an opening beckoned, partially blocked by rocks.

"Check it out!" Ahmad said, raising his voice over the sound of the falls. "I don't know how far or how deep it is. I didn't go in. I wasn't about to get stuck." He gestured to his nearly seven-foot self. "But you don't need to go in to see it. Look."

I leaned toward the dark hole for a better look.

It was another carving.

A rough diamond shape about a meter tall, with a stick figure dead center. Beside it ran a vertical line, an arrow pointing to the sky. Or at least pointing to the top of the cave.

There was nothing else.

"What do you think?" Ahmad asked. He peered over my shoulder.

"I don't know," I said, unsure what to think. All I knew was that I wanted a closer look.

I hauled rocks away from the base to clear a larger opening. Beside me, Ahmad helped me keep the ledge clear. After I'd enlarged the opening enough for me to fit through easily, a thought struck. I leaned back on my heels and looked at Ahmad. "When you checked the Cove for slides, how did you know to look behind the falls?"

Ahmad shifted uncomfortably. "I don't know, man. I just—this is going to sound weird—but I felt pulled toward the falls. Like an urge to check the ledge."

It doesn't sound weird, I thought. *It sounds like Nil.*

I'd been more focused on the island than ever lately, acutely aware of all I didn't understand. My desire to escape warred with my thirst for understanding. It's why I'd spent hours at the Wall in recent weeks, counting the names, searching for patterns and clues, compelled to stare even as part of me ached to stay far away.

And each day over the past few weeks I'd woken with a fierce sense of *wanting*, a sense that the island was urging me toward understanding. Maybe it was all in my head, but it felt real.

For the past few weeks, I'd also been hearing Talla's voice, especially when I was near water. I didn't know what that meant. Probably that I was one day closer to bat-shit crazy.

Ahmad stared at the carving like I stared at the Wall.

"I thought I was going to find someone trapped." His voice was thick. "I really did. And when I came up behind the falls and saw the rockslide and the opening—and it wasn't more than a sliver, just enough to see the open space behind the rocks—I panicked. I was sure someone was stuck behind the rockslide. I shouted, my pulse racing like I'd just finished sprints, but all I heard was an echo. No answer. And I kept clearing rock like a machine. When I saw the carving through the opening, I relaxed. I can't explain it." He shrugged. "It's like I knew no one was in there. That I could stop. Then I cleared off as much of the ledge as I could."

He laughed, a small one of disbelief. "I know it sounds weird."

"No weirder than passing out and waking up naked on an island that doesn't exist," I said.

"Good point." Ahmad chuckled, visibly relaxing.

It was the second carving Ahmad had discovered near a rockslide. It couldn't be a coincidence. Nothing here was a coincidence.

Thad had always viewed the island as a person, as a living, breathing entity hell-bent on making our lives miserable and playing with us every step of the way. On the other hand, most people, like Charley and Jillian, just viewed the island as a hunk of rock, a place that existed where it shouldn't.

My view of Nil hung somewhere in the middle. More than a rock, possibly sentient. But evil? Intent on misery? I wasn't sure, but my gut said no. Something told me that Nil was as alive as we were, or at least the force that brought us here was. It didn't feel random, not to me. And it also didn't feel evil.

Harsh? Yeah.

Cruel? Absolutely.

But not always, because the island had definite moments of benevolence—although I viewed each island kindness with suspicion. Because if I had to pick one word to describe Nil, I wouldn't pick *evil*. I'd pick *calculating*.

And now Ahmad was two for two.

I traced the diamond etching with one finger. Rough and shallow, the carving matched the exact shape of the island that Charley had sketched on her maps. Other than the arrow pointing north, there was nothing else carved into the wall.

The diamond felt . . . unfinished.

There must be more, I thought. *More to this carving. More to this cave. More to this whole damn island.* Maybe I just wanted there to be more, but there was only one way to find out.

Be fearless, the waterfall crooned.

"I'm going in," I said.

"What?" Ahmad's eyes widened. "No way, Rives. You don't know

39

what's in there. You don't even have a light. What if the air inside is toxic? It's a bad idea, man."

"The cave just opened up with the quake, Ahmad, so I doubt anything's in there. And it's been open long enough to vent, so I'm not worried about the air. I've been sitting here breathing it and I haven't passed out yet." I grinned. "Neither have you. Plus, I'm just going to go a little way. I want to make sure we're not missing anything else."

"Don't do it, man. Let's wait. Not today."

"Definitely today. It's the only today I've got, right?" I winked.

A weighted silence dropped as flat as my joke.

Ahmad shook his head. "I don't like it, man."

"Point taken."

I was already climbing inside. Light faded with each step. Slightly bent, I moved slowly, feeling my way, touching both sides of the cave's walls. Moisture clung to them like moss.

The cave narrowed. Soon the walls brushed my sides. I still crouched, but the cave hadn't pushed me to my knees. Yet.

"Rives?" Ahmad's voice echoed behind me.

"Still here," I called back.

"Find anything?"

"Not yet."

I moved farther into the cave, which now was more tunnel than cave. Behind me, a rough oval framed Ahmad's silhouette. Before me the space loomed flat black, like an incoming gate with a rider, only the air ahead didn't waver. Didn't move. It was as if the cave was holding its breath, waiting for me.

Then I felt it.

On my left, a single arrow in the wall pointed away from the Cove. *Come*, it whispered.

"Rives!" Ahmad's voice shot through the tunnel, his tone faint and anxious. "You're making me nervous, man."

40

Every cell in my body screamed to follow the arrow. But the worry in Ahmad's voice made me pause. So did my role as Leader.

The scrabble of rocks echoed through the tunnel, followed by a loud *thunk* and a muffled curse.

"Rives?" Jason called. "You're going to run out of daylight soon. You coming?" The pain in Jason's voice made me turn back.

I tapped the arrow. "I'm not done with you," I said.

Ahmad and Jason waited outside the entrance. When they saw me, their faces relaxed, a tell they couldn't hide. But Jason's didn't relax completely. He gripped his left hand tightly with his right.

I pointed at his hand. "What'd you do?"

"Dropped a rock on it." Jason looked disgusted. "Jammed my finger."

"Find anything?" Ahmad asked. "Or anyone?"

"No people. No skeletons. No bad Indiana Jones moments at all." I grinned. "I didn't even find the end. It was pitch-black in there."

I wasn't sure why I didn't tell them about the arrow.

Liar, the falls whispered. *You know why.*

I did know. It was my discovery, my arrow, and I wanted to be the one to follow it. The urge to turn back toward the arrow was potent, but now wasn't the time.

Soon, I told myself.

Jillian waited by the Cove's edge.

I pointed to Jason's hand. "Jills, will you check out Jason's finger? Says he jammed it."

Jillian's mom was a physical therapist, specializing in orthopedic rehab, and her older brother was in med school. That made Jillian our resident expert in island medicine. As she gingerly felt his finger, Jason's jaw tensed.

"It's broken," she said flatly. "I'm sure of it. I did the same thing when I was eight." She gestured to my waist. "I need your knife and bandana."

41

Two minutes later, she'd sliced the cloth into wide strips and carefully tied Jason's middle two fingers together with a piece of bamboo in a makeshift splint.

He lifted his bandaged hand to Jillian. "Thanks." She waved it off.

"No more gliders for you, Jason," I said. "I promised Thad I'd keep you in one piece." I grinned. "And don't think I'm not telling Miya to keep you out of trouble."

Jason's cheeks reddened. I grinned wider.

I filled Jillian in on the walk back.

"So it's just a long tunnel?" Jillian frowned. "And it dead-ends?"

"I don't know where it ends, or how. It was pitch-black, and I was almost out of voice range with Ahmad. For all I know, it dead-ends into a wall."

Jillian played with one of her braids. Then she looked at me, her sapphire eyes sharp. "But you don't think so, do you, Rives?"

"No. I don't think it's a dead end. I think it leads somewhere, to something. Maybe to something important."

Jillian watched me thoughtfully. "Rives, promise me you won't do something stupid." Her eyes searched mine, her expression worried. "Promise me."

"I promise." I reached over and tugged on one braid.

She rolled her eyes. "Why don't I feel better?"

CHAPTER
6

SKYE
NOVEMBER 16, MID-AFTERNOON

"Nil," I repeated. "What kind of name is that?"

Dad rubbed his chin. "I'm not certain. But Scott references it by name in his journal."

"Dad, if Nil exists, why has no one heard of it? Why has no one found it before?"

"Excellent questions. First, a few things. Scott didn't fully understand the island himself. People arrive through portals and apparently leave the same way. There doesn't seem to be any other avenue of escape. The portals—the teens called them gates—appeared in the lava fields a few times a month, always at midday, and sometimes somewhere else. There weren't that many people on the island. Scott guessed twenty on average, twenty-five at most, from all over the globe. So I'm guessing that perhaps one person arrives each week, possibly two. Extrapolate that and you have approximately fifty-two people per year, 104 at the most. Compare that to lightning. Lightning strikes kill approximately twenty-four thousand people around the world each year. And about two hundred forty thousand globally are injured by lightning. Based on those numbers, the odds of being struck by lightning, let alone killed, are incredibly small. There are over seven billion people in the world, Skye. So put the island against that global back-drop. The odds of hearing about a few dozen or even a hundred people going to some remote island is almost nonexistent." He paused. "Plus, according to Scott, only teenagers made it to the island. And unfortunately, the disappearance of a teen spurs less interest than, say, a child gone missing or an adult. A sad truth, but a truth nonetheless."

I shivered.

"And don't forget," he said, "I know it doesn't seem like it to you, but the World Wide Web connecting the globe is relatively new. So until news searches were available at the click of a Google button, it was up to people sifting through papers and microfilm in libraries. I haven't made strides myself until the last few years."

"Really? You've 'made strides'?" I couldn't help making air quotes around his words. "How?"

"This." He tapped a group of papers tacked at eye level. "Over the past ten years, I've tracked every news story I could find about teenagers appearing naked in odd places, because according to Scott's journal, everyone arrives on the island nude, and based on his experience, when they return, they wake in the same bare state."

Do they always find clothes? I wondered. It seemed a small point, but I'd seen an ad for the television show *Naked and Afraid*, and the naked guy on TV was the scariest thing I'd seen in a while. Plus being naked on an island sounded like an absolute nightmare.

"There aren't many stories," he continued, oblivious to my naked-and-afraid horror, "but the few I've found stand out. Only one mentions an island, but the articles tell me it's still happening." He walked over to the massive map of the South Pacific.

"As you know, I've traveled extensively to the South Pacific. I've spoken to hundreds of islanders and collected volumes of anecdotal information. I've been putting together the pieces for twenty years, Skye. But the big break came last year, in Micronesia. My guide—Charles, the one who hailed from Tuvalu—spoke of a place. Here." His hands traced an invisible circle on the map and stopped at a yellow tack in the center. "Spirit Island, his grandmother called it, a place of magic and mystery only accessed by a select few."

Dad turned toward me, his expression resolute. "And this December I'm going to find it."

"What do you mean, '*I'm* going to find it'?" Something felt off, like I was late to the party. Not that I went to parties, but still.

"I'm heading to Micronesia at the start of winter break. I've got a charter booked and ready. I'll be gone for roughly two weeks."

I processed his words. There were an awful lot of *I*'s. "I'm going with you, right?"

He shook his head. "It's too remote. Too dangerous. You'll stay with your mom."

"No can do, Dad." I fought a winning smile. "Mom's not coming home for Christmas, remember? She's not coming back to the States until spring break."

Dad's expression said he'd totally forgotten, which wasn't surprising. His organization was bad on a good day, and with Mom's surprise departure, Dad was a full-blown parental mess.

"Your mom's not coming back until spring break," he repeated slowly. It was an old trick he used, buying time to think. "Right." He smiled too brightly. "I'll call my sister. I'm sure you could stay with Aunt Meg and the twins. I'll be gone for less than two weeks. More like twelve days and—"

"Stop." I cut him off with a wave. "I'm not staying with Aunt Meg. I'm going with you. End of story. You can't just shuffle me off with your sister because you forgot I'd be here."

He winced. "I'm not shuffling you off. I'm trying to keep you safe."

"Bullcrap, Dad. You forgot, plain and simple. You made plans and now you're stuck. I'm coming with you."

"What about Tish?" Dad's tone was desperate.

"What about Tish?" I said flatly. Tish was my best friend back in Gainesville. I knew where he was headed, but I refused to make it easy.

"Perhaps you could stay with her?" His upbeat tone pleaded for a yes.

I crossed my arms. "So I can't stay with Tish to finish out my senior year in Gainesville, but I can go spend the *entire Christmas break* with her? How messed up is that?" Two months ago I would've jumped at the chance to hang with Tish for two weeks. Now it felt like a consolation prize. I stared at my dad, unwilling to back down.

He flinched first.

"No," I said calmly. "No Aunt Meg, no Tish." *No ditching me like Mom.* "Book another ticket because I'm coming with you. And in case you've forgotten"—I took care to emphasize that last word—"I'm pretty good at taking care of myself. Isn't that what you've worked so hard to make sure of all these years?"

Dad's shoulders drooped, and I knew I'd won.

"Fine." He sighed. "But you'll stick with me at all times on the trip, okay? No wandering off, Skye."

"Deal." I smiled. "So when do we leave?"

CHAPTER
7

Chalk one up in the let's-make-people-suffer category of Nil.

Jason's gritted teeth spoke volumes.

We'd just finished eating. Actually, I'd just finished chowing down on three shrimp wraps, but Jason had barely touched his food.

I pointed at his half-eaten wrap. "Your finger killing your appetite, bro?"

"Yeah. I can't believe I dropped a frickin' rock on it." He sighed. The circles under his eyes darkened in the afternoon shadows.

"It happens." I took a hard look at his finger and frowned. Angry flesh bulged between the tight white lines of Jillian's homemade bandage. Luckily for Jason, his bone hadn't broken the skin, but it obviously hurt like hell. "You're off watch until I say otherwise," I told him. "Try to get some sleep tonight, all right? Hit it early."

He nodded.

Jason walked away, cradling his hand, shoulders stooped in exhaustion and pain. I sighed, knowing he needed rest to heal but cruelly aware that pain and sleep meshed as well as oil and water. He needed a painkiller that would knock him out.

He needed Sabine's deadsleep tea.

It had helped Charley, maybe even made the difference for her. But so many what-ifs here were out of my control, binding my hands with invisible ties.

What kind of Leader was I?

One who's fearless, I thought grimly.

I strode back to my hut.

Behind it, resting on a flat plank, three coconut shell cups sat waiting. By my count, the deadleaf seeds had been soaking in water for a week, the same time frame Sabine had mentioned once. No seeds had been fermenting when Talla had been hurt, and there hadn't been time to soak them. No one knew a shortcut. No one knew Sabine's secrets.

Except me.

I'd sat with her the day she'd mixed deadsleep tea for Charley. I'd watched Sabine's every move and paid attention to her potion. I didn't know a fermentation shortcut, but I knew the process from there.

It was time to experiment.

It was time to wrench this variable in our favor. If not for Jason, whose broken finger was minor by Nil injury standards, then for the next person who clung to life. I was done with watching people get hurt and die.

I picked up the first cup. Using a clean piece of taro leaf, I carefully scooped out all seven seeds and dumped them on the ground like Sabine had done. The remaining water was tinged gold; it was the same translucent caramel shade I remembered. Possibly darker.

Rivessss . . .

The afternoon breeze whispered like a ghost. It blew onshore, smelling like salt and sea and memories. I looked toward the field, where the inked boy had stood, where bleached coral crosses lined the field's edge and marked island graves.

Be fearlesssss . . .

Careful not to spill the amber liquid, I carried the cup into my hut, where a small table, an empty cup, and a gourd of water waited.

Recalling Sabine's methodical steps, I cut the fermented liquid by half with clean water. I sniffed it. Bitter, but not unpleasant. I took a sip. Too sharp, too strong. I added more water and sipped again, twice. The flavor still tasted off. I added a dash more water and drank again. I frowned and took another drink, rolling the tea around on my tongue. The strength felt right—but the tea wasn't.

Something was missing.

I drank another swallow, and a memory hit: fruit juice. Just before she'd given it to Charley, Sabine had mixed fruit juice into the tea, a blend of guava and redfruit juice. I'd assumed it was for flavor, to cut the bitterness, but maybe it was to cut the tea's strength. Maybe it was to neutralize the acidic bite; maybe it was to keep the tea's balance between life and death.

Maybe it was important.

I had this juice epiphany as I realized I couldn't move. My legs and arms were dead weight masquerading as flesh and bone, sinew and muscle. They were attached to me, yet they weren't; below my neck, I felt nothing. My eyelids dropped like blackout shades.

Merde.

The thought ended as I slammed into a wall of black; the black hit me, held me, turned me into stone. Inside my skull, blackness dripped through my brain, thick and heavy. No heat, no ice.

No sensation at all.

No me.

CHAPTER 8

SKYE
NOVEMBER 16, MID-AFTERNOON

"Four weeks," Dad said grudgingly. "We fly out on December eighteenth. Normally I'd be ecstatic to have you come with me, you know that, Skye. But I feel like I'm putting you in harm's way. You're still a kid."

"I'll be eighteen in February, so technically I'm almost an adult." I paused. "But more importantly, I'm a teenager, which—correct me if I'm wrong—are the only people allowed on the island, right? So did it ever occur to you I might just be your best hope of finding it?"

Dad looked less thrilled by the minute.

I changed the subject before he changed his mind. "Dad, say we find this island, Nil. Then what? Not to dash your dreams, but what's the point? Is it just to prove that Uncle Scott was telling the truth?"

"Confirmation of the island's existence is part of it, certainly. The island's existence goes against every scientific fiber of my being, and the scientist in me wants to confirm it for myself. But there's more." He paused. "I think that if I—we," he quickly amended as I arched my eyebrows, "can find the island, then we can save the sanity and potentially even the lives of the kids who end up there. Once the island's existence is acknowledged to the outside world, then the teens won't suffer the stigma of disbelief. And we'll also have the coordinates so all the teens there can be rescued."

I frowned. "One problem. Didn't Uncle Scott say the only way to the island was a portal? So what's the connection between these kids"— I tapped the articles of missing-and-then-found teens—"and this possibly-real mysterious island?" Now I tapped the special yellow tack out in nowhere.

"I'm not sure," Dad admitted. "I can't help but think there might be another way onto the island, possibly a direct route, accessed by boat? Perhaps it's so remote that it's difficult to find? Perhaps something is protecting the island, such as a natural barrier? That part of the Pacific Ocean is enormous. We just need the coordinates, Skye. We'll use the information from my guide, Charles, and the stars to guide us; Scott references specific constellations in his journal. And if we can find Nil, we can save all the kids. We're the answer they've been waiting for." The fanatical news-of-the-weird gleam was back.

Something told me finding the island wouldn't be as easy as Dad believed, and finding a way to save the kids would be even harder.

Maybe even impossible.

Otherwise wouldn't it have already been done?

"Maybe," I said. *Or maybe it's the ultimate island pipe dream.*

I backed up, raising the journal like a shield. "I'm going to go read. Try to find something to help us." *And something to help me believe.*

"Good thinking." Dad's eyes shone, a sign he thought I was fully on board the crazy train with him. The truth was, I *was* on board with the idea of going along with my dad for a Micronesian excursion rather than being left behind over winter break. But as for the mysterious island of Nil and Dad's pie-in-the-sky hope of not only finding this tiny island somewhere in the giant Pacific Ocean, but also rescuing the kids? I wasn't on board with that train wreck at all. Not that I didn't think it was noble and laudable and a lovely Christmas gift for everyone; I just didn't think it was likely, or even possible. I thought Dad was setting himself up for mega disappointment.

Still, a trip to the Pacific Islands in December sure sounded nice.

Weeks later I'd remember that thought. *Nice* wasn't the right word at all.

Risky.

Surprising.

Terrifying.

Naïve.

Deadly.

Anything but *nice.*

CHAPTER 9

SKYE
NOVEMBER 16, EVENING

I opened my uncle's journal and picked up where I'd left off.

Entry #4

    I know she told me to go north, but I sensed she went east.

    I walked up the beach, toward the spindly trees and scrub. Toward where I felt she'd be, knowing I was chasing a vision or a dream or possibly the only person stuck in this nightmare with me. Just past the scrub the island opened wide, a flat black rock field without end. Beautiful and stark and awesome and chilling, as sharp a contrast as an Ansel Adams photo.

    Stark black rock, pale blue sky. Crisp. Clear. Lifeless.

    Dangerous.

    Light flashed ahead, a wink on the black, and I froze; I thought of the glistening air I hit on Oak Street, wondering if this was Burning Air Hell Round Two.

But this light didn't rise. Didn't move. I stepped closer and the light disappeared.

Two more steps and I saw why. Three-foot-wide tunnels snaked through the black rock, full of water, reflecting the sun. No fish. No life. Just water, so clear I could see the rock bottom. I wondered if she'd led me here.

I fell to my knees. Warm water, decently fresh to the taste. I drank until I couldn't.

I sat back, wiped my mouth, and watched the ripples from my hands fade. The surface became a mirror. A boy with spiky brown hair and sleepless eyes gazed back at me. It was the first time I saw myself on the island, and the last time I looked scared.

Now I look fearless.

I spent the rest of that afternoon puking my guts out. I never drank that water again.

My name is Scott Bracken, and this is the truth.

The next few entries described Uncle Scott's search for food, another giraffe sighting, and his obsession with the mysterious girl who may or may not be an angel.

The seventh entry was different. Meticulous sketches of constellations filled the pages. I recognized Orion immediately; for the others I relied on Uncle Scott's identification. I guessed these were the sketches Dad would use to navigate toward the mysterious island.

My turn first.

I pulled up images on Google and tried to match the constellations Uncle Scott drew to the night sky over Polynesia and Micronesia. Beneath them sprawled open water.

Nothing else.

I wasn't sure who was crazier, Uncle Scott or my dad.

That night I dreamed of giraffes dancing on hot lava, and when I woke, I decided I might not be all that balanced either.

And I still didn't believe.

CHAPTER 10

RIVES
DAY 243, ALMOST DAWN

I surfaced from the deepest sleep of my life.

Around me, the air stretched black. Not the bottomless black I'd just woken from, but the rich black of a Nil night. The sky had a swipe of color, enough to hint that dawn would show. Waves crashed in steady rhythm. Otherwise, the island was still, like Nil recharged while we slept.

Beside me, Jillian slumped in a chair, eyes closed. Dex's sleeping form sprawled on the ground next to Jillian, their hands separated by a thin slash of air. Jason lay in Dex's bunk, out cold.

It felt like a deathwatch, only I was alive. More alive and rested than I'd felt in weeks.

I swung my legs over the edge of my bed. Before my feet hit the ground, Jillian sat bolt upright, her eyes red and blinking.

"Rives! You're awake! Thank God." Her eyes narrowed. "What were you *thinking*? You scared the crap out of us. We weren't sure you'd wake up. Ever." Exhaustion etched her face. "I found the deadsleep tea on your table. Only I wasn't stupid enough to drink it."

"Jills, I didn't mean to freak you out. I just—" I glanced at Jason, who was still asleep, his broken, bandaged finger propped on his chest.

"We need Sabine's tea." My voice was flat. "When Talla needed it, we didn't have it. Jason could've used it last night, and who knows how many people will need it in the future. And now I know how to make it." I cocked a slight smile.

Jillian's face hardened. "Jason could've used a night of not worrying you were dead. Make that *two* nights. You've been asleep for almost three days."

"Three days? No way." But the look on Jillian's face told me she wasn't kidding. No wonder my stomach felt like an empty pit. "Man, that tea is strong."

Jillian didn't crack a smile.

"Look. I'm sorry for worrying you, but I'm not sorry I tried it. I'd watched Sabine make it. I guess I drank more than I thought as I worked out the kinks. I forgot to add the juice." I shrugged. "I know we need the tea, and I've been figuring out how to make it."

"By testing it on yourself?"

"Better me than anyone else."

She shook her head. "Talla was bold, but she wasn't reckless. Or stupid. And she wouldn't want you to join her by the field."

"It was quite the cockup, Rives," Dex said. I hadn't realized he was awake. He sat up, bleary-eyed. One side of his hair was mashed flat against his head. "I found you facedown on the bed, breathing slowly, like each breath might be your last. Jillian's the one who told me you bloody well poisoned yourself." He rubbed his hair with both hands, making it all equally spiky, then pointed a long finger at me. "This island is dangerous enough without deadly home brews, mate. And the City needs you."

"Point taken. But now I know. More light breakfast blend, less espresso." I grinned.

Jillian scowled. "So much for your promise not to do anything stupid. Please don't make a habit of self-experimentation, okay?"

"I'll try."

She shook her head, then yawned and peeled herself off the chair. "Since you're back in the land of the living, I'm off to bed. See you in the morning." She sighed. "Which is almost here."

I stood. "Take my bunk. I've slept enough."

Jillian didn't argue. She climbed in and curled into a tight ball.

Dex lay back down. "Glad you're not dead, mate. You scared the piss out of us." His eyes were already closed. "Been a long few days," he mumbled.

A long few days.

Days I'd lost.

Time I'd lost, gone forever.

The urge to return to the Cove hit me full force, as undeniable as the need to breathe. No one carved an arrow unless it was meant to be followed.

Outside my hut, Zane stood a stone's throw away. His back to me, he studied the woods, holding a fresh rock-tipped spear. Ahmad's weapon work, no question. Snatched from Southern California, Zane alternated between looking totally at home to looking completely out of place. Right now, casing the perimeter with a spear instead of a board, he was a fish out of water.

I purposely stepped on a twig as I walked, loud enough to alert him to my presence but not wake the City.

Zane spun. "Jesus!"

"Nope. Just me." I grinned.

Zane pointed his spear at me. "Whoa, bro. You're not a ghost, right? Word is you're in an island coma."

"Boo."

Zane's eyes widened.

"Kidding." I grinned again. "No ghost. No coma. I'm fine."

Zane's stance relaxed. "Dude, you nearly gave me a coronary. No joke."

"Sorry." It was my word of the morning, apparently. "Anyone else up?"

"Just Macy." He pointed toward the Wall, where Macy stood, stretching.

"Morning, Rives." She smiled warmly as I walked up. "Good to see you." As in *Oh yeah, you're not dead.*

"Good to be seen," I replied. As in *yeah, still kicking it.*

"I knew you'd make it." Her calm tone was Macy confident.

"Yeah?"

"Yeah. Your heart was in the right place. You did it for everyone except you." Then she chuckled. "But also, Sabine told me once that deadsleep tea stops a person's heart in ten minutes. Otherwise, it just knocks you out, like what happened to you. So I knew you'd be okay."

"Huh," I said, absorbing Macy's reveal. "I guess I beat the odds."

Another tidbit that would've been good to know. A flash of frustration made my fists clench. Why was everything here so tough to figure out? It was like everybody got a piece of the puzzle, but no one got it all.

Until now, I thought fiercely. *I'm going to add it up, put it together. I'm going to unlock Nil's secrets if it kills me.*

It almost did, the wind whispered.

Macy's eyes flicked over my shoulder.

"Looking for someone?" I glanced behind me, only seeing Zane.

"Kiera," Macy said. "We're going to walk. She arrived the day you left with Thad," she added.

"Any other rookies?"

"Just Alexei. His English is pretty rough but he's doing okay. He's from Georgia. Not Charley's Georgia, but the Russian one."

"Georgia's actually a former Soviet Republic," I said absently.

"Well hello, Mr. Geography!"

I shrugged. "My dad covered a story there in 2008 when Georgia and Russia were on the brink of war."

Mental footage of Dad flanked by armored tanks and troops in flak jackets flooded my head, followed by images of bombed-out streets, children bloodied, soldiers blindfolded. For weeks I'd woken up screaming, terrified that my dad wouldn't come back. But he had.

Are my parents having nightmares about me? They had to be going through hell right now. One more tally mark in the cruel column of Nil.

Foe, I thought. *Because Nil sure as hell isn't our friend.*

Maybe it's neither, the waves whispered.

Maybe the arrow would point me to the answer.

I squeezed Macy's shoulder. "Have a good walk, Mace. Be safe."

The island sun rose quickly, shooting light the color of Nil's lions through the trees. The Cove was a ghost town, like I'd hoped. No need to make small talk or dodge company. Fast strokes, a strong inhale, a clean dive, and I was there—behind the falls, cloaked in liquid cover.

The opening hadn't changed.

I offered up a prayer for safety and eased into the cave.

The tunnel absorbed dawn's light as if starved for it. I counted my steps as I went, running the tips of my fingers across the tunnel walls. Rough, cool, moist. Familiar. The tunnel narrowed. My fingertips brushed the arrow; I didn't stop.

Fifteen steps later, I hit another arrow.

An island blaze, I thought with satisfaction.

Last year my dad and I had hiked part of the Camino de Santiago, starting outside Le Puy-en-Velay. Before we'd set a single foot on the trail, my dad had showed me photos of the red-and-white *balises* lining the route. *Follow the blazes,* he'd said. *They mark our way.*

Why point the way to a dead end?

You don't, I thought. *Not here.* Here death was easy to find. You sure as hell didn't need any help.

I followed the arrow.

Ten steps later, the tunnel widened. Now I could only touch one wall at a time. I slowed, tipping back and forth like a seesaw, checking both sides for carvings and openings, for anything man-made or important. Twice I doubled back and rechecked the walls until the tunnel forked.

Using two hands, I ran my fingers in larger and larger circles over both sides in turn, unsure which way to go.

No arrows. It felt like a test.

I went left.

Twelve steps later, my fingertips brushed a third arrow and I smiled. *You passed, Rives.*

The tunnel curved left, then right. The darkness lifted. No arrows to guide my way; now I had light.

I exited the cave tunnel and stepped into another world, a stunning Nil secret. An underground cavern, lined in black rock, with a three-meter-wide opening near the top where sunlight and water poured in equal parts, falling gently into a wide pool.

To my left, the rock dropped steeply into the water; to my right, a two-meter-wide ledge ran the length of the cavern. Above the ledge, carvings coated the wall like island graffiti. Moons in all phases, stars shaping constellations, suns shooting out rays, and rows of waves and interlocking diamonds were everywhere, along with scattered fish, cats, and simple stick figures. Near the top the number sequence 3-2-1-4 ran like a title. One large diamond stood out from the rest: hanging mid-wall, dead center, it held a sun carving with an eye in its gut. Beside it, a vertical arrow shot toward the cave ceiling, with the letters *N-I-L* running vertically alongside it, with the *N* at the bottom and the *L* at the top.

Now I knew what the shallow diamond carving at the entrance was missing. The *N-I-L.*

On the ledge beneath the diamond, a rock knife lay beside a mango.

A *fresh* mango.

I whirled around, taking in the darkness at my back. The cave tunnel was too tight a squeeze for me to have passed someone without knowing it.

Unless they took the other fork, I thought.

I waited, watching the tunnel exit, expectant. No one appeared. By my mental count, at least ten silent minutes passed. No people, no surprises.

I was definitely alone.

But I didn't *feel* alone.

The air inside the cavern had a presence, a *weight*, a fluidity of time and people and energy and island mojo that I didn't understand but deeply wanted to. Around me swirled silent ghosts and rituals and secrets I couldn't see, but they were as tangible as the carvings on the cavern wall. The weight intensified, like answers hung in the air, pouring in with the falls, pouring into *me*, if I just listened.

I closed my eyes, straining to hear Talla's voice cut through the rush of water.

Waiting.

Searching.

Wanting.

The falls poured in, unbroken.

I snapped open my eyes, breaking the mystique. How long had I stood there, listening for ghosts? Glancing around, I was relieved to find I was still alone.

Moving away from the pool, I studied the carvings, noting the similarity among the images, yet uniqueness, too, suggesting many hands at work. Only one carving looked relatively recent: a moon, its rough edges dripping with something milky white. I sniffed it and gagged.

Deadleaf juice, fresh enough to stink.

I turned away, gulping fresh air. The pool's glassy surface rippled and a head broke the surface, emerging crown first like a baby. The rest of the head followed, and shoulders drenched in ink. When the owner's eyes caught mine, his widened in shock. And then he promptly disappeared.

"Hey," I shouted at the water. "Wait!"

I jumped in. Deep water wrapped me tight, pushing me back even as it pulled me down. In the sliver of light, I caught one crisp glimpse of the kid swimming away, bubbles trailing in his wake.

Got you, I thought.

I followed, swimming fast, knowing that if he could hold his breath, so could I. Light faded. So did the kid's form, and the bubble trail was tough to track in the dim light. I kicked hard, knowing I was seconds away from having to quit and turn back. My lungs burned like I'd swallowed fire.

My hand hit rock. Lungs screaming, I frantically felt around with my hands. My right palm slipped through an opening. I felt the edges, gauging the width, and my fingers brushed the blaze: an arrow, pointing away from the cavern.

Using both hands, I pulled myself through the opening and burst out into rough water with a light-filled ceiling. I dolphin-kicked to the surface. I'd cut it dangerously close.

The boy was already stroking his way through the break. But my time on Nil had served me well. I closed the distance quickly, using the waves' power to take me in.

He strode up the white sand, his intricate tattoos gleaming in the morning light.

"Hey!" I called. "Hold up!"

He spun, his eyes narrowing when he saw me. "You should not be here," he said flatly.

"I didn't ask to be," I said, keeping my tone pleasant.

We stood silent, each sizing the other up. He looked my age, maybe older. He had a fierceness, a thinly contained edge. His heritage was tough to place, like mine. If I had to guess, I'd peg him as Pacific Islander, a bit like me, but here, now, he looked like a Nil native.

Which was something that did not exist.

Then again, neither did this place.

He pointed toward the cliff, the one harboring the secret cavern. "That place is sacred," he said softly. "Do not go back. The Looking Glass pool is not for you."

"The Looking Glass pool? What is that, like the Fortress of Solitude?"

"I do not know your fortress. It is yours. But the Looking Glass pool is not." He stared at me and frowned. "Do not go back." This time it sounded like a warning.

"If it's not for me, who's it for?"

"For those who do not need to ask."

He turned away and blended soundlessly into the trees without a backward glance.

I wondered why he hadn't joined the City, and how long he'd been on the island. And I wondered what he was doing in that cavern and how he knew it existed in the first place.

To hell with his warning, I was definitely going back.

CHAPTER 11

SKYE
NOVEMBER 18, MID-MORNING

Uncle Scott's journal was addictive, like the guiltiest pleasure ever. I felt like a voyeur, but I couldn't stop. I didn't want to think of what that said about me.

Entry #8

For the third morning in a row, I woke to a full gourd of water.

Maybe the girl was an angel after all. Or a genie.

Maybe the island was full of magic. Black magic. Black sand, black nights. Black air that pops out of nowhere.

Let me back up.

I woke up, found a full gourd, drained it, and sat on the beach, staring at the rising sun. I was operating in semi-shock; I just didn't know it. I needed someone to slap me.

So the island did.

The sun licked the sand, making the brittle bits glint like black diamonds. I strolled up the beach aimlessly, thinking about how hungry I was and wondering what the hell I should do and what had happened to the giraffe. As if that mattered.

I didn't want to leave this beach. I knew it was because of her. It was stupid. I know that now.

I was stupid.

I was also hanging on by a thread, so cut me some slack.

My stomach was turning on itself after six days of water. Oh yeah, and urine. Concentrated urine, so foul I'm gagging right now just thinking about it. Think on that, why don't you? I dare you to drink your own piss for a few days, then switch to shotgunning water. NO FOOD. Yeah. How clear would your head be?

The air in front of me wavered, like a warning. Then shimmering air popped at eye level and dropped into a perfect circle that thinned into a wall. All I could think was holy-shit-I-hit-this-air-once-and-it-burned-like-hell so I backed up and tripped. The swath of rippling air glittered like mercury glass, then instantly switched to flat black. Empty black. No light, no glistening, just a black hole hovering in midair. It scared the shit out of me, because the black air screamed life-sucking danger. All I knew about black holes were that they were very, very bad. Like sun-gone-supernova bad.

Two seconds later a walrus fell out of the air. A fucking WALRUS. With tusks and wrinkled brown skin and whiskers just like out of Encyclopedia-fucking-Britannica. The black hole vanished.

The walrus didn't move, but I did.

It was the slap I needed, more like a walrus kick in the ass. I didn't know if walruses—Walrae? Walrus? What the hell is the plural of walrus?—were aggressive, but I didn't want to find out.

Go north, she'd said. Find others like you.

I went north. Correction, I ran north, like an angry walrus was on my tail. With what little strength I had left, I ran. Away from the walrus. Away from the beach with the girl. Toward the best hope I had, which wasn't much.

I never saw the walrus again, but I know it was there.

My name is Scott Bracken, and this is the truth.

Entry #9

I followed the coast, leaving the walrus behind, and as the black beach curved I slowed, my adrenaline rush gone. My feet dragged like cement blocks. The beach rounded into a series of massive rock arches, the most gorgeous island formation I'd ever seen. Black arches, as if carved by the hands of giants.

Then my jaw dropped.

Inside the largest one, a boy stood, running his hands over the rock. Tall, lean, light brown hair cut close to his scalp, fairly light skin and slightly sunburned shoulders, he wore a loincloth like me.

HE WAS LIKE ME.

"Hey!" I shouted. Or tried to shout. My voice cracked, like my lips. Like my tongue.

That's when I saw his spear. He turned, his

expression fierce. I stopped. He hopped down from the rocks as agile as a monkey.

I stood as still as the rock arches, ready to run. For all I knew he was a cannibal.

Turned out he was a German.

"Hello," he said. He'd stopped about five feet away. "I'm Karl. Vat is your name?"

"Scott."

He nodded. "How long haf you been here, Scott?"

"Six days. I think."

He nodded again. Sharp brown eyes flicked over me a second time. He pointed his spear at my waist. "Vere did you get zee clothes?" He sounded suspicious.

"A girl. She brought them to me."

He raised an eyebrow. "A girl." He paused. "Vat vas her name?"

"She didn't tell me. She brought me clothes, and a gourd of water. She wore white clothes and had flowers in her hair." I almost added she looked like an angel, but the last brain cell I had left told me to shut the hell up. "I never saw her again," I added. Karl listened thoughtfully as I spoke. A second of awkward silence ticked by. Then I offered, "But I did see a giraffe. Twice. And I just saw a walrus fall out of the air."

Karl shook his head and sighed, his spear dropping. "Zis place. So shtrange." He looked directly at me, his features relaxing into a smile. He spread his arms wide. "Scott," he said grandly. "Velcome to zee island of Nil."

My name is Scott Bracken, and this is the truth.

And there it was.

Nil.

Why Nil? I wondered. *And why a walrus?* Strange wasn't the half of it. Of course I kept reading. *People* magazine had nothing on Uncle Scott's journal.

Entry #10

I guess by Giraffe Land standards, I got lucky. Karl was a good guy. Smart, honest, and island-savvy. It turns out that he was the Leader of the City. And by City I mean a rock hut village, populated by a ragtag band of misfits, a global version of The Breakfast Club stuck on an island. You had the jocks, the intellectuals, the crybabies, the slackers, you name it. But after a few weeks I learned that people are more similar than you'd ever think. Most are good, especially when working toward a common goal of survival.

Most.

I kept waiting for the Professor and Mary Ann to show up with a coconut-crafted radio to get us the hell off the island or tell us we were all on a new, twisted version of Candid Camera, but it didn't happen. No Professor, no Mary Ann. No adults. Only teenagers got tapped to join the island party, so the over-nineteen crowd was missing. Same for the elementary school set. We were one step above the Lord of the Flies crew.

Barely.

Because in this setting it didn't take long for people's true natures to show.

But like I said, most were good.

Everybody worked together to fish, hunt, and look out for each other, a classic division of labor. We worked in smooth teams to string nets, harvest pineapple, and keep the firepit going; we gave each other privacy at the Cove and collected wood on the way back; we made splints when Dustin broke his arm and we patrolled the City at night. A few days here and you'd see the City was an impressive cohesive unit of kids helping each other and surviving against the odds.

That is, until noon.

Noon was a free-for-all, a get-the-hell-out-of-my-way race for the finish. Because noon is when the gates come. Noon is when you can leave.

And everyone wanted to leave.

Karl delivered the bad news on my Day 6. I had 359 more days to catch a gate or my goose was cooked. Or in his words, "You haf 365 days to catch a gate or you vill die." He accompanied that bomb with a very descriptive slicing motion across his throat. And when I asked for more details, Karl shrugged. His answer? "Zee island vill take you." All I could think about was that scene in the Indiana Jones movie when the Germans opened the chest and all who looked at it were burned to a skeletal crisp. Maybe the island would do the same to me.

I didn't want to find out.

Neither did anyone else.

So we were all one big happy family until noon. Then people took on a feral, crazed look, eyeing the air, the ground, the trees. You could cut the tension in the air with a wooden machete. Then it would pass, and everyone would relax.

But if a gate showed up? All bets were off. Everybody sprinted like a bat out of hell toward the gate. Like the winner would receive a million bucks. But here, the winner got the ultimate prize—a free ride home. Or at least we thought it was a ride home.

Sometimes I wondered where the hell the outbound gates really went. Now I know. But I didn't then. Everything was so unclear when I was there, and yet, other things were so brutally clear, there was no room left for gray. Life. Death. Gates. Running.

That was it.

The first outbound I saw flashed on my Day 15. That was the first time I saw someone—Bobby—shove someone else—Kiefer—out of the way to take a gate. I was shocked. Horrified. Repulsed. The second time it happened—a gentle nudge with an elbow, complete with an "I'm sorry" look, just enough to give Pierre the edge over Sally—I was pissed. The third time? I decided it had to stop. Because the third time, Cathy missed the gate that she was so close to catching. Not because Kumar pushed her, nudged her, or cut her off, but because he simply beat her to the gate. He ran faster.

He won. She lost.

Simple and cruel. Black and white. The next day her time ran out.

Cathy's was the first funeral I attended but not the last. That was my Day 35, the day I fully understood the nature of the island. This wasn't Ancient Rome, or the running of the bulls. We weren't savages; we were better than that. And we needed a better shot.

We needed a system. We needed structure.

And we all needed to buy into it.

The island had rules.

It was time we had some of our own.

My name is Scott Bracken, and this is the truth.

I closed the journal. Nil sounded like an island of nightmares.

What if someone had already tried to find Nil but never came back? Would we even have a clue? The answer was a firm *hells no*. Like the Bermuda Triangle, Giraffe Land had the ability to swallow people without a trace—like Cathy.

For the first time, I wasn't sure whether to hope we'd find Nil or pray that we never would.

"Skye!" My dad's voice rang with excitement. "I think I just found the break we need!"

CHAPTER 12

RIVES
DAY 243, LATE MORNING

I'd broken my own rules.

Look around. Watch your back. Pay attention.

I hadn't paid attention at all.

I'd exited the cavern in an adrenaline rush, focused on catching the kid and not dying. In the dim underwater light, the black rock at the cliff base blended without break. No cracks, no gaps. No sign of a lava tube or exit.

If I wanted a return trip to the secret cavern, it would have to be the way I came in the first place.

Who are you? I thought, keeping an eye out for the kid as I strode through the trees, heading south. *What do you know?*

I tripped on a root, feeling woozy. *Stupid*, I thought. Leaving before breakfast was a rookie move. Hunger had left me weak.

Pay attention, whispered the breeze.

So I did.

I turned, seeing the ground, dusted with dead leaves and ashes of volcanoes past; the tropical woods, harboring squirrels, rabbits, and other small doomed creatures; the tree canopy, an organic web full of holes, letting light peek through, showing off spots.

Black spots, layered on gold. Thirty meters off the path, a leopard lounged high in a tree, eyes closed, paws dangling.

Merde.

I'd never seen a big cat so far from the meadow, but Nil's rules were subject to change without warning.

I'm learning, Nil.

I drew my blade and walked with care, avoiding anything that might make noise as I put distance between me and the cat. Every muscle stayed taut, ready for flight. The path cut toward the sea and I'd just spotted the Cove when something rustled on my left.

I spun, braced to face a hungry cat and found myself facing a boy instead. Thin and rangy, with blond hair and skin as pale as the moon, he wore nothing but an expression of pure fear. He half hid behind a tree.

Slowly, I sheathed my knife and raised my hands. "Do you speak English?"

Ahmad's voice echoed behind me. "Rives?"

The boy startled like a spooked deer. He ran, away from me, toward Nil's interior, where human shelf life shrank dramatically.

"Wait!" I called.

The boy spun back, covering himself, his expression terrified.

My hands stayed raised, my shoulders relaxed. *"Hablas español?"* I asked.

He shook his head.

"Parle tu français? Sprichst du Deutsch?" I asked.

Words burst from the boy's mouth, rapid-fire syllables. Russian. Possibly Ukranian.

"Russian?" I asked.

His eyes lit up. *"Da!"* Then he launched into a run of Russian that was lost on me.

Pointing to my chest, I said, "Rives." Then I pointed to Ahmad. "Ahmad."

Miraculously, the boy got it. He pointed to his chest. "Nikolai." Then he rattled off another string of words, waving one arm around the air.

I bent and touched the ground. "Nil." I patted the ground. "Nil."

"Nil," the boy repeated. Then he frowned. "Nil?"

I nodded. "Nil."

Ahmad stared at me, wearing a total *who are you?* expression.

"How many languages do you speak?" he asked.

"Five, and a bit of Thai. Mostly curses," I said. "But no Russian, which I think Nikolai is. The new rookie. Alexei. Does he speak English?"

"Enough to get by." He ripped a giant taro leaf off a nearby bush and handed it to Nikolai, gesturing for him to use the leaf to cover himself. A second leaf followed the first. It's amazing what a little coverage will do for a person's sanity. But Nikolai needed more than clothes. He needed a Nil tutorial.

"We need Alexei," I said.

"He's in the fields. I've got this. And I'll get Nikolai decked out at the Shack."

"Thanks." I nodded.

I gestured for Nikolai to follow us. He did, louder than I'd like, but I felt better knowing he wasn't running around solo without skivvies.

At the Cove, Ahmad and Nikolai kept walking; I stopped.

Macy, Sy, Dex, Jillian, and Johan all stood in a loose semicircle by the water. When Jillian saw me, she came running, her eyes flashing, her hair wet.

"Oh my God, Rives. I thought something happened to you. Where have you been?"

"Spelunking." I grinned.

Her eyes narrowed. "When I woke up, I went looking for you. I saw you dive under the falls. I followed and called your name into the cave, but you didn't answer." Her blue eyes were wide and accusing.

"So I went back and grabbed Johan. We went in together, and that's when we found—" She shivered, her voice dropping to a whisper. "What was left of him. Or her. Sitting against the wall at the dead end."

The word *dead* hung in the air between us.

"My first thought was that somehow, it was you," she continued in a shaky voice. "That the island had swallowed you, leaving dried bones. I know it's crazy, but I swear, that's what I thought." She took a breath. "We waited for you to come out of the cave. You never came out." Her tone hardened. "So where did you go?"

I explained about the arrows, the cavern, the carvings, and the kid, conveniently leaving out the kid's warning to not go back.

"I never saw the skeleton," I finished. "I'd gone left. Which I guess turned out to be right." I winked.

Jillian glared at me. "Don't think you can sweet-talk your way out of this, Rives. That was a big risk you took going off by yourself and not telling anyone where you were going. The City needs you. Don't pull stupid crap like that again, okay?"

Johan, Sy, and Dex strode up, and I rehashed my morning again. When I was done, Johan looked thoughtful.

"That cave tunnel is ancient," he murmured. "It *feels* old, and that person has been dead a long time. I think that person chose their own dead end."

Dex's eyes widened. "You think that bloke offed himself in the dark?"

"No," Johan said. "I don't think he took his life; I think his life was taken. I think the skeleton belongs to a person who chose to meet his Maker in that place." Johan crossed himself and looked toward the Cove. "May he rest in peace."

"Stop it, Johan." Jillian rubbed her arms. "You're creeping me out."

"I'll pass on the cave tour, thank you very much." Dex gave an exaggerated shiver. "It's a bloody tomb in there."

"It's not a tomb. Well," I clarified as Dex shot me an *are-you-for-real* look, "not totally. It's something else. Something important." I looked at the Cove, thinking of the skeleton and the dozens of carvings. *What else did I miss?*

"Rives." Dex's soft voice made me turn back. He cocked his head at me. "Your own Second gave me a bit of advice on my Day One. Charley told me that all that matters here is survival and escape. And she was right. The cave art is a dodgy distraction, mate. Nothing more. Don't let the island creep in. It might drive you mad."

"C'mon, Dex. Not you, too." I smiled. Now was not the time to mention Talla's whispers in my head.

"Here's the thing. When I woke up in the rainforest, I swear I saw a leopard. Furry, long tail, spots, cat ears"—Dex gestured as he spoke— "the whole bit. It was up in a tree, chewing on something that looked like a corpse. I recognized a foot." He blinked. "I know I was jacked when I landed, so perhaps it was all in my head. But I constantly dream of leopards. Man-eating ones. Sometimes I think I'm actually mental. So when I say don't let the island in your head, I mean it. If you go mad, we're all buggered."

"I won't let the island mess with my head," I told Dex. *No more than it already has.* "And I've got bad and good news." I grinned. "There *is* a leopard on Nil. Near White Beach. It was sleeping in a tree."

Dex paled. "What's the good news?"

"You're not mental."

"Right. I'll take your word for it." Dex exhaled heavily. "I'm not too keen on the leopard though. Bugger me. We've got a bloody leopard as our neighbor now?"

"At least it wasn't eating anything."

"Let's hope he's not hungry, then," Jillian said softly.

We all looked at her.

"What?" She raised her eyebrows. "Well, it's true."

"I do not want to have this discussion now. Or ever. I'm off to fill Jason in on all the fun." Dex saluted grandly, then strode off, muttering about leopards.

"We need to be careful now," Johan said, his eyes on the Cove. "We have disturbed a person's resting place."

"Johan, you didn't disturb anything," I said, exasperated. "The rockslide opened up the entrance, and we checked it out. End of story. You didn't mess with the skeleton, right?"

Jillian looked guilty. "I sort of tripped over it. And"—she gulped— "it rattled."

Johan looked appalled. Sy took a step backward, distancing himself from Jillian. I needed to rein them in, ASAP.

"Listen, that person is long gone." I relaxed my tone. "Don't make this into something it's not, okay?"

"The equilibrium is gone," Johan said quietly. "There's an urgency now. A desperation. An island shift, and it's not in our favor." He looked directly at me. "You feel it, too, yes?"

I hesitated one second too long.

Johan snapped a sharp nod. "We must be more vigilant than ever." He strolled away, crossed himself, and pointed at the sky.

Jillian watched Johan walk away. "Sometimes he's just so intense. I bet he doesn't step on sidewalk cracks at home or stay in a hotel with a thirteenth floor. God forbid he ever drops a mirror."

"Well, there are no sidewalks, hotels, or mirrors here, so I think he's good." But privately I agreed with Johan; I'd sensed the shift in the hour after Charley and Thad left. It was as if the island had woken from a deep slumber and was more alive than ever.

Or maybe that was me.

Come, the falls whispered.

Maybe the inked boy was there, behind the falls. Maybe he had a name.

Maybe he had answers to questions I didn't even know to ask.

"Rives." Jillian touched my arm, her eyes worried. "I know you want to go back in there. I see it in your eyes. Promise me that if you go, you'll take backup."

"Jillian, there's nothing to be afraid of in that cavern. I promise you it's safe."

She shook her head. "That's not what I asked. Promise me you won't go in without backup."

"I can't make that promise, Jills. But I will promise you I won't do anything stupid."

She sighed. "Too late." She turned away. "I've got to show Zane how to stretch the pulp to dry. We're trying to get ahead on clothes."

"Jillian. One more thing. Will you be my new Second?"

Jillian walked back and hugged me tight. "No. I'm not Natalie or Talla or Charley. I'm not a Leader, and if you think about it, you'll know I'm right. You've got Dex and Sy, although why you picked Sy I'll never know. That boy can't figure out how to roast a pineapple or tie a decent knot. People trust Macy; same for Ahmad. I'm not sure you need another Second, but if you do, I'm not your girl." She kissed my cheek. "You know I love you. I'm behind you one hundred percent, just not as a Second."

"You know, you'd be a better Leader than you think."

"Still saying no here, Rives." She smiled.

I laughed.

"Ready to walk back? Or are you going in?" She pointed to the Cove.

"Lead on, Jills. I'm going back with you."

"It's still a no," she said as we walked. "No, no, no."

"We'll see." I winked.

We walked back together in comfortable silence. She'd questioned why I'd picked Sy, whose enthusiasm far outweighed his skills as a Second. At the time, I'd picked him thinking of the adage *Keep your friends close and your enemies closer*. And even though he no longer undermined the City, he still didn't exercise the best judgment. Usually it was no judgment, like he'd forgotten to engage his brain, and it was in the crucial moments when the island forced him to make a call on the spot that Sy waffled or bailed. I trusted Dex like I'd trusted Thad—like Thad had trusted me and Heesham. I'd trusted Talla, too; same for Charley.

Sy, I didn't trust at all, not the way I should.

So now I had one Second I trusted; one I didn't. And the other person I trusted most, Jillian, was unwilling. Jason was too young; same for Miya. Macy was too kind; the tough choices and cruel moments would gut her. Ahmad was my best bet, but I balked at an all-male council; the balance felt off. And Nil was all about the balance.

Maybe Nil was in my head after all.

"Hey, Jillian. Got a favor to ask."

"Still no, Rives," she said, smiling.

I laughed. "I want you to give me a haircut. It's time to ditch the dreads."

She stopped. "Seriously?"

"Seriously." They felt like a weight I didn't want to carry, a link to a boy more carefree than I had a right to be.

Jillian's eyes flicked over my face, unsure.

"Just a hassle," I said casually. "Too much maintenance." My answer satisfied her. Twenty minutes later, she'd hacked them off with Thad's knife and cropped my hair short.

Running my hands over my scalp, I felt lighter. Faster.

Fiercer.

I threw my dreads into the sea. The foaming water curled around the offering like liquid claws. *Take that, Nil. It's the last thing I'll give you. I may be stuck here, but you don't own me. You don't control me—not my mind, not my body, not my spirit. Not my fate. Because I'm finding out your secrets, and when I do, this place will never be the same.*

I *will never be the same.*

The last part was already true.

CHAPTER 13

SKYE
NOVEMBER 18, LATE MORNING

"This is our big break, Skye. I feel it."

I peered over Dad's shoulder at his Mac. An article from a French news site filled the screen.

The headline read: **MISSING AMERICAN GIRL FOUND ON MONT BLANC**.

A seventeen-year-old American teenager who disappeared last August near her Roswell, Georgia, home was found yesterday on the slope of Mont Blanc. Charley Crowder was discovered alive and uninjured, although she is reportedly suffering from hypothermia and extreme shock. According to local authorities, Ms. Crowder was "extraordinarily lucky" to have been found. "She was left for dead in unmarked terrain," said one eyewitness who refused to give his name. Another eyewitness claimed Ms. Crowder was naked, although that report has yet to be confirmed.

Ms. Crowder was reported missing last August and had not been seen or heard from until yesterday. She was reunited with her family this morning. No further information was released.

Dad looked at me, a fierce combo of intellectual curiosity and *I-believe-in-aliens* loony radiating from his eyes. "Charley's story matches the pattern of Scott's, albeit a shorter time frame, but her story suggests she was on Nil. Perhaps she can tell me something specific about Nil, something to help pinpoint the island's location. I'm going to fly to Atlanta and see if I can speak with her in person. With her parents' permission, of course."

He sounded more fanatical than he looked. *Yikes.*

"Dad." I spoke calmly to counter his crazy. "Listen to yourself. You're just going to fly down to Atlanta and do what? March up to her house, introduce yourself to her parents, and say, 'Hi. I'm a professor of astrophysics, and I think your daughter was on a mysterious island that really exists even though it's uncharted and I'd like to talk to her about it'? Do you hear how creepy that sounds? Their daughter just showed up after being missing for months, and you think they're going to let some strange guy who says he's a professor come in and talk to her?" I shook my head. "I don't think so."

He had the decency to look chagrined.

"You haven't thought this through at all, have you?" I asked.

"Not really," he admitted.

I thought for a moment, putting myself in Charley's shoes.

"How about this," I said. "Let's give her time to get home, to adjust. If she *was* on Nil, she's probably freaked out. If she wasn't, she's still probably freaked out because clearly something bad happened to her. Maybe she was kidnapped, or fell victim to foul play." I closed my eyes. *What the what? I did not just use the words* foul play.

Pulling myself back into the real, sane world where everyone else lived, I opened my eyes. "The only way this will work is if I talk to Charley alone. I'll bring Uncle's Scott's journal. I won't press, but I'll give her an opening to talk." I gave him a tough-love look. "I'm not letting you freak out some already-freaked-out girl some more. Let me figure out how to approach her, okay?"

He looked exceptionally guilty.

"Please tell me you haven't called her parents already."

"I may have left a message."

I slapped my forehead with my palm. "Nice going, Dad. Well, let's still go but don't count on any information." I pulled up the calendar on my phone, determined to give Charley some time and protect her from my overzealous dad, who still looked way too hopeful.

"Let's try the weekend of the fifth," I said. "But keep your expectations low, okay?"

Charley, I thought, *if you were on Nil, I'm sorry. And if you weren't, I'm sorry, too.* Either way, lying naked on a French ski slope sounded horrible, especially when you weren't French.

Now I felt like a voyeur AND a stalker.

Two weeks with my dad and I was spiraling quickly into his abyss of crazy.

That night I stayed up to finish Uncle Scott's journal. He described City life, island topography, and people in detail so clearly I could see why Dad believed it was real. Moments of beauty and peace transcended the danger, like the night Uncle Scott danced with Jenny until the fiery orange sun set, and then lay on the warm sand, holding her hand, studying the stars. Moments of weirdness stuck out, like the Brazilian boy who refused to wear a loincloth, opting to go au natural on Nil and leaving his man parts on constant display, or the time a sloth appeared in the City and scared the beejezus out of George. Names repeated and vanished; other entries were laundry lists of animals on Nil. There seemed to be an awful lot of cats. I learned that Uncle Scott cut his face when he was surfing and wiped out on the rocks. Jenny dragged him ashore. I didn't know he knew how to surf.

I also didn't know how he managed to get off Nil, or how he broke. I do now.

And the last three entries gave me chills.

CHAPTER 14

RIVES
DAY 243, ALMOST DUSK

Preparations for tonight's Nil Night fueled the City.

Jason and I sat by the beachside firepit making torches, a mindless process if there ever was one. Beside us sat a basket filled with brown fruit the size and shape of oranges, only these fruits were off-limits for snacking.

The secret lurked inside. Break open the flesh and inside was an oily nut. Dry them out, string them together, and you had a slick bead necklace, but we used these jewels for fire. Take a piece of bamboo, tie a dozen fresh-hulled nuts on it, and *voilà*—a Nil torch. Light the top nut first, then the flame worked its way down. From top to bottom, each torch burned for hours, depending on factors unknown to me.

All I knew was that it worked.

Even with Jason's bum finger, we had a dozen torches fully made when the dark-haired girl with a flower tucked behind her ear walked up with Zane.

"Like the new 'do, bro," Zane said.

"Thanks." I turned to the girl and stuck out my hand, smiled. "Hey. I'm Rives."

"Kiera." She smiled. "I was wondering when I'd finally meet you. It seems that everyone knows you but me."

Her accent surprised me.

"You're French?" I asked.

"Tahitian."

"Your home is a beautiful place," I said in French.

She looked surprised too. "You speak French?" Hers was flawless.

"Yes." I answered in English, aware of Jason's and Zane's eyes, unwilling to make this moment private. "My mother was raised in Paris. We have a flat there."

"You don't have an accent." It sounded like an accusation.

I shrugged. "We travel a lot." With my parents' jobs, we'd lived in a variety of places, always long enough for me to find a local club to play football and sharpen my skills as striker. My last coach said I had pro potential. Even though he was a former scout for Real Madrid, I thought Coach just threw out that line to get more out of me. I wondered now.

"But"—Kiera's lilting French brought me back, still pressing— "where do you live?"

I didn't feel like playing—or defending myself.

"Here." One word, in crisp English, delivered with a smile.

"I meant, where are you from?" she asked. Annoyed tone, tilted chin. I realized I'd misread her posture the first time I'd seen her standing near Dex. It wasn't strength I'd seen, or defiance; it was privilege. I sensed Kiera was accustomed to getting her way.

"Before here?" she added in English.

"Everywhere. I travel with my parents. They're journalists." I could've added that we had flats in Paris, Los Angeles, and Honolulu, and rotated between the three. But I didn't.

Arms crossed, Kiera studied the torch assembly line.

"In Tahiti, we have candlenut trees, too," she said. "I've seen fishermen use the nut oil, but I've never seen anyone make torches. How did you know how to do that?"

"Natalie taught me," I said. "She was the Leader before Thad. I don't know who taught her. Maybe one day you'll teach someone else."

"I'd rather go home," she said.

"Amen, sister," Zane agreed.

Jason looked up from his torch. "I've been thinking about that a lot lately," he said. "Not about leaving but about how much knowledge we lose. You know someone before Charley must have figured out the gate pattern, but then it got lost, like in a bad telephone game." He turned toward me, worried. "What if the next ten people who show up don't speak English? What if all the veterans leave in the same week? What if people forget what these do?" He held up a nut. "What if there's other stuff we don't know, but we don't even know that we don't know?"

"Whoa," said Zane, his eyes wide. "Deep."

Jason tossed a nut at Zane, barely missing his head. "You know what I mean. For all we know, we're still missing tons of information about this place."

"Or maybe we know more than ever," I said. "Either way, I hear you, bro. But you can't worry about the what-ifs." *Because that's how Nil gets in your head.* "All you can worry about is the now."

"Agreed," Zane said. "But I've only been camping here forty-two days, so what do I know? Not much. Just that this place is a total freak fest."

"That it is," I agreed.

I wondered why I'd felt so defensive with Kiera, why I'd shared so little. Maybe I didn't like all the questions. I came from a family that preferred to do the asking.

Maybe, the waves whispered. *Or maybe it's you. Maybe you haven't found what you're looking for. Or who.*

Or who? I wondered, glancing toward the ocean.

If there was someone out there for me, she wasn't on this island. I'd risked my heart once here; I sure as hell wouldn't do it again.

I had absolutely no time for that.

CHAPTER 15

SKYE
NOVEMBER 18, DUSK

Entry #18

Day 202. I stood alone in the Arches, looking at the sea.

Come, the island whispered. Search.

I didn't know what I was supposed to search for. Gates? People? Something else?

I still don't know. But I know we searched for gates every damn day. And the island named the system for us.

My name is Scott Bracken, and this is the truth.

Entry #19

You're not well, they say.

We love you, they say.

You'll be okay, they say.

I'm not sure anymore. Sometimes I think I still hear Nil.

My name is Scott Bracken, and I swear this is the truth.

Entry #20

My last day on the island began like the rest.

Sunrise, I rise.

John sat by the firepit, carving dice. Anne lay curled beside him, asleep. I waved, not wanting to wake her. John tossed me a mango. I caught it and saluted him with it.

He grinned.

I passed the Wall, pointed to my name, and hit the beach. Sunrise in Giraffe Land was stunning. And peaceful. It was my favorite time of day on the island.

Hui was already awake, working on the hang gliders he'd been building for weeks.

The first time I'd gone up, the rush was so intense I didn't want to come down. It had been our project ever since I'd stepped down as Leader. Hui was the engineer; I was the labor. We had two fully functional; two more were halfway complete. The gliders would help us see the island from the air, and since we'd broadened the search area for gates well beyond the City, we were getting spread out. We were losing people to gates, which was good. We were losing supplies to the island, which was bad. And we were running into more wildlife than ever, which was dangerous. Weird wildlife, not what you'd expect on a tropical island. Like hippos. The game Hungry, Hungry Hippos was wrong; it should've been called Angry, Angry Hippos. Hippos were big, pissed-off creatures. And the only thing worse than getting caught off guard by a hippo was running into a snow leopard. An honest-to-God snow leopard, on a tropical island.

Stay away from the meadow, my angel girl had

warned. Probably because it hid snow leopards. A pair
of them. And possibly a cheetah. And, for all I knew,
a walrus. After Jenny and I ran into the leopards in
the meadow and walked away unscathed, we never
went back. Never went close. Even the giraffe knew to
stay away from the meadow. He hung around the City
until one day he simply disappeared.

But the gliders. The gliders were fucking brilliant,
like Hui. The gliders helped us spot danger before it
found us.

Hui went back to get some food. I looked toward
the City, hoping Jenny would show soon. Her detail
was collecting redfruit, but she should be back by
now. Maybe we could go eat at the Arches. It was our
favorite place to hang, close to the City but far
enough away that it felt like ours. I laughed at that.
Nothing here was ours. A total joke. I got up, stiff
from crouching, and decided to jog to get my blood
moving again. I ran by the water's edge, slowly, above
the foam. I'd gone maybe eighty yards north when
I saw the gate; it rose from the white sand and flew
toward me, like it had my name on it.

I didn't even realize it was noon. I didn't even
have to run.

One step later I walked into the gate. No fear.

It burned.

I passed out.

That was it. Totally anticlimactic. Arrive alone,
leave alone, like I'd come full circle, only the boy who
arrived was not the same boy who left.

And when I woke up on someone's frosty lawn, my
first thought wasn't that I was naked. Or that I'd

lived. Or that my time served in Giraffe Land was over. It was that I never told anyone good-bye.

How messed up is that?

So that's it. End of story.

My name is Scott Bracken, and this is the truth. Every fucking word of it.

The next page was the last one with writing. In simple print, perfectly centered, were three words:

I fear nothing.

The remaining pages were blank.

I wondered if Charley still heard Nil, or if she ever did. I wondered if she was fearless. And I wondered if I'd have the guts to ask her.

In seventeen days, I'd find out.

CHAPTER 16

RIVES
DAY 243, DUSK

Nil's unknowns had me jacked.

Tonight was my third Nil Night as Leader in the weeks since I'd taken Thad's place—but it was the first where I couldn't relax. The drive to unlock Nil's secrets was a thirst I couldn't slake, like the island held the perfect well of answers if I could just find it.

I was constantly *looking*. Constantly paying attention.

It was exhausting.

But I couldn't stop.

The moon curved overhead, an arc of white sliced from Nil black. Stars glittered; they knit together into familiar constellations that lulled you into thinking you were safe. Black rocks circled the beachside firepit. Lit torches formed the outer ring, pockets of flame burning holes in the night. Black sky, black air. Black rocks. Nil at night was a dark, dark place.

By the firepit, Nikolai and Alexei sat so close their hips touched, heads together as they talked. Alexei smiled. Ahmad joked with Kiera and Raj. Michael stared at the fire, face intense. Other groups of twos and threes stood listening.

Dex played a pair of drums, rocking out with homemade sticks.

Sweat glistened on his forehead as his hands moved to music locked deep in his head; he drummed with his eyes closed. Jillian sat beside him, mixing it up with gourd seed shakers; Zane played a primitive ukulele. On his left, Macy sang, deep and soulful, an island Etta James.

Her last note trailed off. People raised cups and cheered; Dex waved a stick in thanks. As the hoots died down, I whistled, hard.

All heads turned toward me.

"We've had a big few weeks. First, a farewell. The best kind." I raised my cup and smiled. "To Thad, who kept us safe and kept us together. And to Charley, who connected lost dots and improved our chances. To T and C." I lifted my cup higher amid cheers and whoops. "Second, a welcome. To Nikolai, Kiera, and Alexei, we're glad you're here even though we're sorry you're here. I promise we'll do all we can to help you get home."

Alexei raised his cup; Nikolai didn't move. Kiera's eyes held mine as she mouthed *merci.* Fresh weight settled on my shoulders where my dreads used to be. So many eyes, all looking to me for guidance and hope and direction in a place where the default was simply *run.*

I refocused.

"A few more things. Nil is now a serious cat preserve. Two lions and one leopard are confirmed. No word on whether the tiger is still around. Remember, they usually don't mess with us if we don't mess with them, so give the big cats some distance. We also have a rhino and at least one very ugly hyena, so be aware. Stay alert, especially for those going on Search tomorrow. Two teams head out at dawn. Johan, with Jason as Spotter and Miya and Julio as support. Raj has Pari as Spotter and Carlos as support. That's it." I raised my cup. "Focus on the good, live in the moment. To now."

To now, the City chorused.

The ghosts of friends hung in the evening breeze.

I tilted my head toward the night. Images flickered inside my brain, flashing like falling stars. I fought to grab one; it was a piece of the island puzzle.

"Hey." Kiera's voice next to me shattered my mental mojo.

The fragile outline disintegrated. Gone.

I sighed.

"How long have you been here, Rives?" On her lips, my name had a French lilt, a familiar cadence I hadn't heard in months.

"Two hundred forty-three days."

"So long," she murmured in French. "So the Search system. Aren't you cutting it close? What about just building a raft?"

I stiffened, then forced myself to relax. "Rafts don't work. The ocean always sends them back. The gates are our ticket home, and the Search system gives us the best shot at finding one. Plus, it keeps us alive until we can catch a gate."

My answer seemed to satisfy her.

"You're a great Leader, Rives." Kiera smiled at me, but her gaze didn't draw me in. No spark, no heat. I wasn't looking for an island fling; I never had been. I wasn't even sure if I was reading her right. All I knew was that her eyes held some form of want and I had nothing to give.

"Thanks," I said, wanting distance. *Needing* it. I stood. "I'd better go earn my keep." I smiled casually, the sort of smile that meant nothing. "If you have more questions about Search, you can ask me, Dex, or Jason. Or Jillian. She knows a ton. Probably more than me."

Jillian leaned over. "Still a no, Rives," she said in a singsong voice.

"Eavesdropper." I laughed.

Abruptly, my spine prickled, like I had eyes on my back. I grabbed a lit torch and turned.

"Where are you going?" Jillian asked.

"Just checking things out."

Behind me, Kiera whispered, "He takes his job seriously, doesn't he?"

I didn't linger to hear Jillian's response. Because someone blended with the tree line, watching. I felt his eyes; I felt *him*.

It was the inked kid watching us, or maybe he was just watching me.

I strode toward the trees, toward the darkest swath camouflaged in night. Unfortunately, my torch telegraphed exactly where I was heading, because when I got there, the dense spot was empty. No one waiting. No one watching. But he'd been here; I sensed it.

I turned back, toward the beach. From where I stood, I had a clear view of the firepit through the trees. Careful not to set the trees on fire, I pointed my torch in all directions, trying to see where he'd gone. Nothing. No broken branches, no tells.

No blazes.

But when I looked down, a pale object glinted in the moonlight. Kneeling, I picked it up. A piece of bleached wood, carved into a crescent moon.

Dropped by accident? I wondered. *Or left on purpose?*

Another question, no answer.

Carving in hand, I strolled toward the water, absorbing every sound, every sight. The booming salt spray, the clear night. The endless sea, leading nowhere I could go. The waves whispered, but too many voices in my head crowded out any shot at personal clarity. Johan urging, *Be wary.* The tatted-up boy warning, *Don't go back.* Jillian saying, *Don't be stupid,* and Talla whispering, *Be fearless.*

Kiera challenging, *You don't have an accent.*

You don't know me, I thought.

Who does? the sea hissed.

I couldn't answer the ocean's question. The person I'd been 243 days ago was slipping away, leaching from me like my time on Nil. Lately I'd even questioned myself. I questioned my motivation, my insane need for answers driving my moves with a compulsion I couldn't fight. I didn't know whether it was selfless, or selfish.

I held the crescent moon carving as the real crescent moon shone high. The horizon was lost to the night. Each wave rolled like a shadow, inky black, toward me. Above the water, stars huddled in brilliant groups.

I closed my eyes and the mental dots exploded into shapes. The waves. The moon. The constellations.

The ink on the boy's arm.

Lines of black waves, the single crescent moon, the interlocking diamonds. Shapes in the sky, shapes on his arm. Shapes in the cavern. All a crisp match.

Then I had epiphany number two.

I strode to the backside of the Wall, where most marks weren't crosses or checks, but a mysterious mix of suns, stars, and crescent moons—exactly like the moon I held in my hand.

Get ready, mystery man, I thought, squeezing the wood. *It's time to turn the tables. Because I'm not just coming for Nil, I'm coming for you too.*

I buried the thought that ever since I'd woken under the Nil sky, time had never been on my side.

And then somebody screamed.

CHAPTER 17

SKYE
DECEMBER 5, MORNING

As I drove toward Charley's house, I was as nervous as the morning before a final exam. We'd flown into Atlanta last night, and today I'd talk with Charley if all went according to plan.

To be honest, my plan was a little weak.

I'd decided the best way to approach Charley was to catch her on her way home from school Friday afternoon. Dad didn't teach on Fridays, so he enthusiastically went along with my idea. Suddenly I was the one steering the crazy train.

At least I knew what she looked like.

The international press ran pictures of her with each article, which helped, and having read each one, I had to admit her story was freaky. Star athlete, star student, heavily recruited by major universities to play volleyball, Charley was that girl who had it all going for her, then she disappeared without a trace, only to pop up months later in a foreign country, with no explanation given for her absence. According to the articles, she didn't even have a passport.

Weird.

Like Uncle Scott weird.

I wondered if she had a journal.

Unfortunately, Charley didn't have school on Friday, or maybe she just ditched. She never left the house. I lurked in our rental car in a creepy teen version of a stakeout, while Dad hung out in the hotel. I wondered if I'd missed her, guiltily thinking of the few times I'd zoned out. I returned to the hotel Friday night empty-handed except for Uncle Scott's journal.

Saturday morning I woke with a new plan. Okay, "plan" was generous; it was more like a default. I'd just walk up to her house and introduce myself. Lay it all out and hope for the best.

I'd just pulled onto her street when Charley blew by; she wore tights, a long-sleeved shirt, running shoes, and a fierce *I-will-take-you-down* look. Her long ponytail whipped behind her as she passed.

Crap.

At least I was dressed similarly, for stakeout comfort rather than running, but still. I parked, grabbed Uncle Scott's journal, and took off after Charley.

Holy cow, the girl was good. It took me four blocks to catch her.

"Charley!" I called.

She whipped around, wary. She hadn't even broken a sweat.

"Do I know you?" Her light eyes were sharp.

"No," I said, catching my breath. "And I know this is weird. But please"—I held up both hands, one of which held Uncle Scott's journal—"just give me five minutes."

She glanced at the journal, her entire body tensing. "Are you a reporter?"

"No. My name is Skye Bracken. My dad is an astrophysicist at the University of New Hampshire, and this is his brother's journal." I waved the worn black book. "My uncle wrote it when he was seventeen." I paused. "Here's the thing. Back in the eighties, my uncle claims he was biking down the street and hit a wall of shimmering air. He called it a gate."

Charley's eyes widened, but to her credit she stood her ground, looking down at me. The newspapers hadn't mentioned she was so flipping tall.

"According to his journal, my uncle passed out and woke up on an island called Nil."

Charley sucked in a small breath.

"This island," I continued, "was a freaky place. First he saw a giraffe, then a walrus, then finally some other people." Inwardly, I winced. It sounded more unbelievable when voiced out loud. I kept going, keeping my voice calm and, hopefully, sane.

"My uncle only met teenagers, and he figured out pretty quickly they all had a year to escape or they died. Some kids died, but my uncle made it back home, through another gate. Well, not exactly home. He ended up in Boston. Anyway"—I waved the journal—"he'd been missing for ten months. When he told his parents his story, my grandparents thought he was crazy, and they made him go to therapy, where he wrote this journal. But my dad believes everything in here is the truth." I took a deep breath. "And, after two decades of searching, now my dad thinks he can find Nil and rescue all the kids there."

A million emotions flickered across her face, but the greatest one was grief. Crushing grief. Suddenly I felt awful. Like I was rubbing salt in raw wounds, wounds I couldn't see but that were tearing her apart from the inside out. Pain wrapped Charley so tightly it was a miracle that she could breathe.

"I'm sorry." I took a step back. "I'm so sorry. I don't know where you've been, or what you've been through. And I know this all sounds crazy. I don't know what I thought you could tell me, but my dad, he's got this wild idea that he can find this island and save everyone—" I stopped, aware I was rambling. I never rambled. But the hurt and loss emanating from Charley was so thick it choked all rational thought.

"I'm sorry," I whispered. I turned.

"Wait." Charley's soft voice stopped me.

I looked back to find Charley staring at me, a tear trickling down her face. She made no move to wipe it away.

"If this place did exist"—her drawl stayed soft—"Nil, what makes your dad think he can get there?"

"His brother graphed out the stars—the constellations—and my dad believes he's narrowed down an area in the South Pacific where he's convinced the island is located. It's a long shot, but my dad, well, he's determined. He thinks there must be a direct route to the island no one has found. Yet."

Charley pointed to the journal. "Did your uncle ever mention anything washing up on the island?"

I thought carefully. I'd been through the journal a dozen times already. "No. According to my uncle, everything on the island was made there or came through the gates."

She didn't flinch. "So why does your dad think he can access the island any other way?"

"I'm not sure," I admitted. "If you knew him, you'd know he's prone to wild ideas. Even if he is an astrophysicist."

Charley stared at me intently. "How old are you, Skye?"

"Seventeen."

"If there is another way on the island, your dad won't be the one to get there, because he's too old. You already know that, don't you?" She tilted her head at me. "But you could." Charley closed her eyes, a long, slow blink. The she sighed. "But if you've read your uncle's journal, you also know it's not a place you want to visit. Right?"

"Right," I said. "But what if there were a way to rescue the kids still there?"

She bit her lip before she spoke. "There are good people there," she said. "Some of the best. If there was a way to get there and save them, I would. But there are only gates." Suddenly she strode forward, closing the gap between us and dropping her voice to a fierce whisper.

"Skye, if for some crazy reason you get there, find Rives. Tell him the gates are round-trip. Tell him Charley made it. Natalie too. And Kevin. Tell him"—she swallowed, closing her eyes, fighting emotions so strong her fists stayed clenched at her sides even when she opened her eyes—"tell him I'm still waiting for Thad." She breathed deeply, visibly pulling herself together. "You'll know Rives when you see him. He looks like Ronan from that old *Stargate* show. Built, with bleached-out dreadlocks and pale-green eyes the color of summer limeade. You make sure he makes it." Then the fire left Charley as quickly as it had come. "And if you can't find Rives, find Dex, or Jillian. And if you can't find any of them, God help you, Skye." She smiled. It struck me as grim. "At least you can run."

"Can you tell me anything else? Anything that can help us?"

Charley looked away, like she was deciding how much to share.

"Gates follow a pattern," she said finally. "On both ends. Like a storm. A hurricane. Rives knows how it works on the island. Here"— she gestured—"on this end, the haystack is so big, I don't know how you'd find a gate. The storm cell is too big, so to speak. Maybe if you can figure out the pattern on this end, you could get there. But again, it seems impossible, and honestly, I don't know why you'd want to go. Nil's not exactly a vacation spot." She gave a choked laugh. "I'd like to believe in an islandwide rescue," she said, her voice dropping, almost cracking. "But some things are too big to hope for."

Her pain was back. Crushing, almost suffocating. It was amazing she could run with that.

"Thank you," I said. It seemed inadequate, but it was all I had.

Charley nodded in acknowledgment, then lifted her chin. "One more thing. For the record, I have amnesia." She tapped her head, a wry smile tugging at her lips. "Head injury. Shock and whatnot." She glanced at the journal. "Better forgetful than crazy," she murmured. Her eyes flicked back to mine, her gaze remarkably steady.

I thought of Uncle Scott, stuck with one psychiatrist after another.

"I get it," I said softly. "So this"—I gestured to us—"never happened."

A ghost of a smile crossed her face. "Be careful, Skye. And be careful what you wish for. You just might get it, and it might not be what you think."

"She has amnesia," I told my dad when I returned to the hotel room. "Head injury."

His face fell. "That poor girl. Amnesia is a documented coping response to a traumatic event." He sighed. "Could she remember anything at all?"

I tucked Uncle Scott's journal into my backpack, then I looked directly at my dad. "Dad, I know you wanted Charley to be your big break, a modern-day Uncle Scott. But she isn't. So if you want to go, we're on our own. And you've got to be ready to be disappointed, Dad. We may never find the island Uncle Scott talks about; it's like chasing the Holy Grail, only a scary island version."

"You're very wise, Skye," Dad said calmly. "But even without help from Charley, I have a good feeling about this trip."

That makes exactly one of us, I thought.

We left in twelve days.

CHAPTER 18

RIVES
DAY 265, BEFORE DAWN

I woke to the inhuman sound of terror.

Then, silence.

I peered through the open half walls of my hut, sifting through the darkness to figure out what the hell just happened. My hand gripped Thad's knife tight. I slept with it now.

"What was that?" Dex whispered from across the hut.

"No clue."

I crept outside. Dex followed, moving just as softly.

Ahmad stood next to the firepit, his torch raised high, body tense.

"What happened?" I kept my voice low.

"Not sure. But the goat's gone." Ahmad pointed to the post where the thick braided-twine rope hung slack, holding nothing.

"Bloody hell," Dex murmured. "That's our last goat."

The first goat got snatched two weeks ago at the Nil Night. It was Pari's scream we'd heard. She'd seen nothing but a pair of yellow eyes.

"Same thing happened to the cow a few months ago too." I studied the darkness where the goat had been snatched. No shadows, no movement. Nothing but flat Nil night. "We found the cow dead one morning, being finished by a hyena, but we didn't think the hyena started the dinner party." I paused, remembering the scraggly hyena's arrival minutes after Thad left. I'd thought he'd headed toward the meadow, but it was a guess, not a given. "Another hyena showed up the day Thad left. So now it looks like we have two. And we definitely have two lions and a leopard. Not good."

"Not good at all." Ahmad looked at me, orange torchlight licking his face, highlighting haunted eyes. "I only heard the goat cry out, Rives. No warning at all. It's like the darkness got it, man. I used to sleep like an infant. But here"—Ahmad swiped his torch against the blackness—"I go to bed, afraid I may not wake." He fell silent.

"Sometimes I nap on the beach," Dex offered. "It helps."

Something attacked inside the City, the goat is toast, and we're talking about napping.

I bit my fist to keep from laughing.

"What?" Dex shrugged. "Naps are underrated. And sometimes it's the best way to kill an afternoon. Especially with nights so full of fun." He tipped his head toward the matte black of the island's interior. "It's hard to keep your wits when you don't sleep."

"True," I said. The flicker of humor was gone. I turned to Ahmad. "If you want, I'll finish watch so you can get some sleep."

"Nah. I couldn't sleep now if I tried, man. Something's out there."

"Also true. But whatever it is, it's busy having breakfast. So we're good."

"And by 'we're good' "—Dex rolled his eyes at Ahmad—"Rives means 'we're still completely buggered but just a bit less buggered right at this very minute.' "

"Thanks, Dex." Now I laughed humorlessly. Dex was dead right.

"Rives?"

Kiera crept forward, her eyes wide. Her hair was mussed from sleep, her flower gone. So was her air of privilege. "What was that noise?" Her voice shook.

"The goat," I said. "He decided to take a field trip."

"Because he was being escorted by something big and hungry that wouldn't take no for an answer," Dex said.

Kiera blinked, raw fear ghosting her face, her mouth fixed in a silent O.

"Seriously, it's okay." I spoke reassuringly, realizing she hovered at the fracture point. Her shocked expression read like an open book. *I see it now*, it said. *The nightmare is real.*

She'd finally realized that time here wasn't all fun and games until you hitched a ride home. *If* you hitched a ride home.

"Kiera, you're okay." I spoke quietly. "Whatever it was, it's gone, and it's not coming back tonight. And it might not come back ever. Nothing here is permanent."

Kiera burst into tears.

Dex leaned close. "I think that last line might've been a bit much, mate," he whispered.

I shot him a *shut-the-hell-up* look as Kiera covered her eyes with her hands and wailed.

Dex looked uncomfortable. Ahmad looked at me. Zane looked like he wanted to be anywhere but here. Smart guy.

"I want to go home." Kiera's words burst between sobs. "I can't t-t-take it." She crumpled, and I caught her before she fell. Kiera melted against me like butter.

"You can take it," I said quietly, holding her steady. "You can take it because you have to. And then you'll get home. You're gonna be okay."

We stood there for an awkward moment, Kiera clinging to me as if I were an anchor. As if I were something solid, something unbroken. It took all I had not to pull away; the island pressure had never felt so intense. Or unwanted.

"You're okay," I told Kiera. Smiling, I stepped away slowly, hoping she didn't collapse.

She didn't.

The sky lightened, barely. Just enough to tell me the endless night wasn't so endless, that the sun was actually going to rise after all.

Macy joined our dawn party, coming up beside Kiera and patting her on the back.

"Macy, the goat's gone," I said.

"I heard," she said calmly, still patting Kiera's back. "But we're okay."

I nodded at Macy, grateful. Maybe I should tap her as my Second after all.

"Ready to check out the goat pen?" I asked Dex.

"Not a bit," he said.

"Me either. Let's go."

The pen was undamaged. The only sign that a goat had been here was the fresh streak of red on the dirt. The blood was already darkening, sinking into Nil earth.

"That is *insane*," Zane said. "It's like 'poof' "—he made a magical hand motion—"and the goat's gone."

"Hello?" An unfamiliar girl's voice drifted through the air, dangerously close to the bloody pen. "Anybody there?" She sounded scared.

"My name's Rives," I said, my hand relaxing on my knife. "We're not your enemy, I promise. You can come out."

A wiry girl with stringy blond hair emerged from the dark, wearing a City-made chest wrap and skirt. Dirt covered one arm like a bruise. Her wide eyes flicked across me, Zane, and Ahmad, repeatedly. My first thought: *skittish.*

"He said you'd be here," she said.

"Who?" I asked.

"Him." She pointed behind her, then her hand fell as she squinted at the darkness. "I swear he was right there. A boy was *right there.* And he led me here."

"Did he have a big black tattoo? Here?" I pointed to my upper arm and shoulder.

I wasn't surprised when she nodded.

"Okay, I'm Rives. This is Zane and Ahmad"—both boys raised a hand in turn—"and over there is Kiera and Macy." Macy smiled wide; Kiera waved weakly.

"What's your name?" I spoke softly.

"Brittney."

"Okay, Brittney. Do you know how long you've been here on the island?"

"A few hours? Maybe a day?" She frowned. "I passed out in the yard in broad daylight and woke up naked in the dark." The word *naked* sounded like "nekked." "What happened?"

"You took an unexpected trip, no passport required." I smiled my best reassuring smile. "This is going to sound crazy, but remember that heat you felt? Before you passed out?" She was nodding. "That was a gate. A freak wormhole of nature, a rip in space, whatever, but it's what brought you here, and it's what will get you back home." I paused, letting those bombshells sink in. "Where is home?"

"Blessing, Texas."

I'd never heard of it. I took in her slumped posture, her shifting feet. Her wide eyes darting around. Her shock level reminded me of Dex on his first day in the City.

"Do you travel much, Brittney?" Same quiet tone.

"I went to the big city once," she said. "San Antonio. For back-to-school clothes."

I'd never been to San Antonio, but I was pretty sure it hadn't prepared her for Nil.

"Okay," I said, knowing it was anything but. "Just a few more questions. Do you remember what day it was when you passed out?"

"December second. Or maybe the third." She frowned. "I didn't hit my head, I swear." Her speech accelerated; so did her drawl. "I saw a show last week, you know, the one about real-life EMTs? This man got in a wreck and when they laid him out, the EMTs asked him all kind of questions like that." Now she looked confused.

"Okay, great." *Holy shit.* Nil was going to eat her up and spit her out in days. Talk about unprepared.

I switched up my questions. "And the boy—the one who led you here—he gave you those clothes?"

Brittney nodded.

"What did he say?"

"He threw the clothes at me like I was a dog on the ground. 'From your people,' he said. Then he told me I'd better follow him if I wanted to live. Who was he?"

"I don't know," I said. *But I'm going to find out.*

The sun chose that moment to poke above the horizon. The day would fly fast from here; it was the time between night and dawn that crept like slow lava.

Zane stood beside me, watching the girls walk away. "Dude. She's going to have it rough."

"No rougher than anyone else." I sighed. "No Wi-Fi, no pasta. No high-thread-count sheets. But maybe she'll surprise us."

"Maybe." He sounded doubtful.

Does everyone seem weaker because I've been here so long?

The strongest people were gone, replaced by rookies afraid of their own shadows, not a fair trade.

Because Nil was not fair.

But there was one person who looked fiercer than anyone else on Nil. And he wasn't on the Wall. Problem was, he wasn't even in the City. Then again, judging by the bloody pen, the inked kid was now the least of my worries.

Johan was right. Nil had shifted. And my gut said the worst was yet to come.

Or the best, the breeze whispered.

Merde, I thought.

If Nil liked what was coming, we were more screwed than I thought.

Or maybe just me.

CHAPTER 19

SKYE
DECEMBER 21, MID-MORNING

"So this is it?" I asked, with heavy skepticism.

This island we were circling was as attractive as a hairless Chihuahua. Flat with black rock beaches, the island had a grass-pocked landing strip, a few crumbling houses, and a small harbor with a couple deep-sea-fishing vessels and a handful of pitiful john boats.

"No." Dad chuckled. "This is the last pit stop. Jean Rene, Charles's brother, will meet us at the boat. If all goes well, we should make it to our destination by late afternoon."

If all goes well, I thought. *Hello, big* if.

We'd been island hopping for days, and the elusive island Dad was hunting seemed more mythical than ever. It was supposedly located near the edge of Micronesia, close to Polynesia and even closer to the equator. I had my doubts.

The Pacific is a very big place.

And some of the islands are very, very small.

Wild-goose chase, I thought. And lucky for the locals, Dad was the goose laying the golden egg.

I watched as he handed the pilot a wad of bills; same for the waiting driver. Ten minutes later, we stood at the deck, ready to board the

Mystique, one of the deep-sea-fishing boats I'd seen from the air. The captain wore cargo shorts, a Bob Marley T-shirt, and a flinty look in his eyes that his smile didn't dent.

"Welcome, Dr. Bracken." His deep voice rumbled like the sea. "I have my brother to thank for this pleasure." Only the way Jean Rene said it, it didn't sound like a pleasure; it sounded like a chore.

Don't worry, I felt like saying. *I'm sure you'll get paid well, too.*

Dad smiled as he shook the captain's hand. "Charles was wonderful last year. A good man. I'm honored to have his brother as our guide and our captain."

Jean Rene nodded. "I gave my word to Charles. I'll get you where you need to go."

Need, I thought. *Not want.*

I met his eyes for an instant. The darkness in his eyes had nothing to do with their color. I fought a weird shiver.

"Dad, can I talk to you a sec?"

"Sure. Let me just go over the charts with the captain, then you'll have my undivided attention."

Taking a seat at the front well out of earshot, I tied my hair back in a ponytail, added a few more elastic bands down its length, then wrapped an elastic headband on for good measure, trying to fight the wind as we picked up speed. It wasn't long before the flat island faded completely behind us and the boat was surrounded by water and open sky.

My dad sat beside me and put an arm around my shoulder.

"What is it, Skye?"

"The captain," I whispered. "He creeps me out. Like he could take us anywhere and we'd just vanish. It sounds silly out loud, but weird things happen." *Like Nil.*

Dad squeezed my shoulder. "What do I always tell you when we travel?"

"Think first, panic later."

"Exactly. So yes, we're dependent on him now. But I left our itinerary with multiple people back in the States. And I checked Jean Rene out thoroughly before I hired him, Skye. He doesn't have to be warm and fuzzy to get us where we need to be."

Need, I thought. Dad used it interchangeably with *want* on this trip.

Reaching into my backpack, I fished around for my Sharpie. In careful print, on the inside of my left wrist, I printed the letters *TFPL*.

Think first, panic later.

Right.

Dad leaned back, tucking his hands behind his head. "Based on Jean Rene's estimates, we should be there by late afternoon. The island is the original home of Charles's grandmother. Jean Rene's too. It's squarely in the grid I made using Scott's stars as the guide. If it's not Nil, then someone there must know something about it. Coordinates, how to access it, *something*."

He tilted his face toward the sun. "Do you know why I became an astrophysicist?"

"Because it's the best pickup line ever?"

My dad grinned behind his sunglasses. "Because space fascinates me, especially the sun. When I was five, I saw my first solar eclipse from my neighbor's roof with his dad's high-end telescope. He was a stargazer; I was a sun worshipper. For me, it was always the sun. After all, it's what the Earth revolves around, right? I was obsessed with all things sun related. Eclipses, supernovas, black holes, you name it. And then Scott vanished."

His paused.

"His experience only solidified my fascination with the sun. Because Scott sensed a connection between the sun and Nil. It takes the Earth three hundred sixty-five days to revolve around the sun, and that's the precise length of time kids have to escape from Nil. A rather odd coincidence, yes? And the gates he spoke of only appear when the sun is shining. Scott had no science, just a feeling, but he was absolutely convinced Nil was linked with the sun." He rubbed his chin.

"As scientists, we operate by rules. And yet, there is so much we don't understand, especially about space and the sun. For example, what's the full impact of the sun's electromagnetic radiation on Earth and our climate? We know that solar flares often signal a mass ejection of solar material toward the Earth, and while these ejections comprise a small part of the sun's total irradiation, they can be extraordinarily powerful. In 1989, one tripped a power grid in Quebec, leaving six million people without power. The aurora was seen all the way to Texas. And the Quebec geomagnetic storm wasn't even the largest one ever recorded." He fell silent, lost in thought.

"The Solar Superstorm," I offered in the lull. "Eighteen something."

"1859." He beamed. "The Carrington event. It was spectacular. Massive auroras followed, so did major geomagnetic disturbances. And ice-core sampling suggests the Carrington event isn't unique. Data suggests these storms occur roughly every five hundred years. And my research suggests that the largest geomagnetic storm to ever impact the Earth occurred in 300 AD, at least four times the intensity of the Carrington event, with the greatest impact in Polynesia, with auroras for days. That's what I've been researching, too: anecdotal history of when the night turned to day in the Pacific. Because the aurora would have been so large, it would have lit the night sky like daylight, and such an unusual event would be in island lore. And I don't know what effects such a massively powerful geomagnetic storm could have on our poles and atmosphere."

"But what does that have to do with Nil?" I frowned.

"I'm not sure." Dad ran his hand through his hair. "Call it a feeling. A hunch. One that may be completely off the mark. But if there's any connection between Nil and the sun, any at all, from a geomagnetic storm or something else, I'm going to find it, because if it exists, it's important. It might even be the key to understanding Nil." His voice grew soft. "Sometimes, Skye, even when it seems impossible, you still must try. Sometimes you must take a leap of faith, sometimes you must take a chance. I'm not blinded by my science, nor am I ignoring it. I choose the title hopeful realist." He smiled. "In life, nothing chanced, nothing gained. Even if I just prove myself completely wrong."

I nodded. For a long moment, neither of us spoke. The boat bounced across the water, heading into endless blue. Cool water sprayed across my face, the polar opposite of my mom's recent dry and dusty digs. I hadn't seen her in weeks.

"Do you ever miss her, Dad?" I asked quietly.

He didn't ask who I was talking about. "Every day," he said without hesitation.

"She misses you, too, you know."

"I know." He sighed.

"Promise me something, Dad." I turned to face him. "After this trip, no matter how it turns out, promise me you'll let this obsession with Nil go. It's taken over your life. I understand why you're driven to find Nil, but it drove Mom away. And while I didn't know Uncle Scott, I don't think he'd want you to lose your family over his past. And I think Mom could still be in your future, *if you let Nil go*. Does that make any sense?"

"I promise I'll think about it, Skye. That's the best I can do." He squeezed my shoulder. "Love you, pumpkin. Now excuse me while I go chat with our captain." He squeezed my shoulder again as he left.

I watched Dad slide into the wheelhouse and speak with Jean Rene, no doubt about the mysterious island.

As crazy as he was, my dad possessed an uncanny knack for choosing good people—guides, pilots, hosts, etc.—and he had an equally impressive knack for coming out on top of even the most hopeless-looking situations. Even on the disastrous Kenyan safari trip, he'd managed to extricate our entire tour group—complete with a trio of terrified podiatrists—from the clutches of some less-than-friendly locals toting machine guns; Dad had bartered coin and curios and some impressive karma for our freedom. He never panicked, not at first. Not when it mattered.

I rubbed my wrist and relaxed.

The next few hours passed in a blur of open water.

I dozed off and didn't wake until we slowed. We were approaching an island; actually we were approaching three. One large, stretched wide, with two smaller islands off in the distance, each with a small patchy green peak and black cliffs. The main island had a large emerald peak, a massive sloped mountain, obviously volcanic, not unlike what Uncle Scott had described in his journal. Suddenly I was wide-awake.

I glanced at my cell phone. No signal, but the time read 5:08 p.m.

I made my way to the wheelhouse, picking the side where my dad stood.

"So that's where we're going?" I pointed at the big island.

"That's it," Dad answered.

"What are the other two islands?" I pointed.

"The Death Twins," the captain said flatly. "Barrier islands. The current around the two has crushed many boats, taken many lives."

I glanced back at the Death Twins. Stretching toward the afternoon sun, the islands looked quiet. Peaceful, even.

"Stay away," he said softly, so low only I could hear. "They are not for you."

It sounded more like a threat than a warning.

I liked our captain less by the minute.

We slowed again as we entered the no-wake zone. Near the harbor, the beach glinted warm white in the afternoon sun. The water rippled like liquid glass, crystal clear with a turquoise tint. A manta-ray cruised by, its sleek body brushing the surface. A massive starfish winked from below, so close I wondered whether we were docking at low tide. A man in his late sixties or early seventies waited at the dock, his age alone telling me this wasn't Nil.

I was oddly disappointed.

Jean Rene shook my dad's hand. "Family first. Be safe, young Skye," he said, nodding to me. To my surprise, he actually sounded sincere.

"Dr. Bracken!" The man at the dock waved, his smile breaking his tanned face into a hundred wrinkles. "Charles sent me to take good care of you. I'm his second cousin, Rangi. I will give you the tour. Help you find the island magic you seek." Rangi winked.

You're humoring my dad, I thought, trying to read Rangi's expression. I didn't like it, because I didn't trust it.

Dad didn't miss a beat. "I'm honored to be here. Thanks for the warm welcome."

Rangi shrugged. "We don't get many visitors. Too far out to be a destination for many. Hawaii is where everyone wants to be."

I got the distinct impression that he wasn't the least bit bothered to have his island left alone.

As we left the harbor on foot, we passed a line of black rocks that jutted out into the sea. On the farthest one, a small family of three stood together: a mom, dad, and son. The mom sobbed, one hand on the boy's shoulder, the other dabbing her eyes.

I should've turned away. *Looked* away. Left them to their pain. But hadn't I already established that I was a voyeur?

Something felt—wrong. Or at least very, very strange.

The dad stood upright, arms crossed, bare-chested and showing off impressive black tattoos covering his upper arms and chest, staring down at the boy with an expression of pride, even as the mom wept uncontrollably. The boy, like his dad, wore shorts and no shirt, only the boy wore a lei of yellow flowers around his neck; it hung on his bony shoulders, looking especially fluffy in comparison to his thin frame.

He had a small black tattoo wrapping around one bicep. He stared at the water with no expression, then threw something into the sea. His posture seemed sad, almost defeated. More than anything, he seemed resigned.

Rangi touched my arm. "It's his seventeenth birthday," he said quietly. "An island rite of passage. He's throwing seventeen stones into the sea, one for each year of life. It is time for him to become a man." He paused. "Come. Let them be."

I turned away, feeling horribly guilty for intruding on their private moment.

Then the wind shifted, carrying their words my way. *Spirit Island*, the man said.

My eyes caught Rangi's. He smiled immediately, but not before I caught the flicker of fear in his eyes.

"Come," he said, still grinning. "You have much to see." He pointed at the interior of the island, gesturing for me to follow my dad, who was already a few yards ahead.

Once we got going, the family slipped from my thoughts. The island was gorgeous.

The houses were lovely. Small, pale-colored homes, all sturdily built and well maintained, all gracing quiet streets. This island, as large as it was, had a simple feel to it. Bicycles were everywhere. No cars. The pace felt slow, in the way of comfortable routines steeped in age. Even the palm trees swayed leisurely in the island breeze.

"First stop," Rangi said. "Dinner." He pointed to a beachside shack with a sign that read FISH. "You haven't lived until you've tried my nephew's dishes."

Was everyone related? I wondered. The island seemed too large to have everyone related, but what did I know?

An hour later, I knew that Rangi's nephew could grill fish like nobody's business. Flaky and tender, with a tasty citrus-glazed crust and mango salsa—I'd died and gone to island food heaven. Stuffed, I sat back and listened as the locals regaled Dad with island tales.

But the more people talked to my dad, the more I wanted to leave. I couldn't shake the feeling that people were telling him what he wanted to hear, yet not quite. Maybe he had the patience to sift through the stories for information gold, but I didn't. This was his quest, not mine.

Abruptly, I needed out; I needed *air*. I needed to get away from Dad's crazy quest.

"I'm going for a walk, Dad," I said.

He frowned. "I'll come with you."

I shook my head. "I'm just going to check out the sunset, for goodness' sake. And I have my cell phone and the walkie-talkie you gave me. It's all good."

He hesitated.

"Dad, stay." I patted my backpack, full of all the necessary communication equipment. "I'm *fine*. And it's not noon," I whispered, shooting him a pointed look.

"Okay," he said, relaxing. "But don't be long."

I wandered down to the beach. Twilight was falling, and the sunset would be stunning from here. The fine white sand under my feet was soft. The sand grew chunkier, interspersed with rocks, and without warning the sand turned charcoal black. The beach curved, the restaurant faded from sight, and just as I was about to turn around, I saw the boy. The same one I'd seen earlier with his parents when he was throwing rocks into the sea. He still wore his yellow lei. He held a rope tied to a goat in one hand; his other hand held something I couldn't see. Something small. A basket sat on the ground, and if I wasn't mistaken, it held a cat.

He stood staring at a pair of canoes. He dropped his head, then with his eyes closed, tossed something toward the canoes. It landed in the well of one canoe with a *thunk*.

The boy lifted his head and strode forward. He peered inside both canoes, then reached inside the second one, retrieved what he'd thrown—it looked like a conch shell—and threw it far into the sea. Still holding the goat's tether, he picked up the animal and set the goat inside the same canoe where he'd landed the shell. He did the same with the basket and cat. Then he looked around, furtively, as if to see if anyone was watching. Moving quickly, he reached into the other canoe, picked up a small cage with a chicken, liberated the poultry, and set the chicken in his canoe with the goat. Then he pushed the canoe off the beach, hopped in, and started paddling. He moved swiftly through the break, the nose of his canoe bouncing up, then down, staying true toward the open sea. Past the break, he cut a sharp left.

No way, I thought, my eyes tracking his course.

He was paddling straight toward the Death Twins.

Not for you, the unfriendly boat captain had warned, pointing toward those same islands.

Why not? I wondered.

Sometimes, Skye . . . you must take a chance.

The second canoe sat on the beach, complete with a paddle and no chicken.

I didn't hesitate. Keeping low, I ran across the sand and hijacked the second canoe.

It was time to take a chance.

CHAPTER 20

SKYE
DECEMBER 21, NEARLY NIGHT

Paddling a canoe through the open ocean at twilight was harder than it looked.

The dim light blurred the water. Dark blue waves broke fast and hard, pushing me back, like the ocean was protecting the Death Twins, too. Those were the moments when I was terrified the boy would turn around and see me, and I'd freeze. But then I'd think, *So what if he does? And who can see a thing through this crappy light?* Then I'd dig my paddle deep into the ocean's gut and lurch forward, determined not to let the boy out of my sight.

The gap between us widened and I made a choice: paddle *hard.* Better to keep up with him and risk getting spotted than to lose him. After all, maybe the boy knew a secret route to the Death Twins that would keep me from getting killed. Of the two of us, he was the only one who knew where he was going.

I was an uninvited plus-one.

Oddly enough, he hadn't turned around once; he was completely intent on his destination. Plus he had a feisty goat and a stolen chicken to contend with, so his abridged Noah's Ark trumped my empty canoe as far as distractions went.

I picked up my speed. The sun disappeared. The water darkened to black, and the air cooled. I shivered, wishing I had a sweater, or better yet, a shred of common sense. This impromptu canoe ride suddenly seemed dangerously stupid.

I was as bad as my dad. I guess curiosity was genetic after all.

But nothing about this boy made sense. His bearing screamed the opposite of brave, and yet here he was, paddling out to an allegedly deadly island at night, on his birthday no less.

Most people got cake. He apparently got a goat, a solo canoe ride, and a burst of bravado, enough to steal a chicken. Who steals a chicken?

You stole a canoe, my conscience chided.

I told my conscience to shut the heck up.

And then there were the words I'd heard falling from the dad's lips and carried by the wind: *Spirit Island.*

Maybe that was this boy's birthday gift. But was he running toward it, or away from it?

I had to know.

The moon rose as the boy disappeared behind one of the islands. When I rounded the shore, an empty canoe was pulled up onto the beach, and the boy, goat, and stolen poultry were nowhere in sight. A black cat sat at the tree line, its tail flicking quietly, its yellow eyes on me, watching. The cat creeped me out more than the dark water.

About twenty yards from the boy's canoe, I landed, dragged mine higher on the beach, and draped a few fallen palm fronds to cover it. Ignoring the creepy cat, I jogged over to the boy's canoe and followed the prints. Goat hooves in sand make for easy tracking.

Away from the beach, the darkness thickened with the trees.

I walked faster, and a few minutes later I saw the kid, off to my right. Walking slowly, he still carried the chicken and cat basket and led the goat. He looked as happy as a visitor to a wake. His festive lei was out of place.

I crept along, keeping the boy in sight. The half-moon was bright enough to both guide me and give me away, forcing me to keep my distance.

Eventually, he stopped. The trees ended abruptly in an open area of flat black rock. The boy stood in the very center, turning in a slow circle, still holding the goat's rope. For one terrified instant I thought he spotted me, but he kept turning. Then he dropped to his knees, studying the ground. He traced invisible lines in the air, lines that formed lazy circles and mysterious shapes.

Standing again, he backed up to the edge of the flat rock, dropped his head, and sat down with a sigh. The chicken squawked.

"Shut up," the boy grumbled. "It's not your funeral."

I fumbled for my phone, knowing I should text my dad and tell him I was okay. Just as I fished it out of my backpack, something furry brushed my leg. A cat, this one a tabby.

Weird, I thought. *Cat island*. I wasn't a fan. I'd never been a cat person, probably because I had allergies.

The cat meowed.

I backed up, worried the cat might call the boy's attention to me; same for the glow of my phone's screen. I shielded my phone with my hand.

No signal; I'd forgotten. *Crap.*

I stashed my worthless phone back in my backpack and refocused on the boy.

He hadn't moved. He seemed oblivious to everything but whatever was going on in his head.

I didn't need a degree in astrophysics to know the boy was waiting for something, I just didn't know what. But my instincts told me it was something more important than a birthday cake.

At midnight, my answer rose from the ground.

In the center of the black rock, the ground turned liquid, the surface rippling and roiling where solid rock should be. Without warning, the wavering ground rocketed up into the air and stopped; now it was an invisible wall framed by the night, black on black, the shimmering lines defining where night began and the weird air ended. Then the inside black fell away. A sheer wall of translucent air shimmered in the night like a million specks of diamonds reflecting the moon itself, and yet I could still see through it. Almost.

It writhed in place, waiting.

The boy strode forward and threw the chicken toward the weird veil of shimmering air. The bird hit the air wall and disappeared. The boy waited; I could vaguely see his lips moving. Then he pushed the very reluctant goat forward. The goat seemed to get sucked into the shimmering wall, and then, like the chicken, it too disappeared. Again the boy waited. I realized he was counting to three. Then, with a backward glance at the gray cat in the basket, the boy stepped into the rippling air and vanished.

A white cat shot from the dark, into the glistening wall after the boy. Boom. Gone.

The air still shimmered. Still waiting.

I burst from my hiding spot and ran straight toward the wall, every cell in my being telling me that this was a gate, a gate to Nil exactly like my Uncle Scott had described, only this gate didn't move and *how the heck did the boy know one would appear?*

One . . .

Two . . .

I hit the shimmering air on three and it clung to me like warm sludge; it held me, wrapped around me, and as I fought to breathe, heat poured into every pore . . . every cell . . . every last speck of *me.*

And when the heat washed through my eyes, stealing my sight, I screamed, and yet I didn't. No sound escaped; there was no air.

There was no me.

And yet, I was still here.

Just when I thought I would explode from the heat, every cell went ice cold. I fractured into a billion brittle bits, knit together by invisible thread that I held tight with my mind . . . I grasped it with every ounce of strength I had, holding on in the sheer black *nothingness*—and then it slipped. Drifted away, out of reach.

Gone.

Like me.

CHAPTER
21

I woke with a jolt.

My hand automatically sought my blade in the dark. The sea hissed my name with an intensity that made me sit up.

I was alone.

And yet I wasn't.

The island's presence filled my hut like invisible smoke. The night air vibrated with energy, but it wasn't just the air: it was the ground, the sea, the very DNA of the island itself. It reminded me of the night when I'd woken from my deadsleep coma, fully alive, only right now it was *Nil* that vibrated with life. My blood pulsed in time with an invisible beat.

I'd felt this island vibe once before, but never so potent. Never so overwhelming.

And then it was gone.

Invisible smoke, sucked away by an invisible wind.

Outside my hut, Zane patrolled listlessly. He spun the instant I left my hut.

"What's up, Chief?" he asked, keeping his voice low.

"Did you feel that?" I asked.

"Feel what? A tremor?"

I shook my head. "Not a quake. It was something else. Something powerful, like a pulse. Deep in the island. I'm not sure what it was."

Zane shook his head. "I didn't feel a thing, dude." He glanced toward Mount Nil. "I sure hope she's not going to blow her top."

"I hope not, too. But whatever it was, it's gone."

"Amen," Zane said. He was still looking at the mountain. I wondered if Zane had felt something after all.

"Go sleep," I said. "I've got this."

"You sure?" Shadows of hesitation flickered across his face.

"I'm sure. I've slept. You haven't." I opted not to mention I'd just sacked out minutes before I'd been woken up. "Go." I reached out my hand. "I'll take your torch, though."

Zane didn't protest twice.

I stood near the firepit, alone again.

Assessing again.

Because the same feeling that had woken me whispered that the island's vibe had shifted in a new direction. *Maybe this shift is in our favor,* I thought, sweeping the darkness beyond the City. *Maybe something good is coming.*

God knows we're due.

Actually, we were overdue. I'd just realized there would be no rooster calls at dawn, because the rooster was gone. Snatched, like the goat. The bird had made a tasty midnight snack for something.

Something with fur.

A tuft of coarse gold fur glinted in the torchlight, snagged on the rough wood of the chicken pen. Cat or dog, leopard or hyena, it was a toss-up. I couldn't tell what animal had been the attacker, other than one that was hungry. And a chicken was an appetizer compared to a meaty goat.

I looked at the pair of hens huddled in the pen's far corner. *I'd huddle up, too, if I were you,* I thought.

Then I realized *I am you*.

The only difference between my house and the chicken coop was that mine had a thatched roof. Not exactly reassuring.

And I still hadn't seen Burton.

Michael appeared out of the dark, from the hut Zane just entered.

"Everything okay?" I asked quietly.

"Can't sleep," he said. He looked around, unsmiling. I'd never seen him smile, not once. Then again, Nil didn't lend itself to humor. "How goes the night?"

"Bad for the rooster." I gestured toward the pen.

Michael muttered something in Korean that sounded like a curse.

"Sitting here, like ducks"—he gestured around the City as he spoke—"fire is not enough."

"I know. And the deadleaf barrier isn't enough, either. It's all defensive. We need a better plan," I said. *Before we become prey.*

I glanced at the empty goat pen. Maybe we already were.

"I will think," he said simply, "and try to sleep. Tomorrow night I will take your watch." He nodded, his black hair falling in his eyes. He'd finally been here long enough to need a haircut. He turned back to his hut.

I watched him go, assessing. Michael's build was strong, his footfalls quiet. And he was the best fisherman since Miguel. He'd gained muscle since he'd arrived, not to mention confidence.

Maybe I should trust him with more. His take on sitting ducks was dead-on.

My eyes drifted to the mountain, the highest point on Nil. I had the strangest urge to go there, *right now,* to see the island through Nil's eyes.

Come, the wind whispered. *Come and see.*

I turned away, fighting myself. Fighting Nil. Trying to think and figure out what was coming.

I really needed more sleep.

CHAPTER
22

SKYE
DAY 1, AFTER MIDNIGHT

I came to, my ears ringing with unfamiliar voices. Angry voices.

"Why did you bring her here? Who is she?"

"I didn't bring her! I don't know who she is!"

"She obviously followed you." The first voice. Furious, frustrated. And thoroughly disgusted.

"I've never seen her before, I swear." The second voice. Scared.

Silence.

I kept my eyes closed, unwilling to alert anyone that I was awake and listening. I moved my toe a fraction, just to see if I was paralyzed.

I wasn't. And the awful heat and cold were gone.

"I believe you. Truthfully, I did not expect you. I expected your brother."

"He went to the mainland to school. It is my destiny now." That boy's voice sounded shaky.

Another pause, followed by a heavy sigh. The first voice rumbled through the air, deep and strong.

"Destiny or no destiny, you have changed things, Paulo. You brought a *haole* onto sacred ground. I cannot help you now."

"What?" Paulo's voice quaked with fear. "You can't just leave me here!"

"I'm not just leaving you here," the first voice said. Definitely disgusted. "You *are* here. And you must find your way. That is *our* way. The sun will rise; the clock is ticking." Footsteps. "And you must deal with her. There is a place to take her."

With that, I jumped to my feet. Several things registered: the skinny boy no longer wore his flower lei; his cargo shorts had been replaced by a tan loincloth; another boy with major muscles and intricate black tattoos stared at me with an open mouth; I was naked; the moon was high and the air pitch-black; the ground was equally black and hard, and steam rose on my right.

I sprinted left and hurdled the chicken.

"Wait!" The strong voice boomed over my shoulder.

I didn't wait.

I ran.

Over black rock, down a slope peppered with steps, flying over the ground and expecting a hand to catch me from behind at any moment.

"Hey!" Paulo's voice. Scared.

I ran faster. The rock sloped around to the left, like a spiral track down a mountain, and then spilled me into a wide field of grass, and my spirits sank.

The meadow, I thought.

Uncle Scott's journal said to avoid the meadow. But I couldn't go back, not when the big guy's order was to "*deal with her.*" Nothing good could come of that.

I'd chance the meadow.

I kept running, aware that I was a naked white streak in the night. Knowing you would show up naked is one thing, but actually showing up in a strange place naked? Terrible. Being prepared was no help at all. Ignoring my nakedness, I stayed at my sprint pace, running through the tall grass, determined to ditch the kid I'd worked so hard to track. The irony wasn't lost on me.

Up ahead, stripes shifted in the dark, like living caution tape.

I skidded to a halt, my bare feet sliding on the slick grass and damp earth. When I got a clear look, fear coursed through me colder than the gate. Less than twenty feet ahead, a tiger paced the grasses like a feline guardian.

Turning toward me, the tiger stopped midstride.

The big cat's eyes glinted in the night. They glittered, brilliant facets winking above a mouth lined with teeth that would sink into my flesh like hot knives through butter.

I stood stone still, struggling to remember the material I'd read on tiger confrontations and the optimal human response.

Look big? Or was that only for bears? Curl into a ball and look small? Or was that for bears? Stand still? Walk slowly away? Throw rocks?

Frozen in indecision, I did nothing.

The tiger stared at me for one endless moment, then he swung his huge head away from me and disappeared into the night.

He let me go.

There was no other explanation.

For a long moment, I didn't move. I stood completely still, trying to process what had just happened. Then I gave up.

And I ran again.

CHAPTER 23

RIVES
DAY 277, DAWN

I'd decided Nil was more jacked than me.

All night on watch, I'd sensed the island. Listening, breathing, *watching*, but the weirdest part was that it didn't feel like Nil was watching *me*. I was a sideshow, making me wonder about the main event.

If it involved the leopard, I'd take the Nil sideline any day. Hell, I'd take the Nil sideline *every* day; the spotlight was usually too painful.

Dawn broke as the sun stole the show.

Kiera cornered me after breakfast.

"Morning, Rives." She smiled. "The Arches. Have you been there?"

I nodded as I fought a yawn. "Many times. Why?"

"Macy says the original carving is there."

"I don't know if it's the original one, but yeah, there's a carving. The Man in the Maze."

"Can you take me to see it?"

I hesitated.

"Please?" she asked softly. She rested her hand on my forearm.

I did my best not to flinch.

"Macy talks about the carvings constantly," Kiera said. "The one framed in the Arches. She says it's the most important."

Was the Man in the Maze the most important carving? The urge to uncover Nil's secrets coursed through my veins like the sea, churning and relentless.

Suddenly a trip to the Arches sounded like exactly where this day should start.

"Let's do it."

Kiera squeezed my arm and smiled. Her hand lingered long enough for me to pull away.

"Where are y'all fixin' to go?" Brittney asked as Kiera and I left the firepit.

"The Arches. South of the City. Have you been there yet?"

She shook her head.

"C'mon, then." I waved her over. "Time for a tour, Brittney. You haven't experienced Nil until you've seen the Arches."

Disappointment flickered across Kiera's face, but she recovered quickly. But anything she could ask me in private she could just as well ask in public. I had nothing to hide.

Liar, the sea crooned. *You show what you want to be seen. I've seen the real you.*

For a moment I rethought my decision to head to the Arches, where the sea crashed high enough against the rocks to touch skin. Then I kept walking. Because Talla's ghost lurked everywhere. By the water, in the City, near the Flower Field. I wondered if it would follow me from Nil.

If I left.

I'm leaving, I thought fiercely.

"You're quiet this morning, Rives," Kiera said. We'd gotten all the way out of the City while I was lost in my own head.

"Just have a lot on my mind," I said easily. Which revealed absolutely nothing.

"It must be hard to be the Leader," she said softly. "Do you ever regret saying yes?"

I thought of Thad and Natalie. Both strong, both experienced. Both selfless. Both better Leaders than me.

"No," I said, "I don't regret it." *I'm still trying to live up to it.* "For me, it's an honor."

I left it at that.

I glanced sideways at Brittney, who was as quiet as I was. Only she was looking around, her eyes wide as always.

"You okay, Brittney?" I asked.

She touched the bark of a tree as we passed. "This place is so pretty I can't believe I'm here. It's like I won one of them free vacations you get those phone calls about, only this is real, you know?"

"It's pretty," I said carefully, "but Nil's not a vacation, Brittney, no matter what it looks like, okay?"

Brittney didn't reply. Her rookie status glared as bright as her new City threads. With a start, I realized that the marks I'd first seen on her biceps weren't dirt; they were bruises. Fading to green, the bruises came to Nil with her.

Maybe Nil *was* a vacation for her. A scary thought. And a sad one.

At the City's edge, we cut through the cliff, passing through the Crystal Cavern. It was nearly as beautiful as the Arches.

"Wow." Kiera turned in a slow circle near the exit. Facets winked at us floor to ceiling, the morning light bouncing off the walls. "So beautiful."

"No doubt. They're diamonds. Rough and uncut. But definitely diamonds."

"Diamonds?" Brittney's slow drawl was full of wonder. "Oh my gawd, my mama would go hog wild with this." She ran her hands over the walls.

"Be careful. They're sharp," I said. The last thing she needed was a cut and an infection.

Brittney jerked her hands away. Her face looked wistful.

"C'mon, you two. Let's go see the Man. He's waiting in his Maze."

Twenty minutes later, we climbed around the edge of Black Bay, and the Arches came into view. Five black rock arches in varying sizes, all carved from the volcanic black rock by water or forces I couldn't even comprehend, all framing a piece of Nil sky. Water crashed against the bases, white and frothy.

I led the girls to the biggest arch, where the Man in the Maze lived.

"That's it?" Kiera asked. She stared at the carving, hands on hips.

"That's it," I said crisply. She'd looked more impressed with the raw diamonds than with this carving, never mind the fact that someone had carved a perfectly symmetrical goddamn labyrinth into unforgiving black lava rock, by hand. *No wonder so much info gets lost here*, I thought, abruptly furious. *First you have to care.*

I took a slow breath, dialing down my temper. I wasn't sure why I was so annoyed. Probably because I was freaking exhausted.

"There are three other carvings," I told Kiera. "Not identical, but similar. They all have the number twelve at the top."

"I've seen the rubbings," Kiera said. Still unimpressed. "I just thought in person it'd be different." She shrugged. "Bigger."

Classic.

Brittney touched the carving, one finger reverently tracing the circular lines. "Who did this?" Unlike Kiera, her face read *awestruck*.

"I don't know," I told Brittney. "Someone here long before us."

"I couldn't do this in a million years," she said, her voice full of wonder. "I could draw the stick figure, though."

I stared at the stick figure, at the Man *in* the Maze.

Was this carving more important than the others? If so, why?

"We're going back," Kiera announced. "Are you ready?"

I shook my head. "I'm going to stay. Do you know the way back?"

"Yeah. It's easy," Brittney answered.

Disappointment flickered across Kiera's face—again.

A flash of purple made me turn.

Kiera's flower—the one she constantly kept tucked behind her ear—was in her hand. Three petals were falling into the water below the Arch, dropped by Kiera herself. She looked up, her eyes meeting mine.

"I thought I should leave something." She shrugged. I nodded, impressed. Maybe Kiera had figured out that disrespecting Nil was a seriously bad call.

Maybe there was more to Kiera than I realized.

"Thanks for the tour." Kiera tucked the rest of her flower back behind her ear, a smooth move that hid the missing petals beneath her hair. Self-aware, and calculated. Like Nil, but not.

Maybe Kiera was exactly as I suspected.

"Anytime." I smiled.

Kiera smiled back and turned away, linking her arm through Brittney's.

I turned back to the carving. I squatted down, about four meters back from the Arch. Mount Nil sat perfectly framed. I'd never noticed it before. From this angle, the twelve on the carving pointed toward Mount Nil, the highest island point.

Watching us, are you, Nil? I thought.

Fine, I thought fiercely, my fist tightening. *Two can play this game. Because I'm watching you too. Watching, listening, taking notes and numbers. And I'm getting closer; I feel it. I hope you do, too.*

A hissing on my right made me turn. A black cat with frosted white paws sat on the nearby rock, flicking his tail.

"Well, hello, Burton. Good to see you're not puppy chow." I grinned.

I couldn't help thinking that Nil picked this precise moment for Burton to resurface. A sign of benevolence, a sign that Nil had heard me. A sign that Nil didn't kill everything it touched.

But Nil wasn't in the friend column yet.

Or ever.

CHAPTER 24

SKYE
DAY 1, DAWN

I never stopped running, never stopped moving, and by the time the sun rose, I found myself surrounded by lush trees. Vibrant green leaves canopied overhead; fruit hung from branches for easy picking. Water coated leaves on the ground. I licked a dozen leaves, lapping up every speck of water. Then I carefully studied the trees and fruit, recognizing guava.

Choosing ripe ones, I ate a handful and felt better.

In the early light, the Sharpie on my wrist stood out like a cheap tattoo: TFPL. *Think first, panic later.*

I snorted.

Maybe I hadn't fully panicked—*as if there are degrees of panic*, my mind admonished. *Even partial panic is, by definition, panic*—but I sure hadn't done a great job of thinking. It was more like act first, think later; I'd been reactive rather than proactive. And with the tiger, I hadn't acted at all. I was lucky to be alive. I'd barely given my follow-the-strange-kid plan any thought at all.

Great job, Skye. I brushed aside the nagging thought that landing here had been my plan all along, that on some level I'd known the boy with the lei would lead me here.

Be careful what you wish for, Charley had warned. *Because you just might get it.*

I'd managed to get myself stuck on Nil, like my uncle, the same uncle who died base jumping off the Sydney Harbor Bridge. Apparently the reckless gene ran strong in our family. I just hoped the survival one ran stronger.

But now that I *was* here, now what?

Now I had absolutely no plan at all.

Sorry, Dad, I thought, a lump lodging my throat. *For making you worry, for not listening all the times you tried to share survival techniques.*

For not believing.

Because given my weak performance so far, I wasn't as prepared as I'd thought. My dad must be out of his mind with worry. I hoped that somehow he'd know I was here, that he'd know I'd be okay.

Problem was, *I* wasn't sure I'd be okay. The welcome committee wasn't exactly welcoming. Then I had a frightening realization— neither of the kids at my welcome party had used the word *Nil*.

What if I'm not on Nil?

What if I'm somewhere else?

Panic rose, as swiftly as a gate, a living, breathing, air-sucking beast inside me. I tried to take a deep breath and began hyperventilating instead. *You're panicking, Skye.*

Breathe. Calm down.

Think.

If I had a hope of making it here—*please be Nil*—it was time to start thinking.

Think first, act second. It was my new motto.

Think.

This place had to be Nil. The similarities to Uncle Scott's journal were too great: the gate trip with its invisible burn, the naked arrival.

The black rock mountain, the grassy meadow. The clear blue sky, the lush fruit trees. If the journal rang true, I stood in the groves.

I had to be on Nil. If not, then I was stuck on some freaky replica of Nil that was so similar I was more screwed than I could even imagine.

Fear streaked down my spine, cold and choking.

Breathe.

This is Nil, I told myself repeatedly until the cold subsided. *I'm on Nil. And I'm going to be okay.*

I would operate under the assumption that I was on Nil until I found out otherwise. Plus, my current plan depended on it: I needed clothes, a weapon, and Rives, in that order.

Being naked made me feel vulnerable. I was constantly aware of my nakedness, taking precious mental space that I needed for survival. Just because I knew everyone woke up naked on Nil didn't prepare me for how awkward it was. The sooner I had coverage, the better.

Taking another deep breath, I assessed my surroundings. I catalogued what materials I could use, what I needed to do, my mind replaying a dozen different videos and web pages and parental lectures. I needed a tool.

I found a small, flat black rock, the size of my cell phone, and rubbed the edge repeatedly against a boulder until it was decently sharp. Now I had my tool. Next I needed fiber—the kind to wear, not eat.

I strode over to a thicket of stalks that appeared to be dogbane, or at least a close cousin. *Good enough*, I thought. I skipped the grayed stalks as too old and focused on the brown ones. One at a time, I hacked off a dozen just above the ground. Soon I had a respectable pile.

Moving methodically, I flattened each stalk against the boulder I'd used to hone my rock tool, pressing until the stalk split in two. Then

I broke off each end, gently pulling the outside woody part off, lifting carefully from each end and alternating until the wood fell away completely, leaving me with two three-foot-long ribbons of twine. I repeated this process until I had four pieces of twine. To make the twine more pliable, I rubbed it between my fingers, working my way down the ribbon, just as Dad had taught me, or rather, the myriad YouTube video clips he insisted I watch on making rope in survival situations. Tedious work, but necessary. I manipulated the material until it softened, just enough to make the twine easier to work with. My fingers were already sore. Thankfully, I didn't have blisters.

Yet.

Taking a break from the twine, I gathered green leaves that looked like elephant ears, sharpened a small stick to act as a needle, and pierced the leaves enough to thread the twine through, careful not to tear the leaves. Then I fashioned a wide green-leaf skirt and top, enough to cover myself and give myself a semblance of privacy. It wasn't J.Crew, but it worked.

Next, I needed a weapon, one with better range than a handheld rock tool.

I stripped four more stalks and separated the bark, leaving me eight more ribbons of twine, but this time I skipped the softening process. I didn't want to risk a blister that could rupture and leave me open to infection. Plus, I still had to braid the fibrous ribbons. Working on autopilot, I swiftly wove the material into rope, then crafted a rock sling. A simple but effective weapon, a small cradle held the rock, woven between two lengths of braided cord. Over the course of four summers, I'd practiced this maneuver countless times with my dad, using hemp twine, rope, and a variety of other bark fiber as raw materials. The actual sling took little time to make; it was the prep that took the work. I didn't need practice on how to use it; I could wield it blindfolded by feel. And eyes open, I could hit my mark from 100 feet. Not bragging, just a fact. Some people come home from summer trips with T-shirts; I came back with rock sling accuracy.

I'd never been more grateful.

I draped my sling across my shoulders, picked up three more pieces of twine, and tied my hair back in a long ponytail; it was already an out-of-control island nightmare. Shallow, I knew, but I hated how my hair looked without product—like I'd stuck my finger in a light socket. Tying it back made me feel like I'd accomplished something; it made me feel more like *me*.

Hair barely tamed, I hacked off a branch from a living tree—*Sorry, tree*, I thought, feeling environmentally disrespectful, but I needed a green stick—and sharpened the end into a spear. Rough but decent, and the green stick would be stronger than a dead branch that would snap at the first hint of pressure. I wished I had a pack to carry guava and mango, but I'd taken enough time already. I knotted twine around several mangoes and a handful of guava until they stayed put, then slung the fruit strand over my shoulder. It was the best I could do in such a short time. From what Uncle Scott wrote, the City was on the opposite side of the island from where I was, so I had a two-day walk ahead. I'd go slightly north, tracking the coast. There was no way I was going anywhere near the mudflats and the angry, angry hippos.

I gathered one more handful of guava and held them.

On my left, something snorted.

I turned slowly, slipping off my rock sling as I moved.

At the edge of the fruit trees, a large rhino stood motionless. Twenty feet of grasses separated us, at most.

Think.

Don't panic.

Don't react.

Think.

I quickly worked through what I knew about rhinos. *Poor eyesight, great hearing, killer sense of smell—it's how they sense humans. Sleep during the heat of the day, sometimes sleep standing. If they charge, stand your ground, and at the last second, dive out of the way. Then find cover or run.*

Run, I thought.

Uncle Scott's neat print floated behind my eyes. *Life. Death. Gates. Running.*

Yup, I thought. It seemed like all I did on this island was run. But I didn't feel like running today.

Moving slowly, I eased back into the trees and worked my way north, away from the rhino.

An hour later—maybe longer; I already missed my phone in more ways than one—I ran into Paulo, the younger member of my not-so-welcoming committee, just past the lush trees. He sat on a rock, crying. He looked miserable, and he smelled horrible.

"Are you okay?" I knelt, trying to breathe through my mouth.

His head jerked up. His eyes were red. They widened as he pointed a shaky finger at me.

"You!" he cried. "You ruined everything! Why did you follow me?"

"Why do you care?" I asked.

"Because you shouldn't be here!" Under his breath I caught the word *kapu. Forbidden,* I thought. *Trespasser.*

"I came through the same wall of air as you," I said calmly. "Therefore the island must welcome me, too."

His face paled in shock. "What do you know of this place?"

"More than you think," I said.

Suddenly, he wilted. "I hate this place already. I didn't even want to come. My brother was the firstborn; he should be here. But instead he chose to study Western medicine and I got stuck with upholding the family honor." The way he said "family honor" made it sound like a disease. He glared at me. "And because of you, my mentor ditched me. I've been looking for you all night, and instead, I ran into some monkeys who threw poop at me."

It took all I had not to laugh. "You know, that's a sign of intelligence."

"What?" he said.

"The poop throwing. Scientists say it's a sign of primate intelligence."

"Great. Well, all I know is that it stinks." He sighed. His stomach grumbled. Still holding my breath, I handed him some guava. "Here. Breakfast."

"Where'd you find this?" he asked.

I pointed behind me. "There. Tons of fruit, all within reach. I'm Skye, by the way."

"Paulo," he said.

"I know." I smiled wryly. Then I thought for a moment, choosing my question carefully. "Why did you come?"

"I didn't have a choice."

"You always have a choice."

He shook his head. "You don't understand. This place . . . the tradition . . ." Abruptly he looked wary, like he'd said too much. He glanced around and stood. "There are rules. I can't break them. I'm to tell you to go west, and you'll find people like you."

"People like me," I repeated. Then I regarded him thoughtfully. "Paulo, we aren't so different. There *is* a City to the west, full of kids like us, all trying to make it home. All helping each other." I prayed that what I was telling him was still true. "I'm going there now. You can come with me, and they'll help you survive until you can get home."

He looked at the sky. "A prison is still a prison, even when the walls are beautiful," he murmured. His shoulders slumped. The defeated posture was back. "I can't leave yet."

A thought struck, because he sounded so certain he *would* leave.

"How do you know you'll get home? What do you know that I don't, Paulo?"

His eyes widened and he backed away. "You talk too much, *haole*," he said.

"Skye," I corrected, knowing full well the term for "outsider" was his attempt at maintaining distance. I stepped closer. "I'll figure it out, Paulo. Maybe not today, but I will. And in the meantime, if you need help, come to the City. Come find me if you don't want to do this alone."

"I have to," he whispered. He looked ready to cry again. "It's the only way."

He turned and ran. I watched him go. Something told me I'd see him again.

As Paulo vanished into the groves, I wished I'd warned him about the rhino.

And I wished I'd asked him if this was Nil.

CHAPTER
25

RIVES
DAY 279, BEFORE DAWN

Christmas Eve on Nil royally sucked.

The entire City was on edge, and it wasn't because we were waiting for Santa. Something was out there, something lethal. Something that would probably eat the fat man in the red suit if he got too close.

Animals usually didn't attack humans unless provoked. But if their food sources dwindled, all bets were off. Survival reigned. It was as simple as that. I'd pulled watch off the Shack, unwilling to put anyone at risk so close to the City's edge. As of now, the lurking predator trumped raiders on the threat list.

I cocked my head, listening.

Nothing.

The night had been eerily quiet. I'd heard a hyena and some distant barking, but nothing close. No whispers, not even in my head.

Nothing had triggered the perimeter traps Michael and I had set either.

Despite myself, I yawned.

It was my fourth night in the past week on watch and my second in a row. With two teams out on Search, the City was spread thin. I needed Nil veterans, people used to reading the island in the dark. But

Jillian, Macy, and Dex were spending so many waking hours training rookies and tending crops that it seemed wrong to ask them to take night watch, too. And every time Sy took watch, he woke me up, shaking and wide-eyed, alerting me to a fresh perceived threat. At least Sy didn't sleep on watch, but then again, I didn't sleep on his watch either, so I'd decided putting Sy on watch was pointless.

That narrowed watch duty down to me, Ahmad, Zane, and Michael, but in the end, watch was mine. If I couldn't sleep, I may as well take watch.

It was a toss-up who I was driving harder: me or the rookies.

There was a glut of *new*. New brains to train on the labyrinths and Charley's maps, new bodies to mold. I pushed everyone to get stronger, and more importantly, get *faster*. Fast meant life, or at least a fighting chance. And that was my job as Leader: to give everyone in the City a fighting chance. It's the only way I could sleep, knowing I'd done all I could.

Maybe it's why you're not sleeping, my brain murmured. *Because you're not doing enough.*

That and the fact that the kid from the Looking Glass pool had vanished into island air.

No sightings, no sign.

The drive to find him was so intense, it was screwing with my already-poor sleep. I'd always been able to sleep anywhere, anytime; it was a gift I'd picked up from my dad. It's why Talla's acute insomnia had seemed so unreal. But now, along with a City under attack, I'd been hit with the insomnia jinx, too.

I didn't need Talla's ghost to tell me I'd let Nil get in my head. But I also knew that answers would drive Nil out; I just needed to find them.

The crescent moon around my neck told me that I needed to find *him*.

So where is he?

Dex appeared at first light. "How was it, mate?" he asked, rubbing sleep from his eyes.

"Quiet."

He nodded. "You're off. Get some rest."

"Will do. Going to go take a dip in the Cove. Then I'll grab one of your naps." I smiled.

Dex frowned. "I rather like our new approach to traveling in pairs. Want some company?"

"Nah. I'm good. I just need to clear my head." *I need to get the kid out of my head.*

Dex nodded, his shoulders relaxing. "I'm always a bit keyed up after a night on watch myself. It's Nil in a nutshell, isn't it? Wait all night for something that may never come? Just like noon." He laughed without smiling. "We still have a decent stash of mango in the food hut, so if I were you, I'd pop in and grab a bite before your excursion."

For an instant I thought he'd said "execution."

I cleared my throat.

"Thanks." Grinning, I saluted Dex.

Twenty minutes later, I hit the Cove with the sun. Light bounced off the surface like sparks; near the falls, the water churned rough white. I looked around, noting the stillness. If the inked boy was here, he hid himself well.

I dove under the falls, surfaced, and when I stepped into the cave, I was pleased to find the firebow and torches I'd left last week were still there. Even better, they'd dried.

I'd move faster with light.

Using coconut husk as tinder, I worked the bow until it sparked and the tinder caught, then lit the torch. With firelight to guide my way, I didn't need the arrows; I knew the route cold, but I felt them anyway. And when I came to the bend, I went right. Call it macabre curiosity, call it my newfound island OCD. Whatever it was, I wanted every scrap of information the island was willing to cough up—even a skeleton.

The tunnel curved sharply, and like Jillian said, the passageway stopped abruptly, a dead end. A skeleton lay in a heap against the back wall, facing forward.

Creepy, I thought, taking in the empty eye sockets, the gaping mouth. Clean bones, tinged with brown, leaving no clue whether the person had collapsed into position or had been kicked into that pose by Jillian.

What were you after? Or was Johan right, this is where you chose to die? I moved my torch around the passageway, looking.

Above the skeleton at eye level, a carving gouged the stone. A sun, roughly the size of a basketball, with twelve rays. Inside the sun was an almond eye.

Leaning forward, I stared at the eye staring back at me, wondering what it meant and who the hell it was for. And wondering why it was here, marking a dead end.

I stepped toward the skeleton, choosing my footing carefully, and then I slowly pressed the eye.

Nothing.

Stupid. I shook my head. What did I expect—a secret passageway?

Maybe, I admitted privately. I wanted the dead end to offer up something. But the sun carving was just a sun; the eye was just an eye. Disappointed, I turned away. I glanced down to pick my footing, caught a clear glimpse of the skeleton, and froze.

A circle wrapped the skeleton's wrist: a bleached-out circle that didn't belong. A bracelet. A bone cuff bracelet. Someone on Nil before me wore a bone cuff bracelet.

Ramia, I remembered.

There are no coincidences on Nil.

This cuff was my clue. I didn't need to take it; I just needed to figure out what it meant.

I needed Johan.

He'd helped Thad bury her bracelet. Maybe he'd even met her. If my timing was right, they'd overlapped by a few days. But Johan was on Search again, and for all I knew, he was already gone. I hoped he was still here.

Guilt slammed through me, burning like a gate's shadow.

Selfish, I thought. But it didn't change how I felt. All I wanted was a few minutes with Johan. Ten, max. But it was up to Nil, and what the island was willing to give.

My torch flickered. *Go,* whispered the flames.

Moving as quickly as I could, I made my way back to the Looking Glass pool, and when I stepped into the light, I smiled.

The inked boy sat with his legs crossed, his face turned toward the pool, eyes open, jaw slack. The moment I stepped into the cavern, his head whipped toward me and his face darkened.

"You," he said. He hopped to his feet, his entire body tense. "Why did you come back? This place is not for you! Go back the way you came!" He thrust his finger at the darkness behind me.

I shook my head. "I think I'll stay awhile." I walked closer and held out my right hand. My left still held the lit torch. "I'm Rives."

The boy's dark eyes flicked to the torch before settling hard on me. "Maaka," he said. He didn't take my hand.

I let it drop. "Nice meeting you, Maaka."

He crossed his arms over his chest, regarding me. "Why did you return?" he asked finally. Less angry, more frustrated.

"To find you."

Maaka raised his eyebrows. "Why?"

I pointed to his tattoos. "Nice ink, Maaka. You know what's interesting? Your designs match the ones on the wall." I walked to the cavern wall and touched the waves, the sun, and the tribal face. "But this one intrigues me the most." I tapped the interlocking diamonds, a perfect replica of the ones on Maaka's arms. "A diamond shape, just like this island."

Maaka stared at me, giving nothing away.

147

But you will, I thought. *You already have.*

I pulled the carved crescent moon off my neck.

"This is pretty impressive." I ran my thumb over the smooth wood, then pointed to the carving on the wall—the fresh one that dripped deadleaf juice on my last visit. "And a perfect match. Nice job on both."

His crossed his arms. "What makes you think I was the carver?"

"Because you have the same moon on your left shoulder. Because you were here before me that day, and this carving was still wet. Because I think you were in the woods that night, watching us. And because I think you know more about Nil than any of us."

Maaka stared at the carving in my hand, saying nothing.

Point for me.

I took a different tack. "Why don't you join the City?"

"Because the City is yours."

"Yours," I repeated. "You talk about 'yours' and 'ours,' like the island is divided into groups of people—like the island is divided *among* people."

"Isn't it?" Maaka said quietly.

"No," I said. "All the people on the island are trying to eat and stay alive long enough to have a shot at getting home before their time runs out. That makes us all the same."

He shook his head. "You are wrong."

"Tell me why."

He stared at me. "We are all here for answers, but not the same answers. You have to find yours for yourself, Leader Rives."

Point for Maaka. He knew more about me than I knew about him.

"Perhaps," I said slowly, studying Maaka. "But then why do I feel that you have more answers than anyone?"

Maaka glanced at the water. "I only know what I see. But not everything I see is with my eyes." He turned to me. "What do you see?"

I answered without thinking. "I see a City full of people who are terrified of what else is roaming the island. I see graves filled with people I cared about. I see death waiting around the corner, and I see life, too. I see hungry kids struggling to survive, and people fighting for their friends. I see people working together and lifting each other up, still able to be awed by the beauty here despite the darkness. I see hope and fear and loss and life. And right now"—I kept my eyes on Maaka's—"I see someone who knows a lot more than he's telling."

Maaka nodded. "You see much. But not all. You see the edges."

His cryptic answers grated on my tired nerves.

"Tell me something, Maaka. What do you see?"

Maaka stood for a long moment, studying me. Finally he spoke. "I see a Leader who cares for his people but who does not fully respect what he does not know. I see a Leader who has lost himself in the island and rituals. I see a boy who knows the beginning and the end but does not see the middle, and the middle is the most important part. The middle determines the weight and shape, the form and the substance. Life."

I stared at Maaka, taking in his cool composure, his puzzling words, wondering what the hell were we talking about.

"Doesn't the middle determine the end?" I asked slowly.

Maaka tilted his head. "The end is already written, the path is set."

I shook my head. "No way. The middle shapes the end. It follows in sequence. Start, middle, then end. Done." *Holy shit, I'm turning into Thad.*

Maaka's mouth curved into the hint of a smile, the first one I'd seen. He turned toward the carvings on the wall and pointed at the numbers, 3-2-1-4. "Everything follows a sequence, but it is not always in the order you think."

I glanced at the numbers. A strange, perfect ten. A numerical sequence that meant nothing to me.

"So this is the end?" I raised my eyebrows.

Maaka looked surprised. "This is the middle."

"But not for all," I said, thinking of the Wall dripping crosses. "For some it's the end."

He looked thoughtful. "Maybe. And for others, the beginning."

I couldn't gauge if he was full of knowledge or full of shit.

"What's it for you?"

"I think, the middle."

"You think," I said skeptically.

He looked at me sharply. "Yes. I *think*. If you are not thinking, you are going through motions without meaning. It is the *why* that drives you forward, that drives growth. Without a why, it is simply an empty day."

"I don't think we always know the why," I said quietly.

Maaka's fire faded. "True. But that doesn't mean you should stop seeking it. When you find your middle, you will find your way." He turned toward the pool. Almost immediately he spun back, his dark eyes intense. "If you come back, do not bring fire. Not in this sacred place."

"Sacred to *who*?" I asked, frustrated.

Maaka gave me a long look, as if weighing his answer. He opened his mouth, and then, as if he'd thought the better of it, he gave a sharp shake of his head. He pivoted and in one swift move, he dove into the pool and disappeared beneath the water. I doused the torch in the pool and followed, just like before, only this time, I paused at the exit, mentally noting the shape and placement of the ocean entryway.

That extra time cost me.

I lost sight of Maaka. No head bobbing at the ocean's surface, no one stroking through the waves. Still, I swam toward shore, following the route we'd gone before, wondering where Maaka camped out, since it clearly wasn't the City.

There were no footprints on the sand, no tracks toward the trees. No sign of Maaka at all.

Frustration spiked, layered with fury. I felt toyed with, in a game I wasn't willing to play. A game where I didn't know the rules.

But there were rules; I felt them. And Maaka knew them by heart.

I left the water and strode toward the trees, slowly sweeping the trees, heading right, toward the cliff that housed the Looking Glass cavern. *Where did you go, Maaka? Where are you hiding?*

The island had swallowed him again.

Like the retreat of a wave, my anger gave way to exhaustion. Still, I couldn't help walking close to the trees, hoping Maaka was there. Hoping he was watching me, and that this time he'd be the one to yield.

Behind me, a twig cracked.

Gotcha, I thought.

"Decided to give up some answers after all, Maaka?" I grinned as I turned.

To my surprise, a girl stood on the beach. She had wild, curly blond hair that whipped behind her like an untamed halo. Her light eyes sparked with intelligence, set into a heart-shaped face. A slight sunburn colored her nose and cheeks. Green leaves covered her waist and chest, woven together with twine. But the most impressive part of her island getup was the sling weapon slung across her chest and the sleek spear in her hand.

No, I thought, taking in her expression and stance, the most impressive thing about this girl was her demeanor. Cool and collected, like she held Nil by the balls.

Not a Nil native, more like a Nil natural.

I stared one beat too long.

She strode toward me, raised her free hand, and smiled. "I don't know who Maaka is, but by any chance, are you Rives?"

CHAPTER
26

I'd watched the guy exit the ocean.

Like a merman without the fins, he emerged from the depths, well-built and muscular, dripping water and an air of danger. He strode up the beach, wearing nothing but a pair of almost see-through shorts—I tried not to stare—his eyes tracing the tree line with an intensity that held me completely still. He was clearly hunting something—or someone. He radiated power. He looked a little like Charley described, but this guy had no dreadlocks, and Charley had clearly said Rives had dreads.

He stopped halfway to the trees, his square jaw hard, his broad shoulders braced and tight.

Involuntarily, I took a step back.

Then he sighed heavily, his eyes still on the trees. His fury was gone, taking the aura of danger with it. Now his expression vacillated between worried and frustrated, and standing silently with his hands on his hips, he looked every inch the confident Leader Charley had described. *But no dreads.*

I frowned.

He drew closer, close enough for me to see his eyes.

Rives, I thought.

His eyes were just as Charley described. Pale green—like summer limeade, she'd told me—but they reminded me more of Caribbean water. Troubled water. Underneath his eyes, half-moon streaks clung to his skin, shadows of night that whispered all kinds of tired.

Up close, this guy looked more exhausted than dangerous, like he carried the weight of a City on his shoulders. It had to be Rives.

It was time to take a chance again.

Making sure my leaf ensemble still covered all the necessary parts, I left the trees, gripping my spear like a security blanket and making plenty of noise as I passed through the scrub brush.

The boy turned back, grinning. "Decided to give up some answers after all, Maaka?" he said as he turned. But when his gaze fell on me, his eyes widened and his smile dissolved into a soundless O.

He still looked a little dangerous.

Without pausing, I channeled my uncle's bravery and walked forward, coming close enough to the guy to see the intensity in his eyes and feel the power swirling around him like invisible fire.

"I don't know who Maaka is," I said, "but by any chance, are you Rives?"

"What?" His jaw dropped, but he recovered quickly. "Yeah. Who are you?"

"Skye." I paused, bone-deep relief flooding me with warmth. *I found Rives. I'm on Nil.*

I'm okay.

"Charley told me to find you," I added. "She said to tell you hi."

This time Rives didn't recover as quickly. He stood, gaping.

Over his shoulder, the air shimmered, like an invisible hand had dropped a speck of iridescent liquid in midair, then the drop exploded into a massive, glittering oval of refracting light that quickly thinned into a mirrored wall hovering inches above the ground. An instant later, every glittering speck turned flat black.

153

I grabbed Rives's hand.

"Run!" I yelled.

Rives obeyed without discussion. We sprinted up the beach, with me in the lead; I'd picked the open sand because we'd cover more distance on the open sand than in the trees. Plus, I was dying to see what was coming.

After about twenty feet, Rives pulled me into the brush and dropped into a crouch, pulling me down beside him. We stared silently at the black air. We'd barely stilled when an unconscious, cream-colored alpaca fell out of the black hole. The hole collapsed into a thin line, then a dot. And then it was gone.

The alpaca raised its head, bewildered.

I exhaled as I turned to Rives. "Better an alpaca than a walrus, right?"

He stared at me. "Who *are* you?"

I smiled. "How much time do you have?"

He broke into a slow grin, one that lit his eyes from within; the turbulent Caribbean waters swirled with a different sort of trouble. When he smiled, he was alarmingly beautiful, a fact I was not prepared for at all. "Enough," Rives said, still grinning. "Now start talking."

I looked away, trying to figure out where to begin.

"Start with Charley," Rives said quietly, his smile fading as he pulled me to my feet. "And let's walk on the beach. It's safer."

He didn't need to tell me twice.

We walked on the sand, heading south, the same direction that would take us toward the City, if my uncle's journal still held true. Rives walked on my left, between me and the trees. Every so often, his hand brushed the sheath at his waist, an involuntary movement, as if his palm needed to feel the solid hilt of the knife—like Rives had a security blanket, too. After just three days, the few times I'd put down my spear and sling I'd felt more naked than if I'd ripped off my leaf bikini.

Not that I had any intention of ripping off my bikini.

Holy naked visuals, I thought, blushing, remembering the Brazilian kid who'd walked around the City nude while my uncle was on Nil. That was *so* not me.

I felt an unexpected kinship to Uncle Scott, who'd been here, too, trapped and thirsty and tired and thinking crazy thoughts in this freaky place.

Of course, Uncle Scott was dead.

Which means I'm connecting with a ghost.

Three days on Nil and I was a walking Ouija board.

I pulled my last guava off my twine fruit string, took a bite, then sucked it dry, certain I had low blood sugar and just couldn't sense it. Then, taking a deep breath to pull myself together, I threw the sunken guava rind into the brush and started talking.

"I met Charley three weeks ago," I said slowly, "in Atlanta. Her story was all over the papers. She was found in France, on Mont Blanc, by a group of expert skiers in unmarked terrain. She was naked. But she's okay." I glanced at Rives. "She said to tell you the gates went both ways. And to tell you she made it, and Natalie too. And Kevin. And"—I paused, somehow knowing that this next bit of information would be the hardest for Rives—"she said to tell you that she's still waiting for Thad."

Rives's jaw ticked. He looked toward the sea, like answers would tumble in with the surf. "He made it," he said, his voice hard, his fists slightly clenched. Then, as if he'd caught me staring—or caught *himself*—he relaxed his hands, still facing the sea. "I know it. He had to."

Something told me his words were for his benefit, not mine, because the name Thad meant nothing to me. But it obviously meant something to Rives, something powerful. Pain wrapped him like an ethereal cloak, thick and suffocating and out of his reach, so real and raw I wished I could reach out and tear it away, knowing I couldn't, just like I couldn't help Charley.

The helpless feeling roared back.

How many people will this island hurt?

Rives turned to me, his green eyes full of emotion, a hundred different feelings, all intense, all churning like the chaotic brilliance of a gate. The only thing missing was fear.

"Please. I need to know everything. I need to know answers now. Who you are, how you got here. How you knew to find me. Maybe starting with Charley wasn't the right place. Go to the beginning." Under his breath, Rives muttered something about "the middle" and "the beginning." I'd swear he said something about a macadamia nut getting in his head.

I was losing it more quickly than I thought.

"Okay," I said, trying to figure out where to start. Where the beginning of *my* story was. I decided that, in the end, it all began with Uncle Scott.

"About twenty-five years ago," I began, "my uncle came to Nil . . ."

CHAPTER
27

RIVES
DAY 279, LATE MORNING

I studied Skye as she spoke.

I read her expressions, her posture, her word choices, and her cadence. She spoke calmly, like Macy, but where Macy's tone exuded quiet reassurance, Skye's radiated careful thought. Like she privately considered each of her words before she spoke, judging their weight and how to string them together, carefully calculating their effect on the listener.

Which was me.

In her quiet, methodical way, she'd walked me through her uncle's psych-trip journal, her dad's lifelong quest to locate Nil, her run-in with Charley, and her recent trip to Micronesia. She'd tossed out a suspect boat captain, a tatted-up kid chucking rocks into the sea, a solo twilight beach walk that would have probably pissed off her dad, not to mention a beyond-dangerous canoe trip that definitely would have pissed off her dad, and an insane jump—*on purpose*—into a gate.

A gate that made no sense.

A gate that led here.

I held up one hand. Skye stopped talking immediately.

"Let me get this straight," I said. "So you see a kid—a kid you don't know but you'd seen earlier chucking rocks into the ocean—packing live snacks for an ocean road trip. He takes off in a canoe. You steal a canoe and follow him, in the dark, on open water, to a pair of remote islands called the Death Twins, where you land—"

"One island," she interrupted, uncannily calm. "I landed on *one* island. Since we're being clear. And I didn't steal the canoe, I simply borrowed it."

"Did you return it?" I asked. "The canoe?"

"Not yet," she admitted. "But I intend to."

"Okay, we'll go with commandeered for now. So you commandeer a canoe, and then you follow this loner kid across the open ocean, in the dark, to *one* Death Twin. How am I doing so far?" I smiled slightly.

"Good," Skye said. Her lips narrowed, but her tone stayed glassy calm.

"Awesome." I fought the urge to mess with Skye some more. It was highly entertaining. "Then you stalk this strange kid across the Death Twin island, commence a nighttime stakeout in the dark, and when a shimmering wall of black air rises from the ground, the kid throws in a goat, a chicken, and himself"—I raised a finger in turn, counting— "and then after Casper the cat hijacks the gate, you follow the menagerie. You run straight into a midnight-black wall of rippling air that could either kill you or, for all you knew, take you to planet Krypton."

"I had a pretty good idea that the air wouldn't kill me because of Uncle Scott's journal," Skye said. "And Krypton doesn't exist."

"Neither does this place."

"I'm here, aren't I?" She leveled her eyes on me, her gaze so fierce I couldn't even read their color. Blue, maybe green, flecked with steel.

"Yes, you are." I paused. "Welcome to Nil, Skye."

We walked in silence for a moment. I could grill Skye all day, but I decided I should start with the basic intro.

"How many days have you been here?"

"Today's my Day Three. I've got three hundred sixty-two left." Same matter-of-fact tone, no hint of fear. Complete with a full grasp that her island hourglass had already tipped and her clock was ticking.

Damn, I thought.

She didn't need the normal intro. Hell, she didn't even look hungry. She'd tossed the half-eaten guava away without a sideways glance. Most rookies gnawed down to the rind and then asked if they could eat that, too. But after less than an hour in Skye's company, it was clear she wasn't your average Nil rookie.

She was as mysterious as Nil.

I refocused on her story, on the part that didn't add up. On the single gate, or equally unbelievable, a lightning-fast set of five.

"Okay, so that gate," I said. "The one that brought you here. Are you sure it was just one gate? Not multiple gates, appearing one after another, maybe so quickly they seemed like one gate?"

"It was definitely just one gate. It rose into the air and locked into place, like a liquid door."

I frowned. "It didn't move? It just stood there, waiting?"

"Right. And it was like Paulo knew it was coming."

"Paulo?"

She nodded. "That's the kid I followed. The one with the lei and tattoos? When I woke up in the dark, two people were arguing." She recounted her possum routine and stealth peeks at the two other boys, carefully describing Paulo, the thin one that whined, and a big one with muscles and ink. I privately identified the second boy as Maaka.

Every island mystery seemed to lead back to him. My annoyance with him skyrocketed.

"What were they arguing about?" I fought not to snap.

"Me." She paused. I could tell she was thinking through her next words. "The muscled guy blamed Paulo for bringing me through the gate into a 'sacred place.' " She made air quotes around the last words. "I actually feel bad for Paulo, because he didn't know I would follow him, and because of me, his mentor ditched him. His words."

So Maaka was Paulo's mentor.

Who the hell gets an island mentor?

Paulo, apparently, I thought. *The same kid who knew the gate was coming.* Suddenly two massive pieces of the island puzzle took the hard form of people. People with secrets and ink. I clenched my fists, sick of being one step behind. I breathed deeply, fighting to chill, knowing I needed a cool head to process the clues. And Paulo was the best clue I had.

Besides Skye.

"What else did Paulo say?" I asked.

"The first time I saw him or the second?"

This just gets better.

"Start with the first convo, the one with the muscled kid."

She nodded. "Paulo said that his older brother was supposed to come instead of him, but his brother chose to study Western medicine instead. That this was his destiny now."

"And what did the other kid say?"

"That Paulo had to find his way. And that he was on his own."

Aren't we all, I thought.

"And"—Skye paused—"he told Paulo he had to deal with me. That's when I ran."

"You ran."

She nodded. "Over the black rocks, and down into the meadow. I ran until I lost the boys. And now I'm here." She didn't meet my eyes, a basic red flag.

What isn't she telling me?

"It sounds like you woke up on Mount Nil." I studied her as I spoke. "Do you remember where?"

"Not exactly. It was dark, and for a few minutes I was pretending to be unconscious. So I didn't get the best look around." She met my gaze straight on. "Why?"

"Because," I said slowly, "gates here aren't stationary. Ever. Sometimes they're fast, sometimes they're slow, but they always move. So that wasn't a normal gate. Plus, gates here are always solo trips. One gate, one rider. No exceptions." If Skye's story was true, her inbound broke all the rules.

Welcome to Nil, Rives, I thought. *Again.*

We came to the end of North Beach, where white sand butted against the black cliff, the same cliff that housed the mysterious pool. Right now the girl standing beside me packed more secrets than the Looking Glass cavern. Impossible yet real, another Nil twist.

Maybe her story was real, too.

Maybe.

"Skye?" I said. She was staring at the water. "Are you absolutely sure it was one gate? Because I've never heard of a gate taking more than one person."

She looked at me, her eyes raging with island heat usually reserved for Nil veterans. "I know. My uncle described single gates as racing like fire, invisibly burning up the ground under them, offering freedom for the winner and an electrocution for the second-place finisher. His words." She paused, gripping her spear tight, and I got the distinct vibe she was repressing a shudder. "His journal made it clear that gates took one person, and one person only."

"And knowing that, you just jumped into that stationary single without a clue if it would fry you or send you here?" I held her gaze, not sure whether to commit her or congratulate her. She was either crazy or had balls of steel. Maybe both.

Skye shrugged. "I'd seen the cat follow the boy, and it seemed fine. So I figured I'd be okay, too."

Balls of steel, I thought.

I pointed Skye toward the path, keeping my eyes open for leopards, loners, and anything else that might be a foe. I still hadn't decided which category Maaka fell into.

Or now, Paulo.

"What did Paulo's tattoos look like? I know you said they were all black. But did you get a good look at them?"

"Not really. It was like one really big tattoo; it wrapped around his upper arm. Part of it looked like waves. I'm not sure about the rest."

My money's on interlocking diamonds and moons. Like Maaka's. Like the carvings in the cavern of the Looking Glass pool and the backside of the Wall.

"I think there was a sun," she added. "But I could be wrong."

I doubted that.

"So what else did Paulo say?" I asked. "The second time you spoke?"

She thought for a moment. "He said that there were rules but didn't tell me what they were; he just said he couldn't break them. He told me to go west, to find people like me." She looked sideways at me, humor denting the steel in her eyes. "Which I think means you. I told him he could come with me. He said no. He said he had to do it alone. And he said he couldn't leave yet." She paused, and a full smile broke through her calm. "He also said monkeys threw poop at him. He smelled awful."

Monkeys, I thought. *As in plural.*

Maybe Bart hadn't lied completely after all. But he was still a heartless coward, and selfish as hell. *It changes nothing.*

I ground my teeth.

"My turn," Skye said. She stared at me intently. "What were you just thinking?"

You don't want to know what I'm thinking.

"Rives?"

"That monkeys can be dangerous," I said.

She glanced toward the trees. "Most animals can be," she said finally.

I studied her, stretching her definition of animals to include us. Humans. "True," I said.

I glanced back at the trail, in time to see a porcupine waddle across without stopping. Just a Nil drive-by. Not deadly, not benign, somewhere in the middle. Just your average Nil day in a nutshell.

Skye missed it; she was looking at me.

"Who's Maaka?"

"Good question," I said. "I think he's the boy who greeted Paulo. Intense ink, intense personality. And Paulo's supposed mentor, whatever that means. I've run into Maaka a couple times over the past month, and I think he knows a lot more about this place than he's telling."

"Same for Paulo," Skye said. "So I'm assuming Maaka isn't in the City?"

"Right." The word *City* rolled off Skye's tongue like she'd been here three hundred days, not three.

"And this path. It leads to the City, right? After we pass the Crystal Cove?"

"Right again." I stopped walking and Skye immediately stopped too. I knew she would. "If you listen, we're close enough to hear the roar of the falls."

She cocked her head, her halo of wild hair shifting with her. "I don't hear anything." She frowned. "Except maybe the leaves rustling."

"Close your eyes."

She did.

"Filter the silence. Sift through the silence until you hear what you're looking for."

A long moment passed. I watched her, watching a tiny line appear between her brows, the same line that appeared when she paused at length before speaking. A long curl blew across her cheek. Her grip tightened on her spear.

Looks like Nil finally sent a contender after all, I thought.

She opened her eyes. "Nothing."

I nodded. "It takes time, but you'll get it." I watched her shift her sling higher on her shoulder, a primitive homemade weapon with a one-hundred-meter range if slung well. I'd guess Skye, lean but ripped, could sling it pretty damn well.

"Skye, you're not the average Nil rookie. We both know that. You didn't drop in cold and clueless, and you definitely don't look scared of your own shadow. You know there's a City and a Cove and animals that fall from the air. Some deadly, some not. You know your time here comes with an expiration date written in blood. You had a full Nil preview thanks to your uncle's journal. So knowing all that ahead of time, *why* would you come? Why jump through that gate into Hell?"

Skye closed her eyes again, a long blink. This time I knew she wasn't searching for sounds of the Cove; she was searching for words. I hoped she wasn't an adrenaline junkie looking for a fresh fix. My patience for Nil's theatrics had thinned to a razor-sharp edge.

"I don't know exactly. I didn't really think. I just acted." She rubbed the inside of her left wrist with her right thumb. "It was probably the dumbest thing I've ever done—besides the canoe trip—and my dad would kill me if he knew. Of course, he knows I'm missing by now, and that's probably killing him as it is." She swallowed, her face paling under her slight sunburn. "But in hindsight, it was because of Charley."

"Charley?" I asked.

Skye nodded. "When I met her, pain poured off her in waves. She was grieving and hurting and suffering alone. She'd told everyone she had amnesia. But she remembered everything. *Everything.* And her grief—" Skye's voice dropped an octave. "It was awful." Skye lifted her eyes to mine. "It was because of Thad, wasn't it?"

"Yeah." Now it was my turn to pause. "They were good together. Intense, kind of over the top at times." I smiled. "But—" A memory flashed: Thad's face, his expression fierce, his eyes burning with long- ing and desperation that I'd known had everything to do with the fact it was his 364th day and that within hours, the island would rip him apart from Charley. *Not my back,* he'd said. *Charley's. Promise me you'll have Charley's back.* Thad's words, delivered with an ache that had slayed me back then.

His words killed me now.

Because right now I didn't have her back, or his, because they weren't here. Unless Thad was here after all, lost to the island forever. And if that was the case, I was the shittiest wingman ever.

He made it, I repeated. Because if not, Nil fell so deep into the *foe* category that nothing could drag it out.

"But what?" Skye's words brought me back.

"But they were the real deal." I glanced at her, wanting to believe her story. "Thad's not here, but you already knew that, right? So how did Charley make you take that gate?"

"Her pain." Skye said. "She was suffering, like my uncle had, only differently. And at the same time, my dad had this crazy idea that if he could just find this island, he could save all the kids."

"Really? How?"

"I'm still working on that," Skye said. She was completely serious. "But it has something to do with that stationary gate. In the end, it was the gate that made me go for it. The way it rose, the way it stood still, the timing of it. Tell me, Rives, what gate comes at midnight?"

Merde.

I'd totally missed the fact that her gate flashed at night. At twelve o'clock *midnight,* not twelve o'clock noon. The number twelve capping the labyrinth carvings shifted in meaning again.

Are you playing with us, Nil, or leading us to understanding? All the carvings spun, the labyrinth lines shifting too fast. Like a gate I couldn't catch.

I relaxed my grip on my knife; I didn't remember reaching for it.

"Exactly," Skye said. She'd been watching me like I watched her. "Gates don't come at midnight. Or at least not the ones my uncle saw."

Her thoughtful, assessing look was back, like she'd retreated into herself. "I've been replaying that night ever since I woke up here. I acted without thinking, jumping into that gate, and I think I know why; it just took me a few days to work it out. That gate was different. It rose in the night, and it didn't move. It stood there, Rives, waiting. And it took more than one rider." She paused. "On some level, I think at the moment I chose to take that gate, I already knew: If there's a stationary gate on that end, wouldn't there be a stationary outbound on this end, too? And if that gate—the outbound on the Death Twin—can take two people, a chicken, a goat, and a cat, why couldn't the stationary outbound on this end take a group, too?" Skye's expression was as fierce as Charley's on the day Charley had told me about her storm theory.

No, Skye's was fiercer.

Watch out, Nil. Skye's coming for you too.

"That gate has a mate," Skye said quietly. "A bookend. Here, on *this* side. And it could take everyone off Nil." Her expression dared me to defy her. "We just need to find it."

Warning bells went off in my head like sirens. "Skye, if a stationary gate on this end exists, where is it? Why hasn't anyone seen it? Or heard of it? The island's not that big."

"You could ask the same thing of Nil back home. Why hadn't anyone seen it? I think the answer isn't that it hasn't been seen; it just hasn't been seen by the right people."

Maaka, I thought. *And Paulo.*

She narrowed her lips, a sign I was quickly coming to read as annoyance. "I think the boat captain and our guide knew of this place, and maybe more people than just them. I got the distinct feeling that the locals were stalling my dad, trying to lead him anywhere but here. Paulo definitely knew of it. He was waiting for the gate. Somehow he knew when and where that outbound would show."

"Just like how Maaka knew where that gate would appear on this end," I said. "Because from what you said, he was waiting too."

"Exactly. And I don't think Paulo would've taken that gate if he didn't know he'd get back. He looked resigned, not brave. Not brave enough to jump into that gate without knowing he could get home."

"We've got to find Paulo or Maaka. Or both." *And I need to talk to Johan—if he's still here.*

It was a big *if.*

Skye tilted her head. "I hear the falls," she said. "Finally." A wry smile broke through her calm veneer.

I gently touched her shoulder to slow her down. She was more dangerous than she knew, or at least her secrets were, and I'd barely scratched the surface.

"Listen, I know this is a lot to ask, but can you keep the details about your inbound gate quiet? Until we figure out where it fits." I paused. "The thing is, we have a system for Searching for gates. We Search in teams, with time on Nil deciding Priority. The City supports the Search teams, plain and simple. And we've gotten a lot better at finding gates in the last few months. Charley figured out a pattern to outbounds while she was here—and we're seeing more gates than ever because of it. But your gate is different. And I'm afraid that if people start Searching for a stationary gate, the system will fall apart." *The City will fall apart.*

"Without the Search system . . ." I paused, thinking of the City already on edge. "I don't know," I said finally.

"I do," Skye said quietly. "And it's not pretty."

I raised my eyebrows. The silence stretched to an uncomfortable point, making clear it was still Skye's turn.

"My uncle started the Search system," she said. "Before then, noon was a free-for-all. Nil was a very different place then. Darker, and cruel."

"Don't let the beauty fool you." My voice was sharp. "Nil can still be cruel."

"The island or the people?" she asked.

Crosses on the Wall, crosses in the field. Time cut short by fate, by a bad island hand, or by someone else's. Memories of Li, Bart, and Talla rolled through my head, a mental mash-up in shades of black after too many nights on watch.

"Both."

"That's what I was afraid of."

I regarded Skye carefully. "You don't seem afraid of anything."

Her expression was unreadable. "Everyone's afraid of something."

So says the girl who has Nil by the balls.

"What are you afraid of?" I asked. The island air thickened. Grew weighted, as if Nil hungered for the answer, too, anything to keep the advantage.

Skye shook her head, a slight movement I almost missed.

"I hear voices." Skye shifted toward the Cove. "Is that Dex? Charley mentioned him."

"Yup." I pointed to where Dex stood by the Cove's edge. "He's the guy with serious tats and a half-bleached mohawk."

Dex was deep in conversation with Johan. Selfish relief hit me hard.

As Skye and I walked in silence toward the Cove, I wondered what she was thinking and what she was afraid of.

Because if it scared her, my gut told me we should all be afraid.

CHAPTER 28

SKYE
DAY 3, AFTER NOON

Reading about Nil and actually being on Nil were two very different things. It's like the difference between seeing a documentary about Antarctica and then feeling the ice and snow for yourself.

Waking up in the dark, completely naked, a stone's throw (not that I had a stone then) from two strange boys and then running for my life only to come face-to-face with a Bengal tiger, knowing it was his decision whether or not to make me his dinner.

No amount of reading could prepare me for that.

Yet since then, sometimes the Nil I'd read about and the Nil I was living were exactly the same. Waking with the sun to the cleanest air ever, checking my water traps at dawn, strolling through the groves in awe, and studying trees packed with fruit like a slice of Eden. In those moments, I'd relax, walking through the world my uncle described so well, checking off invisible boxes of familiar. At other times, the two Nils felt eerily identical—but not quite, as if something in this Nil had been tweaked, just enough to jar the scene, just enough to rip away the comfort of familiarity.

At moments like these, the two time frames blurred: The past overlapped the present, making me feel like I had one foot in both and was grounded in neither. Like I'd opened the wrong time capsule.

Like now.

Rives and I had rounded the cliff to the Crystal Cove. The waterfall was breathtaking, as was the cliff, the pool, and the sum of all the parts, just as my uncle described. And the diverse group of people gathered was spot-on—and yet different.

There was no Jenny. No Karl. No Hui.

Still, I couldn't stop subconsciously overlapping my uncle's description of his peers to the people in front of me, trying to make it fit. All the people in front of me wore clothes exactly like those worn on Nil over twenty years ago. Wrap skirts, plain shorts. Chest wraps. All off-white, all simple. All matching.

I was the odd girl out.

Rives was right; I wasn't the average Nil rookie, but I wasn't a veteran, either. I was an outsider with inside knowledge. I was an anomaly. And I was dangerous, or at least my gate was. I also hadn't counted on having to repeat my story to each new group of people; I hadn't factored that in at all. My plan had ended with Rives.

I needed a new plan.

A plan, I decided quickly, that involved more listening and less talking, until I figured out where I fit.

What are you afraid of? Rives had asked.

Not an easy question to answer, but near the top of the list was the butterfly effect, the same effect Dad mentioned on the day he'd handed me Uncle Scott's journal. I didn't want to be responsible for undoing all the good my uncle had done; I would *not* knowingly throw the island into chaos. Not that I really believed I had the power to do that, but based on my uncle's journal, Nil shifts happened quickly, and on Nil, anything could happen. The noon free-for-all wasn't history to be repeated.

I won't let it, I vowed.

But just because I wouldn't talk about the stationary gate didn't mean I wouldn't find it. For everyone.

So much had changed since the moment Dad handed me Uncle Scott's journal; it was as pivotal a moment for me as stepping into that gate.

I gasped.

"What is it?" Rives asked. His body tensed, like he was on high alert.

"I just realized my dad handed me my uncle's journal at noon. It's not a big deal. It's just"—I paused as I dug for the right word—"weird."

Rives said nothing, at least not at first. "An interesting coincidence," he said finally.

"Rives!" Dex strode over, a thin, towering figure with an astonishing number of tattoos and stretched earlobes skewered with black shark's teeth dangling from twine. He grinned at Rives. "I see you took my advice about traveling in pairs?"

British, I thought, inexplicably surprised. Why his thick accent would surprise me more than a rhino was ridiculous.

As Rives snorted, Dex turned to me.

"I'm Dex. You've got quite the island ensemble there. Stella McCartney would be proud. And possibly jealous."

"Only if she landed here. But she's too old, right?"

Dex raised his eyebrows and grinned. "Indeed."

"Dex, meet Skye. Skye, Dex." Rives's eyes traced the Cove as he spoke. He wore the same searching look he'd had when he'd strode from the ocean earlier, only without the fury.

"Welcome to Nil, Skye," Dex said. "It sounds like Rives filled you in on all the crucial details of our lovely resort, yes?"

"No need," Rives said. "Skye already knew. And she's got a very interesting story. But first, a few highlights." He turned to me, his green eyes finding mine. "Cool?"

"Totally." It occurred to me he was asking for permission I'd already given him, only now he was asking in public. A careful Leader move, I decided. I was curious to see what Rives thought were the highlights. I assumed Charley would be number one.

Rives waited until a small crowd gathered. Ten people, including Rives and me.

"Okay everyone, meet Skye." He smiled as I raised one hand. "She's not your average rookie, as you'll find out soon enough." He paused. "She met Charley." Gasps went through the group. One girl with long auburn braids clapped her hand over her mouth, her eyes wide.

One heartbeat later, Rives continued, his voice steady and reassuring. "Now you know Charley made it. She's okay. Same for Natalie, and Kevin. And now we have solid confirmation that the gates go both ways."

A boy with brown hair as wildly curly as mine and freckles across his cheeks and chest raised a hand. "What about Thad?" His deep voice cracked.

"No word. But he followed Charley; I saw him take the next gate. He made it, Jason." The quiet confidence in Rives's voice felt practiced; he'd buried the desperation I'd heard a few minutes earlier. No wonder Charley had told me to find Rives. I felt better listening to him too. "He made it," Rives repeated.

The girl with braids still covered her mouth. Her eyes glistened. She wiped them quickly and looked directly at me, her gaze uncertain and suspicious.

My outsider status had never felt stronger. Worse, I felt like the bearer of bad news, or at least incomplete news. News that wasn't good enough.

Rives kept going without a break. "But here's another Nil newsflash: Just because the gates go both ways, they don't show up in the same place. Charley woke up in France, on Mont Blanc. But she'd been snatched from a parking lot in Georgia. And yeah, she woke up in France naked."

Groans went through the group.

"A few more things. I'm stealing a little of Skye's thunder here." Rives smiled. "But Skye showed up on Nil three days ago." He paused. "At midnight. And the outbound she took on the other end left at midnight, too. Twelve midnight, not twelve noon."

Abruptly everyone started talking at once.

Rives held up his hand. "I don't know what that means, other than Nil has more secrets than ever. Gates still come at noon. Maybe Nil's giving us more chances. Let's think positively until we know differently."

One boy with spiky blond hair stood frowning, arms crossed.

"Last thing. Skye's uncle came to Nil as a teenager. We have her uncle to thank for the Search system. He created it. Skye can fill you in on what it was like on Nil back then. And speaking of Search, welcome back, Johan." Rives tipped his head toward the frowning blond boy. "It's good to see you, although I'd rather you be headed home. And it's good to see your team intact."

Rives paused. "Johan, did you fill Dex in on your Search?"

Johan nodded. "Yes." No inflection, no smile. He looked like he was holding half a breath.

"What about you, Skye?" Dex asked. "See any fun creatures or gates while you were traipsing about?"

I thought for a moment. "I saw an outbound yesterday, a single, at the edge of the northern cliffs." I didn't mention I'd run *away* from the gate, not willing to leave when I'd just arrived and had accomplished absolutely nothing. "And I saw an inbound today, with Rives. On North Beach. It brought an alpaca."

"What's an alpaca?" a dark-haired boy asked.

"It's kind of like a llama, only smaller, and their coats are much softer," the curly-haired boy—*Jason*, I reminded myself—said. "Alpaca fleece is like cashmere. Camels are distant cousins," he added.

"Whoa," another boy said. His ragged bleached hair hit his shoulders in a rough island surfer cut. "Nice little Wikipedia moment, man. Who knew?"

Jason shrugged. "The farm next to ours breeds alpacas. They're pretty cool animals." He cleared his throat as his voice cracked on the last word. "Make some weird noises though."

"Right. Well, maybe we can work some alpaca wool into the fall islandwear collection." Dex rolled his eyes. "We'll get on that straightaway after we make torches and spears and things to keep us alive. Speaking of staying alive and, well, violent death, did you see anything else out there, like, say, big cats?"

"And by cats, Dex specifically means leopards," Rives clarified. He was clearly fighting a smile.

"Like snow leopards?" I asked.

Dex's eyes widened a fraction. "We've got bloody snow leopards? As in plural?"

"No! I mean, not that I know of."

"Dex isn't a cat fan," Jason offered.

"Me either," I said. "They make me sneeze."

Rives coughed behind his hand, like he was hiding something— like a laugh. I glared at him, knowing full well now he was laughing at *me*, which wasn't funny. I'd been highly allergic to cats my entire life. Once I touched a neighbor's cat and rubbed my eye. My entire eye swelled shut, which was the complete opposite of funny. Memorable, horrible, incredibly painful, and unbearably itchy. But not funny. Rives deserved every bit of venom in my stare right now.

Dex cleared his throat, breaking the tight moment. "Back to the big cats, which I'm fairly certain Skye hasn't gotten close enough to determine an allergy to"—Dex turned to me, eyes wide—"did you or did you not say 'snow leopards'? Just trying to assess whether we've got bloody snow leopards at our island party now, too. As if regular leopards aren't enough?"

"I didn't see any snow leopards." This time I chose my words with care. "My uncle saw them, but that was about twenty years ago."

"Which means they should be gone by now," Rives said, winking at me. I narrowed my eyes, unwilling to give an inch.

"Excellent," Dex said. His crisp accent drew my attention. "I'll cross snow leopards off my worry list."

"But—" I paused, thinking of my first night.

"Wait. No buts. Nothing good ever follows the word *but*," Dex said. "At least not here."

"But what, Skye?" Rives asked, all humor gone. "We need to know."

"I did see a tiger on my first night. I'm sure it was a tiger, because I got closer than I'd like."

"How close?" Dex asked.

I shrugged. "Twenty feet?"

"Bloody hell," Dex murmured.

"And?" Rives's eyes stayed on mine.

"He let me go."

"He let you go," Rives repeated. His tone was flat, as in *not possible*.

I shifted uncomfortably. "I'd just arrived on the mountain, and I was pretty freaked out because—" I hesitated, unsure whether I should mention the muscle man who'd suggested that I be "dealt with," and decided to stay mum. *Less is more*, I thought. *Or at least less is best.*

"It was dark," I finished. "So I ran. And I nearly ran into the tiger."

"In the meadow?" Jason asked.

I nodded. "At the far edge. I stopped, not sure whether I should run or scream or what. He looked at me, and then he just walked away." I stopped, knowing it sounded crazy. That *I* sounded crazy. Not the introduction I was hoping for at all. "I can't explain it," I admitted. "I guess he wasn't hungry." It sounded weak, even to me.

"That is *insane*." The blond shaggy-haired boy raised his eyebrows in shocked appreciation. "And a little badass. When you look up *badass* in the dictionary, it says 'stares down tigers.'" He laughed. "Or maybe it says 'Skye.' Sweet spear, by the way." He nodded at my hand, grinning.

Saying nothing, Rives studied me intently.

I shrunk under his gaze. I was definitely not badass. Navy SEALs were badass. Wolverine was badass. The crazy people who swim the English Channel or run hundred-mile road races were badass. Me? I was just a girl in an awkward leaf-kini who caught an early island break.

"Thanks, but I just got lucky," I said.

"Not if you landed here," the girl with braids said sharply. She wore a trio of small white shells wrapped around her wrist with twine. "By the way, I'm Jillian. Been here long enough to know." Under her smile, wariness ran like cool water.

"Nice to meet you." I smiled.

"Zane." The blond boy who complimented my spear raised his hand, his easy grin still in place. "Still a rook. And I'm not ashamed to say I run from tigers."

Jason came up and officially introduced himself, followed by the boy who'd asked about the alpaca, Julio. Both boys had been on Nil for months. A tiny girl with a surprisingly strong handshake and sleek black hair was next. "Miya." Her voice was soft. "One hundred fifteen days. Welcome to the island."

After Miya, a thin boy with dark hair and heavy acne came up. "Sy," he said, offering his hand along with a warm smile. His grip was weak. "I'm one of Rives's Seconds."

This revelation surprised me more than Dex's accent.

"We're glad you're here even though we're sorry you're here," Sy said. Then his smile drooped. "But man, you sure picked a bad time to come."

"Is there ever a good time?" I asked.

"Good point." His posture reminded me of Paulo's.

"Skye, got a minute?" Rives called. He stood beside the other blond boy, the one with the spiky hair.

"See you around, Skye," Jason said. I noticed Miya slide her hand into Jason's as they walked away.

I turned back toward Rives and the blond boy I hadn't met.

"Skye, meet Johan. Johan, Skye."

Johan nodded, his eyes hard on me. They were a piercing shade of blue. "Welcome, Skye," he said softly. "How strange both you and your uncle landed on Nil. Such an odd coincidence." He made *coincidence* sound like a dirty word, and I didn't think it was his accent. His suspicion bordered on hostile.

"I was wondering the same thing," Jillian said. Her tone was slightly warmer, which wasn't saying much. "Your family is exceptionally unlucky."

"I don't know about the luck part, but it's not a coincidence, not really." I kept my tone neutral. "My dad's obsessed with finding Nil. For the past twenty years, he's traveled all over the Pacific and Micronesia, searching for Nil, using my uncle's star charts from his days on Nil as a guide. This time my dad took me. I was in the Pacific, on a very remote island on the edge of Micronesia, when the midnight gate rose up from the ground."

Johan's ice-blue eyes instantly thawed. "So you were looking for the island, and the island took you." He nodded as if it made perfect sense. "Like they say, don't poke the bear, yes?"

Charley's warning floated through my head. *Be careful what you wish for. You just might get it, and it might not be what you think.*

Nil was everything I expected and nothing I expected.

Johan regarded me thoughtfully, his fingers steepled against his chin. "But the island let your uncle go, yes?" he asked, his tone kind.

"Yes." I nodded.

"And what does he think of your father's obsession?" Johan asked.

"I wouldn't know. My uncle died when he was eighteen. Less than a year after he got back."

Johan sucked in his breath and crossed himself, then looked at Rives, who was staring at me with an unreadable expression. I had the weirdest sense that he was trying to read me.

"This place. The balance—" Johan broke off, shaking his head. He muttered a few words in a foreign language I didn't recognize, but Rives raised his brows. Johan crossed himself again. "It is not in our favor. Tell me, Rives, what island takes another from the same family, when one was already lost, found, and lost again?"

Rives held up one hand, his light eyes warm. "Hold up, Johan. We've talked about this. Nil's a cluster, no doubt. A parallel-dimension nightmare twenty-four/seven. But the gates aren't picky; they're random. The island doesn't choose people."

"Doesn't it?" Johan's soft tone gave me chills. Then he turned to me, his blue eyes dark with worry. Or maybe fear.

"Be careful, Skye," he said, his voice still scary soft. "Be afraid. The island brought you here for a reason. Perhaps to keep you, perhaps not. Perhaps because of your uncle—because of something he did or didn't do. This place has a long memory, I fear. Do not let your guard down."

Perhaps to keep you.

A chill crept down my spine, and it had nothing to do with the cool spray blowing off the Cove falls.

"There are no coincidences on Nil," Johan murmured.

I shivered again.

"Okay, now that Johan has completely freaked out Skye," Jillian said, squeezing my hand, "I'm going to take her back to the City, give her the tour, and get her some clothes." She turned to me, her worried expression empty of all traces of suspicion, and she smiled. "No island cashmere, but at least I've got something that won't wilt. Sound okay?"

"Sounds great."

But as we walked away, I couldn't help looking over my shoulder.

Behind me, Johan was deep in conversation with Rives, and Rives's fierce expression looked as troubled as Johan's had moments before. As if he sensed me staring, Rives looked up and our eyes caught. I looked away first. I didn't want to draw Johan's gaze to me.

The island brought you here for a reason, Johan had said.

You're wrong, I thought.

I followed the boy; *I* jumped into that gate.

The island didn't choose me. I chose the island.

But I was still afraid.

CHAPTER
29

RIVES
DAY 279, AFTER NOON

Johan sighed, his eyes on Skye's back.

"I didn't mean to frighten her," he admitted, "but I think in Skye's case a little fear would serve her well. Maybe even keep her alive." His voice dropped to a whisper. "Rives, three nights ago, I felt the island. I felt it *here*." Johan covered his heart with his palm. "I've sensed the island before, but not like that. Never like that. I woke in a cold sweat to a living night, to a sense of anticipation. The intensity—" He paused, running one hand through his hair. "It peaked in the dead of night."

"I felt it, too." *And Skye arrived at midnight, through a stationary gate. A kind of gate I've never seen.*

Johan nodded, then pulled on his hair, hard. A clear tell—of worry and fear. Johan was an easy read.

"Afterward, I couldn't sleep." His voice was soft. "And all I could think was that something had shifted again. That the island no longer slept. I feel like the island is building toward something, Rives. Something big. Something not in our favor." He looked at me, his eyes tortured. "Strange shifts, midnight gates. The island's power has never been greater."

Neither has ours.

I took a deep breath. "I need to ask you about someone, a girl who was here before my time. Her name was Ramia."

"Ramia?" Johan's entire body went stiff.

"Yes. Did you know her?"

"I knew her." Johan's guarded tone was flat.

"Did she have any tattoos?"

"One. Here." He touched his biceps.

"What was it?"

Frowning, Johan pinched the bridge of his nose. A moment passed. "I can't remember."

"Was it all black?"

"Yes. That I remember."

"And she wore a bone cuff bracelet, right?"

"Yes. We buried it. Me, Thad, and Sy." Johan crossed himself. "Why do you ask?"

"Because the skeleton in that tunnel has a bone cuff, too." I pointed at the Cove. "So unless it crept from the grave, it belonged to someone else." I paused. "Johan, I need you to tell me what you knew about Ramia. What you remember. Anything."

Pivoting away, Johan tugged his hair with both hands, then walked in a small circle with both hands on his head. "Ramia is one person I cannot forget, try as I might."

"Why?"

"If you'd met her you wouldn't need to ask." Johan's grin was wry, then it abruptly disappeared. "Ramia had a strangeness about her. And when she spoke, it was as if she looked into your soul. It was disturbing." Johan looked at the Cove. "I met her here, by the pool's edge. I introduced myself, and when I reached out to shake her hand, she grabbed it, holding my hand tight in both of hers. *Strong*, she whispered. *Devoted. Defiant. Oh, the island will keep you as long as it can.* Then she murmured, *You will be here almost as long as me.*"

Johan blinked slowly. "I've replayed that conversation a hundred times, wondering what that last line meant. Wondering whether it meant anything at all." Johan swallowed, looking sick. "I buried her, Rives. And her bracelet. And I'm still right here, with twelve days left."

Guilt ripped me in two.

I'm the reason Johan is still here. Not Nil.

Me.

Because I asked for him to stay. It didn't matter that the request was silent, that no one heard it but me. *I* knew. And somehow so did the island. Because this was Nil, where nothing escaped the island's notice, and nothing *escaped*—unless the island agreed.

Then I had a fresh thought and smiled.

If I made Johan stay, then Maaka's still here, too.

This thought didn't bring guilt; it brought a sense of power. *Dig in my head, Nil,* I thought grimly. *I dare you.* From now on I'd guard my thoughts like I guarded my life. *You will only hear what I choose.*

Johan gripped my shoulder.

I startled, wondering if he'd sensed my thoughts—or my guilt.

"There's something else. Something Ramia told me after the first funeral I attended here. We'd just buried Kelley. I sat by her grave, wondering how evil this place must be if it takes the life of an innocent girl. Kelley was only fourteen."

Sometimes I forgot how long Johan had been here. I'd never met Kelley either.

"Ramia and I were the only ones left," Johan continued. "She dropped to her knees, picked up a handful of dirt, and clenched it in her fist. *Blood runs through this ground,* she told me quietly. *Old blood, fresh blood.* Then she placed both of her palms flat on the ground and closed her eyes. *Feel it, Johan. The heartbeat of the island. It beats in time with our own,* she'd said. Eyes still closed, she'd smiled. *You don't feel it yet. But you will. Remember my words.*"

Johan crossed his arms. "At the time, I thought she was crazy. I'm not sure what I think now." Abruptly, his tone turned fierce. "I want to see it."

"What?"

"The bone cuff."

Surprised, I nodded. "Not a problem."

Johan followed me, his jaw as hard as the tunnel walls. He crossed himself repeatedly as he entered.

My torch pile sat intact. Three were left. I lit one, then led Johan directly to the skeleton.

He bent, and, torch in hand, he inspected the cuff. I noticed he kept a healthy distance from the skeleton. "It is like Ramia's and yet it is not," Johan said finally. "Something is dark. Strange. The feeling of loss hangs heavy here, but I also sense something else. Hope, maybe? Peace? Choice? I don't know. But the darkness—it goes beyond these walls." He stood, then stilled, staring at the carving above the skeleton, the one of the sun with the eye at the center.

"What is it?" I finally asked.

"That"—he pointed at the carving—"was Ramia's tattoo."

Now I stared at the carving.

What do you see? Maaka's question.

I see connections. Bits. Pieces. Part of a whole.

I'll figure it out, I vowed. And I didn't care if Nil heard.

"Follow me," I said, turning away. "I want to show you something."

Johan didn't move.

"Seriously, I think you should see this. Trust me."

Taking the torch back, I led a very hesitant Johan to the Looking Glass cavern. Johan exited first. I stuck the torch in a tunnel crag, just before the entrance to the cavern. Partially because of Maaka's warning, but also because I felt the sacredness of this place, a feeling that grew with each visit. I didn't want to piss off the island any more than I had to. I would pick my battles, pressing when needed. This was not the time nor the place to press.

Johan stood on the narrow ledge, arms crossed, legs braced a foot apart as he looked over the carvings. A good five minutes passed before I spoke.

"So what do you think?" I asked.

"This place is old, Rives. It belongs to another time." He turned to me, his expression as troubled as I'd ever seen. "I want to go." His whisper was so faint I fought to hear it. "This place is light and full of power, but the power is not ours. It's the island's, and yet it is not. Being here feels wrong. I don't belong here."

"But you belong on the island?"

"No. But now that I'm here, on Nil, I have a choice. And I choose not to spend another minute in the belly of the beast."

"Fair enough." I grinned. "Quick question. Do you want to take the shortcut or backtrack?"

Johan didn't hesitate. "Backtrack. For me, one way in, one way out."

Like the labyrinths, I thought. *But the number twelve on the labyrinths doesn't always mean noon. We just assumed it did.*

What else have we assumed?

Fury flared, then exploded into hope. Suddenly I couldn't wait to get back to Skye, to talk about the journal, her uncle, and the midnight gate. Finally Nil had chosen someone who came ready to fight, locked and loaded with inside knowledge. Or maybe Skye hijacked the gate without Nil's consent, surprising the island after all. Old blood, new blood; Skye offered the best of both. But not to the island—to *us*. I refused to let her blood run through Nil's ground.

Nil had taken enough.

I had eighty-six days left to figure Nil out, to save everyone in the City, and myself.

Totally doable.

I actually laughed out loud.

CHAPTER
30

SKYE
DAY 3, LATE AFTERNOON

Jillian filled me in on the City as we walked. Sticking with my new plan, I listened intently and said little.

"Dex is from the UK, obviously. Isn't his accent the best? He's a drummer back home. And from what I've heard here, he's really good." She grinned, maybe even blushed. I couldn't tell because her cheeks were already pink from the sun. "Ahmad's from the Sudan but lives in the US—Minnesota, I think. Jason and Zane are American, like us. Jason's from Omaha; Zane's from San Diego. Johan's Dutch. Uri's Israeli. Julio's from Mexico." She counted off her fingers as she spoke.

"Macy's American, too. I'm pretty sure she's from Alabama. You'll meet her soon, and you'll love her. Brittney's new, same for Kiera. Alexei and Nikolai are rookies too. Alexei speaks some English. It's not great, but it's more than Nikolai, who doesn't speak English at all, just Russian. Raj is from India; same for Pari. Leila's from the Philippines." Jillian paused. "Michael's Korean, he's been here as long as Pari. Cho's new. I think that's it."

"What about you? Where are you from?"

"Maine. You?"

I paused, thinking.

"It's not a trick question," Jillian said. The edge in her voice was back.

"I know. It's just that I was going to say Gainesville, Florida, where I live with my mom, but a few months ago she went to Africa for a dig—she's a professor—and I moved in with my dad. He lives in New Hampshire. I've got enough credits to graduate high school already, so I'm not in school; I'm just doing some courses online for my last year. So New Hampshire doesn't feel like home even though I live there."

"Wow. That would suck to move in your senior year."

"It wasn't great," I admitted. "I wanted to stay in Gainesville with one of my friends, but my dad said no." *Did I take that gate to spite him?* The thought dropped without warning, forcing me to consider it. I didn't think so, but now that I thought about it, I'd been furious and hurt when he wouldn't let me stay in Gainesville. I'd been mad at Mom too, because she didn't fight for me. I'd been left to fight for myself, like now.

Hopefully here I'd do a better job.

I'd better, I realized. The stakes were too high not to.

"What about Rives?" I asked, steering the conversation away from me. "What's his story?"

Jillian's face closed up, a total withdrawal. "Rives holds the City together," she said quietly. "He's an amazing Leader."

"I meant, where is he from?"

Jillian relaxed. "Rives is kind of international. I think he lives most of the time in France, or maybe Hawaii. He travels with his parents a lot. I mean, he did. Until—" Jillian broke off, waving her arm at the obvious, her smile warm and real.

"Right." I nodded.

"C'mon, let me give you the not-so-grand tour," she said, dropping the subject of Rives like hot lava. Her silence felt protective of Rives.

Rives, a boy I didn't know at all, and ironically, he was the person I'd spent the most time with on *this* Nil. Other than Paulo.

Two boys, very different. One strong, one weak. But both with secrets. Personal secrets, island secrets.

Maybe they weren't so different after all.

Two visuals flashed, a Nil study in contrast: Rives, exiting the sea, muscular and threatening, a furious sea god, dripping water and power, and Paulo, sitting on a rock, bony shoulders hunched, stinking to high heaven, already broken.

Nope. Very different. And they were the first two people I'd officially met here.

Was Nil always about extremes?

"Skye?" Jillian asked.

"Yes?" Apparently I'd zoned out.

"Are you hungry or would you rather get clothes first?"

"You pick. I'm good either way."

An hour later, I'd decided Jillian was a fabulous one-person Nil welcome committee. So far she'd shown me the Map Wall, where she'd pointed out the locations of the labyrinth carvings and explained Charley's storm theory for gates; the Food Hut, where she'd given me a mango, a handful of nuts, and explained the basic City meals; and the Shack, where she'd outfitted me in City wear. Now I wore an off-white wrap skirt and chest wrap. Wrapping was apparently the Nil way of life: When in doubt, wrap it. Wrap skirts, chest wraps, fish wraps, shrimp wraps. Fortunately, I could wrap my skirt around me twice. It wasn't going to fall off, and thanks to the double wrap, it wasn't even see-through. All in all, the soft island cloth won hands-down over my homemade leaf-kini. After leaving the Shack, I almost felt normal.

Then we went down to the beach, and the next round of introductions reminded me I was anything but normal. New faces and names, most with questions or comments about my uncle. Word had spread fast.

A boy with straight, dark hair and chiseled cheekbones walked up first.

"Michael." Quick nod, no smile. Hard jaw. "Sixty-one days."

"Leila." Big brown eyes, thick ponytail. A single white shell hung from her wrist. She smiled. "Fifty days. Welcome to Nil, Skye, not that it sounds like you need it." Her smile took the sting from her words.

"Hi Skye! I'm Macy." Huge grin, warm handshake. Gorgeous skin I'd die for. I winced inwardly at my mental word choice. This wasn't the place to flippantly toss around death wishes. "It's gonna be okay, Skye," Macy said, squeezing my hand. "I've been here long enough to know. Your uncle made it, and so will you. It's in your blood. Oh, and you'll be bunking with me, Brittney, and Kiera if that's all right with you."

I nodded. It was hard to disagree with Macy; she was just so—*buoyant*.

A girl stepped up. Wiry and fair, big blue eyes and a chipped front tooth. "Your uncle came here, too? That is *cray-cray*. I'm Brittney. I've been here for three weeks already. The sunrises are the prettiest things you've ever seen." More talking, Texas twang. She sounded giddy, a little *cray-cray* herself.

Then a boy with skin as dark as a Nil night and a smile as bright as the Nil sun walked up. "Skye, welcome to paradise, island-nightmare style. You're like Nil royalty. I'm Ahmad, by the way. Day One Hundred One." I had to tilt my head back to look up at him; it reminded me of when I'd met Charley, only Ahmad made Charley look short. He wore a loincloth like Dex.

"Kiera," another girl said. Proud posture, amazing hair. If anyone was royalty, it was Kiera. The white flower tucked behind one ear seemed both perfect and effortless; I felt underdressed even though our outfits were an exact match. "So Rives found you?" Unlike Macy's, her brown eyes reminded me of the Cove. Chilly.

"Actually, I found him. I ran into him up on the beach north of the Cove."

For some reason, Kiera looked disappointed.

More names, more introductions; it was a frenzy of *new*. Another trio showed up, emerging from the south. Their arrival was met by screams and hugs and blissfully diverted all the attention from me.

I slipped away to the Wall. I needed a minute by myself. I'd gone from zero to sixty in a few hours flat. As an only child, I was used to plenty of alone time. I usually spent my afternoons reading or sketching, or when I was at Dad's, training. On weekends during the year I'd hang out with Tish, but then every summer I'd basically disappear. Summers were spent with my dad, going to crazy places, chasing crazy things.

Like Nil.

Where I was right now.

I ran my fingers over the wood. The Wall of Names stood near the master map. I'd seen it earlier with Jillian but hadn't stopped. Now I strolled alongside it, going back in time, searching for names I knew. I passed Charley and Thad; both had check marks beside their names. I passed Rives and Macy and Jillian and Dex, all still here, all with blank spaces. Then a stretch of names that meant nothing. The only name that stood out was Oliver. I'd dated a guy named Oliver last year, but he was forgettable. Sweet but dull. Once I'd dared him to eat a cricket on a whim after my dad had sent me a box of them along with an article called the TOP TEN EDIBLE INSECTS WITH HIGH PROTEIN LEVELS and Oliver had totally freaked out. He'd freaked even more when I ate one. Even his dimples couldn't save our sad relationship.

I wondered how Oliver would've fared on Nil. Probably not so well.

Then I came to a name that stopped me cold.

Hui.

He had a cross.

I slowed, finding Jenny. She had a check. Then Karl, with his check. Keifer, with a cross, like Ryla. George with a check, like John and Anne.

And then Scott, with no mark at all.

I ran my fingers over the five letters, overwhelmed by a rush of emotion and connection to my uncle. We weren't just connected by blood anymore; we were connected by Nil. The Wall blurred. I breathed deeply, pulling myself together and blinking back tears, because unless I wanted to rip off my chest wrap—which was *so* not going to happen—I had nothing to use to wipe my eyes.

I still wore my sling; it made me feel safe. Tucked inside rested my one tool: my honed rock. I angled it against the Wall, light glinting off the black rock, and slowly carved a check for my uncle. I stepped back to admire my handiwork.

"Looks good," a deep voice said from behind me.

I turned and found myself inches from Rives's chest. His *bare* chest. Automatically, I stepped back and my head bumped the Wall.

"Sorry." Rives's eyes twinkled in amusement. "Didn't mean to startle you." His slight grin said *I totally meant to startle you.* Annoyed that he had, I stepped away from the Wall, toward Rives, intending to force him to move, but he had already shifted back to give me space, his eyes drifting to the Wall.

"Your uncle?" he asked, pointing. Uncle Scott's new check stood out against the grayed wood.

I nodded. "His name was Scott." Voicing his name, I fought a surge of emotion. My connection to a dead man had never been stronger.

I tapped Karl's name. "Karl was the Leader when my uncle got here. He was a good guy. There were other good people, too," I said, running my hand over Jenny's name, reliving memories that weren't mine. "All here, on this Wall of Names."

"We call it the Naming Wall now, but the Wall of Names makes more sense. And there are good people still here, stuck in this deadly paradise. They all deserve to get home."

"But that's only part of it." I faced Rives, the unexpected emotion of carving my uncle's check leaving me raw and vulnerable and hurting and abruptly *angry*; I was furious with an invisible entity that was everywhere. "My uncle caught a gate alone on the beach. No one saw him leave. And do you know what my uncle's first thought was when he got back?" I thought of the last journal page full of words—bitter words, pressed so hard into the paper that it felt like braille. "That he never got to say good-bye."

"I'm sorry." Rives's eyes reflected his words.

"Me too." I traced Jenny's name. "I think he tried to find Jenny after he got back. He met her here, and from his journal, they were close. Maybe even in love. Maybe like Charley and Thad; I don't know. I do know she was from Australia, and I know that about nine months after he got back from Nil, he went there. I can't shake the feeling he was searching for her. I don't know if he found her before he died. I'll never know." *Because he lost his fear. Was he base jumping to feel fear, or to feel alive? I'll never know that, either. All I know is that this place touched him, and changed him. And maybe in the end, it killed him.*

My fingers fell away from Jenny's name.

"I get Nil now," I said softly. "I know I've only been here three days, but I get it. The pressure of time, the waiting. The beauty and the downtime that lull you into forgetting that your clock is ticking. The not knowing. The hope, and the desperation. The camaraderie. The loss." I thought of Charley, her face etched in pain.

"And I get that Nil's reach goes beyond this island. Some people never escape it, even after they get home." I found Rives's eyes with mine, the residual pain of my uncle's Nil turning to fire in my belly. "Rives, we have to stop this. To figure out a way to end it once and for all. And finding that stationary gate is the first step."

CHAPTER 31

RIVES
DAY 279, ALMOST DUSK

Skye was fire.

Skye was ice.

She was all the extremes of Nil wrapped in one, a mysterious package Nil didn't count on.

Just when I thought I had her number, she changed it. A tough-as-nails, sheet-metal exterior that couldn't dent—until it did.

And when I looked at her now, I saw fury beneath the calm, as fiery as the lava flowing down the back of Mount Nil. Her steel-flecked eyes barely held it in check.

"You're right," I said, my eyes on hers. "You've only been here three days, but you do get Nil. Between your uncle, Charley, and now checking out Nil for yourself, you've got the whole picture: past, present, and future." I paused. "I'm all for ending this merry-go-round if we can, and I agree that finding that gate is crucial. But—" I stopped, mentally working through my personal Nil fixation, playing Tetris with my clues.

"Wait," Skye said. "No 'buts.' Nothing good ever follows the word *but*, at least not here."

"Did you just quote Dex?" I fought a laugh.

"At least you're paying attention." She almost smiled.

"Always." I paused. "The stationary gate is huge, no doubt. But"—I emphasized this word, making Skye raise her eyebrows—"it's not the starting place. We need to find Paulo and Maaka first. They have answers that would take us weeks or months to find, and we don't have that kind of time. I think we start with them, and then hunt the gate."

Skye looked unconvinced. "Why don't we go back to the mountain and see what we find? We should go sooner rather than later, while the memory is still fresh in my head. I think I can find the location, or at least get us close. Maybe we do a twenty-four-hour stakeout where I think the gate flashed, to see if it flashes again at noon or midnight?"

"A stakeout?" I fought a laugh, knowing Skye would be offended, but the image struck me as funny. "You do those often?"

Her cheeks reddened but her steely eyes flashed. "Occasionally. When needed."

Nodding, I considered her idea. The meadow was a deathtrap, more predators than gates, and I didn't care to risk it for nothing. "I didn't think you remembered exactly where it flashed."

"I may not know *exactly* where I woke, but I can get us close. Close enough. I wouldn't ask you to go there if I didn't think I could find it." Her tone had a bite.

I believed her—I believed that *she* believed she could find it—but I wasn't convinced.

"I've got a question." Gently, I grabbed her wrist and turned it over. Black faded letters were still visible, scrawled facing her. "What does *TFPL* mean?"

"Think first, panic later." Her cheeks flushed again, barely.

"Is that your motto?" I teased.

"No. It's my dad's."

"He seems tough," I said, holding her gaze.

"You have no idea." Looking away, Skye rubbed her TFPL tattoo. "So what's yours?" I asked.

"My what?" She looked back and frowned.

"Your motto."

Five seconds passed. "I have a few," Skye said. " 'Stay alive. Don't mess with hippos. Let sleeping rhinos be.' " She grinned, then immediately turned serious. "But generally, my new motto is 'Think first, act later.' "

Of course Skye had ditched the panic. It was tough to picture cool Skye in panic mode. But Nil had a way of pushing people to their edge—and beyond. *And there's the but,* I thought.

"What's yours?" she asked.

"My what?"

"Your motto."

"I have a few." I smiled. " 'Stay alive. Avoid the mudflats. Leave sleeping leopards alone.' But generally my motto is 'Notice what others ignore.' "

Skye studied me, her eyes sharp and clear like that first moment we'd met, like it was her motto too. She was always thinking, always *looking.* I wondered if she was even aware of it. And I wondered what she saw.

"That's a good motto," she said finally. "The tricky part would be knowing exactly what others have overlooked, right?"

"That's why I make it a point to notice everything," I said. Then I winked. "At least I do my best."

"That's all any of us can do," she said. "Especially here, where each day is truly a new day, in every sense of the word."

"Well said, rookie-who's-not-really-a-rookie. You just nailed Nil truth number seven."

"How many Nil truths are there?" she asked.

I grinned. "How much time do you have?" Her question, turned back at her.

She rewarded me with a slight smile. "Three hundred sixty-two days."

My grin faltered.

A hell of a lot more time than me.

"And that's Nil truth number two," I said quietly. "You're officially on the clock. Tick-tock."

Skye had Nil's number, no doubt about it. *Maybe she should be my Second.*

But the minute the thought crossed my mind, I dismissed it. The City didn't know her, and City acceptance was crucial. Skye was too new, too untested. At least in the City's eyes.

Skye's face cooled into serious mode, like she'd suddenly realized she was wasting time.

"In case you haven't heard, the other Search team is back," she said. "They're on the beach." Skye pointed, not that I needed the guidance. "I was with Jillian when they came back. Two boys and girl."

Raj's team. Three out, three back. I wondered if it was the same three.

"Thanks. I'd better go check in." I almost asked if Skye wanted to come but didn't. This girl didn't need an invitation. She knew the drill.

She nodded and turned back to the Wall.

As I strolled away, I weighed her motto.

Think first, act later.

Not a bad motto at all, especially if I added *panic never.*

Turned out Raj's team *was* back but not intact. Carlos was gone; he'd caught a gate on the second day of Search. Based on Raj's description, it was like the single that took Sabine. Fast, directed, and unavoidable.

I strode up to the new kid, taking in his loincloth, healthy cheeks, nervous feet. Carlos had worn shorts. So where did this kid get his threads?

"Welcome to Nil City. I'm Rives." I stuck out my hand, leveling my eyes on his. "Have we met before?"

"Don't think so." He dropped my hand fast. "I'm Archie. From South Africa. Have you been there?"

"Actually, yes." *When I was two.* "But I don't think that's where we met." I held his gaze until he looked away, and in his profile, recognition hit: This kid was one of the raiders I'd seen stealing our nets.

Foe, I thought. But I held my tongue. Knowledge was power.

"Word of warning, Archie," I said softly, watching him wrench his gaze back. "Watch your back. Nil's a dangerous place."

I looked around for Ahmad or Dex. Neither was in sight. Sy stood beside Michael, drinking from a gourd while Michael ate. In the late-afternoon light, shadows slashed across Sy's cheeks. His cheekbones jutted like rocks, no flesh to soften their edges. Being thin made you weak, and weak here wasn't good, especially when you weren't strong in the first place. And Sy was nearly skeletal.

I walked over to Sy.

"Sy, got a minute?" I asked him. I nodded at Michael, who raised his wrap at me in acknowledgment. Michael was sharp, as watchful as me. I hoped he'd make it.

Sy wiped his lips and stood. "Sure thing."

We walked toward the sea, out of hearing range but close enough for me to eye Archie. Talking with Raj, Archie had animated hands and restless eyes.

Beside me, Sy stared at the sea. He chewed one fingernail, not that he had much left to work with.

"Are you okay?" I asked. "You've lost weight, and fingernails don't count as food. Talk to me."

Sy shrugged, looking toward the City's edge. "Remember when we found Bart? Remember those claw marks on his back?"

I nodded.

Sy's eyes were haunted. "So do I. It looked like he'd been swiped by something. Like a cat." He swallowed. "I feel like we're being hunted, Rives, like in *Predator*. Here we are, in paradise, right?" He swept his arm around the white sand beach for emphasis. "Blue skies, cool breeze. White sand. Decent food, although it's all self-serve, which gets old. And some of the girls are hot. Sometimes it's so peaceful, I forget where I am. Then all of a sudden I think of Bart, and I almost hurl. Because now I know that catching a gate isn't the hardest part anymore. It's surviving until the next noon."

"True. But you won't survive if you don't eat."

"I know. But half the time I just feel sick."

"I hear you. Maybe focus on the other half, all right? Go get a wrap and some redfruit. Johan's team brought back heaps and it's all ripe. And listen"—I lowered my voice—"keep an eye on Archie, will you?" I paused, long enough to decide to trust Sy with my suspicion. "I think he's one of the raiders who stole the nets."

Sy's eyes stretched into saucers. "For real? So Archie's, like, a spy?"

Spy. The word sounded organized, implying a certain level of intelligence and stealth. If Archie was one of the raiders who crushed half the flowers in the field as they fled, he was as subtle as a bulldozer.

"Maybe. Just keep an eye on him, okay? But eat first."

Sy walked away, his spine a little straighter, his shoulders back. Sy's motto should be *Do more, worry less.* Then he might actually be okay.

Zane came over, smiling wide. "Hey, boss—guess what? Raj and crew brought back a chicken and a goat. Sweet, right?"

I nodded. "Sweet." But I didn't share Zane's stoke. Because as twilight fell, so did the goat's chances of surviving the night. Same for my odds of sleeping. Because I had a possible raider in camp, a hungry predator on the prowl, and fresh meat for the taking.

I sighed.

It would be a long night on watch.

Twelve hours later, I'd realize I was only partially right. The goat turned out to be completely fine.

CHAPTER
32

It was officially the weirdest Christmas ever. I was a stranger in a strange land.

Make that a completely freaky land.

This holiday even beat out the terrible tofurkey Christmas on the freaky meter. That Christmas was the first holiday after Mom and Dad split. We'd still spent Christmas as a family, with everyone acting overly polite and eating the awful organic tofu bird Mom had concocted and all of us pretending the "D" word didn't exist. Ironically, my parents still weren't divorced. But they weren't together, either.

And this year, none of us were together.

The closest family I had here was Uncle Scott. *Haven't you already established he's dead?* my mind scolded exasperatedly.

Yup. I'm connecting with a ghost. Merry crazy Christmas.

I blinked in the dark, wondering what time it was. I closed my eyes like Rives had suggested, filtering the silence, listening for sounds of people moving. Nothing, at least nothing human made.

Breaking waves rumbled through the air like the best sleep machine ever. The air was cool, but Jillian had given me a cheetah pelt as a cover, a lovely yet creepy kindness that kept me comfortably warm. Around me, Macy, Brittney, and Kiera slept. We shared one of the bigger huts, complete with four beds and two tables. Despite the open sides, suddenly I felt cramped, almost claustrophobic.

Outside, I breathed deeply, taking in the space. Overhead, fire lit the sky, each star burning brilliant white in the clearest night sky I'd ever seen: no light, no humidity, no smog—no pollution of any sort to smother the clarity. The firepit's glow dulled by comparison.

I stared at the night, at the stars my dad loved almost as much as the sun, my throat tightening.

"Skye?" Rives's voice. Barely audible, his voice came out of nowhere.

"You're sneaky," I whispered, turning to face him.

"So I've heard. You okay?" Torchlight flickered across his face, cutting his cheekbones with shadows. The dangerous edge was back.

"Yeah. I was just thinking about my dad. He'd love the sky here." I paused. "He's an astrophysicist."

"Impressive."

It was, I knew. But right now Dad's choice of profession seemed driven by this place, and I wasn't sure whether it made his passion more, or less, impressive.

"He loves space," I said simply. I glanced at Rives, automatically smoothing down my hair and feeling it spring right back. I'd lost my pieces of twine while I'd slept. Lovely.

"What are you doing up?" I asked.

"I've got watch."

"Looking for a sleigh and reindeer?" I pointed at the sky.

"I don't think Nil's on Santa's itinerary," Rives said.

"Because we've been naughty?" Beneath the darkness, my cheeks burned.

Rives raised his eyebrows. "Something you want to tell me, Skye?"

"Funny."

"You started it."

"You first," I dared.

He tipped his head, making his light eyes catch the firelight. "I stole a tricycle once."

"No way."

"I was seven. We were in London, and I'd never learned how to ride a bike. I saw this kid park his trike across the street. His whole family went inside a café, leaving the trike outside, and I thought, *Hey, I can ride that.* So I grabbed it and took off. My dad caught up with me, lectured me on the spot, and made me return it with a huge apology. The poor kid was crying. I felt terrible. Never forgot it, actually." A smile pulled at his lips. "Count it as a lesson learned."

"You're definitely in trouble. No presents for tricycle stealers."

"Look who's talking. You stole a canoe."

"Borrowed," I said. "I *borrowed* a canoe."

Rives grinned. "I thought we agreed on commandeered."

I rolled my eyes. "So tell me about watch. Something tells me you're not looking for reindeer after all."

Rives's face hardened. "I don't know what I'm looking for, but it's not friendly. Lately something's been snacking on City livestock. We've lost two goats and a chicken. Odds are it's a hyena or a big cat." He paused. "We know there's a leopard hanging out nearby."

I thought of the tiger, and the snow leopards, melding my uncle's Nil with mine. "My uncle's journal spoke of the meadow. It was full of big cats. And"—I paused, hesitating to throw my uncle under the crazy bus—"there was a girl. In his first few days. She brought him clothes, and a gourd of water. She warned him to stay clear of the meadow, then she pointed him toward the City."

"A familiar MO," Rives murmured. "What else did she say?"

I pictured her, this girl who'd saved my uncle only to vanish as if she were an apparition. "Nothing. He never saw her again."

Rives swept the perimeter with his eyes, even as I knew he'd heard every word I said. "That must've been a hell of a read," he said. "Your uncle's journal."

"It was. So what's with all the cats? Jillian gave me a cheetah pelt. It's really warm," I admitted.

"Want to hear a story?" Rives asked.

I nodded.

"Walk with me," he said.

We started walking, mainly because I think it was killing Rives to stand still. He held the lit torch like Prometheus holding fire, his entire body tense. He didn't relax until we started moving, and by "relax," I mean the muscles rippling across his shoulders stopped twitching. Not that I was looking.

"There's a story Natalie told me. She was the Leader when I got here. Kind yet tough and a get-it-done Leader, day in and day out. She taught me a lot. Anyway"—Rives exhaled, like he was mentally directing himself back on track—"one day she and Kevin and a few other people were sitting around, chilling out by the fire. Up walks a blond kid, streaked with dried blood, wearing a loincloth, and carrying a gutted cheetah around his shoulders like a sack of potatoes. Then he says, 'Anybody missing a cat?'"

Rives paused, smiling. "That was Thad. And you've got the cat."

Another Nil moment, another Nil time. Uncle Scott's journal only told one story: his. I was slowly realizing how little I knew. "That's crazy," I said.

"That's Nil," Rives said. "And Thad." He looked away. I could almost hear his thoughts. *He made it.*

I hoped for Rives's and Charley's sakes that he did.

Rives stopped, tilted his head toward the darkness, which I noticed now was slightly less dark. Apparently satisfied, he turned back to me. "So why are you up? Didn't care for the accommodations?"

"Oh, the Nil Inn was fabulous. Five stars. The cat quilt put it over the top." I smiled briefly. "It's just—" *That I don't belong? And yet I do? That I'm here to do more than just escape?* That sounded pretentious, which I wasn't, or at least I didn't think I was. But I had an urgency, a *feeling*, that I couldn't quite put into words.

Rives waited patiently, for which I was grateful.

"I feel restless," I said finally. "Like I've got something big to do, and sleep is wasting time. It's like the night before a big test, and I'm cramming, only I don't know if the test is tomorrow or the next day or next week." I sighed, feeling I sounded like cray-cray Brittney. At least I hadn't asked about giraffes. "That made no sense. Sorry. Anyway, I couldn't sleep."

"I get it." The intense air around Rives when I'd seen him walk out of the surf was back. "This place makes you want things you didn't even know you wanted, makes you crave answers to questions you didn't know existed." His eyes slid to me. "Nil got to you earlier than most. But then again, the island had a head start."

Abruptly Rives snapped his head toward the darkness. "Stay here," he whispered.

Not a chance.

I followed Rives as he walked toward the darkness, casting his torch out in front of him. I eased my sling off of my shoulder and untied the rock I'd secured with twine. Weapon ready, I had Rives's back.

Twin eyes peeked from the darkness, faceted and glistening and *still.* Tufts of white perked above them. I made out a familiar outline of brown and lowered my sling.

"It's just a deer," I murmured in Rives's ear.

He jumped. *"Merde!"*

The deer bounded away, spooked.

Rives's eyes flamed green. "I told you to stay back."

"And I chose not to."

"I see that. Let me guess: On your report card, the teacher checked 'needs improvement' next to 'listens and follows directions.'"

"I heard you just fine," I snapped. "But it was an unnecessary direction to follow."

"Was it?" Rives's calm tone was dangerously cool.

"Yes." I fought the urge to cross my arms. *Did he seriously think he could tell me what to do?*

Rives's jaw ticked.

From my right, Dex said, "Rives? We've got a situation."

CHAPTER 33

RIVES
DAY 280, BREAKING DAWN

No shit we have a situation.

Skye had just waltzed up to the tree line without a torch. Small in size not spirit, she may as well have told the potential predator, *Hey, I'm breakfast. Hungry much?*

I didn't care that she didn't listen. I cared that she was reckless. And it made me ballistic.

Dex's eyes darted between Skye and me before settling on me.

"That bloke Archie? The one who showed up yesterday? He just left the City from the south end," he said in a low voice. "He's walking like he's out for a stroll, but it feels dodgy. Want me to follow? Or let him go?"

"Is he carrying anything?"

"Nothing I could see."

"I'll go," I said. Archie already knew I had his number. I handed Dex my torch, trying to focus on Archie, not Skye. Lines of pink and gold lanced the air. Archie had timed his departure with dawn.

"Want company?" Skye asked.

Not really. Absolutely.

"Up to you," I said crisply.

I took off at a slow jog, going as fast as I could without making any sound. My gut said he'd go toward the Flower Field, taking the same flight path I'd seen the raiders take before.

I didn't have to turn to know Skye had followed me.

She's quiet, I grudgingly admitted. I didn't hear her as much as I sensed her. I gave the deadleaf plants a wide berth, hoping she'd do the same. She must've, because as I approached the field, she was still behind me.

I raised one hand and stopped, hoping this time she'd listen.

She did.

It took me three seconds to assess the situation. In the middle of the field, Archie strode quickly. He carried three satchels slung over his shoulders, each bulging with stolen supplies. In the distance, two boys were running toward him, smiling. A raider meet-up in the making.

Now I ran.

When I got within hearing range, I yelled, "Archie!"

He spun around, wide-eyed, then turned and sprinted away, moving impressively fast given his stolen load. He handed off a sack to each boy in seconds. As a team, they spun and took off at a full sprint. Archie paused long enough to flip me a slick salute and wide smile, then spun back and hauled ass.

I kicked it up a notch, sprinting all out.

Within minutes, I was gaining ground on the trio. To my surprise, Skye hung with me; she paced me well. The trio's tight group spread out into a line, with Archie at the rear. They were still a solid fifty meters out.

"What's the plan?" Skye asked, her voice breathless.

Get our stuff? Follow them? Find out where their stash is? I was still framing the plan when Archie collapsed.

Swiftly, violently, as if grabbed by the ankle or tripped, he went down without a cry. The boys in the lead never looked back, never stopped running. Soon they were gone, consumed by color and brilliant rising light.

I slowed, watching the spot where Archie went down. Skye slowed with me. The two of us watched, waiting for movement.

Nothing.

Just the breeze, batting the flowers around in waves. Nothing dangerous there. Yet that meant nothing. Nil's dangers often lurked out of sight.

"I'm going to see if Archie is okay. The safe thing to do would be to stay put." I raised one eyebrow at Skye, willing her to sit tight.

I tracked diagonally toward the spot where I'd seen Archie collapse. Raider or not, if he was hurt, he needed help. But if he'd broken an ankle or leg or been bitten on his leg, he was royally screwed. Because winning a ticket home usually meant a sprint to the finish, and if you couldn't run, you weren't even a contender.

I reached the place where I'd seen him fall and frowned. Nobody in pain, nobody hurt.

No body.

Maybe I'd misjudged.

"Where'd he go?" Skye asked. She stood four meters back, her head shifting slowly as she scanned the field. Of course she'd followed. Her other motto was *No fear.* Or maybe it was *I'll do what the hell I want.* Either way, it was a little hot, but more than anything else it was extraordinarily frustrating. She was rolling the dice with her number one motto: *Stay alive.* I'd had enough Nil funerals to last a lifetime.

"Rives?" Skye said. "Which way?"

"I don't know."

I took a few steps forward, scanning the flowers, and caught a color out of place: a few meters away, a slick of crimson smeared across a swath of summer yellow. I eased closer, every smart cell in my head screaming, *BACK THE HELL UP.*

The blood on the flowers glistened, wet. More blood stained the ground.

Fresh blood, too much blood.

My stomach sank, my gut telling me that Archie's hourglass had just run out. Still, I crept closer, ignoring the voice in my head, tracking until I saw drag marks. They pointed east, toward the meadow, away from the City.

The blood trail was gone.

So was Archie's shot at leaving Nil.

"What took him?" Skye's voice, a whisper on my left. Her arms were crossed like personal armor.

"No clue." I'd been so focused on the raiders, I hadn't caught a glimpse of the predator. And if I was completely honest with myself, I'd been slightly distracted by Skye. I needed to get my shit together, and fast.

"Should we go after him?"

"No point. Based on the blood trail, Archie's lost too much blood for us to help him now. The trauma center here doesn't even stock Band-Aids." I sighed, wholly sick of Nil.

Archie may have been a thief, but the offense didn't warrant death.

Skye hadn't moved, her expression looking like she had all the numbers but couldn't add them up. "So he'll die?" Her eyes were locked on the blood trail. "On *Christmas*?"

"Birth, death. Arrivals, departures. All Nil cares about is balance, Skye. The day, or holiday, doesn't matter to Nil. It all comes down to some invisible list, some master plan, with factors only Nil has access to, with scales only Nil can see." My voice sounded tired, even to me. "But balance reigns, always. That's Nil truth number four."

Skye stared at the drag marks. "How can someone just disappear?"

Suddenly I had the thought that Skye would follow the tracks anyway, surprising the beast during its holiday feast, which wasn't just stubborn; it was dangerous.

"Let's go," I said quickly.

To my relief, Skye listened without argument, her cheeks pale. Seeing Nil's dark side had rattled her, denting her tough exterior. Not good. I wanted her sharp, not skittish.

Buck up, Skye, I thought, glancing sideways at her. *First a dent, then a crack. Nil will force its way in, taking all you have to give.* She'd better regroup before Nil found a chink wide enough to blast Skye's armor to dust. Then we'd all be screwed.

After taking a few steps, Skye spun and doubled back.

"Skye, don't!"

Ignoring me, she went another meter, bent down, and when she stood she held up a satchel, the one Archie had carried. It was spattered with fresh blood. "I thought we might need this," she said, striding back. Her tone cool, challenge gleamed in her eyes.

"Thanks," I said. *And thank you for using your head.*

Maybe she wasn't as rattled as I'd thought.

Then again, maybe she was. She was quiet as we walked through the flowers. I carried the satchel. Twice I caught her looking at it, staring at the bloodstains.

As we left the field, she glanced back, and I noticed a tiny streak of fresh blood on her face. It stood out like island paint, where her jaw had brushed the flowers when she'd bent to grab the bag. I reached out and immediately pulled my hand back. I didn't have the right to touch her.

I barely knew her.

"Skye, you've got blood here." I tapped my jaw with my finger.

Her eyes on mine, she reached up and touched her face.

"Closer to your chin," I said softly, moving my finger down my jawline to explain.

Her motions tracked mine. Slowly, carefully, her fingers traced her cheek as she gently wiped away the blood, never looking away from me.

I couldn't move, couldn't breathe, like I'd sucked down deadleaf tea.

"Did I get it?" she whispered, her eyes barely blinking.

I nodded, my eyes on hers. I'd lost my ability to speak. *What the hell was that?*

We started walking. Neither of us said another word.

Dex and Sy waited where we'd left them. "Raider meet-up, pre-planned," I told them succinctly. "Stole three bags, we got one back, thanks to Skye."

Dropping into a squat, I gently dumped the contents of the recovered bag on the ground. Mangos, guava, and rocks spilled out.

"Rocks?" Skye frowned. "Why would anyone steal rocks?"

"No clue," I said. *And why steal food when the groves offer plenty?*

"About the rocks," Sy said. He sounded hesitant. "Last night I saw Archie hanging around the Shack and the Food Hut. He looked like he was up to trouble. Like he might take stuff." Sy flushed, not meeting my eyes. I recalled a time when Sy had been less than honest. My gut said his thoughts tracked mine.

He cleared his throat. "He left the Shack, his arms full of stuff, and when he went into the woods, I saw him stash two satchels at the edge of the Flower Field. Then when he went to bed—he crashed in Cho's hut last night—I snuck back out and opened the satchels. He'd taken sandals—three pairs—shorts, a wooden machete, and food." He shrugged. "I filled the bags with rocks and covered the rocks with food. I figured he could take the food."

"Nice job," I added, watching Sy's posture straighten with pride. "Good thinking."

"So he's gone then? Archie?" Dex asked.

"Yup," I answered. "But his friends might come back. They ran off with two bags." I caught Dex's eye. "Archie didn't make it."

"What does that mean?" Sy frowned.

"It means something grabbed him in the Flower Field. Something strong enough to take down all seventy kilos of him in one bite. And something strong enough to drag him away."

Dex clenched his jaw. "Something with fur, no doubt."

"I'd guess yes."

"It just took him?" Sy looked both bewildered and pale. "Like he vanished?"

"He left a trail of blood," Skye said quietly. She pointed at the satchel, which now lay blood side up.

"Bloody hell," Dex swore.

"That's Nil," I said.

Sy started hyperventilating.

"Breathe," I told him calmly. "Slow and steady. You're gonna be okay, buddy. Just breathe."

I gently led us toward the Shack, Sy breathing loudly, Dex and Skye completely silent.

By the time we got there, Sy had pulled himself together but he still looked ready to puke. I wondered if he'd eaten today.

Working as a quiet group, we inventoried the Shack to see what else was missing.

The answer? Not much.

From our best guess, the third satchel had held a dried water gourd and, of all things, a pillow. Nothing else was missing. Sure, a pillow took a little time to make—the grasses didn't dry overnight—and yeah, the cloth to wrap them was precious, but it was a goddamn *pillow*.

Archie's middle had abruptly turned into his end, *over a pillow*.

And that was Nil truth number six. Don't waste time on stupid stuff. Sometimes it will come around to bite you in the ankle.

Or kill you.

CHAPTER 34

SKYE
DAY 4, MID-MORNING

Christmas in the islands was not at all I what I'd expected.

I had the blue sky and gorgeous beaches, the freshest fish I could ask for, plenty of downtime, and if I was honest, I had hot guys in skimpy island shorts that made me shiver at weird and unexpected moments. And I had people getting mauled by invisible predators and disappearing into thin air.

Merry deadly Christmas.

If Nil didn't like thieves, I was in big trouble.

I hoped that wasn't Nil truth number one.

I watched Rives paddle out, diving under the breaking waves like a pro. I didn't know how to surf, and right now I hoped I wouldn't stay long enough to learn. Noon would show up soon, maybe bringing a gate, maybe not. But midnight would show up eventually, too. I wasn't so naïve as to think the stationary gate appeared every night at midnight; that would be too easy. But if there was a pattern to the rolling gates, why couldn't there be a pattern to the stationary gates, too? And I wouldn't find it sitting here on the sand, watching Rives surf.

My frustration with Rives grew.

Archie's freak death made me want to find that elusive outbound *right now.* To not waste another single second, let alone a day. Not waste time goofing off in the ocean when we had a chance at a City-wide escape, here on land.

Rives pulled up and sat on his board. He faced the horizon, his board drifting, his body still. He made no attempt to catch a wave or come back to land, and he sure wouldn't find the stationary gate at sea.

Why didn't Rives feel the same urgency to find it as I did?

And how long did he expect me to keep the stationary gate a secret?

No more, I thought. He'd had a day. Twenty-four hours, which on Nil was a lifetime. Rives basically said so himself. *Births, deaths. Arrivals, departures.*

It all could happen—and *did* happen—in one day.

Rives had had his chance. Instead, he chose to surf.

It was time to make a new plan. *My* plan, which did not involve piddling the day away on the water.

I spun around and nearly knocked Macy down.

"Hey," she said, backing up with her hands raised, smiling. "Most people only move that fast around here when they see a gate."

"Or a predator," I said. I didn't smile. Less than three hours past dawn and a boy was dead.

Macy's face softened. "True. I'm so sorry for what happened to Archie. Sometimes there are no words, Skye. Sometimes life is cruel."

I noticed she said "life," not "Nil."

Reaching out, Macy pressed something into my hand and squeezed. "It's small, but Jillian and I just wanted you to know that we're glad you're here even though we're sorry you're here." Macy smiled. "Merry Christmas, Skye."

I opened my palm to find a bracelet. Soft twine held a cluster of three small white shells, each unique in shape, none perfect, yet totally perfect for the day. Simple and gorgeous.

Pressure squeezed my chest like an invisible gate.

I had nothing for her or Jillian, and it made me feel awful. I hadn't even thought about gifts, or more importantly, anyone else. My focus had been on the midnight gate and escape. And Archie's death. And me. And not necessarily in that order.

I looked up, feeling shallow and selfish and more resolute than ever. "Thank you, Macy," I said. Tears welled in my eyes; I blinked. "I'm sorry I have nothing for you." *But I will. I have a gate, a surefire escape, I just can't tell you about it. Yet.*

Macy squeezed my hand, a gentle pressure. "I don't expect anything. That's why we call it a gift." Her smile was as warm as her grip. "Given freely, expecting nothing in return. Jillian found the twine; I found the shells. It's from both of us."

I touched my gift. "Thank you." I stared at the bracelet, hearing Rives's voice, his words echoing Charley's. *There are good people still here, still stuck in this deadly paradise. They all deserve to get home.*

He was right, and the sooner the better.

It was time to make some Christmas magic happen.

CHAPTER
35

RIVES
DAY 280, MID-MORNING

I paddled out and breathed.

Out here, I gave in. Gave up, letting the water push me where it pleased. I didn't even try to catch a wave. I decompressed, needing the space to *think*.

Skye's motto. *Think first, act later.* The unspoken *don't panic.*

Talla's motto. *Don't think, act.* The unspoken *follow your instincts.*

Telling myself not to compare the two was pointless. I compared everyone to Talla; she was my standard for Nil badassery. Leila and Pari held their own, rocking a quiet sense of competence, and both had smartly made allies to watch their backs—like Michael, Raj, and Cho. Kiera was weak and privileged and utterly focused on the *I* in *Nil*; Brittney went around with her jaw perpetually dropped in wonder. Neither would notice an elephant on an approach. The only feeling I got around those last two was a heightened pressure to get their butts home in one piece. Macy and Jillian were tough and kind, my Nil sisters like Nat had been. Dex had grown into his strength, like Ahmad and Jason and Miya.

Talla had been different.

And Skye was different.

Talla's *in-your-face* attitude had rubbed others wrong, but not me. There was more to Talla than just toughness, and yet, in the end, you got what you saw. A fighter, unwilling to back down, willing to fight for what was right, even if the battle cost her life. Which, in the end, it did.

Skye was another story.

Skye didn't react like Talla; Skye *acted.* Coolly, with a confidence most people could only dream to channel; her every move was methodically thought through, constantly putting Nil on the defensive. More cerebral, less knee-jerk. More going on inside than anyone could see, giving me hope she might take Nil on and win.

Until this morning. And that's what pissed me off.

Skye had stepped up to the darkness like a rookie dumbass, without thinking. It could've turned out badly. Could've been deadly.

Like Archie.

I replayed the morning and a crisp mental sequence struck. Skye, sliding her sling back on her shoulder, her hand palming a rock.

Had she been prepared after all?

Maybe I was the dumbass. Maybe I didn't give her enough credit. Maybe I owed her an apology for being a chauvinistic jerk.

Maybe I didn't need to protect everyone, but that didn't change the fact that I felt driven to try. Archie had been in camp less than twenty-four hours, and I'd done nothing to protect him. Maybe his death was meant to be. Maybe fate was the foe today, not Nil.

Maybe I'm losing my shit.

Rivesssss . . .

The waves hissed with a ferocity that snapped me back.

The current had pulled me south, past Black Bay, toward the Arches. A single figure stood in front of the Man in the Maze.

Maaka.

I paddled furiously and rode the next wave in. Leaving my board on the rocks out of wave range, I climbed higher, toward the Man in the Maze.

Maaka still stood motionless, arms crossed, a slight frown pulling his eyebrows tight as he faced the carving.

"Morning, Maaka," I said. "How's your middle going?"

Maaka didn't turn. Didn't flinch. Didn't acknowledge my presence at all.

"Why, good morning to you too, Rives," I said pleasantly. "It's great to see you. How's everything going? Lose any friends today?" I crossed my arms, my stance matching his. *I'll talk until you do*, I thought. *I've got time.*

He turned toward me slowly. "I do not think he was your friend," he said quietly. "Unless your friends steal from you."

His gaze flicked to my board and back to me, thoughtful.

"You are not like me, and yet you are. You are *haole*"—he pointed toward the City—"and yet you are not."

"Because I look like you?" I asked, annoyed that Maaka had put me into a club, yet at the same time excluded me. Twice. "Because my grandmother was from the islands? Is that what makes us alike?"

"No," he said. "You are not an islander like me. But there is—something. You act like us. You question like us. You think. You lead, you protect, even at your own expense. We are alike here." He placed his fist over his heart. "The island blood running through your veins is strong."

Which island? I wondered. *Hawaii or Nil?*

"Who are you?" I asked. "Who is your 'us'?"

Maaka dropped his fist and looked away.

"Three . . . two . . . one . . . ," I counted slowly. "C'mon, answer, Maaka. Don't let me get to four." I raised my eyebrows.

"The numbers," he said. "They are not for you."

"Nothing here is for me," I said dryly. "And yet here I am. Feel free to tell me what they mean."

Maaka tipped his head.

"The numbers represent the timeline of the journey. Of our

journey. Of the path we travel. We start with three seasons, then two, then one. A progression, not to zero but to a completion, to a new beginning. To the fourth season, when we return home."

A countdown, I thought. *Just like Thad named the carving.*

Obvious and disappointing.

"You talk about us and them." I studied Maaka as I spoke. "The first day we met, I argued we are one and the same; you told me we're different. In one way, you're right. You come here, knowing you can leave. You don't have to run, you don't have to guess. You don't have to live in fear. Everyone else spends every day running for their lives, trying to catch a gate as it races across the island. We don't have the luxury of knowing a gate is waiting. It's like you've got a first-class ticket and the rest of us are flying standby, every damn day."

I breathed, fighting the constant frustration simmering below the surface. "So you can have your spiritual journey, Maaka, your middle, but we don't get that, either. Because when you're facing down death every day, it's a little tough to find your inner peace and personal path. And some people never get their fourth season, because they die. Here, on this rock." I looked hard at Maaka. The lines of his face didn't change, but at least he was listening. And he didn't tell me I was wrong about the stationary gate.

Point for me, I thought.

"You see much," he said finally.

"Am I still at the edges?" I almost smiled.

He looked through the Arch, toward the island's interior.

"The island only tests those with the strength to survive," he said finally. "The island does not bring people here to die. We are all metal, strong but pliable, forged through fire. That is our middle. The island does not choose those who will burn."

"We all burn," I said, thinking of Talla. "Fire always wins."

"Does it?" The water crashed loudly in Maaka's pause. "Fire may leave a mark, but it doesn't have to kill."

"It leaves you scarred, then." My tone was harsh.

"Perhaps." Maaka sounded thoughtful. "Or perhaps reshaped. Molded. Stronger. Weak points soldered." He pressed his hand flat against the Arch. "Look at the island. Shaped by fire. The land, blistered and burned, reshaped into something beautiful."

His reverent tone made me sick.

"Beauty is in the eye of the beholder, Maaka. I don't think those scarred by Nil would consider those marks of beauty, even if those scars are invisible."

"You don't know that," he said. "How scars are viewed is a choice. Scars are badges of honor. Marks of the path walked to shape you into the person you are to become."

"Back to the journey, I see." I crossed my arms. "People die here, Maaka. People who didn't choose to come."

"Perhaps their choice was made for them," he said softly. "Perhaps their end was already written." His eyes flashed fierce. "But most survive, and those who do are stronger, even if scarred."

He stepped back, like he'd crossed some invisible line.

"I will go now," he said. "Do not follow me."

"Maaka." One word, delivered like a command.

He paused, then faced me like an equal.

"We're not done," I said quietly. "We're not even to the middle, you and me."

For the first time he smiled. "We are definitely in the middle, Leader Rives. Just because you can still see the beginning does not mean it is not behind you." His smile faded. "The island's fire has touched you. It burns inside you. Do not let it consume you."

He turned, dropped into the water between the rocks, and disappeared beneath the froth, leaving me alone with the numbers and carvings.

The island's fire has touched you. It burns inside you. Do not let it consume you.

Easier said than done.

Fire can be extinguished; fire can be also controlled. Harnessed. Like humans had done for centuries.

But Nil's fire was invisible.

How can you harness something you can't see?

CHAPTER 36

SKYE
DAY 4, MIDDAY

After spending the rest of the morning satisfying Sy's rabid curiosity about my uncle's journal—*What did they eat for breakfast? Did they build the fish traps? Did Mount Nil ever blow?*—I finally escaped, begging off to go find Jillian.

Other than Rives and Dex, Jillian was the only other person Charley had mentioned by name, which told me Jillian could be trusted. And I desperately needed to trust someone with my secret. It begged to be shared, because the stationary gate didn't belong to me; it belonged to all.

I found Jillian by the Shack, spreading out sheets of creamy pulp to dry.

"It's so lumpy," she grumbled. "No one beats the pulp flat like Heesham did." She pounded one particularly large knot with her fist, which did absolutely nothing. "Crap." She looked up and wiped her forehead as she smiled. "What's up, Skye?"

In that moment, time's butterfly wings fluttered against my cheek. *Don't cause a ripple you can't undo.* The stationary gate belonged to all, but the secret of its existence was volatile, its effect on the City and the Search system a wild card that Rives had been hesitant to play.

I could at least give him forty-eight hours to figure out how to deal with it. After all, I'd only been here four days, which was a drop in the bucket compared to his 280, or Jillian's 276.

Jillian's hands stilled as she regarded me expectantly.

I patted my wrist. "Thanks for the bracelet," I said, returning her smile. My bracelet matched hers, where the twine wrapped around our wrists twice before being tied. Three shells, two loops.

"You're welcome. Everyone should have a little Nil bling." She smiled wider, then her expression turned serious. "But you look like you have something else on your mind than the bracelet. You walked up with serious purpose."

"I did." I paused, trying to sort out where to go without breaking my promise to Rives. "When I met Charley, she told me to find Rives, or Dex. Or you. You three were the ones she trusted most. Other than Thad," I added. It seemed like I couldn't mention Charley without Thad, and I didn't even know her. Or him.

Jillian nodded. "Thad was Leader before Rives. He was the second person I met here." She paused, like memories had pulled her away. "I trusted them both. They made a great team. It's what tells me he made it. He had to." She shook her head slightly, as if shaking out a mental image she couldn't bear to keep. Then she looked at me. "I trust Rives and Dex and a few others still here. I know you don't know me, but you can trust me, too, Skye. If something's worrying you, or you have a question, whatever we say stops here. Between us." She paused. "Not forcing you, but just know you can bounce anything off me you like."

I nodded, hating that I couldn't confide in Jillian. Friendships weren't easily made, not good ones anyway, and I felt like I was turning down Jillian's with my silence.

If Tish were here, I'd ask her what to do.

But she wasn't.

"And if you don't want to ask me, ask Rives," she added, misreading my hesitation for distrust. "You can trust him too."

You can trust him too.

Those five words made my decision clear. Rives was trustworthy in more eyes than mine, and I'd already given him my word. I'd trust that keeping the full details of my arrival gate a secret was the right call, at least for now.

Jillian was still watching me.

"Jillian," I said, "there *is* something I want to talk to you about, but give me a few days, okay?"

"No problem. Nil takes some adjustment." Her smile was warm, making me glad I'd given what little I could.

"Thanks." I watched Jillian smooth the wet pulp with her hands. "So Thad was Leader before Rives," I mused, fitting pieces of this Nil together. "How long has Rives been the Leader?"

"Did I hear my name?" Rives walked up, a slight curve to his lips. But his smile ended there; his eyes flicked between us, worried.

"Were your ears burning?" Jillian asked playfully.

"Not my ears. My sixth sense," Rives said.

Jillian rolled her eyes. "Don't flatter yourself." She grinned at me. "And Skye, don't flatter Rives. His head's big enough."

Rives clutched his chest. "I'm wounded, Jills. Really."

"No, you're not. And you know I love you. So what's up?"

"Just thought I'd crash your party," he said casually, his eyes drifting to me. His shoulders stayed tight. "Don't let me keep you two from finishing your conversation."

I studied him, fully aware he was pushing to know what we'd talked about.

"Skye was just telling me about Charley. I still can't believe they met. It's so surreal. But awesome." Jillian smiled. "She made it home, and now we know we can, too."

My eyes caught Rives's. I gave a slight shake of my head to say *I didn't tell.*

He relaxed, which irritated me.

222

You don't trust me? I thought, pressing my lips together to keep from saying something I'd regret. I almost wished I had told Jillian— almost but not quite, because if I *had* told Jillian, then Rives's trust in me would've been misplaced after all.

Which also irritated me, because I had no clue how long Rives expected me to bear its weight alone.

"Jillian, do you know where Dex is?" Rives asked, oblivious to my internal fuming. "I've got something I want you two to see. Skye too."

"Dex is filling gourds at the Cove," Jillian said. "Why?"

"Can you take a break?" he asked.

Jillian flicked her hand at the sheet of creamy pulp. "I may as well. This is as good as it's going to get." She sighed. "It's not nearly as smooth as Heesham's, but hey, whose is? At least Zane got it decently thin."

No one said anything else. We headed to the Crystal Cove, the silence strained, at least between me and Rives.

It was a relief to get to the Cove. Sure enough, Jillian was right. Dex had just finished filling empty gourds with water from the falls. They floated in the Cove, tethered to a string.

"Excellent timing!" Dex called when he saw us. He tossed us a wave and a grin. "I could use a hand bringing these back."

Jillian walked into the Cove, and when the water hit waist high, she eased into a smooth breaststroke, swimming toward Dex.

I grabbed Rives's arm and stepped close, grateful for the roar of the falls. "We've got to tell them about the stationary gate," I whispered, locking my eyes on his. "We can't keep it a secret forever. It's not right."

"Not forever," Rives said, his light eyes intense. "Just not yet."

"When?" My voice was sharp.

"Patience, padawan. When the moment is right." He grinned slightly. Infuriatingly. "Right now, a different secret waits."

He strode into the Cove without looking back.

This discussion is not over, I thought, annoyed.

I stepped into the Cove and sucked in a shocked breath. I'd expected the water to be warm, probably because crystal-clear water swirling in a private cove lined with glittering black rocks screamed paradise, and paradise should include a warm pool. But the Cove's water was *freezing*. It would've been nice if Uncle Scott had mentioned the icy water temperature when he'd described the Cove.

I wondered what else his journal left out.

By the falls, Rives spoke in Dex's ear. Dex nodded, looped the string of gourds to a hitch on the rock, and disappeared under the falls. Jillian followed. I stood there, feeling the arctic water bite my calves as I gathered the strength to go in.

Rives turned back to me, raised one eyebrow, and mouthed, "You coming?"

Without waiting, he dove under the falls too.

I sighed, rubbing my triceps. *Time to freeze.*

A hesitant voice behind me said, "Skye?"

I turned around and found myself five feet from Paulo. He looked worse than I remembered. Thin, with shadows under his eyes and cheekbones, all signs of poor eating and even poorer sleeping.

"Paulo?" I walked out of the pool. Paulo backtracked in sync, keeping the distance between us the same. "Did you follow me?"

He ignored my question. "Have you seen Maaka?" he asked.

"Maaka?" I asked, my eyes hard on Paulo's. "The boy who wanted you to 'deal with me'?" I made air quotes around the last few words.

Paulo swallowed hard.

"No." I softened my tone, unwilling to make him feel worse than he already looked. "I haven't seen Maaka. Why?"

"I think he's avoiding me," Paulo admitted.

"I doubt it. Maybe you just haven't run into him."

Paulo shook his head. "Maaka only shows himself when he wants to be seen. Which means he doesn't want to be seen by me."

I studied his posture, his fidgeting hands. The fact that he was *here.*

"You can join the City, you know," I said softly. "We've got plenty of food, and shelter. Decent beds. Even pillows." I thought of Archie and winced.

Paulo shook his head. "I came to tell you something. There's a leopard, a big one. It's prowling around the huts over there." He pointed toward the City. "This morning, it grabbed a boy in the flowers. I saw it."

"So did I. I mean, I saw the boy, not the cat."

Paulo didn't look surprised, which said he'd seen *me*. "Now that the cat has a taste for human flesh," he said, "you're in more danger. It will keep killing. You need to be careful."

"Thanks." It took all I had not to shudder. Then I looked at Paulo, trying to reconcile this helpful Paulo with the one I'd first met. "Why are you telling me this?"

"You deserve to know." He paused. "We're even now."

"Even?" I frowned.

He nodded. "You gave me fruit. On my first day here. Now we're even."

All I could think was *I never told him about the rhino.*

"Thanks, Paulo, but the guava was a gift, freely given. No expectations." I was parroting Macy's words, and they felt right. So did telling Paulo about the rest of Nil, because my instincts told me he was less prepared than me, which was crazier than Nil itself. "You should know there's a black rhino on the island. Rhinos have terrible eyesight, so if you get too close, climb a tree. And there are hippos by the mudflats, so steer clear of them; they can be really dangerous and they charge—"

Paulo was backing away now, hands in the air, eyes wide. "Stop!" he said, stumbling but not slowing. "No more!"

He broke into a run.

I followed. "Paulo, use your brain! Listen to me! The more you know, the safer you'll be! And stay away from the meadow!"

At the mention of the meadow, he spun around, his eyes narrowing. "What do you know of the meadow?"

"I know a tiger lives there, and he's scary. And apparently a pair of lions and a hyena. And possibly a giraffe." I hadn't seen one, but I hadn't ruled it out, either. "They have a wicked kick," I added.

He sighed; his flash of fight was gone. "I can't give you what you want."

"I'm not asking for anything," I said.

"Yes, you are," he said bluntly. "And you know it."

"Maybe I am," I admitted. I stepped closer. "How will you leave the island, Paulo, and when? Where's the gate that will take you home? The gate that can take us all home? Don't I deserve to know about that gate too?"

"Skye?" Rives's strong voice boomed through the trees.

Paulo snapped back around and took off running.

"Crap," I said, resting my hands on my hips. I didn't bother to follow. I'd lost the moment. Rives had seen to that.

You pushed too hard, my conscience scolded.

I circled around, ripping a leaf off a tree in frustration, and came face-to-face with the furious sea god from the ocean I'd met yesterday on the beach.

"Where'd you go?" Rives asked, his voice hard, his eyes unreadable. "We're all waiting for you while you're out here gathering leaves. Rude much?"

"Not really," I snapped. "Sorry to keep you waiting, but I was talking to Paulo. About the stationary gate, which is a conversation Dex and Jillian would be on board with *if you would let me tell them about the darn gate.* And he was just about to answer when you came crashing through the trees like a bull in a china shop. And he ran off. So thank you." I crossed my arms.

"I barely made a noise"—Rives's light eyes sparked—"except for your name."

"Well, since you couldn't sense Paulo, your sixth sense sure could use some work. Same for your stealth."

Rives fought a smile. "Sorry." He looked in the direction that Paulo had fled. "What did he want?"

"To tell me about a leopard. It's what killed Archie, and apparently it's staked the City as its territory."

"And why would he tell you this?"

"Because he felt like he owed me. I gave him fruit on his Day One."

Rives nodded slowly, like he understood. "Did he say anything else?"

"He said that he thinks Maaka is avoiding him. That Maaka only appears when he wants to be seen, and Paulo hasn't seen him." I paused. "I think Paulo followed me and is hanging out near the City. Which means, hopefully, I'll have the chance to talk to him again." I couldn't bring myself to glare at Rives, because I had the sneaky suspicion I'd blown it with Paulo all by myself. I'd pressed and pushed, not my usual style at all.

Was this island changing me already, and not for the better?

Please give me another chance with Paulo. I'll take it slow; I'll be patient. Because it's not about me—it's about everyone.

I hoped whoever needed to hear me was listening. The thought that I'd blown my only chance with Paulo made me feel awful.

Rives gently tipped up my chin, his green eyes intense. "Skye?" A tingle ran down my jaw. Rives's fingers were still Cove cold. "What else did he say?"

"Nothing," I managed. Rives was so *close*, so overwhelming; he filled the space around me with his presence . . . and he was touching me, so softly I barely felt it—but I was wholly aware of it; his thumb brushed the same place I'd wiped the blood off earlier.

Paulo, Rives was asking, but all my mind could whisper was *Rives*.

Rives dropped his hand as if he'd been burned, and I stepped back.

I let go of the torn leaf I'd been holding and brushed my hands on my skirt, getting back to business.

"Now," I said calmly, retying the twine around my hair to give my shaking hands somewhere to go, "don't you have a secret to show me?"

CHAPTER
37

The four of us stood inside the Looking Glass cavern. I was the only one not staring at the carvings.

I stared at Skye.

I still felt the blistering touch of her skin on my fingers. I'd tipped up her chin to make her focus on me, to make her spill the secrets she was hiding.

I'd screwed up big-time.

Skye's skin had felt electric. Powerful. Like Nil's lava flowed through her veins, fiery and dangerous.

I wouldn't touch her again. No more Nil scars for me.

I looked away, aware I was staring.

Nil's playing games, I realized. *Using people as pawns.* Maybe Skye hadn't gotten the jump on Nil after all, maybe Skye was part of Nil's plan.

Maybe Skye was tapped to mess with me.

How freaking conceited can you get, Rives? I thought abruptly, totally disgusted with myself. Not to mention Skye had backed away from me like I was the last person she'd want to touch her. Jillian was right. My head was too big. I needed to take myself down a peg, or ten.

Ten.

"Rives?" Jillian's voice. She was staring at me. I wondered how long she'd been watching.

"Yeah?"

"What are you thinking about?"

"Ten." I cleared my throat. "The number ten. It's the sum of the numbers"—I pointed to the numerical sequence 3-2-1-4 at the top of the wall—"here and on the Countdown carving." Dex and Skye had turned toward me to listen.

"Some people consider ten the perfect number," I continued. "People use ten as the standard of scoring in sports like surfing or gymnastics—because ten represents perfection. You never hear 'she's a perfect nine,' right?" As Jillian rolled her eyes, I grinned. "Pythagoras—or maybe Plato, my Greek's getting a little rusty here—believed the number ten was the most powerful and most sacred number, symbolizing the totality of the universe. And for the ancient Mayans, it represented the end of one cycle and the start of another. Birth and death."

"That sounds like something Macy would say," Jillian said.

"It was. At least the Mayan part."

"Let's hope Macy got the death part wrong, shall we?" Dex said. He stared at the carvings as he spoke. "But she was spot-on about one thing: We all arrive naked as a babe, popped out from a gate." He shuddered. "Nasty visual, that."

"Has she seen this place?" Jillian asked. "Macy?"

I nodded. "I brought her down here last week."

"I bet she loved it," Jillian said, glancing around the cavern.

"She did." I remembered how Macy ran her hands over the carvings, smiling, talking, absorbing all the cavern had to offer, and closing her eyes in the light streaming in with the falls. She'd felt the peace of this place, like me.

I studied the number sequence on the wall, the same sequence found on the Countdown carving, the same sequence Maaka had explained this morning. Picturing the Countdown carving, I thought of the number twelve at the top.

Twelve noon, twelve midnight. One number, with more than one meaning.

What else did the sequence 3-2-1-4 represent?

Maaka knew more than he was telling, that was for damn sure. Because Maaka coughed up his information one painful piece at a time, and sometimes what he didn't say was the most important. Like the fact that somewhere on Nil a fixed gate waited to take him home.

To take us *all* home, if Skye was right.

I hoped she was right.

What else did she know that she wasn't telling me?

I glanced at Skye. She was studying the wall, too, arms crossed but relaxed, head tilted slightly to the right. The only thing at odds with her chill demeanor was her hair. She'd lost the twine she'd tied around it earlier. Half-dry, wild curls flew in all directions and fell down her back, knotted and snarled after a few days on Nil. Somehow I sensed its wildness drove her crazy. Something she couldn't control.

"All right then." Jillian cleared her throat. I turned back to look at her, wondering why the hell I cared abut Skye's hair.

The cavern, I thought. *The belly of the beast,* Johan had said. *The belly of Nil.* And I stood right in it.

With a hard string of silent French expletives, I drove Nil out of my head.

"Why are we here again?" Jillian asked, her eyebrows raised.

"That's the million-euro question, isn't it?" Dex murmured, his eyes still glued to the wall.

"We're here," I said, "*in this cavern,* because I wanted to see if the three of you had seen any carvings like these anywhere on the island, or in Skye's case, in her uncle's journal. Johan feels this place is old and powerful. I agree. These carvings are clues. Maybe they can tell us something to help get us home."

"Let me guess. Johan stayed for all of five minutes, freaked out, crossed himself, and vowed never to return." Jillian snorted.

"Pretty much. Except for the vow part. He didn't stay long enough to make a vow."

"You know what I see?" Dex jerked a thumb toward the cavern wall. "An awful lot of bloody cats. Sure, you've got moons and stars, properly done, and a creepy sun with an eyeball at the center, but bloody hell—have you ever seen so many cats?" He pointed to the letters *N-I-L* running north. "I think we got the name wrong. It should be called Cat Island, or Leopard Land."

"My uncle called it Giraffe Land," Skye said. They were the first words she'd spoken in the cavern. She smiled at Dex. "It was the first animal he saw."

"Better a giraffe than a leopard," Dex said. He pointed at the base of the wall, where two mangoes sat, untouched. "What's with the mangoes? Snacks for later?"

"Something like that," I said. I'd left them for Maaka. A peace offering perhaps, but he never took them. Now I knew why: He'd owe me.

I wished he'd taken one.

I turned to Skye. "Did your uncle mention this place? Or any carvings? Anything that might be important to getting off Nil?" *Anything related to the stationary gate?* my eyes said.

A flash of frustration flicked across Skye's face like she read my mind, then just as swiftly, her expression melted into Skye calm. She took a long moment to think. "No. He didn't. He didn't mention carvings at all."

Disappointed, I nodded. My eyes never left Skye. Her expression told me she wasn't lying, but she wasn't telling the full truth, either. There was more to the journal than she was telling.

Sick of secrets, I turned to Dex and Jillian. "There's something I need to tell you. Something important. But not here." *Not in the belly of the beast.* I turned to Skye. "Can you swim?"

"Can I swim?" She looked surprised. "Sure. I'm no medal contender, but I'm not going to drown."

Her words sliced like ice. Talla had been training for the Olympics when she landed on Nil. Damn this place.

I looked away, unwilling to meet anyone's eyes. "Good." My voice sounded flat. Businesslike. "We're going to go out a different way. That way." I pointed at the pool; the surface near me was as smooth as glass, letting the rocks show from below. The fastest way to leave was through the water Talla loved so much.

Got it, Nil. Irony not lost, and sure as hell not funny.

Skye was staring at the pool with an odd expression.

"Stick together," I said crisply. "No straying off." This last comment made Skye's chin tilt up.

Good, I thought, avoiding her eyes. *Keep your edge. And be a team player.* Nil was not the place to be a one-person show. The finale was usually death.

It was time to take my own advice.

"Want to take the mangoes?" Dex asked.

I shook my head. "Leave them. Let's go." I dove into the pool, pausing underwater only long enough to make sure all three followed.

Twenty minutes later, the four of us lounged on the sand. On White Beach, just north of the City, the same beach where I'd met Skye.

Full circle, I thought. Dex and Jillian would hear of the stationary gate on the same Nil ground I did. It felt *right.*

"Dex, Jillian, there's some stuff you need to know," I said. "That everyone needs to know, but I'm starting with you two, because I trust your judgment and need your advice. Some news is Skye's, some's mine. But you need to hear it all."

With Skye's help, I detailed her arrival through the stationary gate and the conversation she'd overheard between Maaka and Paulo. Then I outlined all my interactions with Maaka, his silent admission to the gate's existence, or at least a lack of denial, and finally, Skye's recent run-in with Paulo.

"Do you have anything to add?" I asked Skye.

She shook her head.

"You sure?" I held her gaze, willing her to give up something.

Her cheeks flushed. I pushed away the visual that they'd flushed when I tipped up her chin, too.

"I'm sure," she said.

"Fine." I looked at Dex and Jillian, who were looking between Skye and me with curiosity.

"All right, then," Dex said. "So we've got a gate that pops at midnight and stands there politely waiting for people and chickens and goats to join the party—"

"And cats," Jillian offered helpfully, biting her lip to contain a smile.

"Right. And cats." Dex shot her a murderous look, making Jillian laugh and forcing a grin from Dex as he turned back to me. "And we've got a pair of inked islanders who packed living snacks and are all secrety-secret about everything and who came here *on bloody purpose*, which is simply mad."

He glanced at Skye sheepishly. "No offense, Skye."

"None taken." She smiled.

Jillian frowned at me. "When are you going to tell everyone, Rives? People deserve to know."

"They do," I said. "But right now the Search system is working, and thanks to Charley, it's working better than ever. I think before we ditch it, we need more info about that gate. Like does this stationary gate come every night? Once a week? Once a month? On a full moon?"

I glanced at Skye. "Was it a full moon that night?"

She looked thoughtful. "I don't think so."

I took that as a no.

"But," she continued, looking at Dex, "there were an awful lot of cats on that Death Twin island, the one that held the stationary gate. I saw at least three, and the island was small."

"Back to the gate," I said, annoyed we were discussing cats and not the gate that could potentially get us all off this rock, "is there a limit to how many people it can take? How long does it stay open? And where exactly does it appear?"

"I don't have answers to any of these questions," Skye said, "but I remember Paulo counting. He sent the goat through, counted to three, then sent the chicken, then after counting again, he went. So I don't think there's a limit, but two things can't go through together. They have to wait."

A limitation, I thought. A twist on the one-gate, one-person rule that we took as a given.

"Anything else you remember?" I kept my tone neutral, even though part of me wanted to snap. Skye doled out info like Maaka: bit by painful bit.

She thought quietly. "Not really. Just that Paulo said he couldn't leave yet—this was on the first day I'd met him—which makes me think that gates don't come every night, or even every week. The way he said it made me think he has to wait for a gate, like us."

Not like us, I thought. *Not like us at all.*

"What if the limit is four?" Jillian asked, frowning. "The limit of how many people that stationary gate can take? Like maybe that's what the four represents?"

"You forgot the cat," Dex said drolly. "Five came through Skye's gate."

"Oh my God, I did," Jillian said. She punched Dex's shoulder lightly. "How could I forget the cat?" She smiled, then squeezed his hand. A long squeeze, almost a hold.

Judging by the slight smile on Dex's face, he didn't mind.

I returned my head to the gate.

"So a big question is, how long does the gate stay open?" I glanced at Skye.

"The only ones who know are Paulo and Maaka," Skye said quietly. Thoughtfully. "We need to know what they know."

"Ya think?" I asked blandly. "If you recall, that was my plan from day one."

"Actually, it was my Day Three," Skye said in the same bland tone. "But in the meantime, I still think we should take a trip to hunt for that gate. To see what we find."

"No," I said. "It's too big a risk. Not until we are sure the City's safe for one, and for two, not until we know exactly where we're going."

"Fine," Skye said, her cool slipping. "You're the Leader."

The Leader. Not *our* Leader.

It wasn't until we'd started walking back that it occurred to me that she hadn't put her name on the Wall.

CHAPTER 38

SKYE
DAY 4, MID-AFTERNOON

Rives kept his distance from me as we walked. He didn't look at me, didn't speak.

I couldn't tell if he was ignoring me or just couldn't fit a word in around Dex and Jillian, who peppered me with questions about the stationary gate, Paulo, and my dad's island vision quest. I wondered if Rives had adopted my new "listen first" plan, too.

But the growing gulf between Rives and me changed my plan. The thickness between us refused to be ignored.

Just before we rounded the bend to the Cove, I pulled Rives aside. His skin was no longer Cove-cold, but my fingers tingled where I grabbed his forearm. He stiffened, his eyes darting to my hand on his arm.

I snatched my fingers away.

"Are you upset with me?" I asked. "Did I say something?"

Rives exhaled slowly, his eyes finding mine. "You didn't say anything, Skye. Not a thing." He looked at me, in that intense way I was coming to identify with Rives—like there was no one else on the island. Just me and him. "But I wished you had," he said quietly.

"What does that mean?" I frowned.

"I mean, this place is hard enough without us keeping secrets from each other. You came here knowing more about Nil than anyone, with an inside scoop no one else got. And still, you hold back. I'll bet there was more to your convo with Paulo, just like I'll bet there's more to your uncle's journal than you're telling."

I bristled. "You think I'm hiding secrets? *I'm* the one who found *you. I'm* the one who told you about Paulo and the stationary gate. *I'm* the one who told you about my uncle and Charley and my dad. And *I'm* the one who wanted to tell everyone about the stationary gate from the start. But no." I poked a finger at Rives's chest. "*You're* the one who wanted to wait. *You're* the one who's been keeping quiet about all your chit-chats with Maaka. If someone's hiding something, it's *you*. Not me."

I crossed my arms and stared at Rives.

A hint of a smile crossed his face, then a wall came slamming down. Invisible. Impenetrable.

"What you see is what you get," Rives said flatly.

"If you say so," I said. "But I say you're the one holding back." My eyes held his. "I just don't know why."

"Everything okay?" Jillian called.

"Fine." Rives's voice was clipped.

We walked in silence.

He stopped, turning toward me. "I owe you an apology." His voice was stiff.

"For what?"

"This morning. When I asked you to stay back. Later I realized you had your sling prepped and ready. Like you could take care of yourself. I was being an ass. I'm sorry."

Stuck behind his polite wall, Rives's apology felt strained. Still, it was an apology nonetheless, although I still didn't understand why he'd gotten so angry.

Then it hit me: worry.

An emotion as powerful as anger, and one that could manifest in the same way. People only worried when they felt a sense of responsibility—or when they felt things spiraling out of control.

Rives was watching me as I studied him, waiting for my response.

"Apology accepted," I said, my eyes on his. I almost reached out to touch his check, to see if the island had turned him to stone when I wasn't looking, or maybe I just wanted to brush off the invisible weight making him tense and say *it's okay*, but I didn't. The barrier between us was too thick; I couldn't breach it. Instead, I added, "I was fine. But—being Leader doesn't mean you have to protect everyone."

"Doesn't it?" he shot back, his wall slipping. Fury and frustration and hurt peeked through. "How would you know, Skye? You just got here."

I wanted to shake him out of this weird funk and into himself. I'd known him all of two days, but Rives was clearly split between roles; Leader, friend, and who knew what else, giving so much of himself, little was left. One person can only take on so much before he breaks.

Is that how my uncle became fearless? To survive Nil and its burdens?

I didn't dare touch Rives. He was wound so tight I feared he'd splinter.

"You're right," I said quietly. Rives's fists stayed clenched, ready to fight an invisible enemy. "I did just get here. But like you said, I got a prep course. A personal one. My uncle was Leader, too. So while I don't know much about your Nil, I know this: Being Leader here is an honor and a burden. It isn't easy, because people always have choices, even if you don't agree with them." My voice stayed calm. "But you don't have to let being Leader consume you. You don't have to lose *you*. Doesn't that make sense?"

Rives stared at me with an unfathomable expression.

"Rives!" Jason's shout broke the moment. Rives took in a deep breath and spun around.

Jason was jogging toward us from the Cove, his curly hair bouncing like crazy. "We've been looking for you!"

"You found me." Rives grinned at Jason. No weird wall existed between those two. "What's up? Good news?"

"The best," Jason said, smiling wider. "Johan caught a gate. On South Beach. Ahmad said a single flashed and Johan had to run for it, but he made it." Jason beamed. "He's gone, with a few days to spare."

Jillian flew into Dex's arms with a shout; Dex smiled and hugged her tight. Rives dropped his hands onto his thighs and lowered his head, exhaling deeply like a massive weight had been lifted off his chest. When he raised his head, his eyes glistened with water, and it wasn't from the Cove's spray.

"Skye," he said, his voice choked. "Maybe I can't save everyone, but I can't stop trying."

Rives's pain was as raw and visceral as Charley's, and just as terrible to watch. Even departures moved our fierce Leader to tears. It made me wonder how long Rives had been here. I'd guessed months but I'd never asked, and now was not the time. Rives didn't need a reminder; he needed reassurance.

"We need to find that gate," I said softly.

"What gate?" Jason asked.

CHAPTER 39

RIVES
DAY 280, LATE AFTERNOON

Skye opened her mouth but said nothing. Her eyes slid to me.

What do I say? her turquoise eyes asked. I'd never seen Skye hesitant. And her hesitation was because of me. She was torn between keeping my secret and answering Jason's question, an awkward position I'd stuck her in for too long.

"I've got this one," I told her quietly.

Relief flooded her face, making her smile. Making me relax. Finally I did something right.

With Jason's question as a cue, I filled him in on Skye's stationary inbound and the two island loners. He listened with wide eyes, taking it all in, saying nothing until I finished.

"Do you think the loners are the raiders?" he asked.

I shook my head. "No. They don't want anything from us," I said, thinking of the mangoes. "Not our food, not our help. But we need theirs. Their help, anyway. We need the island info they're hiding."

Jason nodded. "So what's the plan?"

"Search as usual, find Maaka and Paulo, then find the gate. I don't think we can find it without them. Skye wouldn't have found hers without Paulo."

"That's crazy," Jason said. "And a little badass." He looked at Skye with newfound appreciation; she was too busy talking to Jillian to notice. "She just walked into that gate, following some kid she didn't know, hoping it would take her here? And who wants to come here?" Jason shook his head.

Maaka and Paulo, I thought. But I said, "Skye."

Jason was staring at her. "You know who she reminds me of? T—"

"Don't," I said sharply. "Just don't."

Jason reddened like he'd been burned. "Sorry."

"Me too." I sighed. I put one arm around his shoulders. To my surprise, Jason had gained a few centimeters lately. He still had a way to go before catching me, but he was definitely in range. And his voice hadn't cracked all day.

"C'mon, bro," I said. "Let's head back. And raise a toast to Johan."

I knew something was off the instant we stepped into camp.

Michael, Cho, Uri, and Leila stood by the cold firepit. Nothing roasting, nothing cooking. A dead fire and I couldn't remember who was responsible for restocking it, and the foursome around it didn't seem to notice. Or care.

They stood tight, talking in low tones I couldn't hear. The four turned as one when I said, "Hey."

Michael nodded and broke from the group. He strode straight toward me.

"Archie got attacked by the leopard," Michael said. "Cho saw the cat with"—Michael paused, like he was rethinking his words—"part of the kill. It was Archie. We know."

I nodded. I knew, too. But I said nothing, because I sensed Michael wasn't done.

"Rives, the traps we set? They are not working," he said flatly. "The City is cat hunting ground now. It is not safe." Regret filled his eyes. "We choose to leave," he said softly. "We will test our fate elsewhere.

All we want to bring is a water gourd, the knife I made, and the clothes we wear."

His eyes asked for permission, a gift I felt unworthy to give.

"Take it." I glanced at his bare feet. "Sandals too. And food." I offered my hand. Michael shook it, square jaw tight.

"You are a good Leader, Rives," he said quietly. "It is not you."

It is me, I thought. *I can't keep us safe or together.*

But right now it wasn't about me; it was about Michael, a kid who just wanted a better shot than the one I offered.

"Where will you go?" I asked.

"Tonight we will camp in the cave. The one with the carvings, behind the waterfall," Michael said. "Then we will head to the North Shore. Nothing likes the North Shore."

"True," I agreed. The North Shore screamed island defense. Incoming waves spit high against a harsh black rock wall. Where there was no wall, there were rocks. No animals. No sand.

No room to run.

Then I thought: *Michael knows about the Looking Glass cavern.*

What else does everyone know that I don't? My grasp of City knowledge and City politics slipped farther down the *he's-got-his-shit-together* list. Maybe I hadn't broken my rules, but I sure hadn't followed them.

Look around.

Pay attention.

I hadn't seen this City fracture coming.

Abruptly I thought of Maaka, who never joined the City in the first place. I wondered what Maaka would think when he found squatters in his sacred cavern.

The idea made me smile.

Anything that made Maaka uncomfortable was a good thing, and I needed something good to counter how much I sucked as Leader. I couldn't hold the City together at the first sign of danger.

Michael's feet shifted; he was clearly ready to go.

Regrouping, I gently grasped Michael on the shoulder. "One last thing. Don't bring fire into the cave. It's sacred ground. I know it'll be dark in there, but no fire."

Michael nodded. "No fire. And it is dark everywhere here, my friend."

"True enough." I dropped my hand. "I wish you well, Michael. Get home safe."

He nodded, his face fiercely calm as he shook my hand. "You too, Rives."

I nodded at Leila, who was watching from a few meters away. I'd never really had a conversation with her. "Good luck, Leila," I said.

"Thanks." No handshake, no smile. Just a clear desire to leave.

Same for Cho and Uri.

Sy came up and stuck out his hand. It trembled like he was cold. "Rives. I'm taking off, too."

"Seriously?" Sy was far from a risk-taker, and betting that Nil outside the City was safer than inside was a massive risk.

He nodded. "I can't stay here another night. I'm going to take my chances out there with Cho. And Michael," he added.

I glanced at Cho, who remained expressionless. All I knew about him was that he had a firm commitment to self-preservation that trumped his commitment to the City. Uri faced away, already mentally gone. Sy had never chosen allies well.

"Good luck, Sy. You know we're here if you want to come back."

His head wobbled. "I know."

Still gripping his hand, I lowered my voice. "Stick with Michael. I trust him."

"Thanks." Sy pumped my hand like it might give him winning island mojo.

"Good luck," I repeated. It took all I had not to add *you'll need it*.

As the group walked away, Dex clapped me on the shoulder, his voice low. "You can't save everyone, mate."

"Maybe not," I said.

But I can damn sure try.

I glanced around, wondering if Maaka was watching the City split. Kiera's eyes were on me. My eyes caught hers. She smiled and mouthed, *Let them go,* in French.

As if I could make them stay.

Ahmad stood to her right, his eyes on Sy's back. Skye stood behind me; I sensed her.

No sign of Maaka at all.

I didn't sense him, either. The last time I'd sensed Maaka watching when he didn't show was the night he'd dropped the carved moon.

A gift he'd given.

A gift I'd taken.

I stiffened, struck by an unpleasant thought. *Did I owe Maaka now? What does he want?*

My fists clenched reflexively.

"What's wrong?" Skye gently tapped my right fist with one finger. Like she'd hit a nerve, I released my hands.

"Do you really need to ask?" My laugh was sharp.

She gave me a long look, one that said *yes.* It was moments like these when I wondered exactly how much Skye saw. My gut said *too much.*

"I'm sorry they're leaving," she said finally, as if she'd settled on this as the most likely reason for my worry. Her eyes flicked to Sy's retreating back. "But it's not your fault. This island is bigger than all of us." She paused. "And you're a good Leader."

"Seriously?" I laughed again. I wanted to punch something, like Nil. "Did you see what just happened? A good Leader would've kept the City together. A good Leader would've changed Michael's mind."

"Really?" Skye asked, her eyes searching mine. "I told you earlier, free choice. If Michael doesn't want to be here, it's no fault of yours. Pressuring him to stay makes no sense." She pursed her lips. "Nil doesn't come with a guidebook; it doesn't come with rules and a plan. We're all just doing our best. Same for you. You don't have to be a savior."

I looked at her. "Because that's your job, right?" My voice sounded bitter and I hated it. "You had a guidebook. You came to save everyone."

The hurt in her eyes made me wish I could take it back.

"Not a guidebook." Skye's voice was quiet. "More like a peek into my uncle's head. It was addictive and terrible. And I know I'm not a savior." She looked at me, the flecks in her eyes hardening. Because of me. "None of us are," she said.

"None of us are what?" I asked.

She frowned. "A savior. I don't think it works like that. I don't think one person can do it alone. I think if we're going to leave, it has to be a group effort."

I looked away, because looking at Skye hurt, deeply, for reasons I couldn't explain and didn't want to. And I knew I'd been an ass. Again.

"I hope you're right."

Skye nodded. She looked like she wanted to say something, but she didn't. Then she walked away.

I almost asked for her to come back. Part of me desperately wanted her to turn around, to talk about Nil and island secrets and strategies, because despite her rookie status, Skye got Nil better than anyone I'd ever met. But part of me rebelled, the same part begging me not to play with fire. The part that told me I'd pushed her away on purpose.

I let her go.

I turned away, and the driftwood moon shifted against my chest. A subtle reminder of a debt unpaid.

What does Maaka want?

That disturbing thought clung like a Nil shadow, ratcheting up the mental chaos already in full churn.

I focused on Maaka because it was easier than thinking of

Skye. I didn't know how to get Skye out of my head, or how she'd snuck in so deeply when I wasn't paying attention. But Maaka was my link to the mythical gate, our one shot at an islandwide exit. And I couldn't shake the sense that he wanted something from me, too.

I thought of it on watch, I thought of it while I killed myself with sprints. I thought of it while trying to sleep, which right now was a total Nil joke. Sleep these days was not happening, unless I channeled Dex and napped on the sand in daylight, which was actually going better than expected.

Time passed.

Days passed. One, then two, and another after that.

Today was day number five.

Five days since Michael and crew bolted from camp. Five days since Archie's death, five days of uneasy peace. Five nights of expectant nothing. Five days of no gates, five days of no Maaka, five days of wondering what he wanted from me. Five days of dodging Skye and seeing her everywhere.

I was more wired and exhausted than ever.

Done with today's sprints, I dribbled a crosshatched ball up and down the beach, one of the ones Li had woven, wondering how weak my football skills had become. I hadn't seen a pitch in months. I was used to breaks, but I'd never had a break this long. An extended break, with no end in sight. Maybe a permanent break.

What a shitty thought.

Out of my head, Nil.

When my control slipped, I slumped against the large black rocks by the water's edge, closed my eyes, and willed myself to relax. The ball tucked into the curve of my side like I was chilling on the pitch. The rocks were warm, like the afternoon sun. The feel of the ball slipped away, replaced by the weight of the crescent moon around my neck; it pressed hard on my chest, even though I wasn't wearing it.

Most people wanted something from me. I got it. I was Leader, a position that came loaded with obligations and expectations. But did Maaka want something from Rives, the Leader, or just me, Rives? I could barely separate the two anymore. Lately I hadn't bothered to try.

If Maaka's gift came with strings, I couldn't see them.

My time was the only thing he'd taken, and my gut said it was the only thing he'd accept. Valuable, no doubt, but he'd never shown himself to me at noon, a fact that suggested he valued my time, too—maybe even my life.

It said nothing about Maaka's time, because he had a midnight escape hatch; Maaka didn't thirst for noons like we did.

So what does he want?

Opening my eyes, I saw only Nil sky.

Skye.

Should I ask her? Get her take on Maaka? I considered it. She knew Paulo, and he was a solid link to Maaka.

No, I thought firmly.

Coward, the sea crooned.

My lids grew heavy under the lull of the sea. Try as I might, I couldn't remember the timbre of Talla's voice, just her fierceness and her goodness. Pictures of her rolled through my head, crashing with the waves, bittersweet. For the first time in months, I didn't block the memories, or the regrets. I let them crash in, all of them, until there were none left to fight. And then I let them go.

My thought as I fell asleep was that while I heard the sea, my last vision was of the sky.

CHAPTER
40

I woke before the other girls, slowly opening my eyes to cool Nil air. Light brushed the edges of the sky, just enough to soften the dark. Dawn was close. Curled under my creepy cheetah pelt, I was cozy warm. I didn't want to move. For a long moment, I listened to the ocean, reveling in the peace of the morning. Like Uncle Scott, I'd quickly found that dawn was my favorite time of day on Nil. Its peace was fleeting, vanishing with the rising sun, so I never took the moment I woke for granted.

Movement caught my eye.

Tilting my head, I had a clear view of the firepit. Rives paced like a caged animal in the dark, his face cut in hard lines of worry, like the first day I'd seen him—but worse.

Much, much worse.

He'd taken Sy's departure personally, and Michael's, and if I was right, the whole darn group. Since that moment, something had changed. He'd lost his easygoing edge. A rather frightening intensity had taken its place. Not that Rives was ever sharp or impatient; if anything, it was the polar opposite. It was as if he was determined to single-handedly lighten everyone else's burden by taking on more himself. He stoked the pit, hauled wood, and brought back fish, keeping his conversations pleasant but short, talking just long enough to reassure someone or help out before he was off to the next task, and the entire time his shoulders stayed tight, on full alert.

You'd think with days like that, he'd sleep well, but from what I'd seen, Rives barely slept at all. He'd taken watch every night, and twice I'd caught him dozing on the beach. His days and nights were flip-flopping fast, but the ratio stayed off. The circles beneath Rives's eyes grew.

How long could someone go without sleep?

If Rives's mind was on the predator and City defense, mine was on the stationary gate. But now the two were linked; I felt it. I'd asked Rives about his plan to search for the stationary gate. His answer had come without hesitation, his tone cool and unwavering.

Not yet, he'd told me. *When the time is right.*

All he'd forgotten to add was the *patience, padawan*. But the teasing Rives was gone.

I felt powerless—to help Rives, to help the City. And weirdly enough, I knew that to help the City, I had to help Rives first. Letting him self-destruct could not happen, and yet he'd erected a wall around himself I couldn't breach. Time was slipping away, and it wasn't a good feeling.

The peace of dawn was lost, and it hadn't even arrived yet.

Rives was still pacing.

I reluctantly pushed back my covers and reached for my rock sling. It sat curled beside my pillow, at the edge of my bed close to the open-air sides. Before my hand touched it, I stilled.

Sitting on top of my sling was a braided piece of twine. Dangling from it was a tiny grayed moon, carved from driftwood, delicate and worn. A bracelet, left for me. Kind but disturbing, because it meant *someone stalked me while I was sleeping and I didn't even notice.*

I breathed deeply, fighting a freak-out.

If they wanted to hurt you, they could've, I told myself. *Instead they left you a gift, going out of their way not to be seen.*

Paulo, I thought.

It had to be, and by leaving the bracelet at night, he'd avoided any chance of me asking him more questions or giving him more information.

A gift and a message, both in one.

Now we're even.

And it also meant he was close. Which meant I had a chance of finding him if I could just figure out where to look. I stared at the mysterious bracelet, debating whether to wear it or leave it alone, then slipped it on next to the tri-shell bracelet from Jillian and Macy. I studied the moon charm, taking in its smooth lines, turning it over to find a small pit in the wood on the backside, a dent I could touch. An imperfection, a flaw.

A clear mental picture blossomed in my brain—another small moon, equally imperfect.

The same crescent moon had been doodled in the margins of my uncle's journal.

I closed my eyes, mentally sifting through the journal, searching for the entry marked with a crescent moon and wondering what I'd missed. Wondering what clues Uncle Scott had left that I didn't understand Nil well enough to see.

It was Entry #17.

I remembered it verbatim.

Day 201 in my tropical freakfest vacay. That day stands out for two reasons. It stands out because of two people.

I woke early. The only other person up was Rika. She'd shown up yesterday, but she was on the fence about sticking around. I'd seen enough rookies to know.

I'd asked her the night before if she wanted to

carve her name. She'd shaken her head. "Tomorrow, perhaps."

Now she'd been sitting in front of the Wall of Names for the last twenty minutes, Indian-style, like she was silently singing the Clash song "Should I Stay or Should I Go." Only she didn't look like a Clash groupie. She looked more like my island angel's cousin. Dark hair, big eyes. Distant air. She didn't move, even when I knelt beside her.

"You okay, Rika?"

"Scott." She said my name with precision. "You do much. You lead well. You save many." She turned to me. "Let me see your eyes."

"What?" I asked, not following.

She didn't answer. She grabbed my hands and stared at me, pinning me with a fierce glance that shot through my bones with a creepy chill, which said something, because the island hadn't shaken me in weeks.

"Your destiny," she said softly, like some crazy-ass island tarot card reader. "It wraps the island from beginning to end; I feel it. Don't you? So powerful." Now she looked shaken. She closed her eyes, her voice dropping to a guarded whisper. "Your time ends when the crescent moon rises over the heart of the island. Remember that."

Then she got up and walked away, heading out of the City. I watched her go, wondering what the hell she'd been talking about.

"Hey," I called. "Are you leaving?"

Rika turned around, looking worried. Looking desperate to get away. "Yes. But like you, my journey does not end here. My end stretches beyond, I have seen it."

With absolutely nothing to say to that, I just waved. I wondered whether the island had driven her nuts, or whether she brought her own brand of crazy to Nil in the first place.

That night Rika's words weighed on me like bricks.

I stood alone on the beach, watching the sunset, looking for a crescent moon.

Jenny came up behind me.

"What's wrong?" she asked.

"Rika." I turned toward Jenny, struck again by how beautiful she was. Tangled brown hair, bright-blue eyes, charcoal smudged on her cheek. Rika vanished from my thoughts completely.

I reached up and gently wiped off the charcoal, letting my thumb linger.

"Rika?" Jenny whispered, her eyes on mine.

"I don't want to talk about Rika right now," I said. "I don't want to talk at all." Slowly, savoring every speck of air disappearing between us, I leaned in and kissed Jenny, drowning in the heat of the moment. That was our first kiss, but not our last.

I never saw Rika again.

But I looked for the crescent moon every night. The last time I saw it was the night before I left.

I opened my eyes, pulling myself out of Uncle Scott's Nil and into mine.

When the crescent moon rises over the heart of the island, he'd written. That was the clue, I knew it.

Where was the heart of the island?

Rives, I thought. *He'd know.*

Unfortunately, Rives was nowhere in sight. He'd been replaced by Zane, who was adding wood to the firepit. Sparks glittered with each addition.

"Morning, Zane," I said.

"Morning, Skye." Zane smiled. "You always an early riser?"

"Here for sure."

He nodded. "I get up back home for dawn patrol when the waves call. Here"—he shrugged—"I just get up. It's hard to sleep knowing something's out there." He thumbed toward the woods, where there was just enough light to differentiate the trunks and leaves. The island brightened with each passing minute, making it less scary.

Sort of.

"Do you know where Rives went?" I hoped my mellow tone hid the urgency I felt.

"He went to grab a board." Zane pointed at the Shack. "You might be able to catch him."

"Thanks." I smiled and took off, trying not to run.

As I neared the Shack, I heard voices coming from inside; I recognized Jillian's soft tone immediately. I slowed, listening for Rives.

"I saw you talking to Rives," Jillian said. At the mention of Rives, I froze. "How'd it go?"

"Not well," Dex replied. "He just stared at me with an *I'll-do-as-I-bloody-well-please* expression. I told him he wasn't doing anyone a bit of good by trying to do it all himself. But he won't hear it. He won't let anyone else take watch."

"He's running himself into the ground," Jillian said, clearly upset. "Sometimes I think he has a death wish. It's gotten worse since—"

"Rives?" Kiera called from behind me.

Jillian stopped talking immediately.

Since what? I wondered.

I turned, reluctantly revealing my presence outside the Shack.

"I think he's by the beach," I told Kiera. "But if he's sleeping, let him rest. He's been up every night."

Kiera looked at me, her gaze sharp. "How would you know?"

Because I'm up half the night watching him pace. Because I see the weight he carries during the day spilling into the night. Because I can't bear the thought of him breaking like my uncle.

"I just do," I said.

Kiera turned around without a word.

Jillian walked out of the Shack and watched Kiera stride away.

"I can't tell if that girl wants Rives to give her a pass to the front of the gate line or if she just wants Rives," she muttered. The she smiled at me. "Morning, Skye. What's up?"

I didn't want to admit I'd been looking for Rives too. Instead, I said, "Is Jason around? He said he'll teach me how to fly a glider today."

"He went to the fish traps. He won't be back for a while." She picked up a surfboard as she spoke. "Want to go out with me? This is the best time on the water. Less wind, and you haven't seen a Nil sunrise till you've seen one from the water."

I hesitated. I'd been honest when I'd told Rives I wasn't going to drown, but I didn't love the ocean, either. I preferred the safety of boats.

She cocked her head at me. "Skye?"

I sighed. "I think the ocean's gorgeous, but I don't love being *in* the ocean." I didn't want to admit that during our swim from the Cove's cavern I was the most frightened I'd been since I'd landed on Nil, almost worse than the tiger run-in. The fear definitely lasted longer— a claustrophobic fear as the water held me tight. "When I was seven, I got sucked out by a riptide," I admitted. "I almost drowned. Kinda stuck with me."

"Oh, you definitely need this, then," she said, nodding. "Grab that board"—she pointed to the biggest one—"and a paddle." She turned to me, her eyes shining. "Today's your lucky day, Skye. Today you're going to fall in love with the sea."

CHAPTER 41

RIVES
DAY 288, DEAD OF NIGHT

I was back on watch, again.

I searched the night, like it held answers. Stars winked, the woods stayed silent. No one was up but me.

Bored and restless, I threw my knife at a nearby post, a little late-night target practice. It hit, and stuck.

"Rives." Skye's soft whisper blew hot breath on my ear.

I startled.

Damn, I thought, impressed. No one snuck up on me.

I fought a grin, then lost it completely when I realized I must be more tired than I thought. Or maybe Skye was just that good.

"You're sneaky," I said, turning.

Skye stepped back, but not before I caught the satisfaction in her smile.

"I try," she said. "So"—she paused, her eyes sharp despite the night hour—"why are you the only one taking watch? It's been seven nights running."

Eight, I thought. I shrugged. "I can't sleep. May as well take watch." More honest than I'd planned, but when I was tired, it was harder to guard.

She studied me in her calm Skye way. "Is the cat the only thing on your mind?"

"Are you asking if it's the only thing keeping me up?" I whispered, my eyes on hers, the firelight flickering between us giving me a much-needed adrenaline boost. "Or are you asking if I'm thinking about someone?"

Despite the dark, I saw her cheeks flush. I don't know why I enjoyed rattling Skye so much. Maybe because it took something heavy to rattle her, and it made me feel powerful. Powerful enough to shake Nil, powerful enough to shake *me*.

You're playing with fire, Rives.

I pushed that thought away. I'd kept my distance—until now.

"What—or *who*—are you thinking about?" she asked.

"Maaka." I lifted the driftwood moon at my neck to show her. "He left this for me to find a few weeks ago. Now I'm wondering why, and what he wants in return."

Skye's hand went to her wrist, the one that used to hold the lettering *TFPL*. The letters had faded, replaced by Nil bling. She tilted her head at me. The torchlight made the flecks in her eyes glint like cool sparks. *Fire and ice*, I thought.

"Has he ever accepted anything from you?" she asked.

"No." I thought of the mangoes, untouched by Maaka, no doubt breakfast for Michael and crew by now. "And I don't think he ever will. Which is why I don't understand his gift."

"If it's truly a gift, then there's no expectation of something in return. But"—she paused—"if it's not, the question is why? Has he ever asked you for anything?"

"Not really. The closest thing to a request was when he asked me—more like commanded—to not bring fire into the cavern. He calls it the Looking Glass cavern." I shrugged. "Other than that, we just talk."

"You talk," she said slowly. "About what, exactly?"

"Mostly convoluted new-age crap that makes no sense," I admitted.

"He rambles a lot about how Nil is a 'spiritual journey,' and how we all have a beginning, a middle, and an end, but the middle is the most important, and this is his middle." I shook my head. "It's like the dude drank the Nil Kool-Aid. He worships this place."

Skye absently fingered her bracelets. Her hand stilled and she looked directly at me.

"He wants *you*," she said softly. "Your trust. You're the only one he shows himself to, the only one he regularly seeks out. For whatever reason, he wants you. Not as an ally, more as a confidant. Maybe you're part of his journey, or at least he thinks you are."

Skye had a point. Because as much as Maaka played the loner card, no one truly wanted to be alone. Humans were pack animals, after all.

"Maybe," I said. "But if he needs a confidant, why not Paulo? He's more like Maaka than me."

Skye shook her head, a smile lifting the corner of her mouth. "You haven't met Paulo yet. You two are very different. Paulo"—Skye searched for words—"reminds me of Sy. From what little I've seen, you're more like Maaka than Paulo, at least in the ways that count."

"You mean chiseled and mysterious?" I teased. For an instant I felt like *me*.

"I was thinking more bossy and commanding," she shot back. But her eyes were light.

"Speaking of that, you should get some sleep."

She shook her head. "Not tired."

"You will be if you don't sleep."

She arched a brow. "Speak for yourself."

Her hand left her wrist and in the glint of firelight, I saw the moon. A carved wooden crescent moon, dangling from braided twine. I grabbed her wrist, gently turning it over to expose the bracelet. "Where did you get this?" I asked softly.

She lifted her chin to meet my eyes. "Jealous?" Her eyes flashed.

"Hardly. Maaka and I don't have that kind of relationship."

She almost smiled. "It's not from Maaka. It's from Paulo."

I raised my eyebrow, fighting an unwelcome twinge in my chest. "Really?" My voice was sharp. "I didn't realize you'd seen him."

"I didn't," she said. "He left it by my pillow while I was sleeping."

"He left it by your pillow?" My jaw almost hit Nil dirt. *How the hell did he get so close to Skye without me noticing?*

She nodded. "He left it to make things even."

"Explain," I said curtly, silently reminding myself that Skye was safe. Despite me.

"After he told me about the cat that killed Archie, I told him about the hippos at the mudflats and the rhino I'd seen by the groves and he kind of freaked. I think the exchange of info put him in my debt, even though I was just trying to help. So now Paulo and I are even." She turned to me, guilt flashing through her eyes. "And I owe you an apology. That day I saw Paulo, you didn't make him run away. I did. I pushed him too hard about the gate. It was my fault."

"Apology unnecessary but accepted." I grinned, relaxing. "Now we're even."

She smiled but it vanished quickly. "Rives, you said I was keeping secrets. I wasn't, well, other than my pushing Paulo too hard." She looked guilty again. "That was the only secret I kept intentionally, but I've been thinking of my uncle's journal, wondering what I missed because I didn't know enough about Nil to know what was important. Yesterday after I got this bracelet, I remembered something. He had an entry where a girl, Rika, told him some weird stuff. She told my uncle that his destiny wrapped the island from beginning to end, but that his journey didn't end here. She also told him that his time ended when the crescent moon rose over the heart of the island." Skye paused. "She never put her name on the Wall, and he never saw her again. But he thought she was related to his island angel—the girl I told you about

259

that gave him water. I don't know what Rika's words mean, but they feel important. Especially now that I have this from an islander." She looked at me. "Where is the heart of the island?"

The Looking Glass cavern, I thought. *Or was that Nil's gut?*

"I don't know," I said. "Did your uncle mention Rika having any tattoos or jewelry?"

"No, why?"

I filled her in on Ramia and the skeleton in the Cove tunnel.

"Weird," Skye said. "But related, right?"

I nodded. Rika's words about beginnings and endings also sounded suspiciously familiar. *I see a boy who knows the beginning and the end but does not see the middle, and the middle is the most important part,* Maaka had told me.

Different time period, similar words.

Same us, I thought. *As in* not *us. As in* them.

I scanned the dark Nil sky. The moon was an even half. No crescent.

My mind drifted to the skeleton in the cavern, resting in the darkest place on Nil. Meters away, the woods before us were equally black.

It is dark everywhere here, my friend. Michael's words, dead right.

The darkness shifted. Then it blinked. Twin golden orbs glittered, then disappeared.

"Skye!" I reached for my blade. "Get back!"

The sheath at my waist was empty; all I had was a torch. I raised it high as a growling, snarling blur of spots burst from the trees. The cat stretched long, suspended in the air, teeth bared, claws out.

I raised the torch and lunged. I'd barely moved when the leopard dropped from the air, struck by an invisible force.

Beside me, Skye lowered her arm, sling in hand. Her expression radiated lethal calm.

"Rives! Look out!" Dex shouted.

Meters away, the cat fought to its feet and shook its head, dazed, not dead.

I slammed my torch over my thigh, snapped it in two, and strode forward. Holding my stunted torch in front of me, I drove the other half into the cat's chest. Blood spurted; it stained the golden fur like tar. A gorgeous animal, brought to Nil only to die because it tried to live.

Safaris were a joke compared to Nil.

I stabbed the cat again, feeling ill. The leopard didn't move. I tossed the bloody piece of bamboo on the ground and walked back to Skye, still holding my torch.

"Nice shot," I said.

She nodded. "You too."

"Damn," said Zane. "That was intense." He stood beside Dex, his face pale.

"Did that just happen?" Dex asked, his eyes flitting between the cat, Skye, and me. "Who *are* you people?" He pointed at Skye. "We've got bloody Xena in our camp who just knocked out a ninety-kilo cat with a dog chew toy, popping off a shot like she takes out leopards for a lark while the rest of us are wetting our nappies. And you"—he looked at me, waving his arm wildly—"you're like that nutter who snacks on tarantulas and wrestles crocodiles for fun—" Pinching his nose, Dex paused.

"Bear Grylls," Skye offered.

"Right." Dex pointed at her, nodding. "Bear Grylls. You're like bloody Bear Grylls. Shotgunning deadsleep tea like it's lager, waltzing up to a man-eating leopard and spearing it with an island shiv without even breaking a sweat." Dex shook his head. "Bugger me. That was *completely* mental."

Jason walked out of his hut, rubbing his eyes with one hand and plucking my knife off the post with his other hand as he passed. "Rives, here's your blade." He looked around, suddenly awake. "What'd I miss?"

"Just confirmation that humans are the biggest badasses on the planet," Zane said. "Or maybe just Rives and Skye."

"We're down one kitty, thanks to the dynamic duo here," Dex said, recovering slightly. "Tomorrow Skye is going to wrestle a hippo for kicks, while Rives takes out the rhino with a toothpick. Bloody hell." Dex snorted, then grinned at me. "And for the record, I had your back, mate. I was *this* close"—Dex pinched his thumb and forefinger together—"to going after you and beating off the leopard with my bare hands."

"Perfect," I said. "The next leopard is all yours."

"Right." Dex swallowed. "Well, feel free to jump in early and steal my glory. I don't want to be greedy." Abruptly, he looked at Skye. "No wonder the tiger walked away on your first night in the meadow. You're a bloody force of nature, Skye."

Dex looked like he didn't want to mess with her, either.

Skye turned to me, her eyes as sharp and fierce as I'd ever seen. "*Now* can we hunt that stationary gate?"

CHAPTER

SKYE
DAY 13, MORNING

After the leopard attack, Rives had agreed to head to Mount Nil to search for the stationary gate. His tight tether to the City had died with the cat.

We'd made our plans as dawn broke. Dex would stay back as Leader, and Jillian would stay back as Rives's very unofficial Second. Ahmad too. Our special Search team was Rives, me, Jason, and Miya.

Rives led us, moving with grace and sure feet befitting a cat, which was a scary visual given last night's attack, but it fit. Within a few hours, we'd passed smoothly through a black lava field and made it into a red one. Now broken rocks the color of dried blood stretched for miles, its dull color making the sky extra blue. It was both beautiful and creepy, like my uncle's journal had described. I wondered if I was viewing the island through my eyes or his.

Behind us, Jason and Miya seemed to understand each other without talking, an intensity that occasionally made me feel like I was intruding. It made me think of Charley.

"Lava rock for your thoughts," Rives said, tossing a small black rock toward me. I caught it on reflex. The oval rock was perfectly smooth with a slight indentation in the middle, like a worry stone. "What's on your mind?"

"Charley," I replied.

He gave a weird laugh. "She landed here, you know. In this field."

"I didn't," I said. "I was thinking of how much she missed Thad."

"You got that from this field?"

"No, I got it from Jason and Miya. They're kind of intense sometimes."

Rives shook his head. "Amplify that times twenty and you're getting close to Charley and Thad."

"Wow," I said.

"I know, right?" Rives smiled, and the softness in his expression stole my breath. It was like he'd given me a glimpse into another Nil world, one full of tenderness that touched him, too. Rives was so powerful, so strong, but flashes like these made me melt without warning.

I realized I was staring at Rives, who was smiling at me with an amused expression.

With a very awkward smile, I looked away.

Pull it together, Skye, I told myself. *You're not here to drool over guys, no matter how hot they are.*

"Hey!" Jason shouted. "Rives! Gate at five o'clock!"

Sure enough, a shimmering wall of air hovered over the red rock to our right, rippling and writhing. And then it moved, *fast.*

"Go, Rives! It's yours!" Jason yelled. "It's a single! It won't wait forever!"

A gate.

Rives.

He was leaving.

Suddenly I couldn't breathe.

I looked at Rives; he was looking at me.

"Bye, Rives." I squeezed his hand. "Tell Charley I got what I wished for." I smiled.

Rives stared at me, his light eyes burning.

"Skye," he whispered. Before he said another word, Jason's shout rang through the air.

"Got a runner!" he said.

I turned to see Paulo galloping across the red rocks, running *away* from the gate. He glanced over his shoulder, terrified, then changed direction to avoid the streaking wall of air.

"What the hell?" Rives breathed.

"Paulo," I said.

The gate was too far out for Rives to catch now. It sped away with lightning speed, away from us, and judging by Paulo's ungainly sprint, covering ground quickly in this field wasn't easy. Paulo took an awkward leap off a large heap of rocks and fell out of sight with an agonized cry.

The gate flew on, crossing the field and disappearing into the distance.

Rives gently pulled a curl of my hair. "Let's go check on your boyfriend, shall we?" He winked.

I narrowed my eyes at him. Rives laughed as he broke into a steady jog.

We found Paulo on the other side of the pile of red rocks, moaning on the ground and holding his leg. His eyes bulged when he saw us, his hands tightening on his leg.

"Don't touch it!" he screamed.

"I think he broke it," Jason said, eyeing Paulo's shin. It was already swelling, and the angle looked off.

"No doubt," Rives said, kneeling by Paulo. "Hey, buddy, I'm Rives. And you're gonna have to come with us. We've got someone who can help you. And right now you need some help."

Paulo moaned, tears running down his face.

I knelt beside Rives. "You can trust him, Paulo. I promise. We'll take good care of you." It struck me he was more worried about accepting our help than getting the help he needed. "You can't stay here," I added. "It's not safe. Not when you can't run." *Or even walk*, I thought.

Without a word, Paulo nodded.

Rives pulled out a funky collapsible island stretcher from his satchel. *Had he expected something bad would happen?* I wondered. He caught my eye as he efficiently snapped it together. "Better prepared than not," he said grimly.

The four of us carried Paulo back in near silence. Pale, sweating, and breathing shallowly, Paulo looked absolutely miserable. From what I knew of him, being taken into the City he'd been working so hard to avoid was probably as painful as his leg.

I realized he'd been following us.

With a start, I also realized his arm's tattoos matched the designs in the Looking Glass cavern. Except for the sun one. I'd seen the design before; I just couldn't place where.

I mulled over his sun tattoo the entire way back. It was easier than thinking about the fact that *Rives almost just left.*

"Head to my hut," Rives instructed when we saw the City. A few minutes later, Paulo was moaning on Rives's bed. "Jason, find Jillian," Rives said. "She'll know if we can set it. At least the bone didn't break the skin." He looked at Paulo, who hadn't stopped crying. "But setting that break is gonna hurt like a mother."

Jillian came running. She gingerly felt Paulo's shin, wincing as he screamed. "It feels broken. But clean. I think we should set it. Basically just immobilize it so it can heal. But there are no guarantees either way." Her face looked majorly stressed. "I'm no orthopedist."

Paulo writhed in pain.

"We're going to need some more people to hold him down to set it," she said. "And we're going to need sticks and cloth."

Rives nodded. "Jills, go get Dex to help. Jason, go grab three solid sticks, all just short of a meter. Use my blade, cut branches so we have green wood. Miya, go to the Shack and get cloth. We'll wait with Paulo."

Everyone nodded and ran out, all except me.

The minute the others left, Rives turned to me. "Stay with him, Skye. I'll be right back."

Rives ducked out of his hut, and when he returned a minute later, he carried two coconut shell cups. Both were filled with light amber liquid.

"Deadsleep tea," he said. "Did they have it in your uncle's time?"

"No."

"Well, we do. It'll knock Paulo out so Jillian can set his leg properly." He set one cup on the table and looked directly at me as he held up the other cup. "Skye, I'm going to drink this. And then I'm going to pass out. If I'm still breathing in ten minutes, give the other cup to Paulo. If I'm not"—he shrugged—"don't."

"What? No!" I looked at Rives, appalled. "Don't drink that!"

"Count to sixty ten times," Rives said, backing up toward the other bed. "Make it eleven for good measure." He grinned. "Bottoms up!"

I lunged to knock it out of his hand as he threw back the cup and gulped.

"Too slow," he said, grabbing my wrist and smiling. "This time." Rives's eyes took on a glazed look. "Skye, I want . . . I . . . ." His words slurred. Stumbling, he fell back onto the bed, taking me with him. "Skye."

My name was thick on his tongue.

"Rives!" I shouted.

But he was already gone. I knew it because his grip on my wrist slackened, then let go completely. This was not how I envisioned lying in bed with Rives.

"Rives?" I gently patted his cheek. He was completely unresponsive. Unconscious, maybe worse. I rested my head on his chest, listening. He was still breathing—for now.

What if Rives died?

The thought made me shake; it left me cold and empty and

furious all at once. I couldn't imagine Nil without Rives; it was as if all the colors of Nil had dulled, shifted to a lifeless gray. First the gate had threatened to take him, now the deadsleep tea. A minute ago Rives was the person most alive on the entire island. Now he was slipping away—by choice.

"Stupid!" I punched the pillow beside Rives. "You are so stupid!"

"Oh my God," Jillian said. "He didn't." She'd come into Rives's hut, Dex right behind her.

"That bloody idiot," Dex said. He laced his fingers together on top of his head and stared at Rives.

Jillian's and Dex's expressions were mirror images: shock, denial, and, if I wasn't mistaken, fury. "He told me that if he was still breathing in ten minutes, to give the other cup to Paulo." My voice shook. "That it would knock Paulo out so you could set his leg."

Dex cursed under his breath.

"He called it deadsleep tea," I added.

"I know what it is," Jillian snapped. I knew her anger wasn't for me.

"I tried to knock it out of his hand."

"I wish you'd knocked him in the head instead." Jillian looked close to tears. "Maybe that would help." She took a deep breath, glanced briefly at Paulo, then looked back at me. "So how long has it been?"

I'd totally forgotten to count.

"Crap." I almost burst into tears myself. "I think two minutes."

The next eight minutes were an eternity in hell I never want to repeat. I sat on Rives's bed; Jillian and Dex stood beside it. Every thirty seconds I'd bend down to listen to Rives's breathing. Slow and steady. Rives didn't move. He didn't even twitch. He was, as the expression went, dead to the world.

I'd never use that expression again.

Three minutes left.

Paulo was still moaning. None of us said a word.

Two minutes.

One.

"Time's up," Dex finally said.

Rives's chest continued to rise and fall. The three of us exhaled a collective breath. "I don't know if I want to hug him or wallop him," Dex said.

"When he wakes up, I'm going to kill him," Jillian said. Her wet eyes shot daggers at Rives. Then she turned to Paulo, who was staring at us with wide eyes. "Thirsty yet?"

Paulo drank his tea, passed out cold, and didn't make a peep while Dex and Jillian set his leg. Miya and Jason returned with a trio of sticks and cloth, and Jillian amazed me with her island splinting skills.

"You did great," I told her when she finished.

"Thanks." She looked exhausted. "At least it makes me feel like I'm doing something." She glanced at Rives.

"I know what you mean," I said.

Jillian closed her eyes. "I can't believe he pulled this stunt again."

"Again?" I asked.

"Yup." She blinked. "The first time was after Jason broke his finger. Rives can't stand to see people hurting. But I swear the boy has a death wish. I thought lately it had gotten better." She looked at me sharply. "Dex," she said, still looking at me. "Will you stay with the guys? I want to talk to Skye a minute."

"Your wish is my command, my lady," Dex said grandly.

Jillian gave Dex a quick smile, then gestured to me to follow her. She led me outside, out of earshot of everyone, still talking in low tones.

"Skye, Rives is going to be out for at least a day. Last time it was almost three. And I didn't want to talk in front of him in case somehow he can hear in his deadsleep coma." She looked directly at me. "But when he wakes up, if you hurt him, I personally will kill you." Jillian looked at me like a lethal Pippi Longstocking, then she sighed. Her shoulders drooped.

"Not really. I'm actually a pretty nonviolent person. Before I showed up here I didn't even squash bugs. But you know what I mean." Jillian exhaled slowly. "The thing is, Rives has been through a lot. More than you can imagine. He doesn't deserve any more pain. So don't lead him on, okay? Just know he isn't someone to play with, and he deserves better than to have his heart ripped out and crushed again."

"What are you talking about? I'm not playing with Rives." *Was I?*

"I didn't say you were. I just said don't." She paused, studying me. "You haven't been here long, but time on Nil is compressed. Fewer distractions of meaningless crap, a pressure cooker of survival. And I see how you two are together. I see how he looks at you, Skye. Like you're all he sees. It doesn't take long to connect with someone, especially here."

She studied me. "And I see the way you look at him, too. It's a mirror of Rives. Maybe you don't even know it. Maybe there's someone holding you back. Is there?"

"Is there what?" I asked, stunned by this entire conversation.

"Someone at home holding you back. Someone you're going back to."

I shook my head. "No. My life back home is kind of"—I was going to say crazy, but that seemed to fit my life more on Nil—"different. I dated a little but not much. During the year, I study with Mom and do things her way, and then I spend summers training with my dad and going strange places. This may sound weird, but I'd assumed my life—the one *I* wanted—would start when I went to college."

She nodded. "I'm torn between telling you to stay far away from Rives and encouraging you to go for it." Jillian sighed. "Waiting around for your life to start is a very bad idea, especially here. Like the old saying goes, today is the only today you'll ever have, so why waste it? And here, you may not get a tomorrow. Tomorrow isn't guaranteed for anyone, anywhere, but on Nil? We have a finite number of tomorrows, and sometimes they just don't show."

She glanced back at Rives's hut. "He's more like himself when he's with you," she said softly.

A quiet moment passed. Rives filled my head, even though he lay unconscious twenty feet away.

"I've got a question." I kept my voice low. "I overheard you and Dex talking about Rives being reckless ever since something, but I didn't hear what. What happened?"

She chewed her lip. "I'm not sure I should be the one to tell you. But then again, I think you should know."

I stood quietly, waiting.

"Okay. A few months before you got here, Rives lost someone he really cared about. Her name was Talla."

Talla.

"She got attacked by a wolf," Jillian continued, "and she died. In Rives's arms. He buried her, and it almost killed him. After that, he started taking risks. They've been getting worse. Sometimes I think he's got a death wish, or at least he's lost his fear of death."

My uncle's words flashed behind my eyes. *I fear nothing.* Despite the sun, I shivered.

Jillian looked at me. "Maybe you can talk some sense into him. God knows I've tried. Same for Dex. If he's going to listen to anyone now, it's you."

Everyone's afraid of something, I had told Rives once. I hoped that was the case. Because if Rives was truly without fear, that frightened me more than anything else on Nil.

"One more thing." Jillian hesitated. "Your hair. It's getting really matted." She looked guilty. "Not to get in your business, but if you want, we've got a couple wide combs that I think might help you. Totally up to you, but I think if you don't start working on the knots, they may never come out. And you might have to cut it off." She shrugged. "It's happened before."

I pictured myself like a shorn sheep and grimaced. "I'll take the comb. And thanks," I added. "For everything."

Jillian hugged me. "That's what friends are for."

I sat by Rives's bed the rest of the day, working out the knots in my hair, cursing my curls, but at least it gave me something to do other than stare at Rives's chest. Jillian flitted in and out but seemed content to let me be.

Neither Rives nor Paulo stirred.

In sleep, the hard lines of worry relaxed, making Rives look like your average teenager, not the burdened Leader of a makeshift camp of people stuck on a freaky deserted island full of dangers and death, the greatest of which was simply time. I wondered if that's why Rives looked so relaxed: In sleep, he was blissfully unaware of time's passage.

In sleep, he was absolutely beautiful.

A furious sea god without the fury. I studied his face, as if the perfect lines would help me sort out my feelings, knowing I could take all the time I wanted, that he wasn't going to open his eyes to catch me anytime soon.

Voyeur, my conscience chided.

Duh, I thought. Then I told my conscience to shut the heck up.

Am I playing with him? I lowered my comb and considered the thought.

I was drawn to him, that I knew. I looked for him constantly; I purposefully sought him out. I trusted him more than anyone, even Jillian. I'd had a sense of him before I'd even met him, but the Rives in person was even more impressive than the Rives Charley had described: strong, honest, and downright gorgeous, not to mention an amazing Leader with an endless capacity for compassion that I'd witnessed time and time again. And if I was honest with myself, Rives made my breath catch whenever he got close; he had since the moment I'd met him, even in those moments when he made me absolutely furious. He made me feel things that scared me, things that thrilled me. Things that made me wonder if we could be *more.*

If we *were* more.

I'd known him less than two weeks, but two weeks on Nil was like two months back home. Jillian wasn't kidding about time being compressed here.

No, I decided. *I wasn't playing with him.*

But I didn't know if he was playing with me, or interested at all.

For the first time, it occurred to me that the one thing I'd never expected Nil to break was my heart.

CHAPTER 43

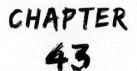

RIVES
DAY 291, SOMETIME IN THE NIGHT

Nothing like a deadsleep coma to give you an adrenaline jolt.

I opened my eyes to the night, wide-awake and fully rested. I wondered how long I'd been out this time.

I looked over and was shocked to see Skye. Someone had wedged a bed between me and Paulo, and Skye was curled in a ball under her cheetah pelt. Eyes closed, she didn't move, didn't twitch, like she'd sucked down deadsleep tea, too. But my gut said she was smarter than that. Smarter than me.

I was damn lucky to be alive. And seriously grateful.

Skye's hair shone gold in the streak of moonlight, spilling across her hands tucked under her head. She didn't look like the lethal badass that she was; she looked like a regular girl. But not average. Nothing about Skye was average. Even sleeping, she looked like the kind who'd turn your head in a pair of jeans and T-shirt. Here on Nil, in island threads, she was the kind who was seriously messing with my head.

I wondered whether she was here for me or Paulo.

I hated that I cared.

That gate in the lava field had thrown me. It was a message from Nil, delivered with the subtlety of a volcanic eruption.

Check your rules, it said.

Pay attention. Look around.

All I saw was Skye. Lying beside me. Squeezing my hand. Saying good-bye. Having the clarity to *say* good-bye. Me, I'd just stood there, shocked that it was good-bye. Shocked that it was my noon.

But it wasn't.

And as insane as it sounded, thank God it wasn't. Because I wasn't done with Nil, not by a long shot. And I wasn't done with Skye, either. There was something about her that kept pulling me back. Something that made me *want*. Something that made me ache.

What are you afraid of? I'd asked her once. She hadn't asked me the same question. But I knew the answer now. I was terrified of the pain I'd felt when I'd buried Talla.

It wasn't a risk I wanted to take.

The end is already written, Maaka had said once.

Is Skye my middle, or was that Talla? And are my end and Skye's the same?

With a deep breath, I cleared my head. Of Maaka and Nil and muddy futures I couldn't see. Then I sat up. In the far bed, Paulo slept hard. His leg boasted a three-prong splint, Jillian's solid handiwork. He was sleeping, not moaning. And not dead. Good signs all around.

"You scared the crap out of me, you know that?" Skye's soft whisper drew my eyes. Hers were open now, trained on me with an intensity palpable despite the dark. "And not just me. Jillian and Dex were *so* upset. You're going to get an earful from them, just wait."

"Let me guess. Dex called me a bloody idiot." I grinned.

"Well, it fit." She bit her cheek and looked hard at me. "Promise me you won't do that again. If you're not careful, the third time could be the charm."

"I hear you."

"Don't just hear me." Skye sat up. Our faces were centimeters apart.

"Promise me," she whispered. "Promise me you won't drink that awful tea again."

"I promise," I said. Now that she was awake, I saw how tired she looked. Guilt hit me hard.

"Have you slept?" I asked.

"A little," she said, glancing away.

"Liar, liar, pants on fire," I whispered.

"I'm not wearing pants." She glanced back at me, a smile lifting the corner of her mouth. "I'm wearing a skirt."

I closed my eyes to the visual that threatened to undo me. "Right."

"Rives." Skye's voice was abruptly serious.

I opened my eyes to hers.

"I'm really glad you're okay. Those ten minutes were the worst of my life. Don't ever do something like that again." Her gaze had reverted to fierce.

"I'm sorry," I said. "But Paulo. They set his leg okay, right?"

"Right." Skye sighed.

"How many days was I out?"

"Almost three."

Same as last time, I thought. I wondered when Paulo would wake. A quiet moment passed. Long, but not uncomfortable.

Out of the dark, Skye said, "I'm sorry about Talla."

I sucked in air, having trouble finding some. "Me too."

Another long pause. The ocean's rumble filled the gap.

"Did you love her?" Skye asked.

I leaned back down and cradled my head in my palms. "I think I could've," I answered finally. "But I never got the chance."

"I'm so sorry," Skye said. She slid back down, too, propping her head on her hand.

Neither of us spoke.

"Did you know that she saved Miya?" I asked.

"No." Skye's whisper was soft.

"She did. Miya was being chased by a wolf. Talla saw Miya running with the wolf after her, and Talla chased them both. She caught up with them and attacked the wolf. It bit her arm during the fight, clean through to the bone. Dislocated her shoulder, too." I fell silent. "She died from the infection. And we didn't have the tea to help her then. I think it would've eased her passing."

I realized I wasn't clenching my fists. The pain had eased, but I still felt the scar. I always would. Bart wasn't worthy of a mention.

"That's awful," Skye said.

"It was. But sometimes I wonder what Miya's destiny is. Why Nil chose her. Miya's brilliant—like Jason, but different. He's got the mind of an engineer. He wants to go to the Naval Academy and fly jets. But Jason says Miya wants to be a surgeon." I stopped, surprised at the info I was spilling. Maybe that's what happens when you sleep for nearly three days. Pent-up words burst out like water.

"She makes the nets, right?" Skye asked.

"Right." I thought about all Miya had done. "She's so much stronger now than she was when she first came."

"Most people are," Skye said quietly.

I rolled over to look at Skye. Her insight was spot-on. "You know what Maaka said? He told me the island only tests those with the strength to survive. It sounds like a crock, but sometimes it fits. Then again, it doesn't guarantee survival, either."

Skye studied me in the dark. "Sounds like a Nil truth."

I nodded. "Number five. Tomorrow's not a given, especially here."

"Or anywhere, really," she murmured.

I wondered if she was thinking of her uncle.

"Can I ask you a personal question?" I said.

Skye nodded.

"What happened to your uncle?"

"What happened to him or how did he die?" she asked.

"Both, I guess."

She was quiet for a long moment. "He was base jumping off the Sydney Harbor Bridge." Her voice was so low I strained to hear it. "His parachute malfunctioned. It opened too late. He hit the water so hard it knocked him out, and then his chute dragged him under. He drowned." She glanced at the cheetah pelt covering her legs. "Since I read his journal, I can't stop wondering whether he was jumping to feel fear or feel alive. Because the last line of his journal reads *I fear nothing.*" She lifted her eyes to mine. Hers looked slightly haunted. "Is that a Nil truth, Rives? That everyone leaves here different? That everyone leaves here fearless? With no regard for living?"

"No." My whisper was firm. "I mean sure, everyone who leaves is different. How can you not be? Every experience changes you in some way. Sometimes for the better, sometimes for the worse. That's more of a life truth than a Nil truth. But no, I don't think Nil makes everyone lose their fear. Sharpens it, maybe. Makes you figure out what's really worth fearing."

The ghosts in her eyes retreated into the past.

"How many Nil truths are there?" Her lips relaxed, almost into a smile.

"Ten." The number popped into my head without thinking.

"Seems to be a popular number here." She quirked her eyebrow. I knew she was thinking of the deadsleep tea minute count. I thought of the number sequence on the cavern wall: 3-2-1-4. A strange island ten. "True."

"You want to know something?" Skye tipped her head, as if she were trying to see the sky. "My birthday is February tenth. I'll be eighteen."

Something inside me twisted.

"Want to know something weirder?" I said. "My birthday is December tenth. I just turned eighteen a few weeks ago."

She looked surprised. "For some reason I thought you were older."

I grinned. "I get that a lot."

She yawned.

"Go back to sleep, Skye," I said quietly, getting up, careful not to step on her as I moved. She was just that close. "I'm gonna get some food. I've slept enough for the night."

"Try not to eat anything starting with the word *dead*," she said dryly.

"Sushi for me then." I grinned. "And keep an eye on your boyfriend." I pointed to Paulo.

Skye picked up an empty coconut cup and threw it at me. I caught it one-handed and smiled. "Thanks. I'd forgotten where I left my cup when I passed out."

With a groan, she flopped back onto the bed. "You're impossible," she grumbled.

I had the oddest visual of Skye lying on top of me. In bed.

Out of my head, Nil, I thought.

Outside, Dex wandered around the firepit, a halfhearted watch in progress. He looked as exhausted as Skye. To my surprise, he wasn't on watch alone. Jillian sat by the firepit, her chin resting on her hands.

They both looked up at once.

"Welcome to the land of the living, Rives," Dex said, waving his torch. "What's on your agenda today? Lion wrestling? Traipsing around active lava vents? Noshing on dodgy berries?" Dex raised an eyebrow.

Jillian walked up and stuck her finger in my chest. "Are you trying to go out in a blaze of stupid? Do you have a death wish? What's going on in here?" She tapped my forehead, hard. "What were you *thinking*?"

"I was thinking you needed to set Paulo's leg," I said. "And you did, right?"

Dex's jaw hardened. "Bloody hell, Rives. Yes, we set the poor bloke's leg. And yes, he's still out. But the risk." He swallowed, his Adam's apple convulsing. "Jills nearly had a stroke, not to mention Skye. The three of us sat around, counting down the minutes, waiting to see if the next breath would be your last. A Nil nightmare, that was. Never again, mate." His voice shook.

I nodded. *Never again.*

Jillian's eyes narrowed. "So do you?"

"Do I what?"

"Have a death wish."

"No."

"I wish I could believe you." She searched my eyes, then sighed. "Would you please give up the damn tea?"

"Done," I said.

"Really." Dex's tone was droll. "Just like that."

"Just like that."

Jillian stared at me, like she was trying to figure it out. To figure *me* out. "Okay, well, good." She paused. "You should know Skye never left your side. I think you freaked her out pretty hard. I don't think you should put her through that ever again. When she wakes, you should tell her you're sorry."

"Already did," I said.

"Excellent," Dex said, walking over. Jillian gave me a long, searching look as Dex handed me his torch. "I relinquish the job of Leader to its rightful owner. I'm bloody exhausted, and you've slept enough for the two of us."

"See you in the morning," Jillian said quietly. She still studied me like an equation she was working to solve. With a yawn, she followed Dex. They disappeared into Natalie's old hut, his hand gently touching the small of her back as he let her go first.

Interesting, I thought.

Another possible Nil shift while I slept.

Alone, I paused to listen, breathing in the Nil night. No chirps, no howls, just steady waves booming onto shore. Above me the moon hung high. Waxing gibbous, if I remembered my astronomy correctly. No crescent.

Skye would know, came the thought.

I walked over to the Wall. Skye's name stood out, the last one carved. Four letters, etched forever.

Somehow her name on the Wall made her presence more real—and more fragile. More frightening. Like Nil had finally laid claim to Skye, like her uncle twenty years before.

I scoured the Wall for Rika but came up empty. She never made it onto the Wall.

But she'd been here, I knew.

Like Maaka.

I didn't have to look to know his name wasn't on the Wall.

How many others came and went but never touched the City? And more importantly, *why?*

CHAPTER 44

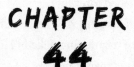

SKYE
DAY 15, MORNING

I woke to face an empty bed. Rives was gone. But I knew he was alive, awake, and more like himself.

I hoped he'd keep his promise.

Jillian swept into the hut with a pitcher and cup as I yawned. "Breakfast," she whispered, grinning. "We come bearing food."

Dex followed, carrying a platter of baked fish, roasted pineapple, and coconut chunks that smelled like heaven. "With all that staring at half-dressed men, you must be famished." He winked.

"Ha," I said, glaring weakly at Dex.

He laughed as Jillian punched him playfully. "Stop," she scolded. Dex caught her fist and kissed it with a grand bow.

Blushing, Jillian turned to me and frowned. "Skye, you're starting to look worse than he does." She waved her hand toward Paulo. "You need to eat, and then sleep."

"I'm okay," I said. "I really did sleep last night. Promise."

Jillian raised her eyebrows. "Okayyyy."

Dex set the plank beside me on the bed. "Any sign of life from our guest?" He tilted his head toward Paulo.

"None. When do you think he'll wake up?" I asked. "Rives woke up in the middle of the night."

"I know," Jillian said. "But as for Paulo, no clue. He's hurt, his body is healing, so does that make the tea last longer or be absorbed faster?" She pulled on one of her braids. "But I'm not surprised that Rives woke first. Pound per pound, he got a slightly lighter dose."

I thought about that. "I don't know. I think Rives drank more; I remember his cup being slightly fuller."

"Idiot," Dex muttered.

Rives stuck his head in and grinned. "You need me, Dex?" His green eyes twinkled.

"We all do, mate. Preferably alive." Dex gave Rives a pointed look.

"At least he's done with that awful tea," I said.

Dex looked at me curiously. "Is he, now?"

I nodded. "He promised me last night he wouldn't drink it again." I glanced at Rives. Lounging against the doorframe, arms crossed but relaxed, he watched me, a hint of a smile touching his lips, his eyes holding that look that gave me chills. The one that said we were alone even when we totally weren't.

"Skye?"

I whipped my eyes to Jillian.

"Yeah?"

"I'm going to paddleboard before the wind kicks up. Want to come? The waves aren't that big today."

I hesitated. Jillian had been right. I loved paddleboarding; it was my new island obsession. Standing on a big huge board, on the calm water past the breaking waves, brought an amazing sense of peace—a peace so *close* to the water, a peace borne of the water—that I'd never expected. Nil had been full of surprises, not all of them terrible. I turned to Jillian, whose friendship was a Nil gift.

"I think I should stay with Paulo," I said reluctantly. I felt Rives's eyes still watching. Studying. "I'm the only one he knows here, and I think I should be here when he wakes up."

"Makes sense." Jillian nodded.

When I looked up, the doorway was empty. Rives was gone.

Paulo woke that afternoon. He sat up with a jolt. "Where am I?" he croaked.

"In the City," I answered. "Here. Drink this."

He thrust out his hand. "No way!" He eyed the cup with fear. "The last time you people had me drink something, the nasty stuff almost killed me!"

"No, that nasty stuff knocked you out so Jillian and Dex could set your leg without you feeling it." I pointed to his splint, a crafty three-prong creation to fix his leg in place. "And thanks to them, you might actually be able to walk again."

Paulo lay back on the bed and moaned.

"You need to drink and eat, and probably use the bathroom. Jason found a pair of crutches for you in the Shack yesterday. They're by your bed." I gestured to the foot of Paulo's bed, where a pair of primitive wooden crutches fashioned from tree branches rested against the edge.

Paulo didn't move. He stared at the ceiling.

"Why were you following us, anyway?" I asked.

No answer.

"Okay, well, why did you run away from that gate? You could've been far away from here by now. And no broken leg," I added.

He jerked his head toward me. "Take a wild portal? Are you crazy? Those portals take people and those people disappear."

I shook my head. "No, they just appear somewhere else. Not on the Death Twin island." I looked pointedly at Paulo. It struck me that each of us had little knowledge of the other's Nil, and some of what we thought we knew was wrong.

"Not always," he said. His voice dropped to a shaky whisper.

"Sometimes the wild portals kill people. Electrocutes them, steals their life force. I've heard the stories. I'm not stupid. I don't want to be here, but I don't want to die, either."

"Those wild portals," I said slowly, "are the only way home for most of us. It's how most people got here, too. You, me, Maaka—we're the exceptions, Paulo. No one else came here by that fancy portal that stood patiently waiting. And those wild portals? They only zap you if two people try to take the same one."

Paulo frowned as the wheels turned.

"Yup," I said, watching his expression shift as understanding dawned. "Those wild portals only take one person at a time. Your portal was different." I paused. "But you already know that."

Paulo said nothing. Sensing we were dangerously close to the *let's-all-take-your-special-portal* territory that made Paulo clam up in a swift minute—*or run*, I thought, not that he could run now—I took a different tack.

"Why teenagers?" I asked. "Why *only* teenagers?"

"If I tell you, will you leave me alone?" he asked.

"Sure."

For now, I thought.

Like he'd read my mind, Paulo sighed. "There are stories back in my homeland, tales passed down for generations. That portal has been alive for as long as my ancestors can remember; it was there when my people came to their island. Some say it is as old as the Earth; others say it was created on the eighth day. No one knows." He shrugged. "It's just always been." He paused. "But many generations ago, as my people explored the islands around their own, someone stumbled across the portal for the first time. Specifically, the son of a king. The bravest of the brave. He walked through it and into this land. His cat—" Paulo glanced at me. "In our culture, each child is given a kitten at age seven, to protect and care for. Cats are a symbol of wisdom and luck." His voice sounded respectful. I thought of the leopard and Archie, and didn't feel that cats were lucky at all. "To have your cat join you is an honor." He exhaled.

"Anyway, the prince's cat had traveled with him in his canoe and followed him through the shimmering door. The king saw what happened, and tried to follow too, but by the time he got to the doorway between worlds, the portal had closed. Disappeared as if it never existed at all. People mourned the loss of the brave prince. The king banned everyone from traveling to the island, saying it held evil spirits. But then the prince reappeared, months later. Older and stronger and wiser, with tales of a beautiful, faraway land where peace was plentiful. The next time the doorway opened, the king tried to enter, but he passed through the doorway like a ghost, still walking on Spirit Island. The doorway denied him." Paulo looked at me. "Our people believe the prince left his mark on the gate. From that point forward, the gate only recognized people on the edge of adulthood. People with the ability to become something more."

Teenagers, I thought.

"Like the prince imprinted on the gate," I murmured. *Had the gate been waiting there, waiting for someone—or something—to pass through? And had the cat altered the gate, too?*

"Please," Paulo said. He sounded tired. "Go. And tell no one what I told you. I've broken our rules by telling you our secret history." He gave a weird little laugh. "But everything's been messed up since you followed me through the door. It's not the way I thought it was supposed to be."

"Most things aren't," I said.

Paulo's story swirled though my mind, another Nil world to mesh with the ones I already knew. The worlds blended and knit, the past and the present, a shifting kaleidoscope of time and people and island scenes, all with meaning I needed to *see*. Potential futures flickered like images I couldn't quite catch.

"Please go," Paulo said. He was watching me, a lost expression making him look younger than Jason.

He still looked broken, in more ways than one. But he was here, with the potential to be *more*.

"Paulo, you're going to be okay," I said softly. "I believe that with all my heart. And I promise I'll always be honest with you. Friendships are built on truth. And because I'm going to be honest, I want you to know that I can't agree to keep what you told me a secret. People who've been stuck here with questions deserve to know; people who didn't ask to come."

Paulo looked ready to cry. "I guess I don't have a choice, do I?"

"You say that a lot." My voice was calm. "But we all have choices, even when it seems like we don't. And this choice is mine. There are so many good people here, Paulo, all wondering why they're here. If what you know helps them sleep at night, I'm all for it. Information is usually meant to be shared." I paused. "But at the same time, I respect your history and your privacy. So I promise you that I'll only tell the people I trust most, okay? Like the people who set your leg. And for what it's worth," I said slowly, thinking of Dad's Micronesian map with myriad tacks, all hunting for the elusive Nil, "I think secrecy is what's gotten everyone into trouble."

Paulo's eyes narrowed.

Abruptly I sensed I'd gone too far again.

"Not secrecy, pride," Paulo spat. "*Haole* pride and power. *That* is what's gotten everyone into trouble." But his inflection on *everyone* matched his inflection on the word *haole*, like the word tasted bitter. "Go."

Paulo said nothing as I left.

Paulo's words ran through my head. *The prince left his mark on the gate. The wild portals . . . steal life force.*

A fully formed theory poured into my head like rain. A fully formed *future*, glittering and seductive and glorious as a shimmery outbound gate.

I broke into a run, heading for the beach, desperate to find Rives.

He stood near the water holding a board. Ahmad stood a few feet away. Kiera and Macy strolled just past Ahmad.

"Rives!" I flagged him over, slowing, willing him to come to me. I didn't want more of an audience than Rives. He dropped his board and walked over, dripping wet, reminding me of that first day we'd met. Fully present, and intense.

"Paulo's up," I said when he drew close. "And listen to this." I recounted Paulo's story carefully, taking time to repeat it exactly as Paulo told me. Rives listened intently as he always did. When I finished, I said, "I have a thought. It's really out there, so let me get to the end before you say anything, okay?"

Rives nodded.

I took a deep breath. "First, let me ask you something. Do you know how people die here? I mean," I said quickly, inwardly wincing at the indirect reference to Talla, "if their time runs out? If they don't escape before one year?"

Rives crossed his arms, a sign I'd learned meant he was thinking. Hard.

"I've never been with someone on their last day," he said finally. "Most people usually go renegade as their clocks run out. Go off on their own, to have privacy or peace or whatever they want or need in their final days. But Natalie—she was Leader before Thad—told me once that people just die. Literally, they just stop living. That when the window between Nil and home shuts, something breaks. It's like some-thing's cut." He took a heavy breath. "She was with Uta on Uta's last day. Problem was, Uta had miscounted. That afternoon, Uta collapsed while they were on Search. Just stopped breathing." Rives glanced toward the Flower Field. "Natalie told me that Uta had landed on Nil in the afternoon too. It was like Nil calculated Uta's time down to the minute." Rives paused. "Why?"

"My uncle's journal said the same thing. That Toby collapsed, out on the red rocks. He also said Toby grabbed his chest as he fell, but by the time my uncle reached him, Toby wasn't breathing. My uncle wrote that it happened without warning, without noise. He wrote that it was like an invisible hand had pulled an invisible string, stopping Toby's heart." My voice was quiet. "I think Nil holds that string, but that somehow, we're connected to the island. Keep this in mind, okay?"

"Okay." Rives's intense expression hadn't changed. Like he just might buy into my crazy idea, too.

I took a deep breath. "Back to Paulo's story. Do you remember what you told me about Nil truth number four?"

"Balance reigns," Rives said.

"Exactly. So the prince's gate imprinted on him, or linked with him in some way—and maybe the cat, too—so that the gate only recognizes teenagers and warm-blooded creatures, right?"

"Right." Rives frowned slightly, not following.

"But the ocean. It only has cold-blooded creatures here, right? No dolphins, no marine mammals." Rives was nodding. "So I'm thinking there's a second gate—a companion gate, a gate underwater on both ends that only transfers cold-blooded things. That *imprinted* on cold-blooded things, like fish. It's the balance to our gate, the counterweight." I paused. "Make sense?"

"A yin and yang," Rives murmured.

"Right. Just like we—all of us—are the counterweight to the island. I don't know if I'm right, but it makes sense. And I keep thinking, what if a counterweight disappears? Gets upset? What happens to the island?"

Rives's eyes widened.

"I think the gates are connected to the sun somehow, but the island is connected to *us*. Paulo mentioned a life force, like the island steals ours. I think that when people die, that somehow the island absorbs our energy, the same energy—like electricity—that powers our hearts." I shivered. "I can't stop thinking that maybe it uses our energy, like a symbiotic relationship. Maybe it's the teens that give this place life. So I'm thinking, what happens if we get all the people off the island at once? The balance will tip too far, right? And Nil's power will be dramatically lost. Maybe fatally lost." I held Rives's eyes, trying not to look as crazy as I felt.

"Maybe we can save everyone at once, and destroy Nil, too." I paused. "Forever."

CHAPTER 45

RIVES
DAY 291, MORNING

Skye was more than fire, more than ice.

Skye was an atomic weapon.

"Damn," I said, fighting to process the killer thought of taking Nil down. "You don't do anything halfway, do you?"

She waved it off. "It's totally crazy. But we can try. So the way I see it, we've got to do three things. One, figure out when and where the next stationary gate will show up. Two, sweep the island for all the kids ahead of time to make sure no one is left behind, right? Number one will save us all, and number two will hopefully crush Nil." She chewed her lip as she looked at the sea.

"What's number three?"

"I'm not sure yet. But good things always come in threes, right? And I don't want to miss anything." She grinned.

"You won't," I said quietly.

"Skye!" Jillian's voice rang out across the sand. "Paulo's up, and he's asking for you. He won't talk to anyone else."

"Crap," she said. "I totally forgot I told him I'd bring him some food." She looked at me, her face bright with hope. "Think on number three, okay? Be back in a bit."

I watched her run up the sand, blown away by her ambition.

Could we do it?

Full Nil destruction was a possibility I'd never considered. I'd only thought of escape.

Waves crashed onto the shore without break. It was like the ocean was hell-bent on fighting Nil ground, day after day. Holding even, keeping the land in check.

A counterweight, Skye had said.

The sea never won. It always withdrew.

A spike of icy fear followed the thought. If we could destroy Nil, what was the cost? Because everything good on Nil came at a price.

One lives, one dies.

So Nil logic begged the question: If we killed Nil, would *we* survive?

CHAPTER 46

SKYE
DAY 16, DAWN

A hand brushed my cheek, startling me awake.

Rives.

"Hey," he said. "Sorry to wake you. But I wanted to say good-bye."

"Good-bye?" I blinked, struggling to focus. "Wait—where are you going?"

"Raj is leaving on Search again today. He asked me to go with him. I couldn't say no. Pari's coming, too. I think he wants to make sure Pari has company on the return trip." His eyes darkened. "Raj has just under three weeks left. So," he sighed, "I'll be back in three weeks."

Three weeks.

Three weeks without Rives. Three weeks to wait to find the stationary gate.

My resolve hardened.

If Rives could go on Search, so could I.

Like he'd read my mind, Rives gently tugged on one curl of my hair, giving me his full—and intense—attention.

"Promise me you won't go off searching for that gate alone, Skye. Or at all." His eyes held mine. The intensity of his gaze made me shiver.

"Not because I don't think you're a badass fully capable of self-preservation, but Nil can take even the strongest."

Are you worried about me? I thought, searching his eyes, hoping for a hint of yes. *Or are you thinking of Talla?*

Rives's eyes never left mine. "I need you here, with Paulo. He trusts you most."

I need you here with Paulo. Not *I need you.*

I was a fool.

"Promise me, Skye." Rives's tone was as intense as his gaze.

"I promise." My tone was reluctant. Rives was right, at least about Paulo needing a shadow. And I was the only one he'd talk to. I was boxed into the job; I may as well embrace it. "Really. I promise," I said, this time with feeling.

Relief flooded Rives's eyes. "Be safe, Skye. See you in three weeks."

And then he vanished into the Nil dark.

Three weeks. Rives only had seventy-three days left. And by the time he got back, he'd be down to fifty-two.

Nil's clock ticked louder than ever.

Paulo's voice cut through the dark. "What does that mean, go on Search?"

I hadn't realized Paulo was awake. I wondered how much he heard, and how he interpreted Rives's words.

"It means they're off Searching for wild gates. Raj only has a few weeks left before his year is up."

Paulo was silent.

"Do you know what happens to people still here at the one-year mark?" I asked.

"They become one with the island," Paulo said.

"If by 'become one with the island,' you mean they die, then you're right." I looked out into the night where Rives had vanished. "They never see their families again, they never have a chance to grow up and grow old. And sometimes they don't get a full year. Sometimes they become one with the island earlier."

Let him think on that, I thought as I climbed out of bed.

Rives's team was already gone.

As the days passed, Paulo and I fell into an easy pattern. I'd bring him breakfast, then we'd go for a walk down the beach, with Paulo sweating as he pushed his crutches through the sand. We didn't talk about the gate, or his history. For once, I didn't push. I guess with Rives gone and my stationary gate quest on hold, the pressure lifted temporarily. Then Paulo would spend the rest of the day sitting by the water until it was time to go to bed. He ate reluctantly, as if every bite placed him further in my debt.

Paulo also refused to go into the City, other than in his hut, and he refused to talk to anyone but me. Not that we talked much at all. We walked in silence, ate in silence, slept in silence.

Until today.

We'd walked to the Crystal Cavern and I'd showed him my favorite place to rest. A small branch off the main cavern, eight feet long at most, it stopped at a wall with a jagged slit for a window and, of all things, a ledge like a seat. We had enough light to see each other, enough darkness to hide our words. Sometimes the dark gives us boldness to say things we never would in the light.

Resting in shadowed glitter, Paulo asked about my family, and so I told him. About my mom, about my dad, and about my uncle.

In turn, he told me about his family. His mom, originally from the mainland, and his dad, descended from island royalty. He told me about his brother, Keahi, who defied his father and refused to come to the island, dishonoring his family.

"Even his noble choice of the healing arts didn't help," Paulo told me. "My dad was furious, because it's tradition. The oldest child, especially the oldest in my father's line." Paulo sighed. "So unlucky me. I got tapped to come."

The spare, I thought.

"Why didn't you say no? Like Keahi?"

"You don't know my dad." Paulo's tone was wry. "Plus, Keahi was always the smartest. The strongest. The chosen one of the family, you know? Everyone expected great things from him." He paused. "I thought this might be my chance."

Getting Paulo to join my destroy-the-island campaign might be harder than I thought. It made Keahi's choice mild by comparison on the dishonor scale.

"My chance to be the brave one," Paulo murmured, "to follow in my father's footsteps."

"It's funny," I said, remembering Rives's conversation with the mysterious Maaka about Nil being a spiritual journey. "The tradition is you coming here to experience peace and to take a personal journey, right?" He didn't say yes, but he didn't say no, either. "It's not a very peaceful island, Paulo. Not anymore."

I paused.

"When I first met you, you told me you couldn't leave, not yet. And I think that's another reason why you ran from the gate, right? To leave too soon isn't honorable either, I'm guessing. So how long do you have to wait?"

Paulo shrugged. "One season, or three. One is acceptable, but three is brave. My father stayed three."

"Why not two?"

Paulo shook his head. "One or three. Those are the choices."

One or three. Not two.

An island thread wove his words into numbers: *3-2-1-4.*

Quarters. Seasons. Dividing lines.

Choices.

A clue was there, I just couldn't see it. Yet.

"Choices." I smiled. "See? You still have some." *And so will we.*

Paulo's smile looked like a grimace. "Not many."

"More than you think." My voice was quiet. "Always more than you think."

For now I left it at that. I was doing a better job with restraint. And I sensed Paulo was done confiding for now.

"Ready to head back?" I asked.

He nodded. We walked back at Paulo's pace, not speaking, only this time, the silence was almost comfortable. The fiery resentment oozing off Paulo had faded to a dull resignation.

I left him at his hut with a full gourd of water. "I'm glad you're getting stronger," I said. "Enjoy your peace."

Then I went to look for Rives again. I didn't know when he'd be back, but it would be exactly three weeks tomorrow. Part of me worried terribly that he wouldn't come back at all, that Nil had flashed a gate and swept him off the island so we couldn't go through with our crazy master plan. It had nearly happened already.

In the east, black smoke rose in the distance, wispy and curling, and then it was gone. *A signal fire?* I wondered. Something had happened, something bad. My Nil sixth sense had finally kicked in.

It's just Michael and Sy, camping out, I told myself. *It's nothing at all.*

By the Flower Field, Dex stared off toward the east, shielding his eyes from the sun with one hand.

"Did you see that, Skye?" He pointed across the island. "Black smoke."

"I saw it. Looks like someone's having a campfire," I said.

"More like a bonfire," Dex said. He looked troubled.

"Dex," I said, drawing his eyes. "Rives is almost late. What do we do if he doesn't come back tomorrow?"

"We pull out the gliders and go look for him." Dex's face was grim. "And we pray to every god and island deity we can think of that he's safe."

Reaching into my satchel, I fished out the black lava rock he'd tossed me in the field and squeezed it tight. *Please keep Rives safe. And please let him still be here.* I whispered the last selfish thought. I knew I could find the stationary gate alone, but the truth was, I didn't want to.

And if I was honest with myself, I wanted Rives.

I was in more trouble than I thought.

CHAPTER 47

RIVES

DAY 315, MID-MORNING

I itched to see the City.

I'd spent three painful weeks on a brutal Search, haunting the eastern side of the island in Quadrants Four and One, the only zones Raj wanted to hit and the only places we'd seen gates. Oddly enough, the gate sets had flashed out of order, a disturbing fact that could mean something or nothing, but I didn't know which. During Charley's time, we'd split the island into four quadrants based on the labyrinth carvings, and since the Man in the Maze sat outside the bottom right, we'd set that as Quadrant One. Then, thanks to Charley, we'd realized that gates flashed in a clockwise motion, like a hurricane, hitting each quadrant in sequence. But the second set of gates flashed in Quadrant Four *after* Quadrant One, like they were backtracking on purpose. Or like Charley's storm theory was falling apart.

Maybe the second gate set was a rogue, a freak aberration.

Then I pushed it out of my head. It was over.

Done.

And all that mattered about yesterday's surprise double was that Pari had caught the second gate of the set yesterday. It almost made up for cremating Raj the day before.

No, it didn't, I thought, cursing Nil's scales. *Not even close.*

Even though I knew it could happen, I wasn't prepared for it, could barely handle it; I'd had enough Nil funerals for three lifetimes. Even worse, I'd seen Raj collapse. No warning, no sound. He just dropped, like someone had flipped the master switch and stopped his heart.

Then it was just me and a shaken and crying and highly pissed-off Pari.

We'd cremated Raj on the beach on the northeast tip at Pari's request, letting the waves take his ashes. Pari had also drawn a symbol for me to carve into the Wall by Raj's name, like she knew she'd be gone. *How the hell did she sense she'd leave?*

But she had. I saw it in her expression when the gate washed over her and she'd waved good-bye. Pure relief, no surprise.

The whole Search had been weird from day one.

I'd asked Brittney to go. Newcomers usually embraced a Search trip like a life preserver, to confirm for themselves that escape was an option, and Brittney had adapted to Nil in record time. But Brittney had said no.

Thanks, Rives, she'd said. *I'm sure honored. But I'm good right here.*

I'd never had someone say no to Search. Ready to roll, I didn't ask anyone else. Then we'd taken off, a silent trio, heading out into a quiet island.

No rookie sightings, no sign of raiders. No sign of Michael and crew or Maaka.

No predators. Few animals, all harmless. Two inbounds, but no riders. No outbound gates at all until the final days.

I felt like we were chasing ghosts.

Since Pari's escape, I'd set a straight course back toward the City. Sweaty, filthy, and despite a dip in the sea, I still felt death on my hands. At the last minute, I'd veered toward the Cove, knowing fresh water was what I needed.

You need Skye, the falls whispered.

I submerged myself in the icy water, grateful that someone had left sandsoap by the Cove's edge. I scrubbed my hands until they burned, then I swam under the falls to chill. I needed some mental space in a quiet place.

On the ledge, I breathed. My eyes drifted toward the carving. Beside the diamond, next to the vertical arrow, the letters *N-I-L* ran vertically, freshly etched into the rock.

Been busy, haven't you, Maaka, I thought. Heat flooded my veins. While I'd been cremating a friend and hiking all over the damn island hoping for gate lightning to strike for Raj, Maaka had been hosting an island art class for one. Carving Nil rock without a care in the world.

Without a care on this island.

Damn you, I thought.

Through the falls, bits of blue sky broke through until soon it was all I could see. The peace I needed wasn't here.

I left the falls without looking back. The Cove itself was still empty. Eerily silent. I had the freak fear that I was coming back to a ghost town, on a ghost island.

Maybe *I* was a ghost.

Get out of my head, Nil.

Nil was not a great place to chill alone. Maybe because it wasn't a great place to chill, period.

The final meters to the City were unsettlingly quiet. I lengthened my stride, breathing shallowly. Dex's distant voice finally broke the silence, but it was the flash of wild blond hair through the trees that made me relax.

By the Shack, Dex was helping Skye pack up a glider. Jason already had his slung across his back. Serious faces, intense moment. No one speaking.

"Going airborne?" I called.

Skye looked up. Relief poured across her face like sweet rain. The glider slid from her hands. "Rives," she breathed.

Dex's head snapped up. "About bloody time."

"Man, you had us worried." Jason slid off his glider pack, his shoulders sagging with a relief as great as Skye's. "We were about to sweep for you."

Skye strode forward, meeting me halfway, and threw her arms around me. "I'm so glad you're okay," she said.

I rested my cheek against her head as I crushed her to my chest. "Me too."

Skye was solid, Skye was *real*. She was fully alive in this world packed with death.

I didn't want to let go.

"You're wet," she finally said. Her lips tickled my chest.

"I took a quick dip in the Cove. Nothing pretty about being Search dirty," I said. *And I had to wash off the feel of death.*

Reluctantly I pulled away from Skye. Dex's and Jason's eyes flicked to the extra satchels; I had brought back three. Alone.

"Pari made it," I said. "Raj didn't. It sucked. Nil understatement." I exhaled slowly. "I never want to go through that again." *I can't.*

I looked at Skye. "We've got to find that gate. Please tell me Paulo's been talking. Please tell me he's given up something."

"He has," Skye said thoughtfully. "Especially the past few days. I think he trusts me, and I think he feels obligated by the City hospitality."

"Good," I said sharply. I was jealous of the time he'd spent with Skye. Here, in the City, away from the death and danger and ghosts lurking behind every rock.

"But"—Skye pursed her lips—"it's like cracking a coconut. Not impossible, just really hard. But one thing I'm certain of is that the number sequence is tied to the stationary gate. How often it appears, maybe when." She looked at me. "Any luck with Maaka?"

"None." I sounded as frustrated as I felt. "The only sign of him was the addition of the word *NIL* to the carving at the Cove tunnel entrance."

"Well, that's a huge help." Skye's frustration matched mine. "We already know where we are, we're trying to *leave*."

Jason was putting the gliders back into the Shack, humming.

"Are you hungry?" Skye asked.

"Yeah. But first I have to carve for Raj. Special request." At the Wall, I carved the Hindu symbol Pari had shown me for Raj, then a crisp check for Pari.

I couldn't help looking at my name. No scar yet on the Wall for me. But the spaces around mine were filling fast.

With a start, I realized I had Priority now. I had fifty days left or it would be me burning on the beach.

Skye gently touched my back. "You okay?"

No.

"Yeah," I said, turning. "Just thinking of Nil truth number one."

"Oh really?" She smiled, her eyes radiating more blue than green in the late daylight. "And what is that?"

"Time here flies faster than you're ready for."

She placed both hands on my chest. "You're going to make it, Rives. We're going to find that gate, and you're going home. That's *my* Nil truth number one."

Maybe a wish, I thought, feeling the heat of Skye's hands on my skin, *but not a truth.* On Nil, wishes were as fragile as time.

CHAPTER 48

SKYE
DAY 39, AFTERNOON

Rives back from Search was even more intense. He kept looking at me as if he wanted to say something, but he didn't.

No, I thought, *he keeps looking at me like I might disappear.* After what he'd described with Raj and Pari, I couldn't blame him. But I didn't know what to say.

Instead, I told him Paulo's family history.

He listened carefully as I recounted every conversation with Paulo in detail, leaving nothing out, hoping Rives might make sense of something I missed. When I was done, Rives looked thoughtful.

"So what do you think?" I asked.

A long moment passed before Rives answered.

"I think Paulo trusts you," he said finally, "and I think his broken leg was a seriously lucky break for us, as shitty as that sounds. I think he might end up being our best hope for finding the stationary gate. And I think we only have about three weeks more of his time, because when he can walk, I think he's gonna bolt."

Three weeks.

We had less time than I thought.

CHAPTER

RIVES
DAY 315, DUSK

The remnants of the City crowded around the firepit.

No sign of Paulo. He was sulking or hiding in his hut. I didn't know, and I sure as hell didn't care. The fact that he only talked to Skye made it clear he felt no loyalty to the City that helped him, and my guess was that his fledgling loyalty to Skye had serious limits—all of which hinged on his broken leg.

"City's shrinking," I commented. "And the Search was weird from the start. Never saw Michael and his crew, never saw a rookie or a raider. And both the inbounds I saw had no riders."

"Odd," Dex said. "Puts the nil in Nil, doesn't it?"

Beside me, Skye stared at the fire, lips tight. Wheels turning. "What does Nil even mean, really?" She turned and pointed to the Wall, where *NIL* ran across the top in all caps.

"Now I'm Lost?" Jillian said, a ghost of a smile tugging at her lips. "That's what Charley joked once."

"Next In Line?" Ahmad asked, tossing a stick on the fire. "No one Is Laughing?"

"That's four words, Big A," Zane said. "I DQ that entry."

"Noon Is Lunch?" Dex offered, his eyes sliding to me. "It was for the grizzly, if my memory serves."

"How about Naked Island Luau?" Zane grinned as Jillian chucked a piece of pineapple at him. He caught it in his mouth and pointed at Jillian as he winked. "A dude can hope."

"I vote for Need Instant Lasagna," Dex said. "I'm so bloody sick of seafood. When I get back, I'm going on a completely unhealthy pasta and biscuit binge."

"I've got it." Zane snapped his fingers. "Now Introducing Llamas." When I shot him a get-serious look, Zane laughed. "What? I saw one last week. I mean, it might've been a camel, but I'm pretty sure it was a llama, Chief."

"Alpaca," Jason muttered.

"Nobody Is Leaving?" Kiera asked.

"No," I said. "People leave. People make it." I heard the fierceness in my voice and forced myself to dial it down. "We definitely can leave, and get home."

"Near Is Light?" Macy said thoughtfully, her voice Macy calm, Macy smooth. "With *light* meaning understanding?"

"I don't think it means anything," Jason said, shrugging. "Nil, nada. Nothing. I think it's because we're here, stuck in a place that doesn't exist, that no one knows about."

"But people do," Skye said quietly. "Some people definitely know." Her eyes caught mine.

"But when we're here, it's like no one can hear us," Jason said, frustrated. "Like we're just—lost."

"That's it!" Zane exclaimed. "Nobody Is Listening!"

Oh, Nil's definitely listening, I thought. My fists clenched. Then I stiffened, feeling eyes heating my back. Nil wasn't the only one listening tonight.

"Be right back," I told Skye.

I got up, turned around, and strode toward the Naming Wall. Behind it, Maaka stood motionless like a living ghost.

"Hasn't anyone told you eavesdropping is rude?" I forced myself to stay calm. I needed to stay calm because Maaka's eyes spewed fire.

"Nil." Maaka spat the word. "You have taken it as your own, put it on a wall, but you do not even know what it means." Disgust dripped from his tone like acid.

"People have taken it," I said slowly, "because they're desperate to make sense of this place. To give it a name gives us desperately needed power over our situation."

"Power?" Maaka's eyes flashed. He took a step toward me, his entire body vibrating with thinly restrained fury. "You seek *power*? It is power that led to the disruption of this place. It is power that led you here. Your people were tempted to harness power they should not. They unleashed a power they did not understand."

I stood my ground and crossed my arms, keeping my shoulders loose. "What are you talking about?"

"Seventy years ago, *haoles* began testing devices in the islands. Devices that unleashed the fires of hell. Many islanders were forced from their homes, their islands. The *haoles* made promises they could not keep, because they did not understand the power they were trying to control.

"For months, weapon after weapon was dropped from the air. Weapons that boiled the sea and made mushroom clouds in the sky. Weapons that melted skin off men's faces."

Maaka closed his eyes. "Horrible stories returned to our island," he whispered. "Tales that we could not believe. But the tales went beyond the men. The tales went beyond *us*." Maaka opened his eyes and looked at me.

"One spring and summer, bombs rained down on the islands for days. Even on our most sacred days. Those were the seasons when unnatural energy filled the air and sea."

Reaching down, he picked up Nil dirt and let it fall through his fingers. "Energy fuels this island. And energy disrupted it. During that time, an elder's son saw the portal tear. He was on Spirit Island, and he watched it happen. It shimmered and fractured and a layer ripped away, a layer thinner than the gate itself. And it kept going, flying faster than the wind, wild and unstable. Then he watched the portal tear again. Another layer peeled away from the whole, and then the layer split, like the *haoles* had split the atom. The layers slowed but kept going. Both of them. He was alone, but he claims it to be the truth. It frightened him enough that he chose not to go through the doorway. He believed the spirits were angry. Despite the shame of not seeking his path, he returned home. He died soon after."

Maaka looked at the stars. "There are other stories, too," he whispered, "stories with many witnesses. Many say in March of that spring, all of Spirit Island glowed as bright as the sun. That glistening light streaked off in all directions, like the sun came to the earth that day. And then all the streaks came back to Spirit Island at once and disappeared. And the island stayed darker than night."

He lifted his eyes to the Nil sky. "I do not know what stories of those are true. But I do know one truth." Now he looked at me. "One of your bombs was dropped on a sacred day. A day when the sun shines the longest and its power is great, when the barrier between the worlds is the most fragile. And it was on that June day when the elder witnessed the portal fracture and fracture again. And"—his voice turned bitter—"it was *haoles* who dropped the bombs. It was *your* people who angered the island spirits. You have brought this place upon yourselves."

I stood mute, processing the informational bomb Maaka had just dropped on me.

Spirit Island. Nuclear testing.

Nil.

Maaka stepped back, clenching and unclenching his fists. "Thank you for caring for Paulo. Your sacrifice was great." Then he strode away.

"Maaka!"

He reluctantly turned back.

"So what does NIL mean?"

He shook his head slightly. "That is your word." He stood, visibly wrestling with his answer, then he sighed. Slowly, he bent and drew the letters *NIL* in the sand, with a vertical arrow pointing toward the sky.

"*N* stands for the beginning, where *we* begin. Low, on the ground—even the shape of the letter itself holds meaning, as does the word it stands for." He murmured an unfamiliar word I didn't catch. "The *I*," he continued, his tone resigned, even tired, "is both a line, symbolizing travel—a singular direction if we are on the right path seeking knowledge and peace—and yet it is also a single *I*, to symbolize each person. The individual nature of the journey. And the *L* is *lani*, the sky, the heavens. Where we aspire to be, where all knowledge flows to and from. It is the everything." He paused, his eyes pained. Deeply hurt.

"These letters do not symbolize *nothing*," he whispered. "These letters, they mean *everything*." He turned and walked away.

The sky.

It is the everything.

And now Skye was on Nil, a girl connected to Nil in unexpected ways, a girl whose name meant everything. A girl with the power to *destroy* everything.

Or save it.

CHAPTER 50

SKYE
DAY 39, NIGHT

Rives stood behind the Wall of Names—*the Naming Wall*, I quickly corrected myself—staring at the woods.

"Everything okay?" I asked.

He spun around, his expression one of disbelief. "Tell me again what Paulo told you about the seasons."

Slowly, carefully, I recounted that key conversation with Paulo, only this time I added my conclusion. "So, the numbers, three-two-one-four? They relate to the seasons. My guess is that the stationary gates open at set times, and only those times."

"I think you're dead on." Rives's voice was tight. "You arrived on the Winter Solstice. You realize that, right?"

I shook my head, feeling ridiculously stupid. How had I missed that?

"Maaka just told me an interesting story. It seems that the Americans dropped nuclear weapons on Spirit Island, on the exact day of the Summer Solstice."

"The day that the sun is directly overhead," I said. "At its highest point."

"Exactly. At noon." Rives swallowed. "Apparently on that day, the doorway between the worlds is both at its most powerful and most fragile, and when the Americans dropped atomic bombs that June day, the portal fractured. Layers ripped away. Hence, the wild portals that roam the Earth."

"Holy crap," I said. I pictured bombs dropping, gates tearing. Collateral damage no one dreamed was happening, damage that lingered to this day. A World War Two legacy, glittering in the sun like an invisible ghost, one that snatched modern-day kids without regard to race, country, or creed.

For a long moment we stood there, not speaking. My mind spun and worked, trying to make all the Nil pieces fit.

Then I frowned. "But my stationary gate was at midnight."

"On the shortest day," Rives said. "I already thought about that. It's got to be a counterweight. Even the sacred days have a balance to stay in stasis, I think. So the Winter Solstice portal opens at midnight; the Summer Solstice one opens at noon."

"And," I said, following the thread of our theories, "maybe the underwater portals open on the reverse. I don't know—I mean, we can't know—but again, the balance of it all."

"Nil truth number four," Rives said softly.

"So," I spoke slowly, "do the stationary portals only open on the solstices? Are those dates the key?" Excitement bloomed in my chest—until I glanced at Rives's face.

Defeat. Crushing defeat.

In that instant I knew: If we had to wait until June, Rives would be long gone.

He had exactly fifty days left.

CHAPTER
51

SKYE
DAY 39, NIGHT

I grabbed Rives's hand before he had time to retreat back into himself. "C'mon. Time for a little chit-chat with Paulo." He didn't argue or let go.

I knocked on the doorframe but didn't wait for an answer before stepping inside the hut.

Paulo's eyes narrowed when we entered. He was looking at Rives. "What do you want?" Paulo sounded peevish.

"Good evening, Paulo." Rives smiled, a dangerous smile. "It's good to see you, too. Are you enjoying the hospitality? This is my hut, after all. And you're in my bed." Rives's tone hardened and his smile slipped.

I shot him a look.

Back down, I willed him. There was enough testosterone in this tent to cause an implosion. *Or power Nil for days.* That thought made me want to shake Paulo, or Rives.

Or both.

Rives raised one eyebrow. *All yours*, he mouthed.

"Paulo." I let go of Rives and sat by the end of Paulo's bed. "Rives has been talking to Maaka." Paulo's eyes widened in surprise. "The two have been talking since before you showed up; they've been chatting for months. And tonight? Maaka told Rives the story of how bombs fell on Spirit Island back in the 1940s in the summer. On the day of the Summer Solstice in June. So." I paused. "The stationary portal, the one you took to come here. It opens on the solstices, right? December and June?"

Paulo hesitated, then nodded.

Answer number one, I thought.

Rives leaned forward, radiating intensity. "What about March? Maaka mentioned that in March one year, Spirit Island glowed. Does the portal open in March, too?"

Paulo looked at Rives. "March on Spirit Island is dark."

"That's not an answer." Rives's voice was thick with ice.

"It is." Paulo looked away. The silence was heavy.

"*Merde*," Rives murmured, a whisper so quiet I knew it wasn't meant for me. I looked up anyway, and our eyes caught. Rives's were full of frustration and fury and fading hope. And, if I read him right, shock.

No, I thought. *Don't quit now.*

Rives's hope balanced his frustration, barely.

Balance.

I turned back to Paulo, a new idea forming.

"Paulo." It took all I had to keep my voice calm, because a fragile hope screamed for air. "Spirit Island is dark in March. But what about here? Does the stationary portal open *here* in March and September? Is that why you have a choice of one season or three?"

Paulo's mouth fell open, then he snapped it shut quickly.

It was the confirmation I needed. *That's answer number two*, I thought.

Then I told myself, *Think.*

"It's the equinox, right?" My voice was steady. "Not when the sun is highest, but when day and night are equal. When you've achieved balance," I thought out loud, "you can leave on the equinox, either in the spring or fall."

And so can we, I thought.

Paulo's expression waffled between shock and fear.

"Does the portal open at noon or midnight?" I looked directly at Paulo.

He stared at me, lips closed.

"Please," I asked. "We deserve to know."

"You deserve to know?" Paulo squeaked. "Why? Why do you deserve to know our history, our secrets? What makes this portal *yours*?"

"I came through it, too, remember?"

He glared at me. "I remember."

"So does it come at midnight again, or noon?"

Paulo shook his head.

"When the crescent moon rises over the heart of the island," I said softly.

Paulo sucked in his breath.

I smiled. "I have secrets too, Paulo. I know more about this place than you think. Maybe as much as you. Different things perhaps, but just as important. Think on that."

He stared at me.

"I'll let you rest, Paulo. In another three weeks you can walk. Then you can leave or stay. But we're going to find that gate, Paulo. Me, Rives, all of us. And we're all going to take it home."

CHAPTER
52

RIVES

DAY 315, NIGHT

Damn.

Skye in action was a little scary. And honestly, a little hot. Paulo looked ready to flatline as she grilled him, only Skye wouldn't let him; she kept reeling him back in, over and over, pulling info out piece by calculated piece. Maybe the CIA was in Skye's future, because the girl could interrogate with serious skill and real results.

As we left the hut, Skye grabbed my arm.

"Rives!" Her eyes found mine. "I just realized something! It's the weirdest Nil coincidence ever."

My blood chilled. *There are no coincidences on Nil.*

"My uncle," Skye was saying, her voice breathless. I'd never heard her speak so fast. "You know, Scott? He left Nil in March. In *March*, Rives. *When the crescent moon rises over the heart of the island*, the weird island girl told him. And he left. Not through the stationary gate, but a wild portal. And yet, that phrase—the heart of the island."

She took a deep breath. "I think the gate flashes in the heart of the island. And I think that's the heart." She pointed toward Mount Nil. "It makes sense. It's where I arrived, and it's the volcano that formed the island. Think of the lava like blood." Skye raised her hands, blushing. "Sorry. Creepy, I know. I'm going crazy with metaphors. But I think Mount Nil is the heart of the island. That the fixed gate will flash there in March, and that's how my uncle's legacy stretches further—through me. And I think tomorrow we need to find it. Not the mountain, but the heart."

"What?" I said, trying to keep up with Skye. The girl operated at Mach force levels on a regular basis. "Go where tomorrow?"

"The mountain. A scouting trip. To see if I can pick out where I landed, because even though the stationary gates open at different times, my sense says the gate is truly stationary, that the doorway is fixed. The time it opens may vary, but not its position. And we need to go look because if I can't find it, then we need Paulo to tell us where it is while he's still here."

"Everyone okay?" It was Dex. He'd come up with Jillian and Zane.

"Yeah. Full details in the a.m.," I said slowly, "but Skye and I are going to take a quick trip to the mountain tomorrow. I'll need you to stay as Leader, Dex."

"I want in," Jason said. He'd materialized from the darkness without a sound.

"Done," I said, feeling the rightness of Jason's offer. Jason had been with Charley when she'd found the carving at the mountain's base. "We're going to look for a Nil answer. For something related to the numbers. We'll be back in two days."

The foursome scattered as quickly as they'd appeared.

I turned to Skye. She stood close, watching me, her face touched by Nil shadows.

"Good night, Skye," I whispered.

She tilted her face to mine. "Good night, Rives." Her lips were so close, a tempting curve defying the Nil night. We stood there, not moving. Barely breathing.

I stepped back. "See you in the morning."

She nodded and turned away. It took me a minute to realize we were walking in step. Skye looked at me.

"You don't need to walk me to my hut," she said. "I promise I've got it."

"Your hut?" I frowned. "I'm heading to Michael's old bunk. I can't bring myself to spend the night with Paulo." *I might kick his ass.*

She turned to me, her cheeks red. "That's where I've been staying. Michael's empty hut. I couldn't stand sleeping near Paulo, either. He's a little whiny." She rolled her eyes.

"What about your old place?"

"Crowded. I think Kiera needed more space." The annoyance in Skye's tone made me laugh.

"So now what. It's you and me?" I teased.

"Looks like it." Skye smiled, her eyes so intense my pulse raced. "I promise I won't attack you in the dark. I save that for the leopards."

Damn, I thought.

We walked the rest of the way in silence.

Michael's hut had four bunks. Skye and I took the ones near the front. I turned the other two beds lengthwise, like a buffer. It made me feel like I was doing something, even as the breeze whispered, *You can't keep me out.*

With a start I realized it wasn't Talla I'd been hearing, it was Nil.

You're wrong, I thought savagely. *Watch me.* With lethal force, I locked Nil out of my head. I would not let Nil consume me.

I'd been warned.

We lay there in Nil dark, the two of us. Me, and Skye. Not speaking, and as for me, definitely not sleeping. Not with her so close.

Time passed, painful and potent.

"Rives?" Skye's soft voice made my chest tight.

"Yes?"

"I can't sleep."

"Me either."

Pause.

"Do you want to walk down to the beach?" she asked. "Sometimes when I can't sleep, looking up at the stars helps."

She didn't have to ask twice.

I got up, grabbed her cheetah pelt, and then I followed her, this insanely ballsy girl who had more brains, looks, and passionate ambition than anyone I'd ever met. A lethal package, topped with a wild, golden halo.

Maybe she was sent to destroy Nil after all. In March we'd find out.

But Nil wouldn't let go easily. Nil would play to win, pulling every last string, messing with our heads until the final second. Nil was the ultimate puppetmaster. Sometimes for thrills, sometimes for kicks. And here was Nil's latest punch line, delivered while Paulo was talking: If I was right, the Spring Equinox fell on March 20.

The joke was on me. March 20 was my Day 365. I'd get one day, one noon.

One shot.

Ha-ha, I thought as I followed Skye out of the hut.

I just hoped that when March rolled around, I got the last laugh.

CHAPTER 53

SKYE
DAY 39, LATE NIGHT

I lay beside Rives on the sand, our hips separated by a breath of Nil air. The cheetah covers were our beach blanket, which Rives had sensibly thought to bring. He'd also brought a torch to guide our way through the trees, to ward off nocturnal creatures, I assumed. Now the torch flickered in the sand beside us. He was the hottest and most thoughtful Boy Scout ever.

If Boy Scouts camped out on deadly islands, I thought.

On Nil, he was better than any Boy Scout, almost bigger than life. The Leader of the City—and yet so much more. He was the most compassionate and driven person I'd ever met.

We lay without talking, studying the stars.

I broke the silence. "Orion." I pointed. "It's the first constellation my dad taught me. And there's Andromeda, who I'm named after."

"Your middle name is Andromeda?"

I winced, wishing I'd kept my mouth shut. I'd forgotten my new motto.

"My middle name is Athena, actually. My full name is Andromeda Skye Athena Bracken. I guess you can figure out why I go by Skye.

That's what happens when you're named by an astrophysicist and a lover of Greek mythology."

Rives chuckled. "That's a mouthful."

"What about you? What's your full name?"

"Rives Jesper Martin-Taylor."

"Wow," I said. "That's a mouthful, too. But beautiful."

"Thanks. My parents named me Rives because I was born near the River Seine. Jesper is my grandfather's name. It's Swedish." He stretched one hand behind his head. "My dad's surname was Taylor; my mom's was Martin. Now we're the Martin-Taylor team."

A long moment passed, with both of us looking at the stars. My heart ached for Rives. His family seemed close, closer than mine.

"What do you want to do?" Rives asked. "After Nil, I mean?"

He sounded so confident I *would* leave. I'd grown less certain. What *would* I do after Nil, if I made it back in one piece?

I stared at the stars.

"College, I guess," I said finally.

"Why?"

"Why college?" The question seemed odd, especially coming from a boy who spoke five languages. I'd heard Ahmad bragging about Rives to Kiera, about our Leader being a language superstar. As if Kiera needed another reason to fawn over Rives.

"Yes, why?" Rives was extraordinarily patient.

Isn't it obvious? "A degree. A good education."

Rives raised his eyebrows. "That's an end. What's the middle? Why college? What do you want to study?"

It hit me like an empty gate, like a question I couldn't answer. A question that *had* no answer.

What do you want to study?

A straight-A student, I excelled at school. I excelled at *excelling.* Past that, I'd no clue.

"I don't know what I want to be," I admitted. I stared at Orion, as if he held a clue. "I just know what I *don't* want."

"Which is?" Rives asked.

"I don't want to live my life dictated by my past. And I don't want to settle. I want to choose."

Rives was quiet. I felt like I'd overshared, but now it was out there. There was no rewind button on Nil.

"Your uncle's past may have pushed your dad toward Nil, but it was still your dad's own choice to search for it, right?" Rives's voice was a whisper.

"I guess." I nodded.

"I guess too," Rives said thoughtfully. "Because your dad's passion for finding Nil was his own. Yeah, maybe it started with your uncle, but somewhere along the way it became your dad's and it drove him. And he let it. Because it fed him somehow. It was his."

I nodded again, slowly this time.

"I don't think your dad settled; I think it was his choice. Both to become an astrophysicist and to hunt for Nil. And Skye"—Rives tilted his head to look at me—"I don't think you should settle, ever. Never settle for anything less than what you want."

The Nil air was thick. Heavy with whispers and echoes and heat, only a fraction of which came from the torch.

I swallowed.

"What do you like?" Rives asked.

You, I thought. My gaze fell to his lips. Perfect lips, set in a chiseled face, sharpened by the night. My voyeurism was now fully confined to Rives.

A smile lifted the corner of his mouth.

"Back home," he whispered, "what do you do? What do you like to do?"

I closed my eyes. "Different questions. What do I do? I train. I run,

I eat weird stuff my dad makes me try, I practice knocking pine cones off tables with a rock slingshot from a hundred feet. Then I go back to my mom's, and I study. I hang with my friends, and I still study. And I still train. Krav Maga, with a crazy ex-Israeli military instructor named Yarin my dad found for me in Gainesville. But what do I like to do?" I stared at the stars. "I love to read, I love to travel. I love to listen to music. But what do I *want* to do? I don't know. Sometimes it's like I don't know me."

I turned toward Rives. He was so *close.*

"You asked me once why I jumped through that gate." I paused. "I think it's because I had to. Like all those years of training my dad put me through, to protect me against this place—it drove me here. I don't know if it was to test my training, or it was just my destiny. All I can say is that I had to take that gate. I felt a pull, and I didn't think; I just *went.* And sometimes I think I jumped because it was finally a choice *I* made, not anyone else. Like in that single moment, I finally did something for me." *Maybe to find me.* I closed my eyes. "But it was selfish, too. My parents are probably worried sick."

A brush across my cheek made my skin tingle and my eyes open. Rives's fingers gently swept hair away from my face, then he traced my jaw. The tingles grew.

His eyes were so light, yet full of green fire.

"You're not selfish, Skye. You're rarely even impulsive. I think maybe Nil *is* your destiny, so how can accepting your destiny be selfish?"

I had no answer for that. Also, my mind was screaming *Rives* and his fingers were exceptionally distracting.

He leaned back and stared at the night. "Want to hear something crazy?"

"Of course. The crazy club is a special one. Come on in. We have snacks," I said. It was easier to think when Rives wasn't looking at me—or touching me.

He laughed, a sweet rumble. "Please tell me it's not fish wraps."

"Nope. I'm talking lasagna bolognese, arugula salad with blue cheese crumbles and a balsamic reduction, fresh French baguettes, followed by homemade raspberry sorbet."

Rives groaned. "Skye, you're killing me."

"Sorry." I grinned. "Over the summer, I do all the cooking at my dad's. He's hard-core Paleo, and I can't take it. I experiment, and I really love to bake. Even my dad breaks his diet for my chocolate chip cheesecake or my crème brûlée—"

Rives placed a single finger over my lips. "You really are killing me, you know that?" he whispered. His eyes were so full of heat I thought I might die. Or kiss him.

Slowly, he removed his finger. "Have you ever thought about being a chef?"

"Um, no."

"Well, the crazy clubhouse has the best menu I've seen in a while." His eyes stayed on mine.

"So what makes you a member?"

"Besides the fact that Nil gets in my head sometimes?" He looked away.

"I think Nil gets in everyone's head." My voice was soft. "My uncle started hearing Nil—or at least talking to Nil—after about the six-month mark." *The second season*, I thought. *Is that why Paulo had to stay? To hear Nil?*

I'm losing it, I thought. *I'm the crazy club prez.*

Rives leaned back, his eyes still on the stars.

"Here's what's crazy." His voice was guarded, yet vulnerable. "Sometimes I think I'm here for a reason. Like I'm the one who's supposed to bring everyone together to leave on time. Not that I'm a savior, more like an organizer. I speak five languages; I even have island blood. And Maaka talks to me. I'm not bragging, I'm just saying maybe I'm supposed to do something important. Something beyond me."

"Something more," I whispered.

"Exactly." Rives's eyes burned mine with an intensity that made me forget to breathe.

He blinked and looked away.

I looked back at the stars, suddenly exhausted, and strangely defeated. "So I'm supposed to find the gate, and you're supposed to lead everyone to it."

"Something like that."

"And we've got until the Spring Equinox to figure it out. How many days do we have?"

It took Rives a moment to answer.

"Enough," he said. "Sleep, Skye. We've got a road trip in the morning."

CHAPTER 54

RIVES
DAY 310, DAWN

Skye lay in my arms.

I was spooned around her, her back pressed against my chest, one arm hooked over her waist. *For warmth*, I told myself.

I eased backward a crucial bit. Then I lay there, thinking cool thoughts. Antarctica. Greenland. Sweden in winter. Waking up plastered to Skye wreaked havoc on my control.

When I'd pulled myself together, I leaned my head close. My lips brushed the edge of her ear. "Hey, sleepyhead," I whispered.

She opened her eyes. "Hey." Then she closed them and curled closer, erasing the slight space I'd made between us and tucking her hands under her head. For a heady moment, it was just me and Skye. But it wasn't. Nil hung around like a third wheel.

Three's a crowd, I thought. *And today marks the beginning of your end, Nil.*

I wondered what Maaka would think of my words, not to mention Skye's plan.

What's number three? I'd asked her.

Now I knew.

"I'm so warm," Skye said, eyes still closed. "Do we have to get up?"

"We've got a trip to take," I said softly. "Remember?"

She sat up immediately. "Right. The mountain. The gate. Let's go."

I laughed. "Patience, padawan. Breakfast first. Then we pack a few things to spend the night in case we need to. *Then* we leave." I paused.

We leave. But Skye dreamed of more.

"Do you remember your three-part plan?" I asked her. "Where part one was we find when the stationary gate opens and where? And two was sweeping the island for everyone to make sure no one gets left behind, with the idea being if we all leave, the island's mojo gets out of whack—maybe enough to destroy it?"

She nodded.

"I know what number three is. It's getting Maaka to join in our annihilation scheme."

"And Paulo," she said, her voice quiet. "We'll have to work on him, too." Then she looked at me, the steel in her eyes flashing in the growing sunlight as she smiled. "But patience, padawan. Don't look ahead. Today, step one."

It was my turn to nod.

"I'm going to wake Jason and get some supplies," I told Skye as we walked up the beach. "Meet at the firepit in twenty?"

"Perfect."

Twenty minutes later, Skye walked up to the firepit. Nikolai followed her like a pale puppy, complete with a goofy grin. Something was up. Skye wouldn't meet my eyes.

"Ready, Skye?" I had a pineapple and three fish, all fire-roasted, thanks to Jason. No time for wraps, but protein was protein. "We're going to eat, then go."

"Rives." Skye came over, and as Nikolai followed, she turned to him, held up one hand, and shook her head. Nikolai stepped back.

"He's well trained, I see," I said. Beside me, Jason snorted.

"I'm sorry," Skye said. "He asked me where I was going and I pointed to the mountain. And he said he wanted to come."

"He said that?" I asked skeptically.

"Well"—her cheeks flushed—"he actually said, 'Me come?' but I know he wants to go. Rives, he's been sitting in this City for weeks. And this gate will be his, too. So why not?"

"Because he's never been on Search. Because he'll slow us down. Because I can't read him and if we get into trouble he's a team variable I don't know where to fit. Skye"—I paused—"this isn't your average Search. I don't think it's a good idea."

"It's not your average Search," she agreed. "A direct scouting mission, not an escape." She glanced at Nikolai, who waved and smiled. "It feels wrong to tell him no, Rives. Why do we get to decide?" she asked quietly.

I didn't have an answer that didn't make me feel like a controlling jerk.

"Fine." I sighed. "Let's go." I turned to Jason. "Will you help keep an eye on the rook?"

"No problem." He looked at Skye.

"I meant Nikolai." I fought not to snap. Skye could handle herself. Plus, my eye was already on her. I waved Nikolai over. "Let's pack and roll."

"And hope the gates roll, too," Jason said. "Wait—scratch that." He ran one hand through his mop of hair. "Let's hope we find what we're looking for."

"Well said, bro. Well said."

I clapped Jason on the shoulder. We ate quickly, then set off on the ultimate Search, looking for the ultimate prize.

Skye and I took lead; Jason and Nikolai took rear. I actually felt better with a foursome as we trekked.

Balance reigned.

The mountain loomed over us, watching.

"What do you want to do?" Skye asked as we worked our way through the south lava field. Smooth ripples of black rock, baked under the Nil sun for enough centuries to crack. The meadow winked grass green in the distance at the black mountain's base. "After Nil, I mean?"

I thought about her question; it was the same one I'd asked her last night.

"Short term? Hang with my parents, I guess, take the *bac*—it's the French equivalent of a high school diploma—play football. Long term? Maybe play football, maybe become a photojournalist. I've lived my whole life traveling. Seeing the world, noticing it. I can't imagine doing anything else. I can't imagine a job where I sit still." I lapsed into silence.

"And by football, you're talking about soccer, right?" Skye said.

"Right. My last club was in Paris."

She looked thoughtful. "I bet France is beautiful." Her sigh was wistful.

"It is."

"I've never been to Europe, just a million tropical islands." She smiled. "But one day."

"One day," I agreed.

Nil fed off our dreams, I felt it. The sun grew hotter, the air thicker, like the island breathed in our words, our hopes. Then it stilled completely.

Noon, I thought, caught off guard. *Merde.*

I looked at Skye; she was looking at me.

"Turn," she whispered, her hand finding mine.

Should I go? Save myself?

Stay? Help the rest? Risk checking out?

Skye's eyes were pleading.

For me to stay? For me to go? For something I couldn't read?

She grabbed my arms and spun me around as Jason screamed.

The shimmering wall flew past me, skimming the ground like a liquid rocket. A furious single flying fast, it rolled over Jason without stopping. The last thing I saw was his face: shock, disbelief, fury, sadness, a roiling mix of emotion twisting his face into a living portrait of *The Scream*.

The gate collapsed into a single black dot—and then disappeared.

Jason was gone.

Our team's balance was gone.

Nikolai stood ten meters away, jaw dangling, arms wrapped tight.

"Holy crap," Skye said.

Should I have caught it?

Was that mine?

Jason made it, I breathed. *That's what matters.*

Skye stared at the place Jason vanished. "I hope he told Miya good-bye," she murmured.

"Me too." Hell, I wished I'd told him good-bye. Told him how much I trusted him, how much I thought of him. That he was more of a man than most I'd ever met. So many words left unsaid. I hoped he knew.

No regrets, Natalie would tell me, even as she hugged me.

I closed my eyes, feeling the lingering strength of Skye's hand, feeling the hole left by Jason's escape.

"Let's get to it," I told Skye. I knew I needed to sort out my feelings for Skye before I regretted something else, too.

Focus.

Pay attention.

Inattentiveness can get you killed.

Mind refocused, I set a strong pace. Nikolai kept up. He even draped a cloth over his head and shoulders as sun protection, a wise veteran move.

But he wasn't a veteran.

The void Jason left brushed cool against my spine. His eyes would be on the rocks, on the grasses, watching our backs.

Time to finally learn to watch your own, Rives.

The island's stillness made me hyperaware. Just like on the last Search with Raj, the lack of small animals was disturbing. *Maybe it's why the leopard staked out the City*, I thought. Nothing moved, nothing chirped.

Not even a rabbit—which used to be a given—to snare.

I pondered Nil's wildlife—or lack of it—as we neared the meadow. To the right, Mount Nil jutted from the ground, a black beast with emerald blotches, butting against the meadow's southern edge.

"The gate has to be on the backside," Skye said as she studied the mountain. "The eastern backside, actually. Which means we have to go through the meadow, or at least around it, because the southern route is blocked by lava, right?"

"Right." The meadow's grasses swayed in the breeze. It looked peaceful, which meant nothing.

"Skye?" I asked. She hadn't moved.

"I'm worried about the tiger." She turned to me. "What if the cats protect the gate? What if they're drawn to it, and they protect it? I know it sounds weird, but no weirder than anything else here. And my uncle's journal? The mysterious island angel girl told him to stay away from the meadow."

"Stay away because of cats, or because it's near the stationary gate?" I frowned.

"I don't know. I've asked myself the same thing. But the cats. They're a problem."

"True. But right now the gate's closed. So they have nothing to protect, right?"

"Right." She nodded. But she didn't move.

"It's your call, Skye," I said quietly. "We can go on and look for the place where you landed, or wait for Paulo and Maaka to give up the coordinates. We have time either way."

Forty-nine days, my mind whispered.

Tick-tock. My Nil clock.

I waited for Skye to make the call.

CHAPTER
55

"Let's do it," she said abruptly.

She starting walking, tacking south toward the mountain.

I followed, hefting Jason's gear and mine, then signaled to Nikolai to follow.

At Mount Nil's base, etched into a black rock boulder the size of a Smartcar, the Countdown carving faced the mountain—like the carving at the Arches. *All* the labyrinths faced the mountain, I realized, all the arrows pointed here.

Another Nil piece locked into place.

Skye and Nikolai were looking at me. Looking *to* me, to lead.

"About thirty meters up is a cave," I said crisply. "A safe house to spend the night if we can't make it to South Beach by dark. We should follow the grassline, using the trees as defense for as long as we can."

"I remember rock steps," Skye said. "Or what felt like rock steps. Let's look for something like that."

Staying above the meadow's grassline, we hiked around the mountain, staying on this side. The backside facing the southern coast oozed lava; it dripped off a hard black shelf into the sea, like molten steel, hissing as it hit the water. On this side, Mount Nil's slope was more forgiving, which on Nil meant it was still a grueling haul, just not instantly lethal. We chose each step with care, hiking without speaking.

"There!" Skye cried.

Midway up the mountain, rough black steps gouged the mountain's side like scars, curving away. The primitive steps led to a black rock platform, a smooth swath about half the size of a football goal but just as deep. It butted against a sheer wall that rose into the clouds.

Skye made it to the platform first and crouched near the center. A carving splayed across the ground, cut into the black rock, the gouged lines filled with pure white sand.

"This symbol," Skye said, kneeling. "The sun, with the eye at its center, and the twelve rays. It was on the ground on the Death Twin island, too, the twin they call Spirit Island. I remember now." She looked up at me, her eyes light. "And it's the same sun that's tattooed on Paulo's arm."

And carved in the Cove tunnel, I thought. *Marking a skeleton's tomb.*

"We did it," Skye whispered. "The heart of the island. This is where the gate will show. I know it."

I nodded. It seemed so obvious now. The eye etched in the sun's center stared back at me. Watching, like the mountain.

Like Nil.

Nikolai bent down. He traced the eye, running his fingers through the sand, mesmerized.

"You know what?" I studied the eye. "We've never come up here, because there's no room to run. But the irony is, if you're here when the gate comes, you don't have to run."

"So now we just need the time of the gate. Noon or midnight. I guess be prepared for both." Skye looked thoughtful.

"I'm hoping noon," I said. *Because otherwise I'm toast.*

"It would be easier," she agreed.

If easier means still alive, then yeah.

Saying nothing, I stood beside Skye, studying the carving.

Staring.

The eye didn't blink. The rays didn't waver.

Inside the eye, a crescent moon appeared, like I'd stared at a hidden picture long enough for the real image to appear.

I blinked, and the crescent moon vanished.

Nikolai and Skye hadn't moved.

I was reminded of my first visit to the Looking Glass cavern, when I'd lost time listening to the water falling, waiting for clarity.

How long had the three of us been staring at the rock?

The sun was fire in the sky, falling fast.

"Skye. Nikolai." Their heads snapped up, eyes unfocused.

"I know we just got here—" I stopped. *Did we?*

"Anyway," I continued, "no gate's flashing tonight. And we need to check out that cave in daylight and set up camp before nightfall."

Without discussion, we backtracked down the steps, then trekked up the mountain to the cave, fighting dwindling light.

The shallow cave was empty, save for a pile of wood and a bleached tusk knife. A lucky break.

When Skye went to touch the tusk, I blocked her. "Leave it. We'll use the wood, but we'll disturb as little as possible, okay?" I didn't add that the skeleton in the tunnel had clutched a similar bone tusk, giving the tusk an aura of death.

She withdrew her hand.

I pulled out the thin groundcover and grimaced. I preferred sleeping on soft sand, not brutal rock, and on this rock, the groundcover did almost nothing. South Beach would've been safer, but we were bunking here. We needed the tri-wall protection, and we needed rest. It was a Nil necessity.

"I can't believe Jason's gone," Skye murmured. She sat on her satchel, rubbing a small rock between her thumb and forefinger. It glinted shiny black.

"You and me both." I watched her hands worry the rock. *My rock,*

I realized. The one I'd kept from my first day on Nil. The one I'd tossed her in the lava field on the day Paulo fell. My chest tightened that she'd kept it.

Our eyes caught and she smiled.

Nikolai tapped my knee. I turned to find him holding out a large redfruit and a small bleached plank.

I raised the fruit in thanks, cut it with my knife, and shared.

Nikolai nodded as he took a slice. He raised it and grinned. *"Spasibo."*

The spooked deer was gone, replaced by a boy finding comfort in companionship and strength in survival. *Did Nil create his newfound strength, or just push it to the surface?*

Another question. No answer.

We added nuts, a mango, and salted fish. Not a bad dinner, considering. Night fell fast and heavy outside the cave; darkness covered the entrance like a blackout shade. We stoked the fire for protection, far enough outside the mouth that we didn't smoke ourselves out.

Any doubts that the hyenas were still here vanished within the hour. They cackled in the distance, an eerie echo. No noises were close. I took the distance as a positive sign. Maybe Nil would let us sleep. Or at least Skye and Nikolai.

With Skye so close, the thin groundcover was the least of my problems.

She curled beside me, tucked between me and the wall; Nikolai slept against the far side. He was already snoring. I faced away from Skye, but my every sense told me she was there.

"Can I tell you something?" she whispered as darkness fell. Shadows clung to her face, like Nil searching for a way in.

"Anything." My voice was rough.

"I'm glad you didn't take that gate today," she whispered. "That you didn't leave. I know it's selfish, that I shouldn't be glad at all. And I know you could be gone tomorrow. But I'm really, really glad you're here."

Here, on Nil? I wanted to ask. *Or here, in my arms?*

I was that man, standing on the edge of a cliff, windmilling my arms to keep from falling.

"Me too."

A thick moment passed. I teetered, then stepped back.

"Good night, Skye."

"Good night, Rives."

CHAPTER
56

SKYE
DAY 41, DAWN

I woke beside Rives, close but not touching, and I almost laughed. It was a perfect representation of last night: good, bad, and completely awkward.

I'd spent half the night terrified something would come inside the cave and eat us for dinner. I knew we were decently safe, but it didn't *feel* safe; it had felt dark and threatening and lethal campout creepy, maybe because the dreaded meadow sprawled below us, out of sight but still fresh in my mind, the same meadow I personally knew was home to a Bengal tiger and that Rives knew was home to a mini pride of lions. Maybe I was claustrophobic; the darkness had felt choking. I missed my hut by the sea with open sides.

The other reason I couldn't sleep? The sleeping arrangements.

Sure, I was warm enough, tucked between the cave wall and Rives, but the rock ground dug into my bones with a vengeance, and comfort was out of the question. And worse than sleeping on a rock was sleeping beside Rives, our bodies so close I could touch him—and to be honest, at one point when I woke, I was completely embarrassed to find myself snuggling closer because he was so toasty warm—and yet there was a wall between us.

Something I couldn't see, but I could feel. It was as real as the rock wall at my back.

It was thicker at some times than others, but it was always there, pushing me away. I wondered if it was Talla's ghost or Nil's pressures. I wondered if it would ever crack.

Like he'd sensed my thoughts, Rives rolled over and looked at me. "How'd you sleep?" I whispered.

"Fantastic. I give the cave a solid four-star rating, taking off a star because the mattress was rock hard. You?"

"Awful."

A smile curved his lips. "Same. Let's grab Nikolai and roll."

We folded the piece of cloth that was just enough to keep the sand off our skin and stuffed it in Rives's bag. There wasn't anything else to pack. Nikolai stood outside the cave entrance on the ledge, toying with the large curved tusk-that-looked-like-a-knife thing as he looked out over the meadow.

"Morning, Nikolai!" I called.

He turned, smiling. The light behind him flickered, like something had blotted out the sun. I caught a glimpse of gold as Nikolai disappeared with a scream.

A chill streaked down my spine like cold fire.

"Rives?" I whispered.

He was already on his feet, knife in hand, face hard. "Load your sling. I'm ninety-nine percent sure that was a cat."

My sling was already in my hand; instinct had automatically kicked in. He strode forward as I fumbled for a rock in my bag. My hands shook, making an easy move hard.

"*Merde.*" Rives's soft word echoed. He still held his knife out like a shield.

"What's wrong?"

"He fell," Rives said, his tone shocked. He walked back to me, his eyes pained. "If I asked you to stay here, would you? It's safer here, but I need to see if Nikolai needs help."

I shook my head. "I'm safer with you than in here alone."

To my surprise, Rives nodded. "You're right. We should stick together. Is your sling ready?"

I nodded.

"He's really hurt," Rives said quietly. "Just wanted to warn you, okay?"

We left the cave and my eyes found Nikolai immediately. He lay at the base of the mountain, unmoving. *Thirty meters,* Rives had said the distance was from base to cave. *How did Nikolai fall thirty meters?* Unbelievable, yet as we picked our footing carefully, I saw how one wrong step could make a person slip.

Dawn on this side of the island wasn't peaceful.

It was horrible.

Strange sounds, weird silence. The grasses glinted like wet knives and our new friend lay deathly still below us. And the closer we drew, the worse it seemed. Nikolai lay facedown at the edge of the grassline, his arms and legs bent at weird angles, his head twisted to one side. His eyes were closed. I had the awful thought that if he vanished, a chalk outline would appear in his place. I started to shake.

"Hang in there, Skye," Rives said.

Please move, I thought frantically, my eyes on Nikolai. *Please be okay.*

I'd chosen to come. My choice. And Nikolai had followed, following *me.*

Rives pressed two fingers against Nikolai's neck, and the instant Rives's head dropped in defeat, I knew Nikolai was dead.

How can someone be so alive one minute and dead the next?

I shook my head. "He's not dead. He can't be. Maybe he's just unconscious, like a concussion or something. Maybe he hit his head . . ." I trailed off when I noticed a red rock on Nikolai's bare back.

Then I realized it wasn't a rock; it was the bloody tip of the bone tusk. It protruded from his back, clean through.

I thought I might vomit. My hand flew to my mouth.

"The tusk," I whispered, swallowing and shaking. "The one from the cave. He fell on it. Is that why he died? How can he be dead?"

Rives gently placed his hands on my cheeks, making my eyes meet his. "Look at me, Skye. It's going to be okay. But we need to move, now."

"Move? We can't leave him! What if he's not really dead?"

"He's gone, Skye." Rives's face was pained. "He has no pulse."

I kneeled, wanting to feel for a pulse myself, needing confirmation, but unwilling to touch him. *Coward!* my mind screamed.

Something warm touched my knee.

Blood.

Dark red, it pooled beneath Nikolai, his blood seeping into the ground, his life leaking out, into Nil. I stared at the blood. On the ground, on my knee. Nikolai's blood flowed as he lay still. It was all so wrong.

Rives knelt beside me. "Skye. We need to go."

I looked at Rives, seeing the blood, feeling it weighing me to the ground. "We can't just leave him here! We need to bury him, or do something."

"Skye. Look at me." Rives cupped his hands around my chin, his voice urgent, his eyes pleading. "We can't stay. There's a puma checking us out from the mountain, a few meters to the left of our cave; I think it's the cat that spooked Nikolai. And in the meadow? An ugly dog duo is on full alert, looking way too interested in us. The lions won't be far. We have to go."

"We can't leave him." I blinked, seeing Nikolai's grin as he shared dinner, unable to reconcile that vibrant Nikolai with the one bleeding on the ground. "It's not right."

"Skye, he's gone." Rives's voice was grim. He pulled a small bag from somewhere, quickly crafted a small white cross beside Nikolai, and murmured a few words. His bag vanished as swiftly as it appeared. Rives turned back to me and cupped my face again, making me look at him.

"We have to move. If we don't, we'll end up like Nikolai. We can't do anything for him, Skye. But if we get back, we can tell the others about the gate and give everyone a fighting chance to escape. We need to go. *Now.*"

He pulled me to my feet. I glanced at Nikolai. Blood seeped from his back, a ruby trickle against his pale skin. His blood ran down my knee.

In the meadow, two scraggly heads bobbed above the grasses, about thirty yards away. "Hyenas," I said blankly. "Those are hyenas."

"I know." Rives spoke calmly; he didn't stop pulling. We walked and walked; Rives talked and talked. I said nothing; it was all I could do to put one foot in front of the other. My mind churned with pictures of Nikolai's body I could never erase. His dry blood stained my knee.

We walked until the meadow was a speck behind us, and then we walked more. Rives led me through a worn path sloping gently down, a wide slash cutting through black rock, alongside the South Cliffs, moving with island ease. When I stumbled, he picked me up and carried me the last few yards. At the cliff base, there was a small pool of three-foot-deep water set slightly back, ringed by rocks, filled with sea water, and fully protected.

Rives eased me into the pool. Using his hand, he scrubbed the blood off my knee. And then the shakes started. Full bodywide, I shook so violently that my teeth clattered together. Rives scooped me up, carried me over to a wide, sun-warmed rock, and held me tight as my body rebelled against itself. He whispered in my ear.

Soon his words sank in.

"You're okay," he repeated. "You're safe. It's okay."

The shakes dulled, tears took their place.

"It's not," I told Rives. My words came in jagged spurts. "He's dead because of me. Because *I* pressed to go on that Search, because *I* told him to come." *The butterfly effect*, I thought. "He told me about his argument with Alexei, and I thought I was helping by having Nikolai come with us. It's my fault," I whispered.

"It's not," Rives said quietly. "It's Nil's. The island brought him here. The island set things in motion. Not you."

"But I played a part," I said. "If he'd stayed in the City, he'd be alive right now."

"Maybe." Rives's voice was soft, but not pitying. "Maybe not. Maybe this is how his fate was meant to play out."

"How can you say that? How can you dismiss his death so casually?" I shook again, for a different reason.

"I know you're angry," Rives said, the muscle in his jaw ticking, "but I'm not the one you're angry with. I'm not dismissing his death. You have no idea how I feel about his death, or anyone else's. People die here, Skye. Nikolai wasn't the first, but God help me, I pray he's the last. Believe me, if I never see another funeral it won't be soon enough."

Beneath Rives's strong words lay pain. I thought of my uncle. *I fear nothing.*

Rives was right; I had no idea how Rives felt about Nikolai's death. Here I was, falling apart after a measly forty days, and Rives had been here for over three hundred.

"I'm sorry," I said, my fury ebbing, leaving behind a well of exhaustion. My limbs felt like Jell-O. "You're right. I'm mad at this place, at fate, and more than anything, at myself. You asked me once what I was afraid of. Now you know. It's the butterfly effect. Me changing someone's fate by coming here. Me interfering. And now Nikolai's dead. And I'm to blame, at least in part."

"No." Rives's tone was fierce. "Don't own his death. He chose to come with us, and fate chose his end. Not you."

I closed my eyes, exhausted. For a quiet minute, neither of us spoke. The sea boomed, a soothing distraction. "Want to know something weird?" I said. "My dad asked me to study Russian. I said no. Did you know that Russian is the fifth most spoken language in the world?"

"I didn't know that." Rives brushed my hair away from my face.

"It is," I said. The sun warmed my face; it felt good to leave my eyelids closed. "Mandarin is number one, then English, Hindustani, Spanish, and Russian. Maybe if I'd listened to my dad, maybe I could've helped Nikolai somehow."

"I don't think so," Rives whispered. "There wasn't time to warn him. The cat startled him; it happened the way it happened." He fell silent.

Maybe, I thought. But the word was too heavy to pass my lips. The sunlight spread through my body all the way to my toes, or maybe that was the warmth from Rives. His arms still wrapped around me, holding me against his chest.

"Sleep, Skye," he whispered in my ear. "You're safe."

So I did.

CHAPTER
57

RIVES
DAY 317, LATE MORNING

After the shock and the shakes, Skye slept for a good two hours.

In my arms.

Even in sleep, she looked fierce and vulnerable. Nikolai's blood was gone from her knee, but it would leave a mark. Skye had her first Nil scar.

Please be her last, I thought.

Now awake, she was exceptionally quiet. I couldn't read if she was taking it all in or blocking it out.

We were skirting around the Southern Cliffs, toward South Beach. When we passed the southern tip, the rocks gave way to fine sand. I pointed at the wide black beach stretching before us. "If we keep walking, we'll hit the City by twilight. Faster, if we don't stop."

Skye studied the coastline ahead. "I want to go slow," she said. "I want to see the water tunnels in the rocks just off the beach, and then see the Arches on the way back." She looked at me. "This is the route my uncle walked on his first days here. Let's take our time and see what happens." Her eyes burned with all the colors of the sea. The steel flecks were there. Different, but still fierce. Like sun glinting off water.

She'd been taking it all in.

"Sound okay?" she asked.

"Sounds like a plan," I said.

I didn't move. We stood there on the black sand, cool water wrapping around our feet. Skye's eyes held mine. I was back on the cliff, teetering.

"Rives, it's almost noon," she whispered, her eyes still on mine. "If you left right now, would you have any regrets?"

And with that, my resolve broke.

It shattered into irreparable bits, raining down into the sea as the invisible wall around me disintegrated and I fell. I pulled Skye close, and gently tilting up her chin, I found her lips with mine. Soft, then urgent. My hands cupped her head, my fingers were in her hair; I was drowning in want and need and *Skye*. I didn't want to pull away.

But I did.

"That," I said, my voice hoarse, my thumbs tracing her jaw as I watched her open her eyes; she looked just as shattered. "I would've regretted missing that. I don't know what we are, but—" I broke off, unable to put the potent mix in my chest into words.

"We're more," she whispered, her eyes full of heat. And then she kissed me.

Later I'd remember I didn't feel the ocean; I'd only felt Skye.

Less a Nil shift, more a *me* shift.

With Skye, I felt like *more*.

I felt something I'd never felt, something I couldn't bear to lose. Something that made me hate Nil and thank Nil and want to scream in frustration that my fate was not mine to control.

Now I fully understood Thad's last slick move. To leave Charley behind would've killed him. Not knowing if she was safe, not knowing if she survived. The stationary gate offered us a priceless gift—a chance at dual escape, a shot at a shared future, a gift only Nil could give.

Before I lost my mind completely, I pulled Skye to my chest. I still couldn't figure out if she was here because of Nil or in spite of Nil.

My gut said the answer was huge, especially given the way this Search had played out.

Our Search began with four, was cut to two, and now Skye and I were one.

If Nil picked a fight with Skye, the island would have to fight me, too. We were a package deal.

I kissed Skye's head. "Ready to see the tubes?" I whispered.

"Lead on." She grinned.

Our fingers stayed entwined, two halves of one whole as we walked to the tubes and sat on the edge of the closest one, letting our feet dangle in the water. A web of tunnels cut by ancient lava flows and filled with brackish water, it was Nil's version of a warm bath.

I wanted time to stop, just for a moment.

For this moment, where we were together, and relatively safe.

But time never stopped on Nil—until you left.

Jason's escape was a shock, but it was Nikolai's unexpected death that unsettled me, more than I'd ever admit to Skye. Was it because he took the tusk? Or because he touched the carving? Nikolai was the only one to trace the lines, to disturb the sand. Had he screwed with some invisible balance? Or was it just an accident, a cruel twist of fate?

More like a cruel twist of Nil, I thought.

Nil was a foe, pulling invisible strings.

Yet without Nil, there would be no Skye. There would be no *us*. And I desperately wanted a chance at *us*.

No matter how hard I pressed, Nil didn't fit into any column I made.

Skye touched my arm. "Rives," she said softly. "Where'd you go?"

I pulled her close and kissed her thoroughly.

She blushed. "Okay, I kinda keep going there myself. But back to the gate. Do you think there's another way to the platform, where the cats don't roam? A back door?"

"I don't think so. That sheer black cliff was solid. I think there's one way in and out."

"Like the labyrinths," she mused. She tilted her head to look at me. "We need Paulo to talk. We need to know whether the gate opens at noon or night, because if it's at night, we need to plan differently. Like more torches—" She broke off, staring at me. "What? Every time I mention the gate's timing, you get a funny look. Talk."

CIA Skye was back.

I looked at our fingers, entwined at the edge of the water. "When I showed up three hundred and seventeen days ago, it was in the afternoon. And the equinox? It falls on March twentieth, which by my count is my Day three hundred and sixty-five." The blood drained from Skye's face as I spoke. She'd already added up the numbers, coming up short like me. "So that noon is my shot," I said quietly. "I don't have until midnight. I have exactly forty-eight days left. Forty-eight noons."

"You can't wait." Her voice was firm. "The risk is too great. You have to go on Search *now*. Dex and Jillian and I will figure out how to get everyone there, but—"

I placed a finger over her lips. "Stop. Let's talk to Paulo, okay? See what he knows. No one has to decide anything today." Except my mind was already set.

I'd roll the dice on the equinox. I wouldn't bail early.

"Let's go," Skye said, getting out of the tube. "Tour's over. Let's go talk to Paulo. And"—her voice sounded heavy—"we need to tell Miya. That Jason made it."

I followed. Skye was right. The island time-out was over.

We had a gate to track.

CHAPTER 58

RIVES
DAY 317, LATE MORNING

We headed straight back.

We blew through the Arches without stopping; same for Black Bay. But as we left the Crystal Cavern, Skye yanked me back, pointing down the path.

"Rives! Incoming!"

A gate popped and dropped, ten meters ahead. Without speaking, we both hit the brush. The gate shimmered, then turned reflective, a mirror over the ground. It glittered, then vanished.

Another inbound with no rider.

"That's the third riderless inbound in three weeks," I said as I stood. "They used to be rare. Or so I thought."

Giving us another clue, are you, Nil? What are you trying to say?

"Odd," Skye said, but she sounded distracted. She tugged my hand and, as we hit the path again, she actually jogged.

"Skye," I said. "It's okay. Chill."

She slowed, barely.

Back in the City, she strode straight into Paulo's hut.

"Thanks for knocking," he said sourly.

"Sorry," Skye said, not sounding sorry at all. "We need answers."

Her voice was flat. If she was fire and ice before, now she was a volcano, ready to blow. "We know where the gate will open in March, but we need to know when. Noon or midnight. And we need to know if you've got any secrets on how to get to the heart of the island without attracting all those cats."

Paulo swallowed. "You found the doorway?"

"The platform. Above the rock steps. It'll open in March," she said. "Now tell me when."

She crossed her arms.

Paulo looked at the ceiling. "If I answer, will you leave? Both of you?" He eyed me sharply.

"Yes," Skye said. I nodded.

"Fine. It used to open at midnight. Over a century ago, the island spirits grew stronger. The sun burned bright in the day and bright in the night, on a day in September when the night approached the day in strength. And that year, the doorway opened twice here on the island—once at noon, and then again at midnight. And the times reversed."

The Solar Superstorm, I thought. *A solar flare impacted the gate.*

"Now the first quarter doorway opens at noon," Paulo continued, "and the third quarter at midnight. So I came in the dark and will leave in the dark."

"But you could leave in the light." Skye was looking at me, her face shining with relief.

"I can't leave. Not yet." Paulo shook his head.

"I know you want to stay for the honor, but this place is not what it once was. It's not what your ancestors first found. It's changed, and not for the better." Her voice had softened. "Thank you, Paulo. We'll go now."

He nodded, studying Skye. I hoped he took her words to heart.

Outside, we walked toward the beach, where voices laughed and Miya might be waiting. Skye stopped me near the path.

"Rives, look at me." She cupped my face in her hands, like I'd done with her this morning. "Paulo's news doesn't change anything. You'll still have to go on Search. You can't wait until the last minute."

"Paulo's news changes everything," I said, my eyes flicking between Skye and the woods behind her. "It means that's my noon. Our noon."

Skye's eyes widened, then narrowed, shooting silver sparks at me. "Don't be stupid!" she cried. She dropped her hands to clench them into fists.

"Ah! Good to see everything's back to normal," Dex said, walking up the path with Jillian. "Skye shouting. Rives being a bloody idiot. What's he up to this time?"

"It better not involve tea." Jillian glared.

"No," Skye said, her voice dangerously low. "But he might just have a death wish after all."

"What?"

Skye ran through the equinox deal, throwing in my expiration date and her ambitious theory about destroying Nil.

"Bloody hell." Dex stared at Skye in awe. "I don't which is madder, Rives's deadly dice roll, or your idea to cut Nil off at the throat. Bugger me." His last words were a whisper.

"I know," Skye said matter-of-factly. She missed Dex's gob-smacked expression; she was too busy frowning at me. "But Rives can't wait. He can't take the risk."

"It's my risk to take." I gently traced Skye's cheek with my thumb as she stared at me. "Remember what I told you when we slept on the beach? Macy once told me we're all here for a reason, but not the same reason. Skye, we're here for different reasons, but they both hold the same end." I paused. "And maybe it can be Nil's end."

"Can you imagine?" Jillian breathed. "A world without Nil? Where no more kids get snatched, sent here to die? I'm all for delivering the death blow. Hand me a spear." She grinned, but it faded quickly. "But Rives, I agree with Skye. You can't wait. Not even to see the destruction of Nil."

Before Jillian had finished speaking, Maaka stepped from the shadows like a ghost.

"Evening, Maaka," I said pleasantly. "I wondered when you'd come out. Eavesdropping is rude, remember?"

His face was hard. He only looked at me.

"Why do you think everything you do not understand must be destroyed?" Maaka said. "Because you do not understand it, you fear it. And then you want to destroy it. It is your way." He practically spat his words. "Are you so arrogant to think that if it does not fit within your own narrow human logic, your fragile understanding of reality as you see it—that it does not exist? That it is not real?" He tilted his face toward the Nil sky. A look of reverence passed over his face. "Do you grasp the breadth of the universe?" he asked softly. "Do you think there is nothing beyond what we see? Human arrogance prevents sight, and prevents understanding."

"I see more than you think," I said calmly.

"You see nothing," he said. "And Paulo is weak. He wastes his time here."

"Time," I said slowly, "is finite everywhere. Is it more valuable here than elsewhere? And is your time here more precious than mine?"

He stared at me, unflinching.

"By the way, Maaka, meet Skye. Skye, Maaka."

Skye raised her hand. "Hi."

A flicker of surprise passed across Maaka's face at her name. After a scrutinizing look, he gave her the barest of nods, like she'd come up short.

I fought the urge to deck him.

"And that's Dex, and Jillian." My tone had cooled.

Maaka stepped back, distancing himself, unwilling to get drawn into the City. He read like an open book. A picture book, easy reading.

"See you around, Maaka. But definitely in March, at the heart of the island. Because if I ran the numbers right, you're in your last season. The equinox gate is your ticket home, right? See you there. In the meantime, enjoy the rest of your journey." I paused. "Word of warning. Steer clear of the meadow. The cats are restless."

Maaka spun around and strode off, too annoyed to pull his silent disappearing act.

"So that was the elusive Maaka," Skye said.

"What the hell was that?" Dex said. "It was as if you were sparring with bloody Confucius, if Confucius was reincarnated as an angry foot-baller with more ink than me. Well"—Dex looked thoughtful—"not more ink. But his was quite impressive, although a bit stark. Anyway," he waved his hand, "do we need him on board with this whole let's-destroy-the-island scheme? Because he might be a tough sell."

"He might," I agreed. Then I smiled. "But he didn't say it couldn't be done."

CHAPTER 59

SKYE
DAY 41, DUSK

Rives called a Citywide meeting on the beach. I think he would've waited until the morning, but the absence of Jason and Nikolai was painfully obvious and begged explanation. So much for our little under-the-radar quick mountain trip.

I still couldn't think about Nikolai without feeling sick.

Everyone left in the City gathered around, except Paulo. I'd invited him, but I didn't expect him to show, and if I really thought about it, he hadn't joined the City, not really. He still didn't engage with anyone but me, he hadn't put his name on the Wall, and he sure didn't lift a finger to contribute.

Rives is right, I thought. *He's going to leave as soon as he's physically able.*

Despite Paulo's slackness, the thought made me sad. I guess I still hoped he would be more. Plus, I wanted him to be okay.

"Okay, people, here's the deal," Rives said. He stood by the beach firepit, which only held a few logs, but it was enough. We were a small group. The orange sun fading over the water was extraordinary, a perfect backdrop to discuss the end of Nil. I wondered if Rives planned it this way.

"As most of you know, Skye's inbound was different." He went on to explain about the stationary gate, our trip, Jason, Nikolai, and the equinox gate, in that order. Miya looked relieved and stoic; Alexei burst into tears. Rives looked every inch the furious sea god and strong City Leader, but he also looked like Rives. The same boy who'd saved my life this morning, who'd carried me when I couldn't walk, the same boy I'd opened my eyes to after my post-meadow meltdown, finding a tenderness in his expression that made me ache.

You can't have the highs without the lows, my dad once told me. I'd just never envisioned them all in one day.

I still felt raw.

I tuned back in as Rives outlined our plan to work toward March, gearing for a Citywide escape. But he still insisted we'd go on traditional Search as usual.

"If the stationary gate fails to open, we need a contingency plan," Rives said. "It's crucial that we don't forget that Search works, that roaming gates have a pattern. That people can still make it home. We can't let Nil slip back into a free-for-all. Everyone still has time."

If the stationary gate fails to open. Everyone still has time.

Not you, I thought, my eyes on Rives. *You'd be lost. Claimed by Nil forever.*

I'd lose you.

The tremors were back. My entire body shook, the last of my strength gone.

Rives glanced at me. "That's it," he said quickly. "We'll meet again tomorrow night to talk through questions." He strode over to me and pulled me into his arms.

"What's wrong?"

I shook my head.

He led me down to the pile of black rocks where I'd seen him sleeping on the beach once.

"Hey." He brushed my hair away from my face, making my eyes meet his. "Talk to me."

"I can't lose you," I said, shaking nearly as hard as I had this morning; I couldn't stop. "I can't. This stationary gate. Everyone's counting on it, because of me. Because I showed up, and changed the rules. It's worse than a ripple, it's like the butterfly effect times one million. You can't wait for that gate. You have to go on Search. If the gate doesn't open, I've got time. But you don't."

He pulled me close, holding me tight. I focused on his heart, beating steady and strong, an energy I refused to let Nil take. Fury replaced fear, and the shakes stopped. Sensing the shift, Rives threaded his fingers through mine, holding us together as he looked me in the eye.

"Timing is everything here, Skye, and the timing feels right. What are the odds that my last day coincides with the equinox?"

"Literally, three hundred and sixty-five. But it happens every time with the islanders, right?"

Rives looked surprised, like that hadn't occurred to him. "Actually, for them it's the solstice. I'm just special." He grinned, making me narrow my eyes. "But Maaka told me the island blood in me runs strong, Skye. Staying feels right."

I shook my head, gripping his hands tight. "It feels wrong. You need to go on Search, at least try. Don't give up yet."

"I'm not giving up," he said sharply. "Can't you see that, Skye? I'm fighting harder than ever. For everyone."

"I do see that." Letting go of one of his hands, I reached up to gently trace his cheekbones, feeling the fierceness and strength of Rives in the lines of his face. "So does everyone else," I whispered. "But I want you to be selfish. I want you to catch a gate now, to guarantee you get home and not wait until the last minute."

The sad truth was, *I* was selfish. I wanted to know now that Rives would make it, that we had a chance to be more on the other side, especially because after watching Nikolai die, I knew things could change on Nil in a swift minute. Forty-eight days meant forty-eight opportunities for something strange and terrible to happen, and the instincts that got me here said putting all our escape apples in one equinox basket was a very bad idea.

"I'll make it," Rives said. "I'm not leaving until I have to. This is why I'm here, Skye. I feel it. Don't ask me to not be me, okay?"

How could I argue with that?

Rives bent down and kissed me, and no one argued at all.

CHAPTER 60

RIVES
DAY 318, BEFORE DAWN

The countdown was officially on.

Forty-seven days.

Forty-seven noons.

I knew Skye was still reeling from Nikolai's death. But our plan had charged the City. Jacked it up with hope and fire and a sense of power, like everyone had sucked down a hundred loaded Monster drinks to prep for an exam that was still days away. The fight in Skye's eyes said that she was all in.

What I didn't tell her was that me going on Search was pointless.

That if Nil chose to let me go, it would be on my last day. And it was a hellaciously big *if*. I didn't tell Skye that on the day Pari left, the first gate of the set had flashed so close that I felt its heat brush my side.

You're mine, Nil whispered, crisp and clear and island cold. *Until I choose to let you go.* Then the gate streaked away, tapping a coal-black cat with snow-white paws instead.

Burton was gone.

But I was still here, and calculating Nil had her reasons.

Maybe I was the counterweight to Skye, or maybe someone else. Maybe I carried no weight at all, but my questions did.

How long will the gate stay open? And how can we make sure we clear the entire island of people?

I didn't know about number two, yet. But number one? Maaka or Paulo had the answer, I'd bet my life on it.

Oh yeah, I already was.

CHAPTER 61

SKYE
DAY 45, SOMETIME PAST MIDNIGHT

I lay beside Rives, trying to sleep. But the ticking of time coursed so loudly through my head I couldn't shut it out no matter how hard I tried. I'd tried counting sheep, but then I'd picture them eaten by lions. I tried counting stars, but without a clear view of the sky, that didn't work at all. And I tried just plain counting, but each time my mind got stuck on one neon number: forty-four.

Forty-four days until the equinox. Forty-four days left for Rives.

The two were wrapped together so tightly now that I couldn't separate them, and Rives refused to let me. He refused to relent about Search. The subject was closed.

I'd been here more days than Rives had left.

In that moment, wrapped in Rives's arms and Nil's darkness, I made a choice. If I couldn't stop the clock, I'd destroy it, whatever the cost.

Even if that cost was me.

CHAPTER
62

RIVES

DAY 325, MID-MORNING

Tick.

Seven days.

Tock.

I had forty-one left.

"It's been a week," I told Dex.

We stood in the Shack, dropping off the morning's haul of bamboo. The focus had shifted to preparations for Citywide escape rather than long-term City sustainability. Weapons took priority over clothes. If Skye was right, somehow we had to appease the feline guardians of the gate, or at least keep them from killing us. Torches were our best bet.

The stockpile of bamboo and oily nuts had begun.

"And your point is?" Dex raised an eyebrow at me.

"We need to send a team on Search. We can't just wait around for forty days, wasting time. The more people leave now, the fewer we'll have to round up at the end."

"Excellent point."

"I agree," Skye said, shooting me a pointed look. She'd popped out of nowhere, carrying an armful of twine. I knew she wanted me to go, but it wasn't happening. I had a date with the equinox gate along with everyone else.

"I'm so glad you agree with me." I raised an eyebrow at Skye, grinning. She dumped the twine in a pile and mashed it down with more force than necessary, grumbling "Stubborn."

I turned to Dex. "You want to go? Lead a Search team?"

Dex shook his head. "I'm with you to the end, mate." His voice was quiet.

His time. His choice.

"Thanks." I swallowed, fighting the knot in my throat. "Let's go see if Ahmad's willing to head up a team. I'd like to see Julio go, too, and maybe a couple of rookies for balance."

"I like it," Dex said. "Ahmad's at the beach firepit. Julio was stocking it with veggies and, I think, the last chicken."

The last chicken.

"Have you noticed that there are fewer animals?" I asked as we walked. "When I was on Search with Raj, I went hours without seeing a squirrel or rabbit or even a cat. It's weird."

Dex looked thoughtful. "Now that you mention it, you're exactly right. And I don't think the lions can take credit for thinning out the island." He paused. "I bloody well hope Nil isn't driving the cats toward us. But I wouldn't put it past her."

"Her?" I asked.

Dex looked sheepish. "When I think of Nil, I think she. I know I'm mental, but sometimes I think she talks to me." He sighed. "I'm totally mental."

I grinned. "Join the club."

"We have snacks," Skye said.

"Awesome snacks," I added.

"Fish wraps?" Dex asked suspiciously.

"Nope. Skye's talking crème brûlée, steak, lasagna, and everything tasty and decadent and not from the sea."

"Cruel," Dex moaned. "The both of you. I was fine this morning. A little roast pineapple, a shrimp wrap—not bad, mind you, even though I've only eaten about, oh, *hundreds* in recent months—but oh no, you two have to come along and tempt me with all the tasty things. Curse you both." He grinned.

Skye laughed. "Sorry, Dex. When we get back, I'll make you something special. You pick."

"Honestly, you know what I miss most?" His voice was wistful. "A good cuppa tea. Not that bloody deadsleep tea." He shot me a dark look. "I'm not stupid enough to dabble in that."

I grinned. "So noted."

We broke out onto the beach into strong Nil light.

Julio was tossing a green coconut to Zane, who lobbed it back. Macy was chatting with Jillian and Brittney; Ahmad was laughing with Kiera.

I walked up to Ahmad. "You up for Search? I'd love to send out a team." I turned to Kiera. "You too, Kiera. You ready for a Search?"

"Absolutely," she replied. "Are you going?"

I shook my head. "I'm thinking you two, plus Julio and maybe Macy or Brittney. What do you think?"

"I'm cool with it," Ahmad said. "But Julio goes first. He's got Priority over me."

I wondered if his words were for me or Kiera.

"Sounds good. Let me check with Julio."

Julio was all in, and to my surprise, when I asked him who else he wanted on Search, he said, "Brittney." He didn't explain why. Then again, he didn't need to. It was his Search.

Brittney declined Search without hesitation. Just a fast, firm no.

"This is the second Search you've turned down." I frowned. "Why?"

"I don't care about leaving." Her voice was a rough whisper. "I'm not like you. Or Skye." Brittney glanced at Skye, who had just walked up. She kept looking at Skye as she spoke. "You've got a mom and a dad, Skye. I heard you talking to Rives once. Telling him about your dad. I never met my dad. I live in a double-wide with my mom and her boyfriend. And he's mean. Yells all the time, takes my money from the Metroplex. Here, it's pretty. Prettier than I've ever seen. I have more room that I've ever had, I have friends, and I'm part of something. I want to stay as long as I can. Like my granny says, it's better to have a few weeks of wonderful than a lifetime of nothing special."

"I think that was from a movie," Jillian said quietly. "But it's wrong."

"Totally," I said. "Brittney, this is temporary. People will leave, new ones will come. It won't stay like this. And if you're still here in ten months, you'll die. You have to go on Search."

"No." She shook her head and cast a longing look at the beach. "If all I have is ten months, then it'll be the best ten months of my life. And if I'm supposed to leave, then a gate will pick me up right here. But you go on. Don't let me take someone's place who wants to leave. I'm happy living right here."

"It's not living." Jillian frowned. "It's waiting for death. What we're doing—going on Search, hunting the equinox gate—is trying to find a way to live."

Brittney looked at her. "It's better than what I had."

"Don't you want more?" Skye asked gently. "Don't you want more for yourself and your life?"

Brittney smiled at her. "This is the best I've ever had."

But the best is yet to come, I thought, my eyes on Skye.

It had to be.

Skye shook her head at Brittney.

"This is just a beginning," she said, rewarding me with a slight smile. "The rest is up to you." Then she hugged Brittney.

When a gate flashed an hour later, Brittney let it streak by. She didn't have to run; all she had to do was step to her left. Literally, a meter max.

But she didn't. She stood rock still. Arms tight to her chest, feet rooted, mind set.

That was the moment that I knew the hardest part of Skye's island annihilation plan was getting everyone else on board. Because participation wasn't a given, even in the City. Not by a long shot.

Right now I freaking hated the idea of a long shot.

Because that was me.

CHAPTER
63

SKYE
DAY 51, ALMOST DUSK

Paulo stared at the Wall, leaning on his crutches. He still used them, but he was definitely moving better. It wouldn't be long until he was strong enough to walk without them. I'd guess a week, maybe two.

"See anything interesting?" I asked.

He turned, startled. "You really shouldn't sneak up on people, Skye. It's rude."

"Sorry. I didn't mean to." I hadn't been quiet, not even close. It made me worry for Paulo when he left. "Are you looking for something? Or someone?"

He tapped the end of his crutch against the Wall, directly on a name. "That's my cousin," he said. "I didn't know any of my people joined the City."

The name he'd tapped was Ramia.

"She never came home," he said. "I wonder what happened to her."

"I think her time ran out."

Paulo frowned. "But she could leave. She shouldn't have been here past the third season."

I thought about that. "Maybe something kept her from going. Or maybe she chose to stay."

"Why would she choose that?"

I thought of Brittney, who refused to go on Search. For all I knew, she'd refuse to join us when the time came to take the equinox gate, too.

"People have their reasons. I'm not saying she did; I'm just saying it's a possibility."

Paulo fell silent. His eyes stayed on the Wall—on Ramia's name. Like me, he had family that had come before, family he'd lost.

My heart seized and in that moment, I knew I'd been approaching Paulo all wrong. *I'd* been the bull in a china shop, not Rives. *I'd* been the one pushing, *I'd* been the one pressing, never stopping to consider Paulo's feelings. I'd treated him like he owed us, and that was wrong.

"Paulo, I owe you an apology, and a thank-you. First, thank you for the bracelet." I raised my arm, where the crescent moon dangled from my wrist beside Jillian and Macy's tri-shell bracelet. "It's beautiful. And it was sweet. And to be honest, it was also a little creepy to wake up and find it beside my pillow, but I know you meant well."

Paulo looked chagrined. "Sorry."

I waved it off. "This is my apology. It's fine. I know you didn't want me to see you, and I know you gave it to me so we could be even. And"—I took a deep breath—"I know it's been hard on you being in the City. You feel like you owe us for taking care of you, and I've pushed you to tell us about the gate and the island, using the fact that you feel obligated, and sometimes I've pushed too hard. I'm sorry for making you more uncomfortable than you already are, because I know even though we're here under different circumstances, you don't want to be here any more than we do. You're my friend, Paulo. You don't owe me anything else; we're even. I'm going to tell you what's going on so you can make your own choices, okay? Choices for your own reasons, not because you feel obligated or guilty, not because you feel honor bound. Choose for *you*. You don't owe me, okay?"

Paulo stared at me and then slowly nodded.

"Okay." I smiled, feeling relief I didn't even know I needed. "The gate will open at noon on the equinox, which you already know, and we're all planning to take it. I know we need to wait three seconds between people; I remember you counting after the chicken and the goat. It will be the end of Maaka's third season, so I'm guessing he'll take it, too. Which means you'll be here alone."

Paulo gulped.

I touched his shoulder. "I'm not trying to scare you. Your ancestors were here alone, too, remember?"

"But they didn't have leopards." Paulo sighed. "Or tigers. Or rhinos."

"True. And it's because of the leopards and tigers and rhinos that we believe Nil has changed; that it's not the place it once was. That it's outlived its purpose. It's no longer the peaceful place where you can find your way. We think"—I paused, knowing I had one chance to say this right—"that if all the kids leave the island at once, that the island will cease to exist. The island has some link with us; we feel it. I know you do, too. And without the kids, the island may not survive. We don't know for sure, but we have to try. I'm not going to force you to come with us. The choice is yours."

"So you're saying the choice whether this place continues to live is up to me?" He looked stunned. "That my vote is the deciding factor?"

"Not totally up to you. Everyone has to leave. If one person stays back, the chance to end this place ends, too. You're not more important than the rest of us, but you're just as important."

I squeezed his hand.

"No pressure. Just telling you what we're planning. You follow your heart, Paulo. I'm your friend no matter what you choose."

Paulo's eyes fell on my bracelet. "Thanks, Skye."

I squeezed his forearm and walked away.

"Skye." Paulo's soft voice made me turn back.

"I don't know, but I think the doorway stays open for one minute. And you don't have to wait three seconds, just two, actually. The beat of one heart." He smiled sheepishly. "I was just being cautious."

"Thanks."

"You're welcome."

"Think about coming with us, okay? I want to know you made it, too."

"I'll think about it. That's the best I can do."

I nodded. It was enough, for now.

I turned to find Rives lounging against a tree by the beach path, a smile playing across his face. The island shrunk to just us. Wrapped in sweet, clean Nil air, under a gorgeous clear Nil sky, it was just me and Rives, connected by something stronger than Nil, an electricity I felt crackle between us as I approached.

"That was kind," he said, tipping his head toward Paulo.

"Thanks." I took one of his hands and pulled him close, close enough for me to find his lips with mine.

Rives groaned, folding me against him, leaning his cheek against mine. "You undo me, Skye." His voice was ragged. "Before I lose my mind, follow me. I've got a surprise."

He led me down the path, then we cut right. He was leading me down to the pile of black boulders at the water's edge, out of sight of the City.

A white cloth covered the biggest rock; it was strewn with gorgeous purple blossoms. Two small planks sat on the cloth, each holding fish, pineapple, and, oh my stars, *bread*. Two torches were stuck in the sand, already lit.

"What's this?" I asked, turning to Rives.

"Keep walking. You'll see."

He led me to the rocks and gestured for me to take a seat.

"Julio made the bread especially for you, and Jillian helped me gather the flowers." Gently, he picked up a lei made of small white flowers and placed it around my neck. "Look," he whispered. He pointed to the beach, where *Happy Birthday, Skye* was written in the sand.

"Rives," I whispered, stunned and moved and falling so deep into the moment I had no words. Instead, I kissed Rives hard, trying to show him all I couldn't say. My eyes were watering as I pulled away.

"This is the sweetest thing anyone has ever done for me," I said.

Rives smiled as he reached up and wiped the tear from the corner of my eye. "I was going to add hula dancers, but I thought that might've been over the top."

"Totally," I said, smiling as I pulled myself together.

"Word of warning: Dex and Zane were vying for the job. Ahmad too. It took all I had to talk them down. Zane was making coconut jock straps." He winked. "I thought you might like this better. More low key, less awkward."

"You know me so well," I said.

"I do," he whispered. "And you know me."

It was the best birthday of my life.

"One more thing." He reached behind him and handed something to me. A bracelet, made of two pieces of twine, perfectly knotted to hold a small rock that glittered in the firelight like a piece of silver ice. "Happy birthday, Skye. I couldn't have you just wearing Paulo's bracelet."

I grinned, amused. "I also wear Jillian and Macy's."

He laughed. "I know. But this"—he tapped the rock—"matches the flecks in your eyes. And at night by the fire, it glitters like a star pulled to Nil." His voice softened. "Like a piece of Orion's belt. I thought you might like something that reminded you of home."

"It's gorgeous." I stared at the bracelet, loving the simplicity, the style, the breathtakingly beautiful crystal, but loving the thoughtfulness most of all. It took me a minute to be able to speak. "Thank you," I said softly, my voice still choked.

"You're welcome," Rives said, his eyes on mine, my hand in his. "Happy birthday, my Skye."

My Skye.

I leaned forward and kissed him, happier than I had any right to be. It was the best birthday gift ever, even if I couldn't keep it. I'd never forget it, or this night.

Please let Rives make it. I can't lose him. I can't.

It was my last thought as I fell asleep that night, and the first when I woke.

My second was Paulo, because when I went to check on him, he was gone.

CHAPTER 64

RIVES
DAY 335, BREAKING DAWN

The insomnia jinx was back.

I'd hardly slept since Nikolai's death. His broken body, lying still on Nil ground, his blood leaching into Nil dirt. That could be me in exactly one month. Hell, it *would* be me if that equinox gate didn't show.

The clock in my head pulsed like an alarm. Ticking with incessant regularity, mourning the loss of another minute. Another hour. Another day.

Another noon.

Tick-tock.

My Nil clock.

I had thirty days left.

A familiar voice I hadn't heard in weeks drifted into my hut. Easing outside without waking Skye, I saw Uri talking with Zane.

"Morning, Chief." Zane nodded.

"Morning." I looked at Uri. "How's everybody doing?"

"Leila's gone. She took a gate. Sy"—Uri shook his head—"is worthless. He's terrified. Cho's taken over. Michael is considering coming back."

"What about you?"

He shook his head. "I came to tell you something. Michael and I decided you should know. Two days ago I heard two boys at the Cove's cavern, fighting. One accused the other of betraying his people, of sharing too many secrets. The other said the first one had betrayed him. They shouted back and forth. The first one demanded that the second one honor the peace of the crescent moon. 'Do not share it!' the first one shouted. The second one said, 'I'll think about it. But I won't promise.' And the first one told the other he'd destroy us all."

Uri looked at me. "What do they mean?"

"I don't know about the crescent moon," I said. "But here's what we're up to." I filled him in on the equinox plan. "Go tell Michael and your crew. Tell them they're welcome to come back, that we're going after that gate. Tell him it appears in thirty days, and we know where."

Uri nodded and left, heading toward the Cove.

The peace of the crescent moon.

I almost laughed. Peace was tough to come by here. Peace on Nil came in fleeting moments that vanished like mist. It came at dawn before the day; it came in the calm before a noon. It came in the absolute stillness before a gate flashed. Even still, peace on Nil was always weighted, like the calm before the storm.

And then it hit me.

The last piece fell into place. The last *peace.*

I'd figured out Nil after all.

CHAPTER 65

SKYE
DAY 59, BREAKING DAWN

Rives woke me with a gentle kiss. I opened my eyes, to find his burning like Nil's sun. With hope and excitement and an intensity that made me instantly awake.

"What is it?"

"I think I know how to make sure everyone gets off the island. Uri just told me about a conversation he overhead between Maaka and Paulo in the Looking Glass cavern."

"Wait." I frowned, clearly still groggy. "Who's Uri?"

Rives waved his hand. "He went with Michael. Anyway, Maaka was demanding Paulo keep the peace of the crescent moon a secret. It got me thinking. Peace here is fleeting, right? And the most peace—I'm talking total stillness—comes right before a gate, in that moment before an incoming appears. So why wouldn't the island have a few *days* of peace before the equinox gate? The wild gates are still linked to the equinox gate, I mean they were born of it, right? So I'm thinking the island conserves all the energy before the fixed portal opens, maybe it *needs* all the energy to open that doorway. The fixed portal is stronger, bigger, and brighter than the wild portals from what you said." Rives spoke so fast I had to work to keep up. "So I'm thinking the fixed doorway needs more fuel. More energy. From the sun, from us. To open and stay open. I think the island might go into a rest status to gear up. And if it does, that's the cue. We can sweep the island from one coast to the other, converging on the doorway at noon, knowing we've picked up everyone along the way."

"Wow," I said. "That's brilliant. It totally makes sense. But—" I stopped.

"But what?" The light in his eyes dimmed. "Nothing good ever follows the word *but*, at least not here." He almost smiled.

"The absolute calm before a wild gate is mere minutes. How do we know it's days, not hours before the equinox gate?"

"I thought about that. The crescent moon. It's a moon phase, which actually is an instant, but to us appears as days, right?"

"Right. My dad taught me that."

"So," Rives said slowly, "I think the crescent moon represents the time period of the peace. It's symbolic."

I sighed. "We still need Paulo."

"I know." Rives was quiet. "He's more likely to tell us than Maaka."

I thought about Paulo. *I'll think about it*, he'd told me.

"C'mon." I hopped up. "I have a pretty good guess where he'd go to think. And definitely to survive."

Ten minutes later, I looked around the Crystal Cavern's ledge in dismay. No people, and no sign that anyone would be back.

"I really thought Paulo would be here. I thought he'd feel safe here since he left, maybe even camp out here." I sighed, frustrated and worried. "We'd come here to talk."

Rives lifted my chin, his eyes full of heat. "Don't doubt yourself. Maybe today's not the day."

But you only have thirty left.

Pulling Rives down with me, I sat on the ledge, leaning back against his chest as I faced the Crystal Cavern. For a few minutes, neither of us spoke.

"Is this your version of a stakeout?" Rives teased. "Because if it is, I can think of a better way to pass the time rather than staring at the dark." He pressed a kiss to the top of my head, then lifted my hair and kissed the back of my neck.

I shivered.

"Cold?" The teasing in his voice grew.

"Hmmm," I said. "I don't think so, but I think you should do that again so I can be sure."

"As you wish, my Skye." As gently as he had the first time, Rives kissed the back of my neck, then the side, then he trailed kisses down my collarbone, making me feel anything but cold.

"How was that?" he whispered.

"Amazing. Your stakeouts are definitely better than mine."

With a low laugh, he wrapped his arms around me, cocooning me in his warmth. He was so real, so solid. So alive.

Mine, I thought, smiling. Our equinox plan *had* to work.

Up ahead, the Cavern glistened like a mirror, like a riderless gate.

As I was tucked against Rives, a languid feeling seeped into my bones, a peace that was all mine—until it wasn't. An odd feeling tugged at my chest, begging me to sleep.

Forever.

And then it vanished.

I turned around so fast Rives looked startled.

"Rives, I just had the creepiest feeling. Like the island was trying to tell me something. I've felt it before, but never as strong, and I think I know why." I took a deep breath and held his hands tight. "I think the island is tired. I know that sounds strange, but every time I think about our islandwide escape plan, I've felt relief. Bone-deep relief, like an exhale, but it's not mine. I think it's Nil's. Like the island has had enough. I think the island knows its purpose has changed, and not in a positive way. I think Nil is ready to go. To let go. And to let *us* go. All of us."

I paused. "And I think maybe that's why there are fewer animals coming. More inbounds with no riders. And more people leaving."

"And more people dying," he said grimly.

I nodded, struck by another thought and feeling its truth. "I think the island *wants* to rest," I said quietly. "And that maybe it's why I'm here. Do you remember what that girl told my uncle? *Your destiny,* she told him, *it wraps the island from beginning to end; I feel it.*" I looked at Rives. "I think I'm part of that, of his destiny. Like ours are entwined, mine and my uncle's. And we're nearing the end. The *island's* end."

Paulo stepped out of the tunnel. He held a cane and still favored his injured leg. He was frowning—not in anger. More like in bewildered disbelief.

"Who told your uncle that? Someone on the island?"

"Eavesdropper," Rives muttered.

"Hi, Paulo." I smiled. "How's your leg?"

"Better, thanks," Paulo said, distracted. "Skye, who told your uncle about his destiny?"

"A girl. Here, on the island. Someone who didn't join the City or put her name on the Wall. Her name was Rika."

The blood drained from Paulo's face.

"Rika?" he whispered. "What else did she say?"

I thought carefully.

"My uncle asked her if she was leaving, meaning leaving the City. Her exact words to my uncle were: '*Yes. But like you, my journey does not end here. My end stretches beyond, I have seen it.*'"

If possible, Paulo's face paled even further.

"There are seers in our culture. Rika was one." He looked at Rives. "I heard what you said. About the crescent moon." He paused, then seemed to make a snap decision. "It's three days. Two nights. Where the island is at peace."

"Three days, two nights, one gate to get home," I murmured. "Three-two-one-four."

375

Rives squeezed my hand.

"And I heard what you said about the island being tired. I feel it too, Skye. Like a warm breeze that wraps around me. Sometimes it weighs on me; sometimes it pushes me. It pushed me away from that gate, the one in the field when I fell. And it pushed me into this tunnel today. Pushed me here." He blinked slowly. "It won't leave me alone."

He looked at me, *only* at me.

"I won't see you until the equinox, Skye. I promise to see you then, to say good-bye. Beyond that, I can't promise anything except that I will think."

As he turned away, I said, "Wait! Paulo, why did you tell us about the peace? About the three days?"

He stared at me. He held a cane but no longer seemed broken.

"Because we're friends," he said finally. "And because Rika was my aunt."

CHAPTER 66

SKYE
DAY 59, LATE NIGHT

Paulo's aunt knew my uncle. My uncle knew Paulo's aunt.

Talk about a shock.

The web of Nil linked Paulo and me, a fluid net cast through time, capturing the past and the present and wrapping the island in the *now*. We'd arrived together, and I couldn't stop thinking that we were meant to leave together, too, bringing our families' destinies full circle. We had a chance for closure, for our families—and maybe even for the island.

You always have a choice, I'd told Paulo once.

I hoped he chose well.

In thirty days I'd find out.

CHAPTER 67

RIVES
DAY 340, DAWN

I floated past the whitewater, trying to get my head straight.

My cerebral clock blared without break. My personal hourglass had twenty-five grains left, and the loss of each one felt more acute. More cutting, more stark. Me, bleeding time.

I had twenty-four cuts left to endure.

Twenty-five days until the equinox.

Twenty-two days until we left the City.

At least we had a plan.

Before we left, Skye and Julio would sweep the island in gliders to look for people and predators. Eyeball any raiders or rookies from the air, and identify any animals that might pose trouble to the sweep teams.

Then the next morning we'd leave. Bail on the City with no plans to return. Broken into teams, we'd sweep across the island, covering all quadrants in grids. We'd carry torches, unlit, and each person would be outfitted with a bamboo whistle. The whistles were Dex's brilliant idea, a way to increase communication across large distances.

Twenty-five days to go.

Tick.

CHAPTER 68

SKYE
DAY 74, EARLY MORNING

Of course everyone was talking about the equinox plan. It was all anyone ever talked about, and it was making me crazy.

Literally.

For the past few weeks, I felt like I was tearing in two. Not torn between the past and the present, but torn between the island and me.

I never heard Nil, but I felt it: The island clung to me like a weight, begging to be released, threatening to drag me under, making my ultimate end match my uncle's.

Lately I'd gone to bed afraid I wouldn't wake up.

Making things worse, my heart was heavy, too. Each time Rives caught my eyes, his had a wistful quality, like something was already lost. Maybe it was just time.

We never had enough.

Now we were putting Rives's fate in one final noon, a frightening gamble no one seemed to grasp except me. With a sigh as heavy as my heart, I tuned back in to the firepit chat.

"I vote for Operation Clean Sweep," Zane said. "Every mission needs a cool name."

Twenty-five days left with Skye.

Twenty-five days weren't nearly enough. Not even close.

I wanted *more*.

Watch out, Nil, I thought fiercely.

In twenty-five days, I'm coming for you.

I'm chasing that gate with everything I've got. Because I'm chasing it for me, for Skye. For us. I'm chasing it for a future that I can finally see, and you're sure as hell not in it.

And then I smiled. Because if Skye had her way, Nil wouldn't be in anyone else's, either.

Fear hit me like a tsunami, rolling over me from behind.

I whipped my head around, watching my back, seeing Mount Nil watching from a distance. If we *could* destroy Nil, I'd yet to decipher the cost. It was the last piece of the puzzle.

An island finale.

The truth was, I didn't really care, as long as Skye wasn't the one who'd burn.

Dex rolled his eyes. "That sounds like my mum tidying up the kitchen," he said. "What happened to the cool part again?"

Grinning, Zane pointed at Dex with his fish wrap. "Okay. How about Operation Island Annihilation?"

"A bit much, don't you think?" Dex raised one eyebrow.

"Operation Exodus?" Zane offered.

"Too short. Plus, a bit heavy on the biblical feel."

"Operation Star Gate? Operation Big Kahuna? Operation Mission Impossible?"

That did it. I got up and strode off, unable to take another minute. Breaking into a jog, I made it about fifty yards down the beach before Rives caught me.

"Hey," he said, coming up beside me. "You okay?"

"No," I snapped. "I am *not* okay. You have fourteen days left, and Zane's back there tossing out movie titles as if that's important." My fists were clenched. "It is not impossible; it has to happen. You have to make that gate."

"I know," Rives said, taking my hand. "We all need to make that gate."

"That's not what I mean."

"I know what you mean." Rives wrapped his hand around mine. "C'mon."

Somehow Rives understood that I needed to move; I was too restless to sit. The waiting was killing me. And maybe so was Nil.

We walked south without speaking, hands entwined like our thoughts. We ended up at the Arches, and when we rounded the cliff, we weren't alone.

Maaka stood in front of the carving, staring at the Man in the Maze.

"Find anything new, Maaka?" Rives said.

"Perhaps," Maaka replied, turning to face us.

I studied Maaka, this boy who saw the island so differently from me.

"Maaka," I said quietly, moved to speak first. "I'm not an islander, or your relative. The island's beginnings belong to you. But I can picture it, how it used to be. A magical place of peace and solitude, where people chose to come, bringing a goat or a chicken for health and luck, intentionally choosing to spend time away from their family, alone in a place where the food is plentiful and so is the time to think. To explore who they are, who they want to become." I paused.

"But the peace is gone. Now predators come, too, like lions and leopards, wild boar and bears. And other people come, too. People who aren't from your islands, people who don't want to be here, who didn't ask to come and who don't have your heritage and hope and knowledge. This island is a very different place now. It's a bit crowded."

Maaka didn't flinch.

"Skye's right," Rives said. "Your people come willingly. They're prepared, at least most. But the rest of us got snatched without warning, totally unprepared. And people are dying, Maaka." Rives's tone was tired. "For what? So your people can continue a tradition started long ago? A tradition that has outlived its purpose?"

"The tradition has not outlived its purpose," Maaka said. "A spiritual quest transcends time. The island," he whispered. "It makes you a better version of yourself."

"Different, maybe, but not always better," I said softly. "And a spiritual quest might be timeless, but this island isn't. The island has changed. Even for your people, the island is no longer peaceful—or isolated. Your island is connected to the world now. Good or bad, it's the reality." I paused. "Don't you see that, Maaka?" I kept my tone soft. "The island no longer serves its purpose. Its purpose has become twisted."

"Because of you!" Maaka cried. "Your quest for power turned the island loose!"

"What's done is done." Rives's voice was calm. "The island is not the same; it's not what it once was, and you know it. You have the choice. You can end it now. Or let it live. The blood of innocents will be on *your* hands now."

For the first time, uncertainty rolled across Maaka's face like a shifting gate.

"My role is to be a protector of the island, not to destroy it," he said.

"What if that's what the island wants?" I asked quietly.

Maaka looked positively stunned.

"The island is tired, Maaka. Tired of living. I feel it; you have to sense it, too. Ask Paulo if you don't believe me." I held Rives's hand tight and took a chance. "Will you help us, Maaka?" I asked softly. "Will you be the ultimate Nil guardian and help set the island free?"

Maaka turned toward Mount Nil. For a long moment, Maaka stood as still as the Man in the Maze. Thinking, searching his mind or the wind or the mountain for words we couldn't see, for answers we wanted to hear.

Finally, he looked at me. Me, not Rives. "I cannot answer you." His soft tone matched mine. "Not today. But I will have an answer when the time comes."

"That's all we ask," Rives said quietly.

With a troubled look at Rives, Maaka nodded and walked away.

CHAPTER 69

RIVES
DAY 363, DAWN

I stole one last glance around the City, my home for the last 363 days.

Images of people long gone flickered like ghosts. I'd been here less than a year, but it felt like a lifetime.

I had three days left.

Three noons.

Tick.

Three . . . two . . . one . . .

Tock.

Done.

I blinked and the City vanished. I was carving Li's cross in the dark; I was kneeling by Talla's fresh grave; I was watching Thad leap over a yawning black hole. I was seeing Raj collapse; I was watching Nikolai fall.

I was cased in invisible cement, my hands bound by invisible ties. I couldn't help them, couldn't block fate. Their die already cast; their end fully written.

So was my end, but I couldn't see it. Each time the future started to take shape, the scene vanished like smoke. Gone, before I ever got a clear glimpse.

I closed my eyes, fighting to *see*.

I was waking to Skye in my arms, feeling at peace; I was tipping her chin, shaking with hope; I was kissing her lips, drowning in want; I was holding Skye's hand, walking down the Avenue des Champs-Élysées, our faces tilted toward each other, the background falling away. No fear, no rush.

No Nil, just us.

More, the wind whispered. *You want more.*

Yes, I thought, my desperation keeping me from locking Nil out.

I want more.

I want it all.

I want Skye.

Beside me Skye laughed. In my head, in my hopes, in the now. I was there, I was here, I was gone. My chest ached, my fists hurt; I wanted *more* so badly I shook.

"Rives." Dex's voice yanked me back to the present. I relaxed my hands. My fingers were stiff from clenching. "You okay, mate?"

"Yeah." I shook out my hands. "Just ready to get this show on the road."

"All right then." He clasped my shoulder and squeezed, his touch saying what neither of us could. "A parting gift." He winked as he handed me a bamboo whistle. "Remember, three quick blasts means danger, and you can switch it into an SOS for help. Three short, three long, three short. One long is the call back signal. All clear?"

"All clear." I knew Dex was nervous. I slung the whistle around my neck, then offered my hand. "Be safe, Dex," I said quietly, fighting the knot in my throat. "See you in three days. Don't be late."

Dex gripped my arm, his expression fierce. "Same to you, my friend. Three days."

More handshakes. More good-byes.

More. More. More.

I fought the urge to clench my fists.

Skye reached up and touched my cheek. A feather-light touch, running down my jaw, a single move that affected me more than Nil.

"It's okay," she whispered, her eyes as fierce as I'd ever seen. "Relax. You're gritting your teeth so hard I hear them."

I grabbed her hand and kissed it.

She grinned and turned away. It took me a minute to figure out she was running a pre-Search check of her gear.

Smart girl, I thought. I did the same.

Everyone split up, separating into their designated teams.

"Operation Clean Sweep is a go," Zane hollered.

"Yeah!" Ahmad hooted. Skye rolled her eyes.

"Let's pack and roll, everyone. Be smart and be safe. See you in three days," I said.

Now Skye was the one clenching her teeth.

The teams split off. Ahmad went north with Kiera and Alexei; Dex headed northeast with Jillian and Zane; Macy headed south with Julio and had even managed to convince Brittney to come.

Skye, Miya, and I were the final team. We'd head southeast and be the first ones at the mountain.

The City was down to twelve, a shockingly small group. The numbers had never been smaller, even with the four still out on their own.

Maybe Skye was right. Maybe Nil was letting go. Yesterday on sweep, Skye spotted Michael near the North Cliffs. But the rest of the island was empty.

It was eerie. Like the island was a ghost town, like time was growing stale. Like the island might have an expiration date, too.

"Ready?" I asked Skye.

She looked like she wanted to say no. But her eyes flashed with steel and her hand crept to her sling. "Let's go," she said. Our eyes met, and I nodded.

We had three days.

CHAPTER
70

SKYE
DAY 88, NIGHT

I'd never sleep tonight. I doubted Rives would, either.

We'd brought the cheetah pelt, which was a pain to carry but definitely made the nights outside better, but it wasn't the lack of cushioning that was the problem. It was the looming day, the coming noon. Tonight was like Christmas Eve as a little kid, knowing that tomorrow was the big day, and you just hoped you'd been good enough for Santa to fill your stocking.

Only I wasn't sure being good mattered here, and we'd already established Nil wasn't on Santa's route. Then again, maybe goodness counted for something, because if Archie hadn't stolen from the City, maybe he'd still be here. Or not. Nikolai was kind and good and lost to Nil forever; maybe Nil chose to keep him *because* he was good. Or not. Maybe Nikolai's death was a fluke after all.

I could drive myself crazy with the what-ifs.

I already am, I thought.

Rives had one day. One noon.

One clear chance of making it off Nil alive.

I couldn't bear the thought of losing him, not when we'd just found each other. Eighty-four days was a drop in the bucket compared to the future I so desperately wanted with him. No wonder my uncle went to Australia to find Jenny. No wonder Charley looked like she might break.

"So serious," Rives murmured. He kissed my shoulder, and I reveled in his warmth. He never missed anything. He was always aware, always noticing. It was part of what made Rives so kind, part of what I loved about him.

I loved him.

The revelation was so crisp and real and deeply true that for a moment, I shocked myself. I didn't know when it happened, but I knew it was true. Not a Nil truth, but a Skye truth.

I shifted back to look him in the eyes, fighting a rush of love so powerful that I struggled to contain it. "Promise me you'll go first," I managed. "Don't wait until the end."

Rives kissed the tip of my nose. "I don't want you to be last, either."

"Why not?" I frowned. *How did he know?* I was totally planning on being last. My gut said it should be me or Paulo.

"Because I'm worried that if we all leave—that *when* we all leave—that the island will exact a toll. Maybe on the last rider, I don't know. But I don't want it to be you."

I thought about that. "You have a point. But whoever goes last needs to know that. And it should be their choice."

"Not you," Rives said. His eyes pleaded in the dark, light pools of hurt and hope.

"I promise to not be last if you promise to go first," I whispered.

He didn't answer.

Stalemate, I thought, watching Rives close his eyes, watching him battle himself.

Be smart, I thought, studying the beautiful lines of Rives's face, willing him to go first. *Because I've fallen so deeply in love with you and can't imagine losing you. I can't leave you behind. Not now, not when we have a shot at more.*

But I stayed quiet. Because Rives had to make the choice, not me.

I lay there, wondering when I'd fallen in love with Rives and why it took me so long to realize it. The fear of losing him was real and awful and right now worse than anything else I could imagine.

If I lost Rives, I'd be fearless. And that scared me, too.

CHAPTER
71

RIVES
DAY 365, DAWN

I hadn't slept.

Hell, I wasn't even tired. The ticking in my head matched the pulse in my veins; I felt primed and awake, reveling in my last minutes on Nil. My last minutes with Skye, the girl I'd pegged as a Nil natural from day one, the girl with the power and will to take on Nil and destroy this Hell for good.

But she didn't destroy me.

She saved me.

She made me laugh and ache and feel things I'd thought were lost; she made me want to *be* more. Her name was a perfect fit. Her uncle got an island angel; so did I.

And Nil brought her here.

I stared at Skye, my chest so tight it hurt to breathe. Her eyes were closed, her hair Skye-wild, her expression so innocent you'd never know she could take down a ninety-kilo leopard one minute and kiss me fiercely the next.

She's mine, I thought grimly, making sure Nil heard. *You can't have her. Can't keep her. You have to protect her, and then you have to let her go.*

Because she's the best thing to ever happen to me.

I watched her sleep until she opened her eyes.

"Hey," I whispered.

"Hey." Skye's eyes held mine.

"Did you sleep?"

"A little," she said. "Not much."

"Me either." I took a deep breath. Emotions I'd held in check for so long threatened to burst like a fissured dam. Natalie's words rushing back to me. *No regrets, Rives.*

Miya lay a few meters away, still sleeping.

Now, whispered the breeze.

"I lay awake all night, thinking," I said. "About today, but mostly about us. About you. I don't want any regrets." My voice was raw. "However this day ends, I want you to know how I feel. Because I'm an idiot—"

"A bloody idiot, as Dex would say," she murmured, smiling. But her eyes glistened.

"Right. A bloody idiot and a slow learner." A smile pulled at my lips. "But I know this. I know it with every part of me, with all that makes me, me." I gently cupped Skye's chin, my eyes searching hers. I needed to see her face, her eyes, to tell her before I lost the chance.

"Skye," I whispered. "You are my sun, my moon, my stars. You are my everything. I love you." My eyes held hers. "You make me *more*. You make life *more*. If we make it back, I can only imagine how amazing our life would be. I hope we get that chance. I hope *I* get that chance."

Skye held me so tight I wondered how she could breathe. "I love you, too, Rives. More than you know. We'll make it. We have to."

I needed that; I needed *her*.

We had five hours left.

CHAPTER 72

SKYE
DAY 89, MORNING

I held Rives's hand, feeling the strength flowing through his veins, feeling his passion and power and *love*. Feeling mine, feeling *ours*, like together we were a force for Nil to reckon with.

The thought made me smile.

I'd swear the island was listening, because it was so deathly still. I still fought a pervasive sense of exhaustion that I knew wasn't mine. It was Nil's.

We're trying, I thought.

And I sensed Nil was helping.

We hadn't seen a single person and only one animal. A bird. A black hawk, winging overhead like a drone. It was weird and creepy.

We'd just reached the meadow's edge when three sharp blasts of a whistle were followed by three short ones. Then three long.

"Someone's in trouble," Rives said, his face like stone. Hard lines, cold fury. No desperation, just pure Rives determination. His hand in mine, we took off running toward the north end of the meadow, the origin of the blasts. The groves gleamed green in the distance.

Now I heard Jillian screaming.

Oh no, I thought, feeling the air press tight. *Please not Jillian.*

It wasn't.

It was Dex.

Bloody and cursing, he leaned on Jillian, dragging one leg that was completely useless, his face drenched with pain. A tourniquet wrapped his thigh. Zane was nowhere in sight. In the distance Ahmad was running toward us, along with Kiera, Alexei, and, if I wasn't mistaken, Michael. Another boy who I didn't know ran beside Ahmad. Macy and her team were nowhere in sight. But they should be coming from the south.

"What happened?" Rives stopped beside Dex. He surveyed his Second, his jaw as tight as his shoulders. His green eyes bled worry as he reached out to support Dex's weight and relieve Jillian.

"Bloody hippos," Dex managed. I bit back a gasp as I looked at his leg. Two deep slashes etched his thigh; I could see bone. It was a miracle he wasn't in shock.

"The mudflats," Jillian said. Sweat streaked her forehead, matting her hair at the temples. "We were skirting them, Sy saw us, came running, waving his arms. One hippo," she breathed, "attacked. So fast. Zane has him. I don't know."

On cue, Zane popped up, a few football fields behind us as if he'd been resting. He supported Sy like Jillian held Dex. Blood ran down Sy's waist and leg, visible from here. His head lolled like a rag doll against Zane.

"Not good," Rives said. His eyes flicked between Sy and Dex.

"Bloody mess." Dex bit off the words. He hopped forward, gritting his teeth, sweating with the effort.

"Dex," Rives said. "Lean on me."

I realized Ahmad was making a hard beeline toward Zane, and Ahmad had backup, more than we had. Macy was heading toward us too, her team in tow. She should be heading toward the Countdown carving, the meeting spot.

"Rives." I grabbed his arm. "You go to the gate. Miya, intercept

Macy. She's headed here, and her team won't know where to go. Light your torches. Lead the way. Ahmad's headed toward Zane, and Jillian and I can help Dex."

He hesitated.

"We have time," I said, pushing at his chest with both hands, making him go. "You don't. *We* don't. Go!"

"She's right," Dex said. Pain rippled across his face in cruel waves. "Don't be a bloody idiot. Not today."

Rives crushed a kiss to my lips, then took off, carrying a load of torches, heading toward Macy.

I couldn't believe Rives actually listened.

But when I looked up, he'd already lit a torch and he ran along the meadow's edge, arm high like an Olympic torchbearer. Miya's torch sputtered to life beside his.

Macy's team was fully visible. Now I saw four people. Finally, a good omen. Miya split off toward Macy as Rives ran on.

I looped Dex's arm over my shoulder. "Hang in there, Dex." *Please.*

"Don't have"—each word was a burst of pain—"choice. Not today." His voice was grim.

Three sharp blasts sounded behind me.

I turned to find Ahmad gesturing wildly and pointing at the meadow to our left.

I looked over, my breath catching. The air thinned, like the island gasped, too.

The two ugly hyenas circled like buzzards, coming for us. Then they split ranks.

"Jillian," I said, my eyes on the predators. "Light your torch. Dex, you're going to have to sit tight for a sec."

We eased Dex to the ground as quickly as we could. He leaned on an unlit torch as Jillian whipped out her firebow and frantically got to work. I loaded my sling without looking, sweeping my eyes around us.

Ahmad's team was a football field away, too far back.

Macy's group was at the mountain base, too far ahead.

Rives was already sprinting up the rock stairs, heading to where he needed to be.

It was just us.

"It's not catching," Jillian cried, desperately working the bow. The coconut husks smoked without fire. *We should've lit the torches before the meadow*, I thought.

Huge mistake.

The hyenas circled, smiling cruelly. A third had joined the pair, appearing from nowhere. All three bared their teeth, defending the gate, or maybe just hungry.

On some invisible cue, all three launched as one, from three directions. Toward us.

The next few minutes were a blur in slow motion, awful and terrible and etched forever in my brain. Three vicious creatures, mouths open wide, all seeking blood.

Three of us, three of them.

Choose, breathed the wind.

I chose Jillian.

I aimed my rock and struck the hyena nearest her between the eyes, inches before it caught Jillian by the throat. It fell as Jillian's torch caught, it fell as Dex screamed, it fell as hot breath brushed my ear. I spun, fumbling for a second rock even though I knew I had no time left, waiting for the slash of teeth sinking into my flesh. Rock in hand, I stilled.

Time stilled.

A full-grown Bengal tiger stood a yard behind me, a hyena dead at his feet.

A second hyena lay burning a few feet to my right.

In my peripheral vision, I saw Jillian screaming, waving a flaming torch at another hyena as it backed away from Dex.

The tiger stared at me, eyes molten and still, then the tiger walked away.

Live, breathed Nil.

The cats weren't guardians of the gate; they were guardians of *Nil*. It was so clear, an absolute Nil truth captured in a frozen moment.

I had to tell Rives.

Rives.

Time sped up, hurtling faster than before.

Jillian was screaming and crying and facing down the last hyena with a fiery torch; the scraggly beast was hunching low, its grin wide, its yellow teeth dripping blood. In the background, framed by crisp blue, Ahmad and his crew were running toward us as a full tribal man pack, spears and torches held high. Zane had Sy in a fireman's carry.

I loaded my sling and shot the hyena in the head, then grabbed Jillian's torch and set the bloody scavenger on fire.

When I turned back to Jillian, she lay over Dex, sobbing.

"No!" she screamed, lying on his chest. His eyes were open, vacant. His throat was a mess. "No, no, no! You can't die, not now. Now when we're so close."

"Aw, shit," Zane said. Still draped with Sy, Zane stood close to Jillian. He looked ready to cry.

"Wake up," Jillian cried. "Talk to me, Dex. Tell me I'm mental. Tell *me* to wake up. Wake *up!*" She patted his chest, then his cheek. More tears spilled. Dex lay still.

This was not happening.

And yet it was.

"Jillian." I touched her shoulder, fighting an overwhelming sense of fatigue and dwindling time. "We have to go. Dex would want you to go!"

Jillian kissed Dex's cheek, and then she punched the ground with her fist, pummeling the dirt as her knuckles bled. "I hate you!" she screamed.

"I know," I said, giving her a minute to vent, losing precious time we couldn't get back. "I know you do. So let's end this, once and for all." I put my arm around her shoulders and gently pulled her to her feet. She wiped her face and nodded.

"Let's kill this thing." Her voice was dangerously calm.

I looked at the sun.

We had minutes, not hours.

And then we started to run.

CHAPTER 73

RIVES
DAY 365, ALMOST NOON

Tick.

I was splitting in two. I was running away from the person I wanted to protect more than anyone else.

Because Skye asked.

Because she was right.

Macy's team needed guidance to find the platform, and I was the Leader.

Rivessss . . .

The whisper came from all sides, from the air, from the sea, from *me.* It grew louder every second. An invisible hand pressed against my back, driving me forward, toward the mountain.

Tick.

My last grain was poised to fall.

I was fully alive and shaking Death's hand.

I was a magnet, pulled by something stronger than me.

I hit the base of the mountain without remembering how I got there.

Rivesssss . . .

OUT OF MY HEAD! I screamed.

I waved Macy's team over toward Miya. Julio gave me a thumbs-up, already turning.

I drove a torch into the ground, marking the start of the steps, and lit it quickly, along with my other three. Then I took the rock steps two at a time. I wedged another lit torch in the cracks beside the steps, another island blaze. Two more torch markers, and then I hit the platform, my last torch in hand, unable to fight the pull to this place. To this *moment*.

Maaka was already there, kneeling, the carving on the ground centimeters from his skin.

"You"—Maaka looked up and frowned—"love to bring fire into sacred places. Do not try to bring it into the gate."

"Your rituals are wearing thin, Maaka. And so is Nil. Where's Paulo?" I asked.

"He will not be here," he said, turning back to the carving. "It is not his time."

"Oh, it's definitely his time. Did you know that Paulo's aunt knew Skye's uncle? And that the future—our future, the one happening right now—was foreseen by Paulo's aunt?"

Maaka had frozen. I had his full attention.

"That's right. Paulo's aunt and Skye's uncle had destinies that extended beyond them, stretching until the island's end, and they're playing out right now through Skye and Paulo. Paulo will show, because this is it. The island's tired; its time is done. The island has seen its own end and welcomes it." The last words were not mine, the magnetic pull was gone.

Maaka stared at me, doubt flickering on his face. I saw it, read it, and without question I understood why I was here. Why I was *still* here, saved for this moment.

I was the counterweight to Maaka. I was here to make Maaka *see*.

"You're thinking that if you stay," I said quietly, kneeling beside him, "if you sacrifice yourself and stay back, the island will live on. That your sacrifice will be for something great, to save this place that is greater than us. But you're wrong."

Maaka's back stiffened, but he said nothing. He listened without moving, as still as the rock beneath us.

"The island wants to rest. To be at peace. It brought Skye, the girl whose name means everything, here for that reason, to make us all *see*." For the first time, Maaka's face paled.

"I don't claim to know all the mysteries of the universe. Hell, I don't understand half of the mysteries of Nil. I don't think we're meant to know everything; I think we're supposed to always retain a sense of wonder. About the universe, about Nil, about our world, about *us*. You said yourself, it's a journey. It's *all* a journey. I may never know if vegetarians eat animal crackers or if Nil was created on the eighth day or eight hundredth. But I know this: I love Skye with all that I am, I know the best is yet to come. I know that I have more to offer the world than making candlenut torches and killing things, and I know *there are no coincidences on Nil*. You and I, we're not so different. And we each have the same amount of power. The power to choose, the power to give Nil what it wants." I paused. "The island's middle is long gone, Maaka. Open your eyes. Look around. This is what the end looks like." I stood and stepped away. "Your choice."

Rivesssss . . .

Tick.

I glanced up. The sun was high; noon was close.

A girl's frantic scream sapped all the energy from the air around me.

The girl's terror was mine.

Skye.

CHAPTER 74

RIVES
DAY 365, JUST BEFORE NOON

I sprinted down the steps and found myself in complete hell on Nil.

The meadow was on fire.

Everything was in motion: people, flames, animals. A giraffe galloped across the rocks, along with a handful of housecats. Flames licked the grasses on the meadow's north edge, ripping south. Like the people. Like the animals. Everything raced toward me.

Macy's team was at the base of the mountain steps: Julio supporting Macy, her feet bare and bloody, a freckled girl I'd never seen cowering behind Brittney, who carried a load of torches.

Thirty meters out, Zane and Michael were hauling ass toward the mountain; together they carried a motionless Sy, Zane's chest and torso streaked with blood.

Uri, Alexei, and Michael sprinted two steps behind. Cho loped even farther back.

Skye.

She was running, too. Toward me, holding Jillian's hand, her free hand gripping a lit torch. Jillian's clothes were soaked in blood. Behind her, black smoke billowed.

Something was burning in the field.

Dex and Paulo were nowhere in sight.

The smoke shifted, and I saw the cat. A tiger paced alongside Skye fifteen meters away, tracking her progress toward the steps.

NO.

I bolted down the steps, blade out, toward the tiger. Skye was shouting at me now, her face flushed, pointing to my hand and shaking her head. The massive cat pressed forward, pacing her.

Two more meters.

I was almost close enough to take a shot. If I could land a decent blow on the cat, it would give Skye time to reach the steps.

I slowed, cocked my arm, willed my blade to fly straight.

"Get to the gate!" Skye yelled.

When you're safe.

"Rives, no!" As Skye screamed, I released the blade and something hard hit my forearm with shocking force. My blade skittered across the rocks out of reach.

"Run!" Paulo yelled. Beside me, he was lowering a stick.

"What the hell?" I asked, scrambling after my knife.

Paulo launched himself at me with surprising speed and grabbed my wrist.

I shook him off like a gnat. "Stop defending this place!"

"I'm not," he snapped. "I'm saving your life. Now get to the gate." He pushed me toward the stairs with all he had.

I looked back. The tiger stood near the edge of the field, facing away from the mountain. Facing away from Skye, who flew to my side and wrapped her hand around mine. She jerked me forward. "The gate!" she cried.

Blood trickled down her right ear.

"What happened?"

I reached up to touch her ear. She swatted my hand away. "The tiger," she said breathlessly, pulling me with a grip of steel, "protects Nil. He saved me."

Above us, Macy's team rounded the stairs out of sight. Ahmad's group jogged a few meters back, almost at the top. Halfway up the stairs, Zane carried Sy, with Michael and Uri's help.

"What happened to Sy?" I asked. We were practically on Uri's heels.

"Hippo," Jillian said. She climbed beside Skye, her eyes blank. Behind us, the meadow burned. Smoke filled the air, choking the blue.

"Move!" Paulo yelled at my back. "It's coming. Can't you feel it?"

I could.

Tick.

Around me the air pressed close, vibrating with an intensity that was still building. Like Nil was sucking in extra oxygen, taking a deep breath before her final exhale.

We hit the platform and paused. The white sand filling the carving's lines glinted in the brilliant Nil sun. Overhead, blue sky winked like freedom: no smoke, no steam. Everyone stood in a loose semi-circle facing the black mountain, including Maaka.

A gap in the circle stood out like a blank space on the Wall.

"Where's Dex?" I asked, panic rising. "He's not here." I swiveled toward the steps. Empty, like the gap in our circle.

"He didn't make it." Skye's soft voice shook.

"What?" I spun back, stunned. *No. Not Dex.*

Skye nodded, her eyes glistening with grief and sadness and guilt.

Beside Skye, Jillian didn't move. Didn't speak. Eyes forward, a single tear ran down her blank face, a cutting flashback of Talla's funeral crashing into the now. Watching Jillian, I knew it was true.

Damn you, Nil, I thought, fighting to breathe. *Why Dex? Why take the energy of one of the best? WHY DEX?*

I didn't choose, the wind whispered.

And then the air stilled.

Completely.

Total calm. Total peace.

Hope and relief warred with grief and shock for top billing as the carving's crisp lines blurred. One breath later, a shimmering gate lifted into the air, bigger and more defined and twenty times more brilliant than any gate I'd ever seen.

I turned toward Skye; she was looking at me. My other hand found hers. Our eyes caught and time stopped.

For an instant.

For a lifetime.

Skye was watching me walk up the beach, her smile making my breath catch; I was touching her cheek, feeling unhinged; Skye was walking behind me, guarding my back with a sharpness that made me proud; I was lifting her chin, drowning in heat; Skye was sitting beside me as I slept, her expression so tender I ached; I was holding Skye on the rocks, my expression defiant; Skye's lips were on mine, making me want; I was writing words in the sand; Skye was cupping my face; I was kissing her; Skye was reaching for me; Skye was mouthing we're more.

I saw a hundred moments and felt a million more; I felt all the love and pride and strength and fear and hope Skye held in her heart, *for me.*

We were *more.*

It was Nil's final gift. Glimpses of us, through Nil's eyes.

I blinked, still reeling. Skye's lips curved into a slow smile, and I knew she saw the same. *Felt* the same.

I didn't have to tell her I loved her.

She already knew.

The gate snapped into place, the glistening air writhing with life.

"Go," she said softly. "Paulo and I will be last. It's right."

I looked at Maaka. "You first."

He held my gaze, then without a word, he nodded, strode into the gate, and disappeared.

One.

Two.

"Go!" I yelled at Julio.

He went.

One by one, everyone vanished. Into the gate, gone from Nil forever.

Jillian turned around to face us as she stepped backward into the shimmering air. Her tears fell like rain, glistening like diamonds as she touched her fingers to her mouth, eyes closed. Then she was gone.

It was just me, Skye, and Paulo.

"Go!" Skye said, her face bloody, her stance badass and her steel-flecked eyes full of more life and fire than any person had a right to have. She was *more*; she was my everything.

I cocked a smile and, pulling her close, I kissed her.

Then I took the hardest step of my life. Away from Skye, toward the gate, knowing it was an argument I couldn't win.

At the last second, I turned, fully intent on pulling a Thad; no way in Nil hell was I leaving her behind with Paulo.

I grabbed her arms, but something happened. Skye moved with ninja speed, putting her own slick move on me, like she'd read me first. It was me flying through air, me tumbling into the gate, me getting wrapped in heat. My last glimpse of Nil was bright blue flecked with silver clouds, steel in the sky. As the darkness flooded my bones and my head, my last thought was *Damn. Krav Maga.*

I smiled, and then I was gone.

CHAPTER
75

SKYE
DAY 89, NOON

My training with Yarin had paid off after all. Rives was gone.

There was no time to savor the relief.

I turned to Paulo, Nil falling away, everything shrinking into the microscope of this black rock platform; it was just me, Paulo, the writhing gate, and my overwhelming exhaustion.

Only the exhaustion wasn't mine.

This was the end. The end of our time on Nil, the end of something set in motion by our ancestors. Tears spilled from my eyes; they tasted like salt and sea, like a drop of something bigger, a fraction of a whole.

"Ready?" I said.

He smiled. "Yeah. Skye, I'm glad you followed me. Now it's my turn to follow you."

"Ladies first?" I teased. "Or afraid I'll throw you in?"

"Something like that." He grinned. I'd never noticed how light his eyes were. Like sun-warmed caramel, his eyes were a gorgeous brown, full of depth and light and quiet strength.

I hugged Paulo hard, this boy who was no longer broken, this boy who was more.

"See you on the other side, my friend." Then I dashed into the gate, spinning backward at the last minute like Jillian had done, so I could give Paulo a wave.

I didn't have to see the gate to know I'd made it.

Heat clawed at me with greedy hands, pulling me deeper and squeezing me tight. Paulo gave me a thumbs-up and a smile, but as he faded, his expression changed. A shadow passed over his face like an eclipse, darkening his eyes from the inside out. Paulo gasped.

Then he was gone.

So was I.

Falling through blackness, plummeting deeper into invisible flames hotter than the meadow's fire. Then the flames turned to ice. A steel door slammed shut behind me, cold and impenetrable; there was no light, no sound. No boundaries.

I drifted away.

Lost.

Pulled not in one direction but two . . . stretched and torn and ready to splinter.

Until, through the darkness, I heard the voice that pulled me back. Pulled me *through*. The barest whisper, streaking through time. Through *me*.

Skye.

With all I had left, I reached for that voice.

CHAPTER
76

RIVES
DAY 365, AFTER NOON

I woke on black rock.

My cheek lay centimeters away from a carving of the sun with an eye in the middle, but this wasn't Nil. A man with cargo shorts, sunglasses, salt-and-pepper hair, and a strong grip helped me to my feet and pulled me away from the gate.

"Here, son," he said, smiling behind his Ray-Bans. I realized he was holding out a pair of black gym shorts and a gray T-shirt. I glanced up, automatically searching for Skye. Everyone had traded their island wear for workout wear, all wearing the same shell-shocked expression. All staring at the gate. All still waiting.

No Skye.

Her ninja move came roaring back.

I spun around, pulse racing. Nil's clock roared in my head, reaching through time and space and *me*, counting down to freedom and life and hope and *more*—or to the deepest, cruelest, most crushing Nil scar ever.

Tick.

No Skye.

It was taking too long.

Barely breathing, I stared at the glittering gate in the air as it writhed on invisible hooks. A silver, iridescent plane, reflecting me. I looked wild and reckless and furious and like hell on Earth.

I was on Earth.

Without Skye.

SKYE!

I screamed in my head, desperate for her. She had to make it. She was in my soul, *in me*; Nil had linked us so completely I couldn't breathe without her.

Tick.

SKYE!

I was that man windmilling on the edge of a cliff, knowing that if I fell, this time I'd shatter, broken beyond repair.

I would not let Nil break me.

I stepped back, closed my eyes, and with everything I had, I reached into the deepest part of me; I reached for Skye.

Skye, I whispered, holding fast the part of me that belonged to her, refusing to give up.

Please.

Like Nil had heard me, the gate turned flat black. Endless, colorless black, like death in the air.

The ultimate reveal.

Friend or foe.

Life or death.

Skye. There was no alternative.

Time stalled.

Tick.

One second.

Tock.

A mane of wild blond fell out of the gate, surrounding a heart-shaped face with closed eyes and wet lashes. Dark blood streaked down the side of her ear, deep ruby slashes against her cheek.

I reached her first, barely.

"Skye," the man beside me said. His voice broke. He threw a fleece blanket over us, covering Skye as I gently picked her up; I cradled her as if she were made of glass. Her heart beat slow and steady, the perfect *tick-tock*.

Behind her, the gate shifted back to a mirror.

The man flipped his sunglasses onto his head and wiped away tears. His steel-flecked eyes were startlingly familiar. He caught my eye and stepped away.

Skye opened her eyes and blinked.

"Rives," she breathed, her eyes finding mine.

"My Skye." The words caught on the knot in my throat. She was radiant, fully alive. In my arms, out of Nil's grip.

"I heard you," she whispered, her voice awed, her eyes full of love and wonder. "In my head. You pulled me through. You pulled me *here*."

"Always." I grinned. "I had to do something after that little Krav Maga move you put on me."

It was Skye's turn to grin.

"We did it," she said.

"No. *You* did it. None of us would be here if it weren't for you."

Over the carving, the gate shimmered.

"You can put me down now," Skye said, rolling her eyes, still smiling. She wrapped herself in the blanket as I set her on her feet.

Around us, all eyes were still on the gate. Its brilliance flickered. Like a power surge.

Paulo, I thought. *The last rider's coming.*

With an eerie hiss, the gate collapsed, snapping back on itself, just like every inbound on Nil I'd ever seen. Nothing flashy, nothing like a Nil finale. Just Nil business as usual, which right now felt monumentally wrong. The gate shrank to a black dot and disappeared.

The doorway had closed.

"Paulo," Skye whispered, her eyes wide with shock. "He didn't make it."

Paulo's on Nil. Nil's still alive.

We'd saved all but one, but it was like beheading the Hydra; Nil would just grow back, strong and powerful, and Paulo was there to fuel the darkness.

"Rives." Skye still stared at the spot where the gate had vanished, like it might pop back up and spit Paulo out any second. "Paulo was right behind me. He was ready to follow; I know it. But at the last second, something happened."

I frowned. "Was he attacked?"

She shook her head. "He was alone on the platform. It was like something changed his mind, or delayed him enough to miss the gate. His expression—" She broke off. "I can't explain it. But it's like the decision wasn't his."

It made no sense. Nil was tired, working toward island rest. Permanent rest. *If Nil wanted to die, why keep Paulo?*

"I don't know," Skye said. "I don't understand it, either." She looked at me, then her eyes drifted over my shoulder and her mouth fell open. "Dad!" Wrapped in the blanket, she ran over and hugged the guy standing beside the grocery bag full of gym clothes.

"Skye." His voice was thick with emotion. "I thought I'd lost you."

"Totally fine here, Dad. You trained me to take care of myself, remember?" She gave him another big hug, then let go and grinned, stepping back to find my hand with hers.

"I also remember telling you to stick with me." His calm tone and fierce gaze was Skye's in dad form.

"Skye doesn't always follow directions," I said, shooting her a quick grin before sticking out my hand. "Dr. Bracken, I'm Rives Martin-Taylor. Good to meet you, sir."

He shook my hand, carefully sizing me up before he smiled. "Likewise." Then he turned to Skye and pointed to her blanket. "How about some clothes?"

Around us, life returned one second at a time, like blood flowing back into numb limbs. Macy was smiling; Ahmad was hugging Kiera; Michael talked with Cho. Uri stood apart, head bowed. Miya looked restless; Maaka was nowhere in sight. Zane held Jillian. Her entire bearing screamed shock.

"Be right back." I squeezed Skye's hand, then walked over to Jillian, knowing Skye and her dad needed some space and I needed to make sure Jillian was okay.

Zane looked at me as I approached. "Hey, Chief." His eyes were bloodshot.

"How're you holding up, Z?"

"Okay." He nodded. He let go of Jillian. She turned to me, her gaze both hollow and hurt. Relief took a backseat to her pain.

"Jills," I said. "I'm so sorry."

She hugged me, hard. "Me too. It just sucks, you know? So close, Rives. We were *so close.*"

"I know." I didn't ask for details. Part of me didn't want to know, didn't want another bloody visual I couldn't erase. It didn't matter how it happened; it was over. Dex was another Nil casualty.

A gap on the Wall. Another Nil scar, for all of us.

"You're gonna be okay," I said quietly.

"I know." The fierceness in Jillian won out. "And I know more of my friends made it back than died. But I still hate it. It's not fair. I think"—she swallowed—"we could've been something."

Something more, I thought.

Sometimes Nil's unknowns followed you home.

"Where's Sy?" Zane asked sharply. He was looking around. "Michael and I tossed him in the gate. He wasn't conscious, but he was breathing."

Michael's head turned at the mention of his name.

"Sy?" I called, letting go of Jillian.

Michael walked over, shaking his head. "Didn't make it. Lost in between."

Jillian shuddered. "That's awful."

"Dude, I didn't even know that could happen," Zane said. "I thought gate trips were a given."

I thought of Heesham, throwing Miguel in the gate. I'd always assumed Miguel made it through. I gritted my teeth, reminded of how nothing on Nil was guaranteed, not even in escape. *Nothing's a given*, I thought. *Not when Nil's involved.*

Standing here, free of Nil, I'd never been more grateful.

Skye's dad whistled. "I'm Skye's dad, for those I haven't met. When you're ready, the boat's at the beach," he called. "It's stocked with food and drinks. No fish." He winked. "Take your time." He pointed toward a path through the trees, waved, and started walking.

Zane grabbed Jillian's hand. "C'mon, Jills, Skye's dad said he's got chips and Coke. Man, I've been jonesing for a Dorito." She didn't smile, but Jillian followed Zane. Macy linked her arm through Jillian's, whispering in her ear. Slowly the group dwindled to two.

It was just me and Skye.

I placed my hands on her waist; her hands rested on my shoulders. Our lips were centimeters apart.

"Do you hear that?" I said softly.

She closed her eyes, listening. "What is it?" she whispered.

"Silence." I brushed a kiss against her forehead, then another on her eyebrow and one on her cheek. "No clock." I kissed her other cheek. "No rush."

Her lips met mine, and in that moment I knew. *She* knew.

The *tick-tock* was gone.

All that was left was *more*.

EPILOGUE

SKYE
SIX WEEKS LATER

Reentry has been swift and strange and impossible to completely process. My uncle's journal didn't prepare me for the weeks post-Nil. I don't think it could've, not really. My post-Nil world is totally different from his, just like my experience on Nil was not the same.

I have support he never had—Rives, and Jillian. And they have me.

And yet, Nil still creeps into this world.

I still stiffen as the sun sits high, just for a second, surprised that I don't need to run. I still think of the Wall at random moments, wondering if Paulo filled in the blanks. I still wake in the night reaching for my rock sling.

Nil habits die hard, and new ones are hard to break.

I still dream of blackness, the hollow blackness of the doorway between worlds. I dream I'm lost. Fading, until I reach for Rives. Always, I reach. And always, I hear him.

Jillian still dreams of Dex.

His death overshadowed the boat ride back.

Dad did all the talking. The rest of us sat around and ate, staring at nothing and everything and struggling to grasp that we were free of Nil. I never let go of Rives's hand, and he never let go of mine.

Dad was our island savior in waiting.

After I'd vanished that night, he'd taken an indefinite leave of absence from his job. He'd set up camp out on the Death Twin island, after finding, of all things, one of my blue hair ties in the woods near the carving. He'd watched, waited, and paid special attention to every astronomically significant event, realizing I'd disappeared on the Winter Solstice. He'd also paid a private captain a ridiculous amount of money to bring a large boat to the island fully stocked with necessities—including two bins of clothes. When I asked why he had so many clothes, he smiled, saying, "Hopeful realist, remember? I took a chance."

We all did, I think.

Mom and Dad are talking again. He's making plans to visit her in Africa and considering quitting his job altogether. He didn't say it, but I'm pretty sure he's finally given up his island quest. When it's been found, what's left?

The rest of us have made a pact. Among ourselves, and with our families. Not to go public about Nil, because we all agreed the exposure would give Nil power over our lives here, and we've already given the island enough. And we honestly can't figure out how going public would do anyone any good. Gates are impossible to avoid if one has your name on it. But we'll stay in touch, and stay together. Our bonds are island-made, island-strong. I guess we have to thank Nil for that.

Rives and I are definitely *more.*

I've met his parents and he's met mine; we'd all spent a week together in the islands after our return. We don't know what we want to do yet, or where we we'll go, but we have time, without pressure.

And we have each other. Here, in this world, in the *now.*

Right now we're in Kona. Tish will meet us in Paris next week, but this stop is just for us. For Nil survivors. A reunion, and a good-bye. Kiera's dad bought everyone's tickets and paid for the hotel, too. It turns out she's got more money than the rest of us put together.

As twilight fell, we walked to the edge of the sea, leaving our mark in black sand the color of a Nil night. Rives and I stood beside each other, fingers entwined like two halves of one whole. Charley and Thad stood to Rives's left; Zane, Jillian, Ahmad, Kiera, and Macy were to my right. Jason couldn't come; his parents said no. *Too young*, he grumbled over the phone to Rives. *Maybe I'll catch the next one.* Same for Miya and a few others.

The next one.

Because there would be more Nil reunions. We have time.

We all faced the water, cups in hand, our feet grounded in safety, a bittersweet peace that still felt unfair.

The setting sun brushed the water, and Rives raised his cup high.

"To Dex," he said quietly. "A bloody good friend. I'll never forget you. I hope you're up there, raising your cup, too. We love you, man." He tipped up his cup and drank.

"To Dex," I murmured. Dex finally got his cuppa tea. Grief and guilt mingled with free will and fate. I had chosen, like Nil. Like Dex.

Rives dropped his cup on the sand and wrapped his arms around my waist.

"You okay?" he asked me, his eyes brilliant green.

"I will be," I said, reaching up to pull him close.

He nodded. I knew he understood, that he felt the same way.

We will be.

Rives kissed me, then slid his fingers through mine.

Thad clapped Rives on the shoulder. Something unspoken passed between them. The first time Rives and Thad saw each other this afternoon, they had hugged long and tight with no words. Sometimes there are no words, I've decided. Sometimes you need to feel what's real.

Thad looked at me, his blue eyes glistening in the fading light. "I can't thank you enough for saving my boy, Skye. This is a good man here." He squeezed Rives's shoulder.

"I know." I smiled. Rives winked.

Thad grinned. "And hell if it doesn't feel good to know you out-foxed Nil. Beat her at her own game."

Did we? I thought. I wasn't sure. I wasn't sure if we'd won or lost or just broke even. Sometimes I wondered if we'd just reset the clock.

Charley walked up, her golden eyes sad and warm in the setting sun. "You did it, Skye," she said, smiling. "After you left that day, I had the craziest feeling you would. You got what you wished for." Her eyes slid to Rives, slightly mischievous. "Or maybe something better?"

"Definitely better." I smiled. "Something I never imagined."

"I know what you mean."

Her eyes found Thad. They were always finding Thad.

Charley and Thad together were intense. Like crazy intense. They had some kind of silent communication, and heat crackled between them. A small ring graced Charley's finger. *A promise ring,* she'd said with a smile.

My hand crept to my neck, finding my gift from Rives. A rough unpolished diamond on a simple silver chain, a replica of the stone he'd given me for my birthday on Nil. I like that most people have no clue it's a diamond; they think it's just a pretty rock. But it's so much more.

I know.

I glanced at Rives. He was watching me, his eyes full of fire and heat just for me. He smiled, his dangerous smile I knew so well, and I felt luckier than any person had a right to be.

"Geez." Jillian rolled her eyes. "You two are as bad as they are." With a laugh, she tipped her head toward Charley and Thad before glancing back at Rives. "It's like you read his mind."

Sometimes I do, I thought. I squeezed Rives's hand. *Sometimes we do.*

Nil changed everyone; it's a basic Nil truth. Rives and I are linked, a connection forged through fire and love and pain and something else, something powerful Nil created in our final few moments.

A final gift.

I know now what Charley had lost. I'm deeply glad she found Thad on this side. And I'm glad Rives and I saved as many as we could. But I still wake thinking of Nil, wondering why Paulo stayed. Why Nil lives, why we failed.

I hope one day I find out.

My name is Skye Bracken.

And this is the truth.

ACKNOWLEDGMENTS

The word *Acknowledgments* seems so paltry in light of the hundreds of pages before it. ☺ Epic hugs, billboards proclaiming my thanks, and a lifetime supply of cookies all sound much better . . . for without the following people, *Nil Unlocked* would not exist.

Jennifer Unter, my rock star agent, who cheers me on without fail. Who believed and supported me when I told her this book was already written in my brain, that I just had to put it on paper. I adore you, Jennifer, and am so grateful you're my agent/friend/cheerleader/champion. Thank you for making my publishing dreams come true (again!).

Kate Farrell, my brilliant editor, who makes each book better than the last. Who, when I outlined my idea for *Nil Unlocked* over the phone, said "Let's do this!" and we did! I love working with you and am so grateful for your keen eye and wise words, and am so honored to have Rives's and Skye's journeys shaped by your hand. THANK YOU SO MUCH!!! I can't wait to see where we go next!

All the amazing people at Macmillan and Henry Holt, who have so much love for books that I think the Flatiron Building must radiate literary magic. Thank you for your endless enthusiasm and your dedication to the world of Nil. I'm so very grateful!

Every copy editor who struggled with the day count (again), thank you for your sharp eyes, and I'm sorry. ☺

April Ward, who designs the most captivating covers ever. I love them both and am so honored to have your talent touch the world of Nil.

Ksenia Winnicki, my publicist extraordinaire, and all the marketing lovelies at Macmillan—including the amazing Fierce Reads team!—who have worked tirelessly to share Nil's secrets with the world. I am so grateful for y'all's unwavering support and excitement. Y'all have helped me touch readers' hearts, and I thank each of you for that gift.

All my writer friends and book cheerleaders, especially the YA Valentines (Sara Raasch, Bethany Hagen, Lindsay Cummings, Bethany Crandell, Phil Siegel, Sara B. Larson, Amy Rolland, Anne Blankman, Paula Stokes, Kristi Helvig, Jen McConnel, Jaye Robin Brown, Kristen Lippert-Martin), who make up the best writers' support group EVER. There are not enough words; I love you all and your books. Hugs for life.

Kristen Lippert-Martin, Kristi Helvig, and Becky Wallace, extra thanks for your brains, support, and enthusiasm for Nil Unlocked as it all came together; Tonya Kuper, Sara B. Larson, and Lindsay Currie, for always being there with an ear and a kind word; Lindsay Cummings, Paula Stokes, Phil Siegel, Bethany Crandell, Amy Rolland, and Vivi Barnes, who made touring a blast; Mary E. Pearson and Kasie West, who embraced the Nil world from book one; and Laura Stanford, Eliza Tilton, Jay C. Spencer, Natalie Whipple, Charles Martin, and Jessie Harrell, who supported my writing from word one. Y'all are THE BEST.

The All the Write Notes crew, for musical musings and writing support. You rock. ☺

Artists Pendulum, Thirty Seconds to Mars, Snow Patrol, Rise Against, and Lana Del Rey, for providing inspiration rich enough to fuel an entire crazy island world.

All my wonderful Twitter friends, booksellers, librarians, and book bloggers—especially super bloggers Nikki Wang and Eli Madison—whom I've chatted with (both online and IRL!) since the launch of Nil.

I'm deeply grateful for your support. Books are sold one book at a time, and you've made the #NILtribe real!

The #NILtribe, for embracing all things Nil and being so amazing. Extra special thanks to Lauren Goff for her creative #WinNIL answers, which worked their way into this story—you helped give Zane life. ☺

My friends who have supported me and the Nil world with such love it makes me cry. Sims Wachholz, Gina Donahoo, Christy Gillam, Kelly Anderson, Phaedra Avret, Amy Grant, Mary Claire Miller, and Leigh Smith, thank you for letting me bounce all my wild ideas for *Nil Unlocked* off y'all and jumping into my crazy; Kelley, Natalie, Kat, Allison, Meg, Avery, Lindsey, Julie, Erin, Heather, Margaret, Isabelle, Susanna, Mary, Susannah, Nicole, Annie, Darden, Kasie, Laddy, Virginia, Debbie, thank you for picking up my boys or encouraging my writing (or both! ☺). And thank you to all my dear college and high school friends for Nil love from afar: Rebecca, Michele, Stacy, Lani, Shannon, Angela, Devon, Susan, and Jennifer . . . and all my other sweet friends I forgot to mention in my writing haze. I love you all and am so grateful to have you in my life.

My family, who make my world go round: Ki (best sister ever), Penny, Mom, Ryan, Baz, Max, Mark, Jill, Blake, Kerri, Grandma, Bev, Beepsy, Jim, Johnny, and Aymi. I love you all! So, so much!

My boys, Caden, Christian, Davis, and Cooper, who have my heart. You inspire me and fill me with hope. Thank you for sharing me with Rives and Skye this year, and for being the wonderful individuals you are. I love each of you more than all the words in the universe.

My best friend and my true love, Stephen, who makes life *more*. Thank you for your support, for your belief in me, and for being by my side each step of the way. You are my everything, my love!

And to my readers, thank you! My gratitude, forever. Nil belongs to you now, and so does this book. Island cookies for life, on me.

3 1901 05773 8116